The ROAD of SILK

*To Vickie,
One of the friends,
I love, and care.
Matt Afsah*

By
Matt Afsahi and Barbara Dysonwilliams

The Road of Silk

Copyright© 2004 by Matt Afsahi and Barbara Dysonwilliams

Printed and bound in Colombia by Imprelibros S.A. All rights reserved. No part of this book may be reproduced in any form or by any electronic or mechanical means including information storage and retrieval systems without permission in writing from the copyright holder, except by a reviewer, who may quote brief passages in review.

ISBN: 0-9747644-6-9

Published by

2525 W Anderson Lane, Suite 540
Austin, Texas 78757

Tel: 512.407.8876
Fax: 512.478.2117

E-mail: info@turnkeypress.com
Web: www.turnkeypress.com

To Nenita, for all your love and support of my dream
- Matt

To my son, Joseph, who put the rainbow in my life.
- Barbara

There was a time when people knew many things closer to the true way of life. Unfortunately much of that knowledge fell victim to the relentless march of time. Mighty civilizations rose and fell. Peoples came and vanished. For many ages, this knowledge from those distant times was kept alive by the ones who remained pure in heart. Handed down from generation to generation, this knowledge was revered, respected and, most of all, believed. But believers become fewer and fewer, destroyed by conquerors and by progress demanding facts and data that delegated such things to the arena of folklore or fairy tales and, unfortunately, destroyed simply by the growth of human greed.

This ancient knowledge had a profound effect on those who lived during those olden days. In essence, it was the belief that if one lived his or her life honorably, it created a promise land, a paradise. Each rock, each blade of grass, each thing in this promise land was created by a life from this earth. On earth, each vow honored, each love that remained steadfast, each principle that was upheld created something in this paradise. And through the middle of this land ran the road of silk. It was a beautiful place, but it was a borrowed land with borrowed time. It existed on a higher plane but could also interface with the physical world. Back then, there were those with the knowledge of how to call that place to earth—if they were brave and true of heart. You see, this paradise would not tolerate any intruder who lived a dark life. Those who tried to use it for wrong, failed or died.

But today, even today, if there is one who is true of heart, one who believes, one who is not tainted by greed or egotism, that one might find the road of silk …

Chapter 1

Soldiers! Soldiers are coming!

The small boy ducked among the reeds along the river. His drab, homemade clothes blended so well with the foliage he was virtually invisible. He squatted and peeked through the tangled vines to watch the large squadron.

Their language sounded harsh and guttural as the officers shouted to the foot soldiers. The men were tall and looked fearsome in their dark armor: the huge, black horses pranced and strained against the strong grip of their riders. The boy could see the whites of their eyes as the animals pulled against their bits. He could even see the puffs of breath from their nostrils in the cool morning breeze. To him the horses appeared as formidable as their masters.

Monsters. Men and horses. Even at the age of six, Mata knew danger when he saw it. He had to warn the village.

Crouching low as possible, he backed out of the rushes carefully so moving weeds would not reveal his position. Gaining solid ground, Mata got to his feet, staying bent in order to remain screened by the tall foliage. He remained that way until he reached the rocky outcrop marking the beginning of the road leading to his village.

He ran.

Fast.

Faster.

Twice he nearly fell headlong into the narrow ditch running by the road but regained his balance at the last second. Holding tightly to his slingshot, he veered from the dusty lane and hurried toward the field, his eyes seeking his father among the workers digging neat rows in the fertile, black soil. Exciting things seldom happened in the village, and his thin chest fluttered with the importance of bearing such urgent news. He tried to ignore the other flutter causing his heart to pound so. Fear. Raw, feral fear.

Finally, he spied his father—a tall, thin man nearly as rough and scarred as the wooden handle of the hoe with which he worked.

The boy ran across the long rows so laboriously dug that morning as he headed toward his parent. Several men grimaced as the child uprooted some of the tender plants and shouted at him. Mata ignored them.

"Father! Soldiers! Soldiers are coming!" he shouted as he jumped the last row.

Bothwyn had been about to scold his son for undoing much of the work finished that morning, but as he heard these words, his reprimand died. He dropped his hoe and knelt to grab the boy by both arms when Mata reached him.

"What kind? How many?" He clutched his son as he searched the horizon. Seeing nothing, he returned his gaze to the child. "Mata, their insignia?"

Mata, excited earlier to be the bearer of important news, felt the thrill disappear when he looked into his father's worried eyes. The fear overtook the thrill and he trembled. Already breathless, his fright made him unable to speak. Glancing around, he saw each of the farmers quit his labor and hurry toward him. Suddenly, he didn't want to be the center of attention. Not this way. He simply wanted his father to hold him and tell him everything was going to be all right. His father gently shook him, interrupting his thoughts.

"Mata! Don't be a babe. Quickly now. The soldiers. Describe them."

Mata saw the apprehension filling his father's faded eyes. Despite his young age, a part of him realized at that moment his world was about to change. He struggled to get the words out.

"B-black. The soldiers are in black. And t-they have f-funny looking hats on. Not like ours. Theirs are shiny and black with a dragon."

The boy's father shot a worried glance at his friends. A murmur of dread and anger rumbled through the small crowd.

"It is as we feared," he whispered, then focused again on his son. "How many?"

"I-I don't know, Father. Lots. There are some on horses. Big, black horses."

"Think. Were there as many as the fingers on my hands or more?"

Mata screwed his eyes shut, trying to figure a way to tell what he had seen. When he opened his eyes, they were wide with wonder. "More than all of the people in our village. Maybe two times as many people. Not all of them were on horses. Maybe this many were riding." Dropping his slingshot, the boy quickly held up both hands and flexed his ten fingers three times. "I could feel the ground grumble with their footsteps. Who are they, Father?"

"Threescore," the kneeling man mumbled to himself. He scanned the horizon. "Trouble, Mata. Where did you see them?"

"The river. At the shallow part, where the rocks show. On the other side. I was in the tall reeds looking for a grosnook. I thou—"

"So close! We must hurry and warn the others. Quick. Now." The man grabbed the hoe he had discarded and hefted its weight in his right hand. "If fight we must, we will. We must protect our wives and children. Get home and tell your neighbors on the way. Tell them to meet in front of the castle. We must protect her."

Each of the men sprinted toward the village. Grabbing his son's hand, Bothwyn ran, dragging Mata after him.

"We must warn your mother and sister." The fear trembled in his voice, and he didn't scold his son for the tears trickling down the boy's cheeks.

It didn't take long for word to spread through the hamlet. By the time Bothwyn found his wife and daughter and gotten to the village, the town square was full. Shops were closed, windows shuttered and boarded. Small children whimpered and clung to their mother's long skirts. Every man had brought some kind of weapon with him, a meager collection of rough-hewn hoes, scythes or simple wooden stakes crudely sharpened to a point. The defense was paltry, the fear obvious, the courage, high. It could be seen in the set jaw, the tight lip and the firm grip on the makeshift weapons. Even the day seemed to sense the ominous threat. Dark clouds drifted across the sky, blocking the bright rays and casting dark splotched shadows on the countryside. The tiny village seemed to shrink as shadows gathered in the corners and grew. The only exception in the darkening landscape was the glorious castle standing on the hill above the village. Built from yellow stone, it almost appeared golden. Against the darkness, the castle took on a light of its own, almost glowing in the growing shadows. It stood alone yet was part of the village. The castle was the essence of simplicity. Its beauty lay in the simple lines that let the beauty of the natural rock shine.

Mata gazed in awe at the marvelous sight but quickly became aware of the turmoil around him. It scared him. He wished he could hold his own mother's skirts like the other children. But he was six and too old for such behavior. He tried to act brave, all the same he moved closer to Bothwyn.

"What is it, Father? Why is everyone here in the square? Who are these soldiers?" Mata whispered.

"Soldiers from King Amir of Dragonval. He wants what we hold most precious, and he'll stop at nothing to achieve his goal. We will fight to the death to keep him from succeeding. He is ruthless, heartless as are his soldiers. No good comes from Dragonval. It is a taint that ruins everything it touches."

"But what—"

"Hush, Mata. We must prepare. If something should happen to me—"

Fear gripped Mata's heart. He could not imagine his world without his father in it.

"No, Papa, you—"

"Enough!"

Seeing the terror in his son's eyes, Bothwyn felt pain sear deep in his heart, and he knelt to soften what had to be said. "Mata, if something happens to me, it's your responsibility to take care of your mother and sister. You will be the man of the house. Understand?"

Mata nodded but could not keep tears from gathering in his eyes. Bothwyn hugged his son fiercely and rose. Better to let the boy know the truth than live a lie. Still, it hurt him to see those tears. He had no desire to die, to leave his family, but he had a duty and he would be faithful to the end. For Her. As everyone in the village would do.

For Her.

He gently pushed Mata in the direction of the boy's mother. "Go to your mother. Remain close to her and sister."

"But Father, I want to stay here, with you. I can fight."

Pride surged through Bothwyn. He allowed himself the time to gently ruffle the boy's hair. It could be the last time. "I am proud of you, Mata, but I need to know Sheviere and Fleuise are safe. You can help me more by going to your mother and sister. It makes one less worry for me. We must prepare. Go."

As if in response to Bothwyn's words, a low rumble wove itself among the villagers' whispers and murmurs. The ground trembled under the onslaught of hundreds of marching feet. The children drew deeper into the long skirts of their mothers, and the smallest began crying. The villagers drew closer, forming a human wall before the small path leading to the golden castle. All eyes turned toward the dusty road. Large waves of dust rose in the distance and grew nearer.

The reputation of the approaching army was known far and wide. In truth, the bravest of hearts felt a tremor of fear at the mention of these fierce warriors. They were known for their cunning, their ruthlessness and their ferocity. Many times they had destroyed villages as thoroughly as a plague of locusts, leaving not a blade of grass behind. It was rumored many murderers and thieves were inducted, valued for their ability to do the most heartless deed without hesitation.

The thundering grew louder. At last the first of the column appeared around the bend in the dusty road. The villagers edged closer to each other and tightened their grip on their weapons.

The column was headed by two huge men, both well over six feet and muscular. Like the rest of the soldiers, each was covered in thick, black leather from head to toe. The leather had been polished with bear grease until it gleamed. Like the rest of the soldiers, each commander wore a bowl-like, black helmet with a golden dragon on the front. Unlike the rest, each of the two mounted soldiers had red ribbons streaming from the crown of their helmets. The ribbons fluttered and danced in the breeze, creating the illusion of blood spewing in the air. Each of these two soldiers also had gold metal dragons on the front of the armor indicating their rank. The smaller of the two—if indeed, small could be used to describe him in any way—had one gold dragon indicating he was a *matadoron*, the first rank above foot soldier. The other had four gold-encrusted dragons on his chest, the highest rank an officer could obtain: *Demolisherian*. Few soldiers in King Amir's army lived long enough to reach this status. Those who did were said to be feared by their own men, quite a feat for anyone in King Amir's army. The *Demolisherian* was over six and a half feet tall, a giant in the land of Gwendomere. He was muscular, with hands large enough to easily hold a melon in each palm and strong enough to grip a skull and squeeze it until it popped. His face was rough-hewn angles and planes, dominated by shrewd, dark eyes that missed nothing. His black beard was wooly like a bear, and he had filed his canines to accentuate the look. He rode tall in the saddle, and the horse beneath him was as impressive. Its black mane had been laced with red ribbons as had its tail. The horse's black skin rippled as the muscles moved beneath. Its hoofs were the size of a *tamaroon*, a round watermelon. The horse snorted and fought its bit incessantly, its huge white teeth snapped the air. But as powerful as the animal was, it could not overcome the power of its master's hand.

As the column rounded the bend, the *Demolisherian,* Goliagoth, pulled his horse in abruptly. Surprise flickered in his eyes. He allowed himself a small smile before he turned to his second in command. "Well, Nemoith, it appears our sheep have decided they're wolves."

"Ay, Sir. That's good. My sword has not felt my hand for a few days. It grows lonely. Maybe I'll have a chance to reacquaint the two." A low, coarse growl of a laugh rumbled from deep in his belly.

"Perhaps, Nemoith. Perhaps. I, myself, long for the smell of fresh blood in my nostrils. Has been far too long. But King Amir made his wish clear, although before Altera, I cannot understand why it should make a difference whether we take what we came for by force or consent."

The Road of Silk

"I hope by force."

"It may come to that. But I vowed the King we would avoid conflict if possible."

"King Amir grows soft in his age."

"Guard your tongue, Nemoith, or I'll have to cut it out. That sounds close to treason."

"I mean no disloyalty, Sir. Only that tongue-wagging is not the King's usual way. He has the power to seize whatever he desires."

"Our duty is to follow orders not question motives. Our orders are clear."

"Aye, Sir. But I'd be sore tested to ignore a rotten potato or *toma* thrown at me."

Goliagoth glanced at the gathered crowd then back to Neomith. "The King's orders are not to *instigate* a slaughter; however, he will not stand the insult of one of his men being the target of a projected missile, whatever its nature. I believe he would want that particular *individual* duly punished. But we tarry, let's get this mission accomplished and be gone from this forsaken land."

"Aye, Sir. Give me hot-blooded women and men strong and worth fighting instead of this sheep-filled hole."

"On that we agree."

The two men urged their horses forward. The foot soldiers again picked up their pace, black shields locked in side position and sword arm free.

Goliagoth was positive once he and his force reached the village square, the crowd would disperse; therefore, he was mildly surprised when he and his troop reached the center of the village that no one moved from his path. He urged his mount forward, using it as a physical bulldozer through the crowd. Still, the villagers did not move, except for a few moving sideways from the physical on-slaught of the horse. Suddenly, Goliagoth realized that although he had made some headway, the crowd was still there. They had simply moved and now surrounded him and his second-in-command. A faint flicker of something distantly akin to respect skimmed across his consciousness. These people were nothing, weaponless, facing the best fighting men in the world. Perhaps it was still possible to be surprised. No doubt, *She* would be the same. Besides, she had no place to run. His reverie was broken by a soldier's shout. He twisted in his saddle and saw a second rotten vegetable hit a soldier. The man started for his sword as did his comrades.

"Hold!" Goliagoth shouted. At his command, each soldier stopped in mid-action. Goliagoth stared at the stricken soldiers. "Who threw it?"

The men hesitated a second, then shook their heads. "Don't know, Sir. But it came from that direction." One of them nodded to his left where several people stood.

The *Demolisherian* stared at the sullen faces. There was no clue as to who had thrown the potato. He looked back at his soldiers. "Stand down." The men hesitated. They were not use to being insulted. In truth, Goliagoth wanted to slice the face off each person standing there, but he had his orders. Again, the *Demolisherian* shouted, "I repeat, stand down! First soldier drawing his sword without my permission will find his sword *and* his hand on the ground. Stand down."

Slowly, the soldiers relaxed their swords back into its scabbard. Goliagoth swiveled back in his saddle and faced the crowd. "I am *Demolisherian* Goliagoth, sent by King Amir. He spoke loudly, the language of Gwendomere flowing easily from his tongue. Although the language of Dragonval was not so different, he wanted to make sure the villagers understood him clearly. He would carry out the King's orders as implicitly as possible. "Who is your spokesman here?"

A wall of silence met him. "What's this? Cat got your tongue? Or do none of you have the backbone to speak?"

The silence continued.

The faint amusement Goliagoth felt began to fade. Irritation swept through him like a raging river. *By the gods, these sheep aren't brave, just stupid.* In one swift movement, Goliagoth dismounted his horse and pushed his way toward a thin man standing in front of him. He sensed his second-in-command do the same and come up behind him. Goliagoth towered over the lanky man. "Perhaps you can tell me."

Bothwyn looked up at the man looming a full head taller than him and silently prayed he would have the courage to not show his fear. He remained mute.

Goliagoth's massive hand whipped out and slapped Bothwyn. The force drove the older man to his knees, but he slowly stood back up. A small trickle of blood leaked from the corner of his mouth. Bothwyn ignored it and stared at Goliagoth defiantly.

"Perhaps you forget? Well, this should refresh your memory." Even as Goliagoth had struck the thin man, his quick eye had missed nothing. A small boy had started forward, but a worn-looking woman had grabbed him and pulled him back. Abruptly, Goliagoth shoved his way through the crowd to the young child. Seizing the boy, Goliagoth held him high over his head. The woman screamed and frantically grabbed for the child. Goliagoth hit her one hard punch, and she collapsed into an unconscious heap.

Angry murmurs rippled through the crowd as the *Demolisherian* shoved his way back toward Bothwyn. Several of the men tried to step in his way, but he simply pushed them aside, his eyes never leaving Bothwyn's face. A white-haired, old man stepped directly in Goliagoth's path.

"Put the child down," he shouted. "He's a baby."

"Out of my way, old man," Goliagoth growled. "Move."

The elder drew himself up to his full height, dignity shining in his eyes. "At least I am a man. I do not make war on women and children."

"You're a fool," Goliagoth snarled. Faster than a cobra Goliagoth's free hand shot out and twisted around the old man's neck. With a flick of his wrist, he snapped it and dropped the elder as if he were a bag of garbage. Ignoring the crowd's gasp and the body, he closed the remaining distance between himself and Bothwyn. The thin man's eyes were glued to Mata high above in Goliagoth's upraised hand. Bothwyn did not move, but his face paled and beads of sweat broke out on his brow.

"You're trying my patience. One more time. Who is your spokesman?"

Bothwyn licked his cracked lip and whispered. "We have no spokesman. But I will try to answer your questions if I can. Please, put the boy down."

"Answer me and I will. You must have a spokesman or a mayor, perhaps a *duergue?* " At Bothwyn's blank look, Goliagoth amended the last word, "a 'judge'?"

"No. We have no mayor or judge."

Goliagoth glanced back at his second-in-command and gave a mirthless laugh echoed by Nemoith. He turned back to Bothwyn. "How can you have a town without a spokesman, a leader?"

Bothwyn hesitated, his eyes flickering up to his son who struggled in Goliagoth's huge hand. The big man made as if to pitch the boy up into the air. "I said, how can you have a town without a leader?"

"We, we have a leader. We are guided by our leader."

"And who might that be?"

Again Bothwyn hesitated. He glanced at his friends and neighbors, saw the pity and the fear in their eyes. Clearing his throat, he whispered, "Our Queen."

"What? I can't hear you."

Bothwyn cleared his throat again and spoke a little louder. "Our Queen. She is our leader. She rules."

"Ah. And where might this queen be?"

Bothwyn thought his heart would burst. At any moment he would fall dead at the feet of the giant before him. He loved his Queen. He loved his son. At last concern for his child won. Silently he nodded in the direction of the castle. "There," he whispered. "Please, sir, let the boy go."

Goliagoth turned toward his second-in-command. "Four men. Come with me." He turned toward the castle, determined to push through the crowd before him.

Frantic for both his wife, who had not moved since being hit, and his son, Bothwyn clutched at the arm of Goliagoth. "Please, Sir, the boy. Please let him go."

For a moment, Goliagoth stared deep into the eyes of Bothwyn, then a bruised smile twisted his lips. "The child? Your son, I presume. I promised I would, didn't I?"

Bothwyn barely shook his head. "Yes, Sir."

"I always keep my promises." Goliagoth opened his hand and let Mata drop to the cobblestones. The tiny figure didn't move. "Men, follow me." Goliagoth started forward.

He had underestimated the love and loyalty of these people. A thin keening rose from Bothwyn who knelt on the cobblestones holding his son's limp body. The keening was quickly picked up by the crowd, becoming a raucous wail. Suddenly, the commander found himself surrounded by screaming villagers beating him with whatever they could grab. From what he could hear, the same was happening with the rest of the soldiers.

"You killed him!" someone screamed. A rock sailed through the air and hit Goliagoth in the shoulder. Angry shouts rose amid the shriek of metal against metal as the soldiers began pulling out their swords. Ever mindful of Amir's orders, Goliagoth did not pull his weapon but simply used his mighty arms as clubs on those surrounding him. *This is going to get ugly fast*, he thought. His plan to get in and out without bloodshed appeared futile. He ducked as a toothless, old man swung a scythe at him, then grabbed him by the throat.

"Stop it! STOP IT, I command you!" a woman shouted.

Everyone, including Goliagoth, froze at the sound of that voice. No one could mistake the authority in it. Goliagoth looked for the source and was astounded by what he saw. A young woman was running down the path directly into the middle of the battle.

"Hold," he shouted to his men, afraid they might hurt her. Instinctively, he knew this was the one he sought. His life would become a living hell if anything happened to her. King Amir would see to that.

But that fear wasn't what tied him to the spot. His entire life Goliagoth had had any woman he desired, by voluntary or involuntary means. He could understand why King Amir wanted her. She was beautiful. She was almost, he mentally searched for a word, she was almost *magical*, unearthly in her beauty. But she was more than beautiful. She was a *queen* in every sense of the word. It was in every movement, the turn of her head, her voice, her eyes. Goliagoth managed to close his mouth but could not take his eyes off her.

She was tall for a woman, tall and willowy, unusual in this land where most inhabitants were short and dark. Her skin was fine porcelain, so pale it almost glowed from within. The faintest of roses bloomed on her cheeks. Her eyes were wide and almond shaped, the color of the sky at dawn. He had never seen such eyes. The irises were blue with flecks of pink in them, just like the clouds at sunrise. And her hair, her hair almost defied description. It was long, hanging to her waist and of a color he had never seen. It reminded him of snow and ice in the winter sun. Goliagoth wanted to touch her—not from physical desire but to simply see if she was *real*. She was the most beautiful thing he had ever seen in his life.

Something deep within him moved. He had no name for it. He could only feel a hollow ache where something should be.

"You must stop, all of you."

Yasamin continued to move toward Goliagoth, yet her glance took in everyone—her people as well as his soldiers. The giant soldier stood transfixed as she came directly to him. Tears glistened in her eyes as she stared up at Goliagoth. Without hesitation, she slowly reached up and loosened his hold on the old man's throat. The elder sat abruptly on the ground, coughing and gasping. Goliagoth felt his own breath catch in his throat and again the hollow ache in his chest. Her touch was both fire and ice where her hand rested against his hand. Oblivious to everything but the woman in front of him, Goliagoth vaguely heard someone shout "It's the Queen." But he already knew who she was. Yasamin took a deep breath and spoke to Goliagoth. "You are here to take me, not to kill my people, *Demolisherian*."

Suddenly Goliagoth found himself doing something he never thought possible. He bowed before the Queen, sinking to one knee as her villagers had done only moments before.

"Your Highness, I regret the bloodshed, but your own people started it." He flushed and rose quickly, knowing his soldiers must think he'd lost his mind. Perhaps he had, or perhaps he had been bewitched. He had never knelt before a woman, even the Queen of his own country received only a token bow.

"Truly, *Demolisherian*?" Yasamin withdrew her hand from his arm and moved toward Bothwyn and his son. The villagers continued to kneel as she passed them, and the soldiers remained motionless. When she reached the father, she knelt beside the crying man and whispered something in his ear. She briefly laid her hand on the tiny child's head, then rose and returned to Goliagoth.

He expected anger, even danger if she ordered her people to attack. He did not expect the heaviness in his chest when she turned sorrowful eyes toward him. "And how did that child threaten such a giant as you, *Demolisherian?* What did he do to deserve such a fate?

"I—he, his father would not cooperate. I did my duty."

"Your duty is to take me to your King, *Demolisherian*, not hurt my people. Has King Amir withdrawn his promise?"

"No, your Highness."

"Then understand this, *Demolisherian*." Yasamin moved closer to Goliagoth until mere inches separated them. She looked deeply into Goliagoth's eyes, and as she did so, the sorrow receded and was replaced by anger. Her eyes turned to ice. The irises were no longer blue but cold steel. Goliagoth almost shivered from the blast emanating from them. Her voice remained low and lilting, but each word struck him like a blow. "I will not allow anyone—*anyone*—to harm my people. I will do whatever it takes, *whatever* is required of me to protect them and my country." Yasamin's voice quivered slightly. "If I have to give my body or if I have to give my life to save them, I will do so without hesitation. There is no need for your violence. Do you understand?"

"Yes, Majesty."

"Then understand this, and you will obey as you are the cause of it."

"And that is?"

"Your soldiers will dig the graves of the people killed here. And you, *Demolisherian*, shall personally dig the grave of the child you killed. Then you and your soldiers will retire and camp outside the village, while we grieve our losses. Once that is completed, I will prepare for my voyage. We will leave with the morning light to go to your ship in the harbor. Do you understand?"

"Your Majesty, the King expects you within

Yasamin interrupted. "If you had kept your temper and better control of your men, we wouldn't be spending the rest of the afternoon preparing our dead, I'd be preparing to leave. I will bury them and I will grieve for them. And I will say a proper farewell to my people." Head held high, Yasamin turned and faced the villagers. "Put down your weapons. You mean well, but no more violence will be done in my name. I have given my word to King Amir. I will keep it. The soldiers will dig the graves for those they killed then retire from the village to let us grieve in peace. At sunset I'll say my farewell to you. Now go home until time for our mourning ceremony. You know what you need to do to prepare.

Head high and back straight, Yasamin turned and walked up the path to the castle. Neither the villagers nor Goliagoth saw the tears staining her cheeks.

Chapter 2

Yasamin hugged the faded blue, velvet dress against her, then buried her face in the soft folds as she had so many times the last seven years. Occasionally she thought she could still detect the faint whiff of *moonlitea*, the sweet fragrance that had been her mother's favorite. Today, the ache to be held in her mother's arms was almost overbearing. The wish was impossible. The Queen had died seven long years ago, killed by a virile, wasting disease that had racked her body and slowly destroyed her beauty. Yet it had never touched the beauty living inside her. The Queen had watched over her people and her daughter with love and dignity until she no longer had the strength to sit on the throne. Even then, she continued to train her daughter how to be a good ruler, a good person and, most of all, how to love. When the Queen died, her people mourned her as they had no other, for they had loved her as fiercely as they had come to love her daughter. Rulers from countries as far away as Adajawai, more than 500 miles, had come to show their respect for this beloved ruler.

"Oh, Mother, I miss you. I need you more than ever. I do not wish to do this terrible thing, yet I must for my people to survive," Yasamin whispered. "I only hope I have the strength to do it."

The young woman buried her face deeper into the soft cloth trying to draw power from it. In her mind's eye she could see her mother clearly. The Queen had been even taller than her, with the same hair, so fine it looked like spun silver. Most of all she remembered her mother's beautiful eyes, full of love, laughter and quiet dignity. Even when the Queen became a mere shadow of her former self, her skin stretch taut across the bone, the love burned in her eyes, and she bore the pain with the same nobility she had lived her life. The day her mother died, Yasamin felt as if the sun had ceased to shine. It seemed the coldness and emptiness never left her.

"Are you all right, Highness?" The soft voice sliced into Yasamin's reverie. She turned to see her nurse, Nitae, standing at the door, her arms full of clothes. The woman had been with her since her birth, just as she had been at the Queen's. No one was sure of the woman's age, but she must have been at least seven score. Her face was so wrinkled it looked as if it had been pieced together with tiny stitches, like a quilt. Despite her age, Nitae stood straight and strong as any woman half her age. Her golden eyes usually sparkled with humor, and on those rare occasion when her anger flared, it seemed red sparks flamed in their depths. At the moment, her homely face was without its usual smile and worry lay like a heavy blanket on her features.

Yasamin managed a faint smile as she sniffed away the tears. "Of course, Nitae."

"Hmmph," the old woman snorted. "I can see you are just jumping for joy." She came into the room and laid the clothes on the huge canopied bed. Nitae was one of the few who spoke her mind to the Princess and knew she would get away with it—most of the time. After all, she had diapered and cleaned the behind of the girl when she was a baby, paced the floor with her when Yasamin had had the colic and nursed her through the common childhood diseases. No title, no crown changed that. More importantly, on her deathbed, her beloved Queen had charged Nitae to watch over the young girl, and she would as long as there was breath in her body. Her golden eyes drifted toward the blue, velvet dress the girl hugged and softened. She started to touch the dress but, on second thought, withdrew her hand. "You have so much to do, Highness. If you wish, I can pack that dress in with your personals."

Yasamin smiled. "Yes, I would. I have a few other things I will want to carry with me as well."

"Of course, Highness. I will take care of everything. I only hope when you arrive at your new home they will take as good care of you."

Yasamin actually laughed, a sound like tiny bells tinkling in a light breeze. "I know I shall be well taken care of, Nitae. Of that, there is no doubt."

Nitae frowned. "How can you be so positive, Highness?"

"Nitae, stop being so formal. Call me by your pet name. I need something familiar at the moment. This is a very hard day for me."

"Of course, High-, forgive me, Yase. Why are you so positive you shall be properly attended?"

"Because, Nitae, you are going with me as my personal maid."

"Me!" For a moment Nitae's eyebrows rose so high Yasamin thought they would disappear into her hair. "You are taking me to Dragonval?"

"Of course, silly, did you think I'd leave you here?"

"I ... well ... I'm ... I thought you would take Shichicia or Drudiania. They are much younger and most capable. I'm an old woman and can't think as fast as I used to."

Yasamin placed her mother's gown on the bed and walked to the old woman. Gently, she took hold of each shoulder and looked deeply into the nurse's eyes. "Nitae, Shichicia and Drudiania are much younger and faster and quite capable, but I need someone at Dragonval I know, someone I trust. And there is nothing wrong with your thinking. You always speak honest words. Nitae, you have been my second mother. The Queen would have wanted this also. I can't leave you behind. My cousin, Dreylenwill bring his own court and council. So, unless you don't want to—"

"Oh, no, I am happy to go with you. I prayed to the gods for this. Thank you."

Yasamin smiled gently. "You may not thank me so readily once we reach Dragonval. It sounds like a dreadful place."

"Aye, it does. All the more reason I should be there with you. I will let no one harm you. They shall not lay a finger on the hair of your head unless it is over my dead body!"

"Nitae," Yasamin laughed nervously, "I don't think it will come to that. King Amir has given me his word that all be well."

"That snake! I don't believe any words sliding from his lips."

"Hush, Nitae. We must hope, we must believe, King Amir will be a man of his word. We have no choice but to believe, because if we are wrong, then I—" Yasamin's voice broke and she hugged herself. "Then I—"

"Oh, Highess, forgive me. I'm just a foolish old woman who knows nothing. And very stupid. I shouldn't speak of things of which I know naught. He is a *King*. Of course he will keep his word. A King should be an honorable man. After all, he rules his people and, therefore, is wise and just. I am an old woman who listens to gossip and lets it fog my mind. I should not have said such a thing. Please forgive me."

Yasamin looked at the old woman standing before her. Worry etched the lines deeper into Nitae's face until it seemed it would collapse into itself. In all of her twenty years, Yasamin never remember the nurse looking more vulnerable. When had the old woman's skin become so thin, her hair so white, her hands more frail? Wrapped in her grief, Yasamin had failed to notice the changes in Nitea.

"It's all right, *Mamia.*" This had been Yasamin's pet name for the old nurse when she had been a baby. For a second, its mention took Yasamin back to those days when her only worry had been whether it would rain so she couldn't play in the lush, green fields surrounding the castle.

But that was then.

This was now.

"Nitae, shortly I must prepare for the funerals of our people killed today."

"Yes, and may the gods have mercy on their souls."

"I'm sure they will. The old man was trying to save the boy, and the boy was a mere baby. I doubt he had ever done anything so terrible as to keep him from paradise."

"Of course. I was thinking of the soldier."

For an instant Yasamin could only stare at Nitae. The old woman never ceased to amaze her. "Yes, yes, you are right, *Mamia*. Perhaps they will have mercy on his soul as well when the time comes. But, as I was saying, before I prepare for the funeral, I need you to do two things."

"You have only to speak."

"Prepare my coronation gown. I will wear it tonight."

"Your coronation gown? It would not matter to them if you wore but a sack, Yase, they love you."

"I know; however, I wish them to see me as they did when I assumed the throne after Mother's death. I wish to leave them with a vision as well as my words. I want them to remember me. After all, what I do is for their well-being."

Nitae sighed deeply. "Yes, Highness. But do you truly believe you must do this deed? Is there no other way?"

Tears formed in Yasamin's eyes as she stared at some distant point invisible to Nitae's vision. "No. I *know* I have to do this. King Amir has left no doubt as to the consequences to my country if I don't."

"But it seems so wrong. He already has a Queen. Now he wants you as well."

"In Dragonval it is the custom. If the King's wife is unable to conceive an heir, the King is allowed a second wife."

"But that puts you in second place. Medusimia will still be his first wife."

"But it is the only way I can save my people, the only way I can help my country. What I don't understand is why me? I have no dowry. I met him once when I was but a child, yet he now seems besotted with me. He will have no other but me to become his wife and bear his children."

"But still, it seems-"

"Nitae, listen. But first, swear you will speak of this to no one."

"Of course, Highness, I would never break any confidence you share with me. They would have to rip my tongue—"

"Nitae, I believe you." Sometimes the old woman became zealous showing her loyalty. If Yasamin didn't get her to stop now, they could easily spend the next half hour with Nitae swearing her loyalty despite all tortures. "I received several messages from King Amir, most of them the usual type of thing about finding me desirable and all that. But one night he sent a messenger to me. He arrived very late—"

"I know nothing of any messenger. No one—"

"Nitae, listen! That's exactly the point. The man made sure no one saw him. He was dressed all in black and somehow climbed the wall to my chambers. He waited until I was alone."

"Oh, my gods, why didn't you call for help?"

"I was so stunned I was speechless. By the time I thought to cry out, he had covered my mouth with his hand and told me he was there to deliver a private message from King Amir. He said that if I called for help, he would kill whoever came through the door, even my maids. He said he would chop their heads off and take them with him as proof to show King Amir I would not receive the message."

"Oh, my." Nitae grew pale when she thought of the danger the young woman had been in. "Did he threaten you in any way?"

"He never touched me except for putting his hand over my mouth and whispering in my ear to not make a sound. When I nodded agreement, he removed it. But the warning was clear in his eyes. He wouldn't have hesitated to hurt me or anyone else. In fact, I had the feeling he almost hoped someone would show. Violence surrounded him like a cloak."

"What did he say?"

"First he repeated the things King Amir had already said—how he had fallen in love with me the first time he saw me. He said the King had realized I was the only hope he had for becoming a better man. If I married him, he could develop that love because he had never had such feelings for anyone, not even his Queen. Then the man told me King Amir said to make sure I understood he wouldn't take no for an answer. If I did not come to him willingly and marry him, he would give himself up to the dark side to get what he desires. He would come to Gwendomere and take me by force. And if he had to come to Gwendomere—" Yasamin's voice trembled and she stopped.

"What? What is it, Yase?"

"He would take me and destroy my country. He would slay every man and boy child, and every woman and girl would be taken into slavery. He would kill the livestock, raze the buildings, kill every blade of grass. He would destroy everything. And then he would sow salt so deep that nothing would ever grow here again. And worse—"

"What else could he possibly do?"

Yasamin look at Nitae, her eyes wide with horror. What little color was in her face drained and tears filled her eyes. After a moment, she whispered, "He said he would dig up the grave of my mother. He would, he would—"

"Go, child, go on." Nitae placed her gnarled hand on Yasamin's arm. She could feel the young woman trembling.

"He said he would—" Yasamin lowered her voice even more, "he would piss on my mother's bones, then scatter them to the winds. She would never rest in paradise."

"Oh, ye gods!" Nitae signed to ward off the evil eye. She started to put her arms around Yasamin, but the young girl held up her hand to stop her. She straightened her back and once more spoke in a normal voice. "I will not let that happen. It does not matter about me, but I will not let him dishonor my country, my people nor my mother."

"And if you marry him?"

"King Amir will leave Gwendomere alone, and my cousin may reign in peace. The country will be left alone unless it uprises against him. Gwendomere will continue to exist as it always has. He says he has no desire for a land of sheep."

"You believe the word of such a monster, such a beast, such a heartless liar—"

"Enough!" Yasamin seldom raised her voice at the old nurse. Seeing the pain it caused, Yasamin softened her tone. "Nitae, I believe what he says is true. I can help him become better. I have to believe it. I have to try. I have to do this for my people. I will not let him slaughter them. I will not let my country be destroyed and erased from history. If I have to live with a 'monster' to keep this from happening, then it will be so. My mother would have done the same to save them. You know this is true."

"Yes. It is." The old woman bowed her head for a moment. When she raised it, her eyes glistened with tears. "I was present at your birth, and you were such a beautiful baby everyone was overcome with love for you. I watched you grow into a sweet, young girl, then a young woman who has seen much sadness. And now, I see that same young princess has become a Queen. Your mother would be proud of you."

"Thank you, *Mamia*. I will always treasure your words. But now we must hurry. After you prepare my coronation gown, there are some special things I need you to pack." Yasamin hurried to her dressing table. "All my jewels." She gathered small boxes and placed them in a stack. "These were my mother's, but I seldom wear any of them. They'll have to be my dowry. We'll pick out clothes later. Oh, and I want this and this." She hurried around her room picking up several books, a tiny figurine and a music box. "Pack all of these. Oh, and especially this." Yasamin hurried toward the huge tapestry hanging on the wall beside the fireplace and pushed the corner of it aside. Behind was a small door built within the rock. Opening the door, Yasamin carefully lifted out an ancient, wooden box and brought it to the bed. The box was carved from cedar, a wood seldom seen in Gwendomere, and there were traces of gold paint from a design long worn away.

As simple as the box appeared, there was an aura about it which sent tingles down Nitae's spine. "What is it?" she whispered.

Reverently, Yasamin placed the box on the bed and gently worked the lock to open it. Inside was a small book so old the parchment had aged corn yellow. The leather binding was well worn. "I don't know really. It was my mother's, and it was very important to her. She said to hide it in a safe place because some day I would need it."

"But what is it? Her journal?"

Yasamin shook her head. "Not a journal. Some of the words seem familiar, but others I do not recognize. I just know she said it was very important, and I would need it someday. That I would know when the time came." Gently, she opened the book and touched the worn pages. A whiff of *moonlitea* enveloped the two women.

Nitae came around the bed and bent for a closer look. The words were faint, written in gold ink. Nitae drew in a sharp breath.

"What is it, *Mamia*?"

"The language, it is Gwelosharin."

"Gwelosharin? What is that?"

"A very ancient language once spoken here. A long time ago there were many who knew this language, but their numbers have grown few. Rumor is there are only a handful who can speak and read it. Much of our own language is based on Gwelosharian. That's why you recognize some words. But why would your mother have this?"

Yasamin glanced at Nitae. "Why does it surprise you?"

"As I said, there are very few who speak or read Gwelosharian," replied Nitae. She dropped her eyes to the floor and would not look at Yasamin. Not so with the book—it was a magnet. Slowly, Nitae's eyes slid back to it. She tenderly touched one of the pages.

"What are you not telling me, Nitae? There is more. I see it in your face. Speak."

"I was a very little girl, Highness. Much I have forgotten."

"Tell me what you remember."

"It is said in ancient times, long before our land became settled by our father's father's father, an ancient people lived here. They lived simply, but their knowledge was much beyond that in the known world. The language they spoke was Gwelosharian. Their way of life was very different from all their neighbors. Their beliefs were so powerful many people were afraid of them and called them wizards and witches because they did not understand these people. Perhaps they were, I do not know. But one thing I do know, these people were good. They did not walk in the darkness. They used their powers only for good, but it didn't matter. They were constantly attacked by other peoples who were afraid of them and their power or by those who hoped to gain access to that power for their own selfish ends. Many were killed, and finally, they retreated to distant mountains or deep forests to escape. However, some remained and mingled with neighbors who tolerated them. They wrote their beliefs in books with golden ink because they believed their way was the true way to light. I, I Nitae hesitated.

Yasamin was fascinated. She gently nudged Nitae. "Go on, Mamia. What?"

"I remember once when I was very young, a woman came to our village. She was beautiful, but it is her eyes I remember most. They were like silver metal in the sunlight. She was one of the ancient ones. Many of the children were sick with a disease that was killing them. This woman healed them. She performed some kind of ceremony and, and—it was like magic. Every child was cured. Instantly. All of them at once. Later that night I slipped out of our house and went to find her. She was in a cave just outside the village. Everyone there had tried to give her their house in which to stay, but she preferred the cave. I was quiet as I slipped up, quiet as a little mouse. She was sitting in front of a fire, dropping herbs in a boiling pot. It was a wonderful smell, very sweet, so sweet it made my mouth water." Nitae closed here eyes and breathed deeply. In her mind, she could smell the broth.

"Go on, Nitae," Yasamin whispered. "What happened?"

"Well, child, I'll tell you. Perhaps she was a witch. I made not a sound, not a peep or crack of limb, yet she suddenly called out, 'Nitae, come closer to the fire, so you will not chill, and I'll give you some of this delicious *babashe*'. I don't know how she knew my name or that I was there, but she did."

"Did you go?"

"Of course. I wasn't scared of her. I went and sat by the fire. 'What are you doing here, Nitae,' she said. 'I came to find you. I want to know how you did your magic today and healed the children.' I told her. 'No, not magic, Nitae,' she told me. 'It is more like faith, that which I call upon.' I said, 'But the book you had, it had spells; did it not? And how do you know my name?' She smiled. 'I know your name because I heard someone call you. And my book, well, maybe you could call them spells, but I prefer to call them formulas. They help me concentrate on the particular need I have.' I interrupted her. 'Well, then how did you know I was here? That has to be magic.' And do you know what she told me?"

Yasamin shook her head as she gazed at Nitae. Even after so many decades, Yasmin could see the wonder shine in the old nurse's eyes. "What?"

"She said she 'felt' me. She *felt* me in the woods."

"How could she feel you?"

"That's what I wanted to know. She said everything on earth has its own distinctive aura. Each blade of grass, each rock, each bird, everything, much like the print you leave when your hands are dirty and you touch something white. She was very smart. I wanted to be just like her, and I told her so. She said for me to come sit beside her and I did. She pulled out her little book and read some passages from it. I didn't understand a lot of them, being a child, but I knew what she was reading was important, had some special meaning. It was so beautiful I wanted to cry. She let me hold the book for a few minutes. I shall never forget how it looked. As I held it, I could feel a tingle in my fingers as I traced the letters on its cover. Yase, I wanted to go with her and learn more about her ways. I had forgotten my mother, father, my sisters—everyone. All I could think about was going with this woman and learning everything I could."

"But you did not."

Nitae shook her head. "No, I didn't. When I told her I wanted to go with her, she smiled and shook her head. She said I had a very important mission in life, a *crucial* mission, and I must follow that path. It was not meant for me to be one of their leaders. But she said if I believed in what she told me, I could do some of the things she did. I wish I hadn't been so small. When she spoke about more than one world and borrowed time, it didn't make much sense to me. Eventually I fell asleep in her lap. When I awoke the next morning, I was in my bed."

"And the woman?"

"I ran back to the cave. She was gone. There was nothing but a tiny silkworm weaving a nest. From that day, I have never heard these people mentioned."

"Until now."

Nitae looked at Yasamin and nodded her head. "Yes, but that is not all."

"What else?"

Nitae reached out and gently closed the book in Yasamin's hand. Reverently, she traced the faint letters on its front. "This is the same cover, the same words that were on her book. It is one of *their* books, so how did your mother obtain one?"

"I don't know. Nitae, can you read this?"

"Not really. Like I said, I don't remember much of what she told me. It was too complicated for a baby." Again, Nitae traced the letters on the cover. "I do know this much. This book contains their beliefs, and I know what the cover says."

"What?"

"*The road of silk.* That is all I know."

Yasamin gently returned the book to its box. "We'll talk again. Perhaps you will remember something else. But now we must hurry. Time has flown. I have to prepare for the funerals. Be sure to put all of these things in a safe place, Nitae. When I return from the funeral, I'll prepare to say my farewell to my people.

As soon as Nitae had dressed Yasamin for the funerals and the Queen had departed, the old nurse returned to the bedroom. Carefully, she opened the worn box and touched the book. The memories of that night were as fresh in her mind as they had been more than seventy years before. She could almost hear the fire's crackle, the song of the crickets and smell the sweet herbs. If only she had gone with the woman, she might be able to help her beloved Queen. Somewhere along the way she had failed because in the decades that had passed, she still did not know what her important mission was. Tears ran down the nurse's wrinkled cheeks as she gently traced the golden letters on the cover. She could still feel the tingle in her fingertips. So much knowledge. So close. If only she knew how to use it.

Slowly, she closed the lid, and with a long sigh, she began packing her Queen's possessions.

* * * * *

The last of the sun's rays grasped at the blazing red clouds like the fingertips of a lover loathe to release the hand of the beloved. But leave it must, and gradually, the orb slipped beneath the horizon. The glorious reds and oranges faded to pinks, lavender then indigo and, finally, black. Stars twinkled in the black velvet, echoed on the ground by the hundreds of fiery torches surrounding the courtyard beneath the castle's balcony. The torches threw their glowing arms upward, casting back the darkness. More of them twinkled in the distance as people moved up the path toward the castle. The square glowed almost as bright as day as hundreds of people crowded into the area. The more agile had climbed the trees in order to see the young queen. Every possible perch, every foothold had been confiscated to accommodate someone a better view.

True to his word, Goliagoth had kept his soldiers out of the village for the funerals, but seeing the mass of people coming for Yasamin's farewell, he decided to stand guard. Taking twelve of his best men, he posted them throughout the area to prevent a riot from breaking out. Not only had all the villagers come, but those from the surrounding areas drifted in as well. The people seemed harmless enough, but in vast numbers, Goliagoth had seen "harmless" people become bold. After the day's earlier events, Goliagoth was hoping there would be no more violence, whether his men wanted it or not. The entire afternoon he had noticed the surreptitious glances of his soldiers, and he knew they were wondering what had possessed him to agree to Yasamin's terms. More importantly, he knew they were wondering what had possessed him to order them to dig graves for mere peasants. Anger ran close under the surface. It would not take much to fan it into action.

Waiting for the queen to appear, Goliagoth glanced around. The crowd had children as well as elders, but regardless of their age, all stood quietly, expectantly, waiting. For the most part, the villagers ignored him as well as his men—it was almost as if they didn't exist. More than likely, at the moment, the soldier's didn't exist. All minds were on one thing.

Yasamin.

Goliagoth leaned against one of the castle's abutments. He had the advantage of being in front of the crowd but could also have a good view of the queen. His second-in-command shared a similar position on the other side of the entrance. If necessary, they could keep anyone from going into the castle. Or, if need be, keep anyone in.

Ever alert, Goliagoth became aware of a stirring among the villagers—the low murmurs became louder, turning into a shout. All eyes turned toward the balcony. Goliagoth followed their glances upward and again felt his breath catch deep in his chest.

Yasamin.

He had thought her beautiful earlier that day, now she was glorious. Her long hair cascaded over her left shoulder in glimmering silver waves. The light of the torches reflected in the curls, giving her hair a life of its own. It gleamed, glittered with every movement. The golden light of the torches warmed her porcelain skin until she seemed to glow. She wore a very simple gown that clung to her body in soft folds. It was made of silver silk threaded with hints of blue that matched her eyes. She wore no jewels and needed none. She *was* the jewel. Standing above the torch-encrusted courtyard, she was a phoenix rising from the flames.

As she moved to the edge of the balcony, the shout grew until it became a mighty roar. Listening, Goliagoth felt the slightest of shivers run across his arms as the many voices shouting one name washed over him in waves.

"Queen Yasamin! *Salutia*, Queen Yasamin! *Salutia*, Queen Yasamin!"

For a moment, Yasamin could only stand and look at the mighty ocean of people before her. She could not remember seeing so many people at one time, not even at her own mother's funeral. A lump rose in her throat as she fought back the tears. Her love for her people threatened to overwhelm her. Finally, she raised her slender arms and waited for silence.

"My people." She halted, drew a deep breath and began again. "My people. Tonight I stand here to bid you farewell. Tomorrow I leave for Dragonval to marry King Amir. Even though our land is poor compared to Dragonval, King Amir has declared he shall marry me and no other. And though I have no dowry—"

A middle-age woman from the crowd interrupted Yasamin with a shout. "My Queen, I have little, but I give you what I have for your dowry." The woman threw a small pouch of coins toward the castle door where one of the Queen's guards stood.

"As do I," replied another who pulled a gold bracelet from her arm and tossed it toward the pouch. The bracelet had been in her family for years, hoarded for a time of famine when it would have been used for food.

"And me," shouted an old man from the edge of the crowd. He pitched a small bag onto the growing heap. The rotten cloth split. Gold coins peeked through the tear.

The voices grew as each cried and tossed whatever they had of value. For a full five minutes the crowd shifted and swayed as those farther back came forward to add their contribution to the ever-growing heap.

Again, the hollow ache hit Goliagoth deep in his chest. He had never seen such a sight. The only loyalty he knew was born through respect, or more likely fear, for someone stronger. These people were loyal but for neither reason. He had heard the word, but never in his entire life had he experienced the power it could have.

Yasamin was speechless. She had not expected such a display from her subjects. Her lips trembled, and tears welled in her eyes as she fought for control. She had known her people loved her, but never had she guessed the depth of that love. It was overwhelming and humbling.

She could do no less than to honor them by accepting their gifts. To do otherwise would be an insult to their love.

When the gifts had ceased, she began again. "My people, thank you for your generosity. What you have done here is the greatest honor I could ever receive and worth more to me than all the treasures of Dragonval. I shall present my dowry to King Amir with the greatest of pride.

"As I had been about to say, although our country is poor, I shall take with me a wealth of memories of a wonderful people. Tonight, what you have just done here is priceless. You and Gwendomere shall forever live in my heart, more precious than any jewel.

"You know my cousin, Mezodale, who will assume the throne. I believe he will be good to you for he is a good and just man. I ask that you give him the same loyalty as you have given me.

"I was very small when my mother returned here with me. I remember nothing of my former residence, but I remember your welcome. Because of your love, Gwendomere *became* home. I may live in many places, but this country is the only one I shall ever claim as *my* home." Again, Yasamin's voice wavered. Drawing a deep breath, she reached for the strength she needed. Her people would see her as a Queen of whom they would be proud. "It does not matter if I have to live forever in another country, in my heart, whenever I am lonely, whenever I am sad, I shall call upon my memories of you and Gwendomere and draw comfort.

"And this is my gift to you. I agreed to this marriage with one condition. The King has given me his word, his oath. I will become King Amir's wife, and in return, he will never harm you nor Gwendomere." At this declaration, Yasamin glanced down at Goliagoth and a few of his soldiers. Drawing herself to her full height, she became the Queen he had met earlier that day. Yasamin raised her voice so that it rang clearly throught the plaza. "I will make sure all nations are advised of this promise and will do everything in my power to see they protect you if the King fails in his pledge. King Amir will not rule this country. This marriage does not unite Dragonval and Gwendomere. I have made this clear to the King and his counsel and had a document drawn and witnessed to this effect. I want this country, I want—" Yasamin lost her voice. She stared at the faces before her as if to memorize every one. One hand covered her mouth so they would not see her lips tremble as tears threatened to overwhelm her.

Nitae had been standing behind her. Now she moved forth and whispered something in the Queen's ear. Yasamin waved at her people and returned to her quarters.

* * * * *

At daylight Goliagoth met Yasamin and Nitae at the castle door. Quickly, the *Demolishserian* barked orders to his soldiers. He pointed to a young recruit. "You. Get the Queen's trunks."

"*Demolishserian*," Yasamin spoke softly.

The huge man glanced at her. "Highness?"

"Make sure someone you trust carries that chest," she nodded toward a small, ornate chest with a lock. "*That* is my royal dowry. I will hold you accountable to see it gets to King Amir."

"It will. I give you my word."

"The word of a *Demolisherian*? We shall see."

Goliagoth bit back the retort that sprung to his lips and yelled to another soldier. The man hurried to him. Goliagoth rapidly spoke rapidly to him in their native tongue and gestured toward the small chest. The man blanched, then saluted and hurried to heave the chest to his shoulder.

"What did you say to him?"

"Frankly, Your Highness, you don't want to know. But rest assured your dowry is safe. Now we must hurry."

The troop quickly formed around Yasamin and Nitae. With Goliagoth leading, they stepped outside into the bright light. Yasamin gasped. The entire village waited before her. They must have stayed all night in order to see her leave. The convoy moved forward. No one spoke, but as the Queen passed, each man, woman and child bowed before her.

Just before the group reached the edge of the village where the rest of the soldiers waited, a tiny girl ran out and grabbed the *Demolisherian's* leg. She tenaciously clung to Goliagoth with one hand and beat at him with the other.

"You killed my brother and hurt my mama, and now you're taking the Queen away. I hate you! I hate you! I won't let you do it!" she screamed.

The troop halted unsure what to do. Goliagoth looked down at the child. Her black curls bounced with each blow, and her face flushed crimson with the effort.

"Well, well, what do we have here?" The giant reached down and picked her up with one huge paw. He lifted his arm until child hung inches from his face. Still she screamed and tried to hit him in the face. Her tiny arms were too short to reach. Goliagoth threw back his head and laughed. "I have to say, here's one sheep who has some spirit. 'Tis a babe, but I see more spunk in her than all the men in the village." He grew quiet and his eyes narrowed. "And how do you think you can stop me, little one?"

The small child quit screaming and looked him in the eye. "I'll stop you. I'll ... I'll kick you and make you fall down. Then I'll stab you. I'll take a big, long knife like yours and stab you through the heart with it." The small child was deadly serious; the giant could see it in her eyes. He considered her a long moment. His voice lowered until it rumbled in his chest. All laughter left his eyes. "That wouldn't work."

"Why?"

The *Demolisherian* brought the little girl closer to his face, his eyes never leaving hers. "Because I do not *have* a heart. But I do like to eat stew made from the hearts of tender ones such as you."

Yasamin drew in her breath. She was terrified for the child who had suddenly hushed. The child's anger had evaporated and been replaced by fear.

"*Demolisherian*", Yasamin whispered.

Goliagoth swiveled his eyes and saw her fear, not for herself, but for the child.

"Will you break your word before you leave my village? You promised."

Goliagoth was aware of the restlessness among his soldiers. Too much lenience on his part could jeopardize his command over them. Yet he had given his word. For a long second, he stared hard at the slender woman. At last he spoke. "So I did, Highness. But I'll not stand for insult either." He walked over to Yasamin with the child suspended high in his hand, just as her brother had been the day before. Yasamin held her breath, unsure of the child's fate. Goliagoth glanced once more at the little girl, then thrust her into Nitae's arms.

"She insulted an officer of Dragonval's army. As *Demolisherian* of this squadron *I* decide the punishment. She's young, but she is feisty. She will serve well in my country. Your Highness, as the wee one seems attached to you, she is now your slave." A snarl of a grin twisted his lips. "Consider it my wedding present."

Goliagoth whirled and faced his men. "Let's march. We've wasted too much valuable time in this god-forsaken village."

The queen gave one last look and then turned to leave.

A strong voice broke the silence. "Your Highness, wait!"

Yasamin turned. A tall, dark-haired stranger stepped through the crowd which parted before him. With a heavy sigh, Goliagoth twisted his neck to see who had spoken. He turned quickly to face the approaching man and rested his hand on the hilt of his sword. He had seen this kind before. Strong. Brave. Usually the kind who acted before thinking. Most of the time, men like this meant one thing—trouble.

Removing his hat, the man stopped in front of Yasamin and knelt on one knee. He bowed his head, then looked up into Yasamin's face.

Her heart quickened as she stared into his dark brown eyes. She felt she was drowning in them. They were so piercing she thought he could see straight into her soul. Suddenly, she realized he was staring at her, waiting for permission to talk. Quickly she gathered herself together. "Speak."

"Your Highness, I am Arash, from Pars. Forgive our tardiness. We planned to arrive last night but, unfortunately, were detained. We have an urgent message for you."

"We?"

The young man rose. "Yes, your Highness. I escorted Shar. She said it most urgent you receive a message."

At this, the man looked back toward the crowd, and Yasamin followed his glance. An old woman, looking as ancient as the hills surrounding the town, approached through the parted crowd. In spite of her obvious age, the woman stood tall and straight as she slowly advanced toward them. She was dressed in a long, dark blue cape and hood. Spikes of snow white hair stuck out around her face, but most noticeable were her eyes. They were as silver as Yasamin's hair. They gleamed. Yasamin heard a slight gasp behind her and looked over her shoulder. Open-mouthed, Nitae was staring at the old woman. All color had drained from the nurse's face. The queen frowned and glanced back to the approaching woman. The stranger did not seem threatening in any way, just ... *different.*

The old woman walked straight to Yasamin. Unlike Arash, Shar did not bow. Yasamin stared at the old woman. Her face was far more wrinkled than Nitae's, the skin thin over high cheekbones. It was a strong face, a face without fear. In her hand was a metal cane with a strange knob. In a flash of recognition, Yasamin realized the knob was shaped like a silkworm.

Shar stared deeply into Yasamin's eyes. For a second or so, it seemed to the Queen she and the old woman were the only ones in the universe, all else had ceased to exist. Then Shar looked at Nitae. The slightest hint of a smile touched the corner of Shar's mouth, then disappeared so quickly Yasamin thought she had imagined it. The old woman glanced at Goliagoth and his second-in-command. If their massiveness intimidated her, it did not show. Dismissing them with the slightest narrowing of her eyes, Shar returned her glance to Yasamin.

"Queen Yasamin, I am Shar. I came as soon as I received word of your marriage to King Amir. This marriage is an abomination, and I condemn it for the facade it is. Do not always believe what you see only with your eyes or hear with your ears. You must see with *this*." Shar touched the spot over her heart. "You have a great mission, but you also have the choice as to whether you will fulfill it. One road is easy; the other full of many trials and tribulations. If you have a true heart, child, I will guide you as much as I can. If you choose to fight evil, you must not flinch. You

"Silence, crone! You are interfering where you don't belong and your words are treason," shouted Nemoith. Several of the soldiers muttered agreement.

Shar merely looked at the giant man. "Silence? Truth will not be silent. I have the power to stop you this moment if I so choose, but the choice is the Queen's to make," she hissed. "You and your comrades are a plague—hateful, spiteful creatures who destroy everything in your path. And the blackest of all is the one who rules your country. You think I fear you, you frail human being? You are pitiful against the force of truth. Your ships will be destroyed on this voyage and *you* will drown."

Nemoith's face deepened to a bluish-red. "Shut up, you lying bitch. You dare threaten me?" he screamed. Before Arash or Goliagoth could move, Nemoith grabbed the spear of the man next to him and threw it at Shar.

Faster than a thought, the old woman whipped her unusual staff between her and the oncoming weapon. The spear bounced harmlessly off the metal and fell to the ground.

Shar returned her gaze to Yasamin. The light in her silver eyes glowed brighter. "Yasamin, the time will come, remember the road of silk." With a soft *swish*, the old woman burst into thousands of silver butterflies that flew up into the air and disappeared into the bright sunlight.

Yasamin and Nitae gasped as did the villagers. The only one who moved was Arash. He jumped forward and knocked Nemoith to the ground. Both men fell in a jumble of arms and elbows. Goliagoth grabbed Arash and pulled him off the soldier. No matter hard Arash struggled, he could not pull free of the huge man's grasp. Nemoith jumped to his feet and made to draw his sword.

"Hold!" roared Goliagoth, but Nemoith, in his rage, continued to draw his weapon. "Seize him," the commander ordered. "Cast him in chains if his blade clears his scabbard."

Nemoith hesitated, then let the sword slide back. He glared at Arash through slitted eyes filled with hate. "He hit me. You will allow a foreigner to get away with the insult?"

Goliagoth stared hard at his second-in-command. "He will pay, but not by your blade. It is a hard voyage filled with danger. He's a strong man and full of piss and vinegar that we'll use to our advantage. We'll put him on the oars." Goliagoth released one of Arash's arms and swung him around, so Arash was forced to stare up at the giant. "You are young and strong but foolhardy. You've just earned yourself the chance to see Dragonval's splendor—if you survive. Cause any more trouble and I'll cut your throat with my own blade." Goliagoth shoved Arash toward the two nearest soldiers. "Put him in chains. Keep a close watch on him. Tonight bring him to my cabin. I want to question him about the hag. Now, let us go. We're behind schedule."

Goliagoth moved to the two women. "I obtained a cart. You two and the child will ride in it, along with your trunks. 'Tis not fancy but will save your feet." He lifted Yasamin into the wooden cart before she could open her mouth and turned toward Nitae. Seeing what had happened to her Queen, Nitae slapped at his hands, protesting she could get in by herself. Goliagoth ignored her and lifted the nurse with one hand, the child with the other and deposited them beside Yasamin.

Once again, the ground trembled as the soldiers marched. The villagers gazed at the troop until they disappeared from sight. Yasamin looked back once, but the expressions on her people's faces ripped at her heart, and she turned her gaze back to the broad shoulders of Goliagoth in the lead. Whatever lay ahead, she had to face it, not only for herself but for Gwendomere as well. She wondered what her trials would be and if she had the courage. Most of all, she wondered what Shar had meant by "remember the road of silk."

Had she known what lay before her, Yasamin might have never have left Gwendomere.

Chapter 3

"I will not stand for it. How dare you!" The young woman stormed into the large chamber and marched toward the two men at the oak desk sifting through parchments. Hearing the strident voice, the older man, bending over the shoulder of the younger to point at a lengthy passage, cringed, then bowed low. Remaining bowed, he discreetly moved to the other side of the younger man, in the hopes it would provide him some protection from the approaching terror. The younger man merely glanced in her direction, then returned his attention to the document.

This seemed to anger her even more, if such a thing was possible. She moved to stand in front of the desk and slammed both hands down on it. The old advisor jumped and moved back another two feet. The younger merely glanced at her with annoyance, then returned to reading the parchment.

She swatted at the document, knocking it out of his hands. "Amir, I'm speaking to you. Answer me!" she screamed.

Amir calmly gazed at his wife, Medusimia. By the gods, she was beautiful even when angry. She was tall and angular, with a mane of curly blue-black hair and skin pale as snow. Her eyes were the color of honey, and when she was angry, like now, flecks of red sparked in them. He could see the scarlet specks now, along with the bright red splotches on each high cheekbone. Her black curls trembled with her barely-contained fury. A sliver of desire stirred in Amir's groin, and he was half tempted to take her there on the desk. He loved the fire in her, but he had important work to do.

"Amir!" There were times her husband drove her close to the brink of insanity. Medusimia glared at the calm man. He was a full head taller than she, slim but well-built. His hair was jet black with wings of silver at the temples; his face was lean and angular with high cheekbones. He trimmed his black beard close and into a point on the chin. That and the thin mustache added emphasis to his full, sensuous mouth. But it was his eyes that captured one's attention. They were dark, so dark there was no discernible difference between the iris and the pupil. His eyes had fascinated her the moment she had met him. When he was angry, she swore she could see movement of something even darker stirring in them. He was a dangerous man, which only excited her. At the moment, though, all she could think of was the insult he had delivered to her. "Do you hear? I will not have it."

Amir cocked a ebony eyebrow. "Really? It's done." He returned his concentration to papers before him, picking up the one she had knocked from his grasp.

"It is not. I said I will not have it!" Medusimia ripped the document from his hand again and threw it to the floor. Then she swept all of the documents from the desktop. Like a frightened flock of doves, they flew in every direction. "It is not done, I tell you." She glanced at the trembling advisor who had retreated several more steps during her tirade. "Get out!" she screamed at him.

The old man bowed and turned to go.

Amir's generous mouth tightened. "Melrex, stay. We have work."

The old man stopped and looked uncertainly at the Queen.

She shrieked at him again, "I said get out!"

"Stay, Melrex."

The advisor swallowed hard and turned the color of a mushroom. Both of these people terrified him, and when they were angry, he couldn't think of a word capable of describing his fear. He stumbled, taking one step forward, then two steps backward, only to step forward again as he tried to follow both commands.

Medusimia glared at her husband. "If you wish to air your dirty laundry in front of anyone, it matters not to me. I *will* have my say. Now." She straightened and crossed her arms across her chest.

Amir knew she would. Medusimia had no qualms when it came to getting what she wanted. He knew she would do whatever it took. But clever as she was, she was not as smart as he. A headache burst behind his eyes and tugged at his temples. He had a lot to do in a short time. Better to be done with it now. He glanced at his advisor. "Melrex, leave us for a few minutes. Wait in the hall. I'll call you when Her Majesty and I are finished."

The old man bowed. "Yes, Your Highness, of course." He hurried from the room as fast as his arthritic legs could carry him.

The door had barely closed before Medusimia whirled on her husband. "I cannot believe you have insulted me thus!"

"I have not insulted you."

"Liar! I have to hear from the maids' gossip that you have sent Goliagoth to Gwendomere."

"We had this discussion before. I told you I would send him to escort Yasamin to Dragonval several months ago."

"Yasamin! That stupid, mousy, little sheep! I told you she isn't suitable! I can't believe you wo

"She is *my* choice."

Medusimia darted around the desk to stand before Amir. "What kind of choice is she? Look at me, Amir." She moved closer and leaned her face toward him. "I am beautiful, am I not?" She stood back up and held her arms out as she did a slow pivot. "Look at me, Amir." Slowly Medusimia ran her hands up her bare arms. "Look at my skin; it's as smooth as *sashamin*." She ran her hands over her breasts and lifted them slightly so they budged against the top of her low-cut gown. "My breasts are perfect, like honeydew melons. How many times have you buried your face in them and moaned with pleasure?" She ran her hands down to her waist. "And my waist is tiny, perfect, small enough your hands reach around it to hold me on you." She continued to trail her hands down toward her hips and thighs. Amir again felt the tingle of desire stir in his loins. Medusimia leaned down so they were face-to-face. Her voice became husky. "And my legs, long and strong so I can draw you deeper and deeper into me until you are groaning in pleasure. Look at me, Amir, *I* am perfect. I am a Queen. I am *your* Queen."

Amir's eyes had followed Medusimia's hands as she had traced her body. Now he raised them to hers. Lust minced his voice with hoarseness. "Yes, you are beautiful."

The queen grasped his hand and lifting it to her breast whispered, "I am. I am all you need. I am *your* Queen."

"You are, and you shall remain my First Queen."

"Your *First* Queen!" Medusimia thrust herself away. "Your *First* Queen. I am your *only* Queen. You cannot unite yourself with this milk-sot, whimpering wisp of a girl. She has no dowry, no value. Compared to my beauty and perfection she is ugly as well as an oaf. You will not unite with her. I forbid it!"

Before Medusimia could blink, Amir sprung from his chair and gripped her wrist. Ruthlessly, he twisted her arm behind her until Medusimia was mashed against him, and she was forced to look up to see his face. A small shiver darted through her stomach as she stared into his eyes. In them she saw something blacker than black swirl.

"YOU forbid it," he hissed. "Don't forget who is King, Medusimia. *I* am the ruler, not you. I enjoy your spark, but don't make the mistake of overstepping your bounds." Amir tightened his grip. He knew he was hurting her. He knew it because he could see it in the wincing of her eyes, the tightening of her mouth. He wanted to hurt her. He wanted to dominate her. The thrill of domination excited him. "You may be beautiful, Medusimia, but you are not perfect. You can not give me what a common milk maid or a whore could give me—a child. You're as barren as the island of rocks to the west of Dragonval. No seed grows in your plowed field, and by the gods, I will have what I need. I grant you the privilege of First Queen, and for that, you should be grateful. Yasamin is *my* choice, and she shall give me what you cannot, a son, an heir. So watch your tongue. If she can produce an heir for me, I might consider making *her* my First Queen."

"You wouldn't dare," Medusimia whispered. "Everyone knows your alliance with my country is too important for you to do such a thing."

"I will do *what* I wish *when* I wish. It will bode you well to remember that. Now go. I have business to attend to." Amir thrust Medusimia from him and sat back down in the chair. "You have made a mess. It'll take me twice as long to finish this."

"You will regret this, Amir."

He glanced at Medusimia glaring at him, while she rubbed her wrist. "If I do, so will you. And remember this, I don't care if you like Yasamin or not. In public you will treat her as my second wife, just as you will do in my presence. I will not listen to you two arguing. And you will do nothing to harm her. If she comes down with a case of poisoning or any unusual accidents, I will know who is behind it. Listen and heed what I am saying. Now go. Tell Melrex to come in as you leave."

Amir sighed and laid his head against the chair. His closed eyes made it clear that he had nothing more to say to her.

Assuming a regal stance, Medusimia whirled and went to the door. Jerking it open, she barely glanced at the elderly advisor who stood just outside and wondered if he had overheard any of the conversation. Without a word she turned away and hurried down the hall. If her husband would not listen to reason, she knew someone who could help her. It was dangerous but she didn't care. She would remain the *first* and *only* Queen. In the end Amir would thank her.

* * * * *

Medusimia glanced over her shoulder to make sure no one followed.

The graveled path was empty. No sound broke the waiting stillness. Drawing her dark cloak tighter, Medusimia hurried into the thick grove of trees bordering the path. Among the trees the darkness was tangible. Slowly, she searched for the tiny trail leading to the bottom of the ravine. Finding it, she picked her way down. The more she descended, the more difficult it was to see. A thick, ropy fog coiled around the twisted tree roots. Twice Medusimia stopped to listen. The only sound was the occasional trickling of pebbles loosened by her downward journey. No chirp, no owl's hoot, no scurrying of small feet, broke the silence. She glanced up at the full moon. A dark cloud drifted across and obliterated its pale face. Total blackness enfolded her. For a moment, Medusimia's courage almost failed—failed until she remembered her earlier confrontation with Amir. Her fury and resolve returned. No one, not even her husband, would insult her in such a shameless manner and get away with it.

He would pay.

He would pay dearly.

Straightening her back, Medusimia plunged forward. Amir had no idea of her numerous resources. Not only was she beautiful, she was much more clever than her husband would ever imagine, and she would do whatever it took to obtain her goal.

Reaching the bottom of the ravine, she slowly moved forward, feeling her way more than seeing. It had been a long time since she had been here, but Medusimia was confident she would find it.

At last, she broke into a small clearing. She was close. A satisfied smile played across her full lips. No woman had the backbone to do what she was about to do, which only proved she should be First and *only* Queen. The knowledge that she alone had the ability to win the help of the one she sought made her giddy with power.

She carefully moved toward the ruins of an ancient tower. The entrance to the cave was near it. She found the first of the large stones and began to count. At the sixth boulder, Medusimia turned left and counted six paces. There, among the twisted vines before her, lay the way. Walking to the edge, Medusimia drew a deep breath and called in a loud voice, "*Vuturia ulta comsemu auna thrata!*" Having uttered her call, Medusimia sat on the large stone and waited.

In a few moments, she detected a stirring of the thick, dark air and the faintest whisper of wings. The sound sent chills rippling across her skin, but she straightened her back and rose. The sound grew louder and at last a huge *buzimorian* appeared. Dark blue-black feathers covered its vulture-like body. Its head, supported on a long, skinny neck, was little more than a skull with deep-set ruby eyes that glowed through the darkness. The huge beak dominated its face, the curving upper bill capable of ripping a man's arm from his body. Each leg ended in a three-clawed toe tipped with razor-sharp talons. It was believed the talons emitted a poison when they tore flesh. The faint odor of decay followed the bird.

Slowly, the *buzimorian* circled Medusimia, its blazing eyes examining her closely. Finally satisfied, it lifted its head and cawed, "*Xxxxxaiexxxx.*" The harsh sound echoed through the silent woods. With a last look at Medusimia the giant bird retraced its flight through the thicket. Quickly, Medusimia pursued it, fighting her way through the tangled vines. Occasionally, the *buzimorian* glanced back, making sure she followed. Thus they traveled, bird and woman, through the dark woods for three fingers of time.

At last, Medusimia detected a faint, red glow shining from the base of a hill. The *buzimorian* perched on top of a rough boulder at the mouth of the cave. It curved its huge wings inward and watched Medusimia approach. When she reached the bird's perch, the buzimorian swiveled its head toward the cave's entrance. Slowly, Medusimia entered.

The first thing she noticed was the smell, strong and similar to sulphur and mixed with an undertone of something she didn't want to acknowledge. It was easier to see in the cave because of the faint red glow. The tunnel twisted downward, and the further she descended, the brighter it became—warmer as well. Going around a sharp corner, Medusimia entered a huge underground chamber. The light came from dozens of fissures in the ground which issued fire. Hotness filled the room. The smell of sulphur was almost overwhelming. The remains of hundreds of bones were scattered around the room. Most were animal's, but even Medusimia's inexperienced eye could ascertain some were human. She raised her gaze and searched among the stalagmites and stalactites. Even with the many fires, dark shadows danced and shimmered, leaving most of the room in blackness. One shadow seemed to move more than the others, and Medusimia focused on it.

A larger form detached itself and moved forward. A massive man began to materialize in the light. He was over seven feet tall, with shoulders so enormous they measured four feet from arm-to-arm. Rock-hard muscles rippled beneath bronze skin. His hands were huge, capable of lifting a full-grown man in each, but instead of nails, each finger ended in a pointed talon. Despite his gigantic size, it was his face that commanded attention. His uneven ears were slightly pointed and his features were angular. He looked as if he were hewn from the rock of the chamber in which he lived. The one exception was his mouth, which had full, moist lips. Despite the distance between them, Medusimia could see the tip of his rust-colored tongue dart out and lick them. His eyes were deep-set under a tangle of dark eyebrows. They were cat-eyes—bright, yellow and all-knowing—with pupils slitted like a snake. As he moved farther from the shadows the lower half of his body materialized. From the waist down, bronze scales covered his body. Behind his muscled, powerful legs a dragon's tail slithered along the littered floor. He continued to move toward Medusimia until a few feet separated them. She could feel the heat emanating from him and the lust in his gaze was palpable.

"*Queen* Medusimia." His voice was deep, with a hiss-like snakes whispering in each syllable. "What brings you to my humble abode?"

Medusimia knew Vulmire lusted for her: he had from the moment he had seen her. He hated King Amir simply because Amir could have her body while he could not. It was why he always sneered at her title. He didn't care for her designation of rank, but he understood her desire for the power she obtained by it.

He knew about power. He had once been a normal man who lusted for power. To obtain it, he had given himself to the dark side. Now he had the power, but he had paid a great price. He was a man-beast for all eternity. He was the equal of a wizard, but he was so ugly he chose to live in the bowels of the earth and let those brave enough to face him come to ask for his help. If they became sniveling cowards in his abode, then *they* paid with their lives. That was *his* price.

"I came because I desired to see you, Vulmire."

The giant threw back his head and laughed until his moss-like, black hair quivered. Beneath the laugh was a sound like the hiss of fire when one throws water on it.

"You *desired* to see me? Choose your words more carefully, Queen Medusimia." The pupils in Vulmire's eyes narrowed.

The tall woman studied the monster. She was quite aware of his power and strength. He could kill her with one blow of his massive hand, but she knew he would not because of his desire.

"Vulmire, I speak what I choose. I came because I *desired* to see you. If I didn't, I would not have walked through this godforsaken country, and I wouldn't be here alone."

Slowly, the giant's slit eyes resumed their normal size. "You have courage. Tell me then, *Queen*, why you *desire* to see me, certainly not for my handsome body." The man-beast glanced down at his body. The slightest of sneers curled his full lips.

Medusimia forced herself to take a long, meaningful glance that traveled up and down the giant. She saw past his ugliness. She saw the power and strength in him and recognized their kindred spirits. Neither would hesitate at destroying whatever stood between them and their goal. She loved power and control. If she could rule this man-beast, she would be a formidable queen. All would bow before her.

"It is said beauty is in the eyes of the beholder," she whispered.

Again, the giant's eyes narrowed. "You mock me, Queen."

"I do not."

Medusimia moved until she was mere inches from Vulmire. She raised one hand and gently ran it up his bare arm, letting it come to rest on his chest. From his sharp intake of breath, Medusimia knew if she followed her plan she could control him. Tracing small circles on his expansive chest, Medusimia slowly raised her eyes until she stared into his. In their dark depths, she saw sparks of fire dance.

"If I valued a handsome face or youthful body I could have any man in the kingdom. That is not what I value. I look for strength and power. That makes a man," she whispered.

"And what of your husband, *Queen* Medusimia?" sneered Vulmire. He was having a hard time drawing air into his lungs. Any moment now he would awake and discover this was just another of his many dreams about the beautiful queen.

"I married Amir for political reasons. It is a good union between our countries—each benefits. I thought he was a strong ruler, but now"

"Now? What are you saying?"

"I am not so sure. I'm beginning to think he is weak. He lets himself be distracted by things of no importance."

"Like the young Yasamin?"

His remark threw Medusimia off guard for a moment, and she drew back. "How would you know of that?"

Vulmire smiled. "I have my ways. Don't think because I choose to live here," he indicated his surroundings with a slight nod, "that I am not aware of all that happens."

Medusimia smiled. Perhaps she would gain more than she had dreamed. Again, she placed her hand on his arm and traced the veins bulging against the skin. "I should have remembered you are as intelligent as you are powerful. Admirable. I have no tolerance for weaklings."

"Flattery gets you nothing. I am no fool. You want my help."

"Yes. I am clever, but there are things I cannot do and you can. I wish your help."

"And how do you propose to pay me, *Queen*? I don't need money. In fact, there are few things I need."

"I'm sure there must be some things you desire?" Without taking her eyes from Vulmire's, Medusimia grabbed his hand and pressed it against one full breast. She moved a little closer. "Isn't it true, Vulmire? Aren't there some things you desire?" Although her breast was the size of cantaloupe, his hand engulfed it. He squeezed and rubbed against the velvet. They were so close she could feel the heat in him rise and became aware of his hardness thrusting against her. "Isn't there, Vulmire?"

For a second the man-beast lost his control and fondled her large breast, then he jerked his hand from her grip.

"Perhaps there is. Perhaps there isn't. What precisely do you want of me?"

"Rid me of this milksop girl. She'll be the ruin of Amir and Dragonval. I will not have it."

"Yasamin?"

"Of course, what else could there be?"

"To avenge yourself against the King? You are First Queen. If he marries this girl, he has insulted you. I think you wish to insult *him*."

"He *has* insulted me. I do want to hurt him, to make him sorry."

"If I help you by destroying Yasamin, you remain First Queen, a*nd* you'll return to Amir."

Medusimia felt a small thrill. Vulmire was *jealous* of Amir. "He *is* the King and my husband, but if he's not a fit ruler, then someone who is strong enough should be." She walked past Vulmire toward a large, black rock hewn into a rectangular altar. It was filthy with the soot from the fires. She stared at it. "If Amir is not strong enough to be a ruler, then he needs to be declared unfit. I would take his place. I would be an excellent ruler. But I need the help of the right person. Someone ... like you." She turned and stared at Vulmire. "You're strong, with powers like no other. You

"I have powers even you haven't dreamed of. I know things of which you are unaware. Do not toy with me, Medusimia." He moved toward her until he was only a few feet away. "Observe."

He pointed one clawed hand at a stalagmite. Fire burst from his fingertips and blasted the formation to shards. He pointed a finger at the black rock, and a white beam of fire shot out. The fire surrounded the rock, heating it until the blackness glowed red. She could feel the warmth against her legs. He closed his hand and the fire ceased. Vulmire stared at her.

"You are a woman, Medusimia. Strong-minded, strong-willed but still a woman. Perhaps a foolish one. You come to my home and ask me to help you. In return you hint you will favor me with your body. What makes you think I cannot just take you? I can have what I want now. I can easily overcome your weak protests."

The moment of truth had arrived. In a second she would know whether or not she had been right. Drawing herself up to her full height, she slowly raised her eyes to Vulmire.

"Yes, Vulmire, you could take me here on this filthy floor. You could overpower me, rape me, even kill me, and no one would know what happened because I came here alone. I know this, just as I know the story of what you were and how you came to be. But if you take me against my will, it isn't the same, is it?"

"The same?"

"The same as me coming to you willingly. To fully give myself to you. I am not blind. You desire me. Can you deny it?"

Vulmire stared at her without replying. What she spoke was the truth.

At that moment, Medusimia knew she had won. She reached up and untied the strings of her cloak. Slowly, she unbuttoned the singled fastener of the loose garment she wore. It dropped to the grown with a faint whisper. She wore nothing underneath. Her alabaster skin glowed pale in the cave. She let him look at her; his gaze traveled from her face to her breasts to her long legs. His bronze skin began to glow, and she could see the bulge rising higher beneath his loin cloth. Never taking her eyes from his face, she moved toward him.

"I am beautiful, all men want me, but I choose who will have me. Tonight that is you."

Still Vulmire remained mute, his eyes drinking in her beauty. "Medusimia." The word rumbled with desire. "Speak true." He reached out a hand and traced its talon against the snowy whiteness of her long neck. "Do not mock me."

A faint, red line glowed where he touched. She could feel the heat of it and, fast on its heels, a surge of animal lust. Closing her eyes, she raised her neck.

"Vulmire," she moaned.

The man-beast lowered his head and kissed the red line. He licked and nipped at her neck until he had covered every inch. He steadily worked his way down to one of her breasts, his breath coming in ragged gasps. She could feel the searing heat of his mouth, the moist trail of his lips as he licked her skin. Then, his mouth found her nipple and began to suck greedily. She moaned as he eagerly switched to the other nipple, then sucked both at the same time. A mere human could never please her in such a manner. She thrust her breasts forward wanting more.

"Help me in this, Vulmire. I am yours tonight," she whispered. "Serve me, Vulmire, and I will come to you freely. I speak of a union, you and I. With your power, I can obtain anything ... *We* can obtain anything. With my beauty and your power, you and I could rule Dragonval."

Vulmire raised his head and stared into Medusimia's eyes, seeking the truth of her words. He saw only her lust. Within his own dark eyes the red sparks flamed. He waved one hand at the ebony altar, and the dust spewed from it, leaving it like black velvet. He ripped the loin cloth from his body, and Medusimia had a quick glimpse of his rigid manhood glowing ruby red before he lifted her to the rock. He held both of his hands before him and spread his fingers. The sharp talons curled downward until they cupped the ends of each huge finger, leaving each digit rounded.

Medusimia lifted her arms above her head and spread her legs. She wanted him to see every part of her—to touch, lick and smell every inch of her. She moaned and arched her back. Vulmire lowered his head and began sucking her breasts again, all the while his hands eagerly roaming her body. His touch left hot, red trails welting her skin until she felt as if she were on fire. And still she wanted more. She shivered in delight as his hands roamed lower, touching her waist, her legs, her womanhood. Never had she experienced such craving. She thought she would burst.

Suddenly, Vulmire climbed the rock and straddled her. Resting on his knees, his hungry eyes drank in her beauty open before him. Medusimia stared back. Now his eyes were pools of fire. She looked at his manhood. It was rigid, thick as a man's arm and glowing red. She ran her tongue over her lips as another surge of need ran through her. She felt cold without the hotness of his mouth and touch. She moaned and lifted her arms to him, wanting to feel the hotness, the strength, the power flowing from him. With a low growl, Vulmire plunged deep into her while his lips and tongue again sought her breasts. Forgetting she was a queen, forgetting everything but the raging desire rising in her, Medusimia spread herself wider and wrapped her legs around the monster's legs. Still fondling and sucking her breasts, he lowered one huge hand beneath her hips and pulled her closer. Again and again he thrust into her. She could feel the rock beneath her shiver from his power, just as she could feel him tremble as he struggled to keep himself crushing her beneath him.

Time ceased to exist. All places ceased to exist. The only thing real was the cavern, the black rock and the huge beast thrusting himself into her. Moan after moan escaped her lips, and waves of pleasure skimmed through her like an endless tide. All she could think of was getting closer, of merging into Vulmire. She met each aggressive thrust with one of her own. Swiftly, she untangled her legs and spread them around his shoulders attempting to suck him in even deeper. She wanted every inch of him. Her nails dug into his bronze skin. Her soft moans became animal grunts of lust. Dots of light danced behind her eyelids. Still, she dug for more. All of her lovers, even Amir, were nothing compared to this beast who tirelessly hammered his way deep into her womanhood. The dots behind her lids became a wall of fire. Her universe condensed from the room, to the rock, to the pit of her stomach where a glow burst into flame and engulfed her. Suddenly, wave after wave of blazing fire and pleasure enveloped her. She was a conflagration of burning need, desire, craving, feelings for which she had no name. As she climaxed, her screams pierced the darkness.

Outside the cave, the *buzimorian* waited. Six separate times during the night a faint sound deep within the cave had disturbed its sleep. It stretched its neck, shifted its weight on the limb, then settled again. Patience was one of the *buzimorian*'s few virtues. If it took all night, it would wait for the one it had brought. If she returned from the cave, it would guide her back to the ruins.

Chapter 4

The water was boiling. Good. She would be arriving soon. He could feel her in the air, could see the shift in its color. They all belonged to the light, but each had a different aura. Hers was almost as strong as his. He was anxious to hear her words.

Slowly, he rubbed his hands in front of the cheery flames to warm them. There was still much to do. He hoped he would be able to complete his task. It had been a long time since he had felt such hope; it surged through his veins filling them with song. Humming, he limped to the cupboard and pulled down a box of rare *berrirouge* tea. It was their favorite, his particularly, but he saved it for her visits.

Swirls of silvery dust stirred the air. One spot became lighter then burst into silver sparks and she appeared, smiling and as beautiful in his eye as the first time he had seen her. His topaz eyes glowed golden.

"Greetings, old friend. Come, have a cup of berrirouge tea and tell me all."

"As we had thought. He was there. She is more beautiful than I dreamed."

"Her mother was beautiful."

"Yes. But the child, the child is *different*. I almost missed them. The dark ones were already there. Devastation and death as usual. They do try my patience."

"And mine. Perhaps some day they will learn."

She laughed and took a sip. "When piglets fly through the air."

"Stranger things have happened. But the message, did you get it to her?"

"Not all of it, however. I believe she will come to understand."

"Good. And the other? He was with her?"

"Yes, but not under the best of circumstances."

"If he is with her, he will succeed in bringing her."

They drank in silence, savoring each other's companionship. With a sigh, she spoke. "I need to ask something of you."

"It must be of great importance. You have the wisdom; you seldom need to ask."

"It weighs heavily on me. I want, need, to help her."

"We cannot influence her decision. She must choose. Only then will we know if she is The One."

"I understand, but there are so many of *them*. And the dark one who rules is extremely strong."

"Has been for many years. Still, she must make the choice."

"I know. I wish only to buy her some time. She needs time to see more of the world. She's a lamb among quarreling wolves. I believe experience will better help her make her choice."

"Hmm. Perhaps. You have a plan?"

"Yes. But it needs to be put into action immediately, and I wish your permission to observe her. Danger is rampant. She needs protection."

"Drink your tea and let me contemplate this." He rose and limped to a dark corner. As he neared, the rocks glowed softly and brightened with his approach. He stood there so long she began to worry he might not agree with her proposition. At last, he turned and returned to the seat. His tea had long since grown cold, but he drained the cup before he spoke. "You may proceed—"

"Thank you."

"However, understand it most vital you do nothing which takes her choice from her. Create whatever circumstances you deem helpful as long as they leave her path to her. You may observe her and protect her ... to a point. If called to action, be discreet. Do it in a manner it seems nothing more than luck. She is not to see you. I cannot stress enough that it is vital she makes all decisions, so we can see if she has the heart. Is this clear?"

"I understand. Thank you." She rose and started to bow, but he raised a gnarled hand and stopped her. "No need for such ceremony. You and I have known each other far too long. Hurry and return to her. There is much darkness afoot. Let's pray she has the heart for what lies ahead. If she is as you believe, then there is hope for us. Godspeed, my friend."

"And may you be in the light."

In a burst of silver sparks she disappeared.

Chapter 5

The weary convoy plodded into the small town located near the sea. They had battled flash floods and an unusual sand storm. The soldiers were fatigued and on edge. They were used to fighting flesh and blood; it made their adrenalin flow through their veins faster, but they were at a loss when trying to battle the elements. All of them were glad to be back at the port where their ships lay anchored. Yasamin and Nitae were anxious to get out of the cart. The wooden floor had worn both skin and patience thin.

Goliagoth dismounted the black stallion, which snorted and stamped at the sand-filled winds, and headed toward the two women. The small child had been sleeping with her head in Yasamin's lap, and she stirred as the Queen shifted position.

"Nemoith, a squad to the prisoner ship to make sure all is well. Set camp there." He pointed to a slight depression to the west of the village. Place the tent for the Queen and her maids fifty paces east of the camp. I'll select three men to stand guard there. Free the prisoner's hands, but shackle his ankles. Move! It will be night within two hours. I want the men settled and ready for first light."

"Sir." The second-in-command saluted and turned to carry out his orders.

Goliagoth looked at the darkening clouds along the sea's horizon. "We'll have another storm before morning. Ill fortune. The voyage is rough enough without bad weather." He reached up and lifted Yasamin out of the cart before she could protest. "In a short time the men will have a tent for you. I'll send soldiers to the village to appropriate food. I prefer the villagers didn't know your identity, but I doubt we'll be that lucky. Word travels. I suggest you follow my orders, and we won't have another incident like the one yesterday. If we do, it's on your head." He reached back into the cart and lifted up the child. Nitae scrambled over the other side before he could reach her and came to stand beside the Queen. Yasamin held out her arms for the little girl who twined her arms around the slender woman's neck.

"There will be nothing on my head. *I* gave my word and I will keep it. You control your soldiers. I would hate to report to King Amir you failed to follow his orders." Yasamin trembled inside as the huge soldier glared at her, but he finally gave a brief nod and turned to go. "*Demolisherian*" Yasamin handed the clinging child to Nitae and moved closer to Goliagoth until she was only a few inches away. "Have you taken my people as slaves?"

"What?"

"You said to check on the prisoners in the ship? Have you violated the agreement between King Amir and me?"

Goliagoth stared at Yasamin. She was exhausted. Blue shadows tinted the skin beneath her eyes. Her face was drained of all color. He was sure her delicate skin was bruised from bouncing around in the wooden cart for more than ten hours yet here she stood, tall and straight, concern for her people foremost in her mind. He felt a stir of respect for this slight woman. It surprised him. He had never thought of a woman as someone to be respected. He *acted* in a respectful manner to Queen Medusimia but only because of her title and his loyalty to King Amir. It was something to be mulled upon when he had time.

"Highness, there has been no violation of the agreement. The only prisoners we have taken from Gwendomere are the child and the man—they attacked us first. The Code of behavior mandates they be taken as prisoners."

"Yet you have a ship full? Who are they?"

Again amazement sifted through Goliagoth. Normally he would not have the time nor desire to explain himself to anyone, especially a woman, but found now he did. "Prisoners taken on the trip here—none on Gwendomere soil. The voyage is long and arduous. We need galley slaves."

"I see. So, you took this child," Yasamin nodded at the little girl in Nitae's arms, "prisoner because she 'attacked' you? Couldn't you have left her with her family?"

"We obey protocol. When attacked or provoked, age or sex doesn't matter, we have two choices—kill the attacker or take that person prisoner."

"That's a very limited code."

"It is our way. The voyage is long, grueling—grown men die. Before it is over you may have wished I had killed her—it would have been more merciful. Now I have duties, unless you have another question?"

"I will never wish that you had killed her. While there's life, there's hope."

"There is much you haven't seen, Queen. You may find that isn't true." He turned to go, then looked back at Yasamin. "I was inducted into King Amir's army when I was around the age of that child. Most times there are no choices. If you need me, my name is Goliagoth. I will post guards at your tent tonight for protection—your protection. We will leave at first light. Be prepared."

Goliagoth gave Yasamin a small bow, "Your Highness." He turned abruptly and walked toward the milling soldiers. Yasamin stared at the broad back of the retreating soldier, trying to imagine him ever being the size of the little girl. Strangely, she felt a sadness for Goliagoth. It surprised her. He was the enemy. She had seen him do savage things, yet in her mind's eye, she could see a little boy, lost and alone, thrown into the midst of heartless and soulless men.

"You're wrong, Goliagoth," she whispered, "there is always a choice, if you seek it." Turning to the old nurse and the child, Yasamin smiled bravely. "Well, we have things to do. Let's get what we need for the night. Soon we'll have a tent and some warm food. If only we could have a nice warm bath, it would be almost like home."

"Hummph," Nitae grunted as she set the little girl on the ground. "It may seem like home to you, Highness, but these old bones prefer the nice soft bed in my old room to this hard earth. I guess we should be thankful we'll at least have a roof over our heads, even if it is only cloth." She cast a quick glance in Goliagoth's direction to make sure he wasn't near. She had no intentions of letting the giant lift her into the air again. Seeing him busy with his men, she lifted her skirt and slowly climbed back into the cart.

* * * * *

It had not taken the soldiers long to set camp. Yasamin rested on the pillows which her old nurse had spread on the ground. She had eaten some fruit brought to the tent by a soldier and it had refreshed her. Now she was restless. Nitae and the child lay on the other pallet napping until the same soldier would later return with a warm meal. Yasamin peeked through the flaps of the tent. The evening sun was painting a beautiful montage of reds, yellows and lavenders on the western horizon. She glanced toward the camp. It was a beehive of activity: soldiers repairing torn gear, tending horses and cleaning their weapons. A few were practicing sword maneuvers—new recruits she imagined, and a handful of older soldiers gathered around Goliagoth discussing the upcoming voyage. Yasamin was thankful to see the village going about its daily activities. So far the soldiers had left it alone. A sudden yearning to take a walk overcame her. This was the last time she would ever be on Gwendomere soil. Soldiers had not yet arrived to guard her tent, so there was no one to stop her. Yasamin picked a course along the perimeter of the camp and headed in the direction of the village. Several soldiers observed her but made no move to halt her. Moving slowly she continued, occasionally stopping to watch a soldier weave a broken sandal strap or patch a hole in his shield. It amazed her how proficient they were in maintaining their equipment while marching, relying on things they found en route. Reaching the outermost limit of the camp, she spied Arash leaning against a large rock. His hands were free, but the soldiers had shackled his ankle to a huge outcrop. He was dusty, his clothes were torn, yet there was a quiet dignity around him. She studied his handsome profile and again felt the faint flutter in her heart. It was obvious he had been ignored—there was neither bowl nor platter near him. Glancing around, Yasamin saw a large water jar. She picked up the drinking gourd and filled it with the cool liquid. Slowly, she walked toward him. Intent in his observation, Arash didn't hear her approach until she was beside him. When he saw her, he struggled to rise to his knees.

"Stop. Don't waste your energy." Yasamin leaned toward him. "I brought you some water. I-I thought you might be thirsty." She shyly offered the gourd to him.

Arash sank back against the rock and reached for the gourd. He drank deeply. Yasamin leaned against the rock and watched him. He was one of the most beautiful men she had ever seen. His muscles were hard and bronzed from the sun. His shoulders were broad, his waist and hips slim. She looked at his hands; they were large with slender fingers. She found herself wondering how they would feel touching her face.

"Thank you, your Highness. I am most grateful."

"What?" His voice startled Yasamin. Her mind had been somewhere else.

"Thank you for the water." Arash was holding the gourd toward her. "My throat was caked from all the dust today." He continued to hold the gourd out.

"Oh, yes." She took it but remained leaning against the rock. She found she didn't want to leave. "Would you like more? If you do ..."

"Thank you, Majesty, I am most grateful. It was gracious of you to bring me a drink."

"It was nothing. I mean, I just thought you might be thirsty. It didn't look like they had done anything except chain you here." Yasamin felt herself blushing. She felt like a tongue-tied child and it upset her. She tried changing the subject. "It's just like soldiers. They're heartless. They don't even think about simple things like giving a prisoner food or water."

"We try to treat our prisoners as humanely as possible."

"Of course, I didn't mean *you*. I mean I didn't mean *your* army. I was talking about this one. They're known for being heartless."

"I see," Arash sighed. "You're right. That's why most countries fear King Amir so. I guess I'm lucky to be alive. I'm not sure why the *Demolisherian* didn't just run me through. " Arash looked back toward the village and became silent.

Yasamin continued to rest against the rock. She wanted to say something, but every time she opened her mouth things came out the wrong way. She wanted to stay with him a little longer, find out more about him.

"What is she doing?" Arash asked.

"Who?"

"The young girl over there." Arash nodded his head toward the village where a girl of about twelve sat on bench with a small loom in her lap. She leaned over a swatch of woven silk that shifted colors in the late afternoon sun. Beside her were different skeins of yarn-like threads.

Yasamin followed his nod and saw her. A soft smile settled on her mouth. "She's making her *dremhopa*."

"Her what?"

"*Dremhopa*. Don't you have them in your country?"

Arash looked from the girl to Yasamin. He wanted to stare at Yasamin the whole time but knew that would be improper. She was the most beautiful woman he had ever seen. If he were honest with himself he would have to admit he had lost his heart the first time his eyes had met hers. It galled him to think she was on her way to marry a ruthless tyrant more than it did to be shackled like a common criminal. It was a battle to keep his face blank as he talked to her. She must never suspect his true intent.

"Perhaps but not by that name. I've never heard it. What is a *dremhopa*?"

"It will be her wedding dress. It is the tradition in our country. She may not begin it until she has her Yasamin blushed again, trying to think of a way to tell the story. She had never been at a loss for words, but something about Arash made her unsure of herself. She continued. "Until she becomes a woman. Once she has, her family will buy skeins of silk to make her a wedding dress. Sometimes, if the family is poor, the father will sell a goat or a cow or anything they have of value in order to purchase enough silk for the *dremhopa*. It is a matter of honor for the father to do this for his daughter. Before the girl begins the dress, she must go through the *shalbegi* ceremony."

"What is that?"

"The father will build a tiny hut not far from the village. The mother will wash her daughter in a bath containing *sweshema* blossoms—they're from the plant that our silkworms eat. These blossoms must be free from blemish, although they can be fresh or dried. As the mother bathes her daughter, she will sing a special prayer."

"And then what?"

"The daughter is led to the hut by her mother. There she will have to stay for a fortnight. She may have only water and honey and cannot speak to anyone. Sometime during this period, she will have a dream, or some believe it is a vision. Once she has had that she may return home. Then she will weave her wedding dress. It is the physical expression of her very heart. The design will contain elements of her vision. While she weaves, she will be weaving all of her dreams and hopes and desires into the garment. If she doesn't already know a boy, she will weave the hope that the right one will come."

"And if she already has one?"

"In that case, they can be friends only. She must remain a virgin, until the boy has asked her father for her and weds her. It would be a sacrilege to wear the dress if she has already been intimate. There is an old story that if a girl lies with her lover before she marries, during the ceremony the dress would turn to ash and fall from her so that all would know what she had done."

"Do you believe that?"

"It must be based on something. I don't think people would just make a story like that up."

"Hmm." Arash glanced back at the young girl who continued to weave the silk. "I would think the silk would be too expensive for these villagers." He looked back at Yasamin. She was a flame, and his eyes were moths drawn to her face.

"It is not as expensive here as some countries because we have the silkworms. Still, it costs more than most of these people make in a year. But it's not just the money, it is a matter of honor. A father will sell whatever he has to in order for his daughter to have her wedding dress. It is the most important and most beautiful thing that will ever happen in the girl's life."

Arash nodded thoughtfully. "I understand. It is a beautiful custom. Our name for the wedding dress is *dremlesa*, but we have no ceremony like yours. First, we have to import our silk. The wealthy hire skilled people to make the wedding dress—the more money, the fancier the dress. The less fortunate make their own, but there is no ceremony involved. I think I like your custom. It is beautiful and meaningful. But tell me, what happens if the girl has no father or if she makes the dress but never marries?"

"Whether she marries or not, she will be buried in her *dremhopa*. The dress contains *her* hopes and dreams and what she saw in her vision. It is hers and hers alone. If she does not have a fath

"What are you doing here?" The harsh voice was a sword cutting through the air. Yasamin dropped the gourd she held and whirled to find Goliagoth glaring down at her. His face was as crimson as the sweet winter beets she favored, but there was nothing sweet in his face. His lips were a tight slit, and she could feel the anger emanating from him.

"Nothing. I went for a walk. I needed to stretch my legs."

"Down here to the prisoner?"

"I didn't know he was here until I saw him. He had no food or drink. I brought a gourd of water to him."

Goliagoth's eyes narrowed. He swiftly bent and grabbed the gourd and just as swiftly brought it up and slammed it across Arash's jaw. The gourd shattered, and blood spurted from Arash's lip. Goliagoth grabbed a handful of the young man's clothing and pulled his face close to his own. "And you, swine, what are you doing? Trying to sweet talk her into letting you go? You're a piece of trash not fit to wipe my boot on. I should ..."

"Stop it. Stop it this instant." Yasamin cringed at the bright blood spilling from Arash's mouth. It covered his shirt and ran over Goliagoth's hand. She had seen the giant's anger and knew Arash could be dead in an instant. "Goliagoth, let him go. He's shackled and has neither said nor done anything. *I* brought him the water. Your men left him like this. It's no way to treat a human being."

Goliagoth glared into Arash's eyes. "He's trouble. I can smell it as clear as I can smell the ocean in the air. I should have killed him back at the village."

"*And* violated the agreement. Goliagoth, let him go. If you're angry at me for taking a walk, for the gods' sake, don't take it out on an innocent man. Let him go! I command it. You are still on Gwendomere soil."

Goliagoth swiveled his head toward Yasamin, contemplating her words. She was right, and he had no desire to stir up any more trouble. Slowly, he let go of Arash's shirt and thrust him away. Straightening, he faced Yasamin.

"You must return to your tent for your own safety. I wish no further incident to mar this voyage. Warm food is waiting for you. If you wish to take a walk, advise me. I will make sure you have a proper escort. If you will, Your Highness." Goliagoth held out his arm indicating Yasamin to leave. She looked past him to Arash who lay against the rock with the edge of his shirt held to his lip. Concern worried fine lines across her brow.

Goliagoth moved forward slightly blocking her view. "He'll be fine, nothing more than a split lip. I'd wager he's had much worse in fights. If it will ease your mind, I'll personally see he has food and water. Now you must return to your tent, Highness. It grows dark, and it isn't safe for you out here. You need rest before we board in the morning."

Yasamin knew she would get no farther with Goliagoth. She was lucky he was offering to see that Arash got food and water. As much as she disliked the soldier, she had already come to realize he did keep his word when he gave it.

"It would ease my mind, *Demolisherian,* see to it."

She reluctantly turned and made her way back to her tent. Silently, the giant soldier followed. He occasionally cast his eyes to the darkening sky and felt a shiver goosebump his flesh. For some reason he could not fathom, fear curled and settled in his stomach. In the distance, thunder grumbled like some gigantic beast awakened from its sleep.

Chapter 6

On her knees, head to the ground she almost blended in with the rocks. Finally, she straightened from her prostrate position and stood. She placed the bag hanging from her shoulder onto the ground and began withdrawing items. Reverently, she placed a piece of woven silk on the flat boulder. Then she placed a small silver urn in the middle. Engraved around its lip were ancient symbols that twinkled in the occasional flare of lightning. Lastly, she began putting a variety of herbs into the bowl. A sweet and woodsy smell mingled with the fresh scent of coming rain filled the air. She was ready.

Picking up her staff, she stretched her arms outward and raised her face to the sky. "*Nobelum isa chideia decolum,*" she intoned, "*adori ische declaritum powble*". A powder-like substance appeared in the silver bowl. "*Nobelum isa dictatorium summona. Nobelum isa dictatorium santitonium adori ische declaritum powble.*" The powder began to swirl and glow as she chanted. The more she sang, the brighter it became, until it looked like stardust. The wind rose. At first it teased the long cloak covering her, then grew stronger, until the heavy fabric swirled around her. She continued, her voice growing louder with each line. "*Nobelum isa dissantictea Arim. Proventea a protectea. Dictatea nobelium isa decolum te Yasamin. Conjurea winbloea pangeria a oceneia.*" The wind increased, whipping her cloak around her. Dark clouds rolled across the horizon. Hundreds of feet below, the waves crashed against the cliff's base. The ocean became a maelstrom of swirling waters—rising, twisting and foaming, a beast gone mad. The heavy clouds grew closer. Twisted forks of lightening flashed in them. Funnels descended from their bottoms until the heavens twisted with a tangle of black, angry clouds. The bowl glowed from within as the powder twisted and frothed like the sky above it. *"Arbortea haileata,"* she shouted. Anger roared from the gathering storm. *"Neptumanium haileata,"* she cried. The ocean grew more agitated, and the waves dashed higher against the cliff, appearing to climb the rocks. She closed her eyes and pointed her staff at the writhing clouds above her. *"Unitatea a arbortea sanitatorea, sancitatea, SANCITATEA!"* she screamed. A bolt of white lightening issued from the silver urn and speared into the whirling clouds. Each billowy cloud reflected the light. The heavens thundered until the ground shook beneath her feet. *"SANCITATEA!"* she uttered once more. The lights coalesced and sent a blazing white light into the ocean below her. The ocean hissed and steamed. The waves hammered the cliff's wall, knocking rocks loose. The light sank beneath the water, and it became quiet.

Then a low rumble began. Slowly, the waters began to swirl, forming a giant whirlpool. Faster and faster the dark waters spun until the bottom of the ocean was visible. Fish and seashells flew into the air, only to drop back into the murky malestrom. *"Unitatea a arbortea sanitatorea Yasamin, santatorea. Emen."* She pointed her staff in the direction of Gwendomere. The thunder and lightening ceased and withdrew into the dark clouds. The whirlpool disappeared beneath the surface. In union, the clouds and a large swell in the ocean slowly moved out from the cliff and toward Gwendomere. Within seconds all was as before. There was no trace of storm, wind or light around her, only the gentle settling of a few leaves. She gathered her things, replaced them in the bag and again sank to her knees to place her forehead to the ground. It was done. Now she must wait.

Tomorrow would tell her if she had succeeded. Tomorrow would begin Yasamin's trials. Slowly, she rose and moved away from the cliff. There was still much to do. Tomorrow was only the beginning.

And, hopefully, not the end.

Chapter 7

The morning dawned dark and heavy, with low bruised clouds pregnant with rain. Any moment their swollen bellies would burst, and the downpour would begin. The ocean within the cove rode high with waves indicating even rougher seas once they hit open water. Goliagoth gazed at the horizon. If he had the choice, he would postpone the departure. The day did not look promising. In fact, all of his senses screamed danger, but he had his orders to get Yasamin to King Amir as soon as possible. With an unreasonable fear curled around the base of his spine, the *Demolisherian* ordered his crew to set sail.

Yasamin and Nitae along with the child were aboard Goliagoth's ship where he could keep an eye on them. He had sent the prisoner to the galley. He didn't trust Arash and had thought to put him on a different ship but finally realized that he would be more worried if Arash were where he couldn't be watched.

With the supplies loaded, the three ships sailed out of the natural harbor. Once past the mouth of the bay, they would join the three other ships anchored at sea. Goliagoth was confident no country would dare attack six ships from Dragonval.

The path home was clear in Goliagoth's mind. They would follow the coast of Gwendomere for two days, then turn west into open sea. It would take them a fortnight before they would see land again, a rough jag of rocks and mountains that thrust into the sea between them and home. This was a very dangerous area, full of hidden rocks and reefs that had been created as the land built up from a volcano. They would have to circumvent this peninsula. Once around it, they would turn north toward Dragonval. But the danger wasn't over. There was the Dragon's Mouth they had to sail through. This was an area where two ocean currents met. The waters were particularly vicious. There was no way of avoiding this route. It lay directly before the inlet leading to Dragonval proper. Many ships found themselves caught in the Dragon's Mouth and were torn apart by the opposing currents of water—in fact, this is how the area originally earned its name. The rough waters tore unwary ships apart as surely as they would have been by real dragon's teeth. Goliagoth had been through the Dragon's Mouth more times than he could count on his fingers, but he was still as fearful of it as he had been his first trip.

As the ships sailed out of the bay, Goliagoth sighed with relief. He had managed to leave Gwendomere without any more incidents. He continued to keep an eye on the sky. It looked like winter was well on the way, although it was much too early for the heavy storms and strong northern winds that came with that season. He hoped they would be able to reach Dragonval before any bad weather or an early winter hit. Being a soldier, he was much more comfortable on land with firm footing than a tossing ship where the floor shifted beneath him. If he were a religious man, he would sacrifice to the gods for good fortune and a safe trip, but he had long ago ceased to believe in anything other than his sword and his own wits.

The first two days passed with only the normal problems. There was the usual seasickness of those who had not gotten their sea legs. Several ropes broke, and two of the galley slaves died. Both men were old and little more than skeletons. Goliagoth had suspected they would never have survived the trip but was surprised they only lasted a day. Again, he was thankful he had not killed Arash. The man might mean trouble, but he was strong as an ox and pulled with the strength of two. As long as he was properly restrained, he could do little harm.

Goliagoth searched the horizon with his spyglass. Nothing broke the sea's surface. The dark clouds covered the sky as far as he could see.

"What is that thing you're holding?" The soft voice broke the worry nibbling at his mind. Goliagoth turned to see Yasamin beside him.

"Your Highness, you should not be up here. Please return to your quarters."

"I cannot tolerate being down there any longer. It is too dark and too close. Poor Nitae cannot keep anything down. She looks green and swears she is dying. I do not know how to help her. And the child is almost as bad. Both of them are heaving and retching their insides out. I fear they have caught some awful disease."

"'Tis no disease, only the sea sickness. Many people get it when aboard a vessel and not use to its motion. They can neither eat nor drink without vomiting. Most swear they are dying. It goes away once they get use to the ocean's movement."

"Then they're not dying?"

Goliagoth allowed himself a small laugh. "No, Your Highness. I've seen many grown men think they were at death's door with this very thing. Once they became accustomed to the rocking, they were eating and swigging ale with the rest of their comrades. And you, Queen Yasamin, how are you feeling?"

"Quite well, actually. I have had no sickness at all. If anything, the sea's air seems to make me more hungry."

"Then you are one of the few lucky ones. Count your blessings. But you need to return to your quarters. You will be safe there."

"*Demolisherian*, I cannot and will not sit in that dark hole and listen to the moaning and retching ... at least not now. I'll remain right here by your side. I should be just as safe here as down below."

Goliagoth couldn't think of a retort. "Very well. Perhaps a bit of fresh air is good, but if something happens and I order you to go below, you will go."

"What could happen?"

"I don't expect anything. I am only clarifying the point that if something should, you will go and not question my orders.

"If something happened, I would rather face it up here in the open air than in that dark hole." Seeing Goliagoth's frown, she quickly amended her retort. "All right, I give you my word. I'll go below if the need arises."

"In that case, I am honored by your presence."

"So, what is that?" Yasamin nodded at the instrument in his hand.

Goliagoth held the spyglass up. "This is a *speglasea*."

"What does it do?"

"It doesn't *do* anything. You hold it up to your eye like this." The soldier demonstrated. "It brings far away things up close, so you may discern what it is."

"How unusual. May I see it?"

"Be careful. It is heavy and hard to replace the glass if it gets broken." He handed the instrument to Yasamin.

She held the spyglass in her hand a moment. "It is heavy. How do I use it?"

"Just lift it to one eye and focus on something far away. There, see that bird in the distance? Aim the scope at it, close your other eye and look through it."

"And it will be easier to see the bird?"

Goliagoth nodded. "Probably its feathers."

Yasamin hefted the spyglass to one eye and did as she was told. Instantly, she almost dropped the instrument as she ducked, stepped backwards and tripped over a rope.

Goliagoth sprang forward and grabbed her arm. "Are you all right?"

Yasamin uprighted herself and laughed nervously. "How did it get here so fast?"

"What?"

"The bird? Didn't you see it here on the deck?"

"The bird's still over there," he nodded, and Yasamin saw the dark spot on the horizon.

"But, it was—" she lifted the spyglass, looked, lowered the instrument, then looked again. She grinned with delight as she glanced at Goliagoth. She tried the spyglass twice again. "Amazing. Absolutely amazing! I *can* see the feathers! How wonderful."

Goliagoth found himself staring at Yasamin as she tried the spyglass on different objects. At the moment, it was easy to forget she was a queen. She was more like a young child with a new toy. Goliagoth found himself grinning at her simple delight. He had used the instrument for so long, he had forgotten the wonder of the thing.

"Sir." The one word instantly brought him back to reality. He wiped the grin from his face before he turned to the soldier behind him.

"What?"

The soldier saluted and glanced at Yasamin.

"Speak, soldier."

The young man looked back at the commander. "Sir, the *pilotte* reports we are at the turning point."

"All ready? We have not sailed two days' time."

"He has doubled-checked the coordinates, sir. We are there. He thinks it is because of this high wind. Our sails have been full blown the entire trip."

"A first. Very well, tell him to proceed to the correct coordinates."

"Yes, sir." The young man continued to stand, shifting his feet.

"Is there something else?"

"Sir, yes, sir."

"Well, spit it out before we all grow old."

The soldier shifted his eyes toward Yasamin. "It's something you should know."

"Obviously, you nitwitted pig. What?"

The man lowered his voice. "We have had three more slaves die, and we have had word from one of the ships that they have sprung a leak, nothing serious yet. They are working on repairing it. And

"And? By the gods, speak, man. I haven't got all day."

"Our own ship has a leak. The *pilotte* believes it is—"

"Leak? The idiot *pilotte's* duty is to check this ship before we sail to make sure something like this doesn't happen."

"It was, sir. Everything, top to bottom. The *pilotte* says he believes it's the current. It's the roughest he's ever seen—almost as bad as the Dragon's Mouth. The tug of the current has worked some of the *legons* loose. What do you want to do?"

Goliagoth rubbed one large hand over his face. The good luck seemed to have turned. "I need to check it. Get the dead overboard before anyone gets the death sickness." Goliagoth turned to Yasamin. "Visit's over, Highness, I need to solve these problems now. Return to your quarters. I'll send a soldier to escort you."

Yasamin handed the spyglass back to the commander. "I can find my own way. Attend to your problems." Yasamin turned and headed back to her room. She hated to go into the darkness below deck. Whenever she awoke she suddenly felt as if she were in a coffin, a dark, close coffin. With a heavy heart, she descended the stairs.

If it were so terrible in her rooms, which were the largest and most comfortable, what kind of hell must Arash be in? She hoped he was all right.

* * * * *

Yasamin awoke with a start. Something had roused her, and she lay in the dark cabin trying to figure it out. Nitae and the child had finally fallen asleep, exhausted from their sea-sickness, so it was not their moans which had awakened her. She stared at the swaying lamp above her bunk, watching its feeble light cast gyrating shadows against the worn wood. Suddenly, she bolted upright. It wasn't a noise that had awakened her; it was the ship. The monotonous up-and-down motion was gone, and in its place, a chaotic movement shivered the ship. She could hear the creak of the boards straining against the waves that beat against them. Deep within the boat, she felt a shudder that had not been there before. Quickly she jumped from her bunk. "Nitae, wake up. Wake up."

The old nurse moaned, opened her eyes, raised her head then fell back against the pillow. "Oh, ye gods, will this cursed sickness ever end?"

Again Nitae raised her head. "Your Highness? Do you need something?"

"No, Nitae. I think something is wrong. The ship feels different. Don't you—" The boat gave a sudden lurch, and Yasamin fell on top of the old woman. Frantically, Yasamin sought her footing. "See? It has never been this rough."

Nitae's eyes widened with fear. "Highness, are we sinking? Oh gods, do not let me die in this watery grave. I should die in my bed of old age on good solid ground. What are we to do?" She struggled to rise to a sitting position while Yasamin held onto a timber as the ship gave another wild lurch.

"I don't know what's happening. I'm going above to find out."

At this, Nitae's eyes grew even wider. "Oh no, Highness. Don't go up there. It is too dangerous."

"I must, *Mamia*. I have to know what's happening. Perhaps it is just a rough sea, but I have to see."

"But Yase, you might get washed overboard, or a sea monster—"

"Nitae, there are no sea monsters! And I'd rather be washed overboard than die in this hole."

Nitae gasped. "Don't say such a thing. Let me go with you. I don't want to die down here either."

"No. Stay here. Wake Fleuise and be prepared. If we must abandon ship, I will come for you."

Yasamin turned to go, but the old nurse grabbed her hand. "Yase, please let me go with you. Don't leave us down here."

Yasamin turned and took the old woman's hand in both of hers. "*Mamia*, you must stay here with the child. She cannot go on deck, she is too small. I will come back after I know what's happening. If it comes to abandoning ship, I *will* come back for you. No matter what, I swear this." Yasamin reached over and gently wiped a tear trickling down the old woman's cheek. "I promise, *Mamia*, I will come back to you. Now I must go. Wake Fleuise and wait for me."

Yasamin quickly headed through the cabin door and into the narrow hall. She fought her way toward the steps leading to the upper deck. The rocking ship slammed her from one wall to the other as she inched her way forward. Grasping the handrail, she climbed the stairs and thrust the door open.

Wild, howling winds smashed her against the wall behind her. The wind was a living thing; it tore at her hair, her clothes and tried to drive her to her knees. Raindrops beat against her skin like pebbles. Gasping for air, her eyes sought Goliagoth.

At last she spied him standing aft, shouting orders to his men. The soldiers were running helter-skelter in an effort to keep the ship afloat. Through the roaring winds, she heard a faint scream and looked up. A soldier on the mast was trying to secure a sail. The wind ripped him from the pole and he fell. Arms flailing, the wind tossed him into the raging sea as if he were nothing more than a rag doll. Yasamin gasped. The decks were slippery with crashing waves, but she grasped a rail and slowly pulled herself toward Goliagoth. As she left the meager shelter of the wall, the wind hit her full force and drove her to her knees. Determined to reach Goliagoth, she tried to rise. Her hand touched a rope. She quickly looped it around the rail leading toward the soldier and then tied it around her waist. Gritting her teeth, she crawled toward him. It seemed for every inch she gained, she lost two, but she slowly neared him. Now she could better see the storm around them and stared open-mouthed. Black, heavy thunderclouds swirled around the boats. Long, dark, funnel clouds dropped from the clouds' heavy bellies and whirled the ocean into a frenzy. Thunder roared and lightening speared the ocean, which spewed gigantic gouts of steam and water. The water was murky and filled with living things. It rose in waves higher than the ship's mask. Goliagoth frantically shouted an order for the ship to face the oncoming wave. She saw it coming and held her breath. They would never make it. The wave was gigantic, seething and sucking at the ship. Yasamin closed her eyes. She suddenly felt herself rising up, up, up. Despite her terror, she opened her eyes and saw that they had miraculously ridden to the top of the wave. Now they were sliding down the back side. Yasamin's stomach twisted. It was such a deep trough. They would plough right into the water and to the bottom of the ocean. The ship groaned and shuddered and somehow managed to stay afloat. Had it not been for the giant soldier's knowledge, she was positive they would have sunk long ago. Through the sheets of rain, she could only see two other ships. The others had sunk or been driven out of sight.

Terrified, Yasamin continued her trip toward Goliagoth. He was drenched, his hair plastered to his skull. He had wrapped one leg around a post, and stood defiant against the elements. A smaller wave hit them from the side as he bellowed another order. Despite his loud voice, at times it was impossible to hear him. The wave slid across the deck and dislodged a soldier. The man slid across the wet boards screaming and tried to seize something solid. As he washed past Goliagoth, the huge man grabbed him with one hand and pulled him to safety. "Get back to your post. The rest of the sails have to be secured. Get men up there now."

The soldier pulled himself up and fought his way back to the group surrounding the mast. Seeing the man make it, Goliagoth wiped the water from his face and looked to sea.

"Goliagoth!" Yasamin shouted. The wind ripped the words from her mouth and tossed them into the air. She took a deep breath and screamed again, "Goliagoth!"

The huge soldier turned and saw her. Shock filled his eyes. He loosened his hold and hurried toward her. "Highness, what are you doing here? Get below, now."

Yasamin shook her head. "No. It's no safer there. I cannot stay in that hole.

I have to see what's coming, not hide from it."

Goliagoth stared at her. Part of his brain understood, and he couldn't blame her. He preferred seeing what lay ahead as well, and he didn't have the time to physically carry her back. From his short acquaintance with Yasamin, he knew that was the only way he'd get her to her cabin. He gave a brief nod. "As you will, but stay close to me. What's this?" He looked at the rope.

"I tied myself to the boat to keep from being washed overboard."

"Good, except you don't have a knife. If we were to sink, you'd go down with the ship. Once that rope's wet, it's hard to undo." He reached into his belt, withdrew a small dagger and handed it to her. "Keep this with you. You may need it."

Yasamin looked up at him with wide eyes. "Are we sinking?"

Goliagoth shook his head. "Not yet. But the ship cannot take a beating like this for long. We've already lost two."

"What are we going to do?"

Goliagoth pointed to the west. There's a finger of land over there that points into the sea. It's not all that hospitable, but if we can get close enough, the sea won't be as deep, so the waves won't be as rough. Maybe we can ride out the storm out."

"What if the ship still breaks up?"

Goliagoth hesitated. He knew this woman preferred the truth and would want him to be honest rather than fill her with false hope. "If we get close enough and the ship breaks up, we can use the lifeboat. This far out they're no good; the waves would sink them within seconds."

"Are we going to make it, Goliagoth?"

"I don't know, Highness. I've never seen a storm like this. It's like a living thing. If you believe in the gods, I suggest you pray."

"Don't yo—" Yasamin was interrupted by a large *kaboooom, craccccck*. A shaft of blue-white lightening struck the mast. For a moment it sat there, a blazing candle atop the ship, then slowly, it began to topple.

"Look out!"

Yasamin suddenly found herself thrown to the deck with Goliagoth upon her. The sounds of the storm receded as he wrapped himself over her head and body. She could feel the heat from his body. For a moment, she felt safe, secure and warm. For a moment, she wished she could remain there. No sooner had she thought it than she felt him pull away and rise to his knees. The cold hit her again.

"Are you all right?" Goliagoth held out his hand to help her stand, and she took it.

"Only a bruise or two. What happened?"

The soldier's face was grim. "We lost the mast and all the sails. If we survive the storm, we have only the slaves to rely on for movement. That'll slow our time to more than half."

Yasamin turned and looked. There was only a charred, splintered base where the tall pole had stood. Several soldiers lay on the deck with others trying to pull them to shelter. Her stomach churned, and the bile rose in her throat. "This is really bad, isn't it?"

He nodded. " I lost a lot of good men up there trying to secure sails. Not only that, the mast helped balance the boat. We're fast becoming disabled."

"How far are we from land?"

"A *dectare*, more or less. If we can make at least half of that, we'll have a chance to ride out the storm."

"Do you think we'll make it, Goliagoth?"

"Truthfully? I don't know."

"If it can be done, I believe you can do it, *Demolisherian*. If we don't and somehow you survive, don't blame yourself. I know you'll do your best. It is the gods' will whether we make it or not."

For a long moment, Goliagoth stared at Yasamin. It was the closest thing to a compliment he had ever received. Something burst in his chest, and a spark of warmth spread through him. "Thank you, Your Highness. I will do everything in my power to see you are safe."

Yasamin nodded. "I believe you. Now do what you need and don't worry about me. I'm fine, and I have the knife. Go."

Goliagoth bowed his head and hurried toward the ruined mast. Yasamin looked up at the sky. Never had she seen such a sight. The heaving, murky clouds looked like a witch's boiling caldron. She counted at least five swirling funnels reaching down from the heavens like long, gnarled fingers. Wherever they touched the ocean, the water spewed and frothed. A chill ran through her. The whole scene was uncanny. Her eyes scanned the distant horizon seeking the land Goliagoth had mentioned. At last she discerned a distant cliff. It was a black rock pointing to the sky like a lone finger. He was right. It didn't look hospitable, but it represented the only chance they had at the moment.

She shook her head. At first she thought she had hit it when she fell and that was what was causing the sound. Then she felt it in her feet. Whatever the source, it wasn't inside her. The ship developed a new shudder. She glanced up at the sky and gasped. The five funnels had moved. They now formed a tight circle directly in front of the boat. She felt Goliagoth beside her.

"What in the—" The giant soldier stared at the sight, his mouth a tight line. "Nemoith," he roared, "Now!"

The other soldier appeared. "Sir?"

Goliagoth merely pointed at the funnels whipping at the ocean. A large whirlpool was forming. Fear pinched the second-in-command's face. "What is that?"

"Whatever it is, it lies between us and safety. We have to circumvent it. It'll destroy this ship and the others. Get to the head of the galley and replace Stemoroi. You follow my directions faster. Move."

Nemoith stood transfixed at the sight. Goliagoth shoved him. "Now."

"Sir." Nemoith whirled and headed toward the area where the slaves were laboring with the oars. Goliagoth shouted again, "Nemoith."

"Sir?"

"Unshackle the slaves."

"Why waste the time? They're worthless."

"They're men. Shackled, they've nothing to fight for. They know they're fated to go down with the ship. Free, they will work harder because they have hope of surviving. It could make the difference. Do it."

"Aye, Sir."

Goliagoth turned to Yasamin. "Keep your knife handy. If we hit that whirlpool, this ship will sink fast. Your only chance will be to swim. I have to get on the *stocascen* to coordinate." Goliagoth hurried to the small cubicle positioned five feet above the deck.

The next fifteen minutes were a blur to Yasamin. She alternated between watching the vicious whirlpool and Goliagoth shouting orders from the *stocascen*. The ship slowly began to move to the right of the swirling vortex. It appeared they would clear it by five hundred or so feet. It was close but apparently manageable. A few minutes later they were on the other side and nearing land. Yasamin relaxed her shoulders. She had clutched the knife so tightly the pattern had imprinted itself on her palm. She shifted the blade and wiped her hand. Hopefully, the worst was over. The rain and wind didn't seem quite so fierce. Perhaps it was the protection of the approaching land. She could see Goliagoth shouting orders to Nemoith, but he didn't appear as tense. Soon she would go below and comfort Nitea and Fleuise. Her old nurse must be frantic with worry.

Yasamin never knew what it was that made her turn. Perhaps it was something in Goliagoth's body language. Perhaps it was instinct, but she suddenly had a terrible foreboding. She turned and looked back at the whirlpool. There was an awful howl of wind, and it blew the second ship to the edge of the vortex. For a second, the boat perched on the edge, then slowly began circling the circumference of the whirlpool. Even from this distance, she could see men jumping from the decks. The vessel continued to circle the vortex, gaining speed with each loop. It reminded her of a leaf she had once seen as she had watched a large vat being empted. The leaf had twirled in the tiny whirlpool and gone through the hole with the rest of the liquid. Only this was not a leaf. This was a tremendous boat tossed as if it were nothing more than a splinter. Faster and faster it went, tighter and tighter the loops. The ship hit the center and disappeared from sight as if it had never been. She gasped. It had happened so fast. She felt giddy and took deep breaths. So many lives lost so quickly. Tears prickled the back of her eyelids. She blinked. Then blinked again. Her eyes must have deceived her.

For a heartbeat all sound ceased—no wind, no rain. Nothing. The silence was almost unearthly. With a terrible shriek, the wind began again. The five funnels merged into one. It foamed the water hundreds of feet into the air, then lifted. As it withdrew from the ocean, the tip of it caressed the whirlpool and curled toward them. It grew smaller and disappeared into the heavy belly of the clouds. But it wasn't the funnel that frightened her. With disbelieving eyes, she watched as the foaming vortex began to *move* toward them.

Her mind could not believe what she was seeing. The knife fell from her numb hand as she watched the swirling mass *methodically* shift position. From a great distance, she heard Goliagoth's voice. He was suddenly beside her.

"Highness, you must jump. There's no escape." Yasamin heard but stood transfixed, refusing to believe the sight. "Highness!" Goliagoth grabbed her and forced her to look at him. "You have to jump. Head for land. It is your only chance." He seized the rope tying her to the rail and snapped it with his hands. Picking her up in his arms, he ran for the opposite rail.

All about her was chaos. Soldiers were screaming and dashing mindlessly. Some were already jumping from the stern. Suddenly, Yasamin came to life. She began struggling.

"Put me down. Now. Let me go!" She beat ineffectually against the giant's chest. "Let me go. I have to get Nitae and Fleuise. They're below. Put me down. I promised her I'd come for her. I have to go."

The giant paid no attention to her slaps and blows nor her tears. He knocked the crazed soldiers out of his path. "I'll get them, Highness. I swear. But you are off this ship now."

"*Noooo*. I promised Nitae I'd come for her." Yasamin tried to hang onto the soldier's jacket.

For a moment, Goliagoth and Yasamin locked eyes. "I have a better chance. You cannot swim and carry two people. I can." His voice was husky with fatigue. "Forgive me, Highness, it's the only way."

"No, Goliagoth, no. *I* promised." She struggled in vain as Goliagoth extended his arms over the rail and threw her as far as he could from the boat.

He was strong. Yasamin landed in the water closer to shore than any of the soldiers. She hit the surface and dropped below, into its murky depths. It was cold and water swirled around her, chilling her to the bone. It pulled at her, trying to draw her into the waiting darkness below, but her will to live was stronger. Holding her breath, she fought her way to the top and treaded water. Not five feet away was a huge boulder; she swam to it and held on as she watched the ship. The waves fiercely beat the reef all around her, but she could still hear the screams of the men and the groaning of the ship as the maelstrom neared. She wiped the streaming hair from her face as she struggled to peer through the falling rain. The mighty ship was buckling. The hidden reefs ripped planks from its sides as the vessel bashed against them. Men continued to jump. She couldn't see Goliagoth. The whirlpool overtook the boat. It ripped the ship, twirled and tossed it against the underlying rocks. The helm tore open, exposing the inner compartments. The boat shuddered and slowly up-ended, exposing its underside. With a deafening groan, the ship raised high in the air, like a mighty beast in its death throes strains upward for its last gasp of breath. The vessel hung suspended for a moment, then silently sank below the surface. Yasamin hung her head and cried for all those lost.

For her family.

For herself.

Even for the enemy who had saved her.

Chapter 8

She became aware of the softness beneath her. The sun was warm on her skin. At first, she thought she had had a terrible nightmare. She raised her head, and pain shot through her body. She felt as if someone had been beaten her with a stick. Shading her eyes, Yasamin looked around, and the nightmare became reality. She lay on the beach, the soft sand cradling her body like a pillow. The sky was a blue bowl without a cloud and the wind nothing more than a whisper of a breeze.

But the beauty of the place was marred by the bodies. Bodies were everywhere: some on the shore, others rolling in the waves and further away floating in the water among the debris. Horror swept through her. Yasamin struggled to her feet, ignoring the pain wracking her body.

"Hello? Hello," she spoke through stiff lips. No one answered. The silence was overbearing. She ran to the nearest soldier and shook him. "Can you hear me?" She fell to her knees and shook him again. With great effort, she managed to turn him over. The fish had already been at work on his face. He stared at the sky with sightless eyes.

Yasamin fell backward and scrambled crab-like away from the body. Bile rose in her throat. She got to her feet again and began running up and down the beach, stopping at each body. She shook each but lacked the nerve to turn it over. Fear grew and squeezed her heart, until she struggled for breath. She bit her lower lip to keep from screaming. Surely someone had survived beside herself.

She retraced her steps and began running in the other direction toward the cliff. "Hello?" she shouted. "Can anyone hear me?" Her eyes frantically searched the beach and the rocks nearby. "Can anyone hear me?" A low moan reached her. She turned toward the sound.

A soldier lay on the beach. The dark green water washed over him with each wave. He feebly moved again, trying to pull himself farther onto dry land. Yasamin ran to him and grabbed his arm. Half stumbling, half-falling she pulled the man toward higher ground. When she had him at a safe place, she turned him over.

A long, ugly gash ran across his forehead and blood flowed from it. She scanned the beach trying to find something to staunch the flow. Seeing nothing, she ripped the lower edge of her gown and wrapped it tightly around his head.

"Hold on. Everything will be all right." She wasn't sure if she was trying to reassure herself or the soldier. He was semiconscious.

Clamping her teeth together to keep them from chattering, Yasamin continued her search. She found two other soldiers caught on the rocks; both more dead than alive. With great effort, she brought each man back to the spot where the first one lay. Her efforts might be fruitless, as the injuries to each man appeared severe. Still, Yasamin refused to give up. She continued her search.

As she neared the base of the giant cliff, movement caught her eye. Someone was moving in the water. Without hesitation, Yasamin ran for him. This one seemed in better shape—he was attempting to stand. She grabbed his shoulders and helped him ashore. They fell to the ground as the waves tripped them. Coughing, the man rolled over, and Yasamin found herself staring into the eyes of Arash.

"Oh, thank the gods, you are all right!" Just like the waves lapping at her feet, relief washed over her. "I was afraid you were dead."

Arash managed to sit. "Thought I was going to be. The ship went down fast. Had I been shackled, I'd be at the bottom of the sea right now." He shivered. "I feared you were in the cabin. If you had been—"

"Don't talk about it now. Let's get you back with the others."

"Others? Some made it?"

"I've found three soldiers alive, all hurt badly. I tried to help them, but I don't know what to do."

Arash struggled to his feet. "Three—five—out of so many. The ship sank too quickly."

"We need to get you back to the others and build a fire or something. Maybe someone will see us."

Arash ached from head to toe but knew he couldn't rest until he had made a search for any remaining survivors. "You go. Stay with the others. It's warm enough in the sun, and no one would see a fire in this bright sun. Daylight?" Arash looked up at the sky. "I don't understand. It can't be more than thirty minutes since we sank. There isn't a cloud in the sky. That storm, how did He stared at Yasamin with bewilderment in his eyes. "I don't understand how it cleared so quickly."

"Neither do I. Nor how a whirlpool can move."

"Move? Whirlpools don't change positions."

"This one did. It came directly at the ship."

"Surely you're mistaken. Must have been a trick of light or rain."

Yasamin didn't want to argue. She knew what she had seen, but it didn't matter now. "Do you think there's a chance for more survivors?"

"Possibly. That's why I'm going to search this area. With all the rocks, some may have caught purchase on them."

"I'm going with you."

"You should go back to camp."

"No. I'm going with you. Two can look twice as fast. Anyway, look at you. You're shaking and you're blue. What if you faint and fall in? I don't want to lose you again. I'm going. I've spoken."

Arash sighed. In his heart, he knew she was right. He *was* weak. His shirt felt as if it weighed ten stones, and his knees trembled with the effort of standing. "All right, Highness. I'll look in this area Arash pointed to the spot in front of them where the water was deep and frothy. "You check down there near the cliff."

Yasamin headed for the area. Several times, she found bodies but little more. She saw a chest floating in the breakers and waded in. Pulling it out, she opened it. The chest was full of dried food—rations stored for long trips at sea. She carefully moved it to higher ground and continued her search. She would get Arash to help her move it on her way back. At least they wouldn't starve.

Yasamin walked all the way to the base of the soaring cliff. The rocks were plentiful here and huge. There was little tide, as the natural boundary of the boulders cut it off, but the water was deep. She stared out to sea. Arash was right, the ship sank so fast most didn't have time to escape.

She sighed, and guilt fell heavily on her shoulders like a cloak. She had let Nitae and Fleuise down. She had not kept her promise and gone for them as she had said she would. Tears filled Yasamin's eyes. And she was responsible for Goliagoth's death as well. If he had not sworn to go back for the nurse and child, he might have jumped while there was time. She bowed her head to say a prayer and heard the noise. If the tide had been louder, she would not have heard it—a small whimpering noise and an occasional groan.

She quickly ran to the water's edge and scanned the ocean. At first she could see nothing. She shaded her eyes against the bright sun, and there it was. A tiny, dark spot that popped up and down at the huge boulder fartherest from the shore. She pulled her gown to her knees and headed to the smallest boulder nearest the shore. The way they sat, she could almost use them as stepping stones until she reached the largest one at the end. With as much speed as possible, Yasamin made her way from rock to rock until she reached the last one. She ran to the edge and looked down.

Shock rendered her speechless for a moment. Just above the waterline was Goliagoth's head and shoulders. He had a grip on an outcropping and was trying to pull himself up. On his back was Fleuise, arms wrapped around his neck. This was what had caught her eye: each time Goliagoth tried to raise himself, the top of Fleuise's head rose above the rock.

"Arash," Yasamin screamed. "Come here, quickly!" She dropped to her knees.

At the sound of her voice, Goliagoth looked up. Cuts and bruises covered his pale face. A deep gash ran across his temple. His lips were blue, deep bruises against his white, water-logged skin. "The child," he croaked, "grab the child."

Yasamin reached down for her and whispered. "Fleuise, come to me, sweet. It's all right." The tiny child whimpered and tightened her grip on Goliagoth's neck. "It's is all right, sweetplum, give me your arms. I'll pull you out of that cold water. Come to me. I promise I won't drop you."

Fleuise looked up again. Her blue eyes were round with fright. She slowly let go with one arm and reached up toward Yasamin. When Yasamin got a firm grip on it, the child let go with the other and let the woman pull her up. Once on the rock, she wrapped herself around Yasamin.

"It is going to be all right, Fleuise. You're safe now. Thank the gods, you are safe." Yasamin looked over her head and saw Arash limping toward her. "Arash, hurry!" she shouted. Then lowering her head, so she was on the same level as the child, Yasamin spoke softly, "You need to stand right here, sweet. I must help Goliagoth. I'm not going anywhere, but I need to help him. Do you understand?" Fleuise nodded and put her thumb in her mouth. "Good, girl," Yasamin whispered.

She quickly turned and leaned over the rock. "Goliagoth, give me your hand."

"Your Highness, I'm too heavy. I'll pull you in. I will pull myself out. Just need a minute to catch my breath."

Yasamin glanced back over her shoulder. Arash had started on the first boulder. "Hold on, Goliagoth. Help is almost here. We'll get you out." The soldier took a deep breath and somehow forced himself up to another outcrop with one hand.

Suddenly, Arash was by her side, lying on the rock. She looked at him. "I think he must have a broken shoulder, he's only using one hand. We have to get him out."

Goliagoth glanced up and saw Arash. A thin smile crossed his lips. "Well, well. The man I put in chains. The fates have a way of having the last laugh. I guess you now have your chance to get even."

Arash stared at the giant a long moment. "It would seem that way."

He watched the giant struggle for another hold closer to the top. The rock was wet and slippery. The giant's grip began to slide. Arash's hand shot down and grasped Goliagoth's wrist.

"But not today. Today we are all dependent on each other." He began to pull. The veins on his neck bulged with the effort. Goliagoth regained his hold. Arash reached down his other arm. "Can you give me your other hand?"

"No."

Arash shifted so he could put both of his hands on Goliagoth's right arm. "I'll try to pull you up. Hold on to each outcrop as you rise. It will help disperse the weight."

Groaning, Arash struggled to pull the giant up. Yasamin added her help as well. After ten minutes, they had managed to get him only another few inches closer to the top.

"We need to find some rope or something. This isn't working," Arash panted. He looked at Yasamin. Her face was red from the exertion, but she still looked beautiful. He blinked away the thought. "Did you happen to see any rope or anything we could use?"

Yasamin shook her head. "Nothing."

"The two of you cannot pull me out. I'm too heavy. Best you go and take care of the others. I'll get myself out."

Arash stared down at the giant. "You are a stubborn, pig-headed goat. We *will* get you out of here. Your body's warmth will lower in this cold water, and you'll die. You're already looking blue. I don't particularly want your ghost to come and haunt me for letting you go to the underworld."

"Watch your words, slave. When I get out of here I will show you who the goat is, and I won't worry about your ghost haunting me." Goliagoth strained to inch up another notch.

"I'll make you eat your words." Arash grimaced as he pulled with the giant. He glanced at Yasamin. "Highness, take another quick look on the beach. See if you can find anything we can use."

"I'll try." Yasamin rose and cast one quick glance at Goliagoth. It was then she saw what she couldn't see before. Before she could speak, the giant's hand slipped and he fell. Arash struggled to hold onto Goliagoth's arm. He slid a few inches before he was able to lock himself against the boulder. Yasamin dropped to her knees. "What is in your other hand?"

The giant raised his head to look at her. A cold glaze filled his eyes. "Your chest."

"My chest? What are you talking about?"

Goliagoth was breathing heavily and gasped out the words. Arash was slowly losing his grip on the soldier's arm. He frantically searched for a toe hold to keep from sliding any more.

"Your dowry. Promised it would get to King Amir."

"Drop it, Goliagoth. It's pulling you under."

The man's words were slurred. "I swore an oath to you, Highness. I will keep …"

Yasamin cast a troubled look at Arash. "It's pulling him under. He must have come all the way from the ship with it."

Arash squinted. He could just make out the chest below the waterline. Without it we might be able to pull him out. "You heard the Queen, drop the chest."

Goliagoth shook his head. "No. I must—"

Yasamin grabbed onto the giant's arm again. His eyes were becoming dreamy.

"Goliagoth, drop the chest!"

"No, Highness, you entrusted me with—"

Yasamin shouted, "*Demolisherian*, drop the chest! I command you! Do you hear me? I command you!"

Goliagoth looked at Yasamin, and his eyes focused briefly. She took advantage of the situation. "Drop it, I command you."

"It is your dowry."

"'Tis a tainted one if another life is lost over it. I command you. Drop it. Now!"

Goliagoth sighed and opened his hand. The chest disappeared quickly. With the added weight gone, Arash began pulling again.

"Give me your other hand." The soldier lifted his arm and Arash grabbed it. Yasamin kept her hold. "Now pull."

The two of them began pulling and inching backward over the rough rock. The giant slowly edged upward, occasionally pushing with his feet. At last, they heaved his upper body over the edge. It was enough to keep him up. Arash and Yasamin lay on the rock, gasping for air. Gradually, their breathing eased. Goliagoth lay immobile on the rock. Arash moved to check him for a pulse.

When he touched the giant, Goliagoth growled. "I suppose you expect me to thank you."

Arash withdrew his hand and smiled at Yasamin. "He's alive. From the sound of him, I expect he'll recover." He glanced at Goliagoth. "It would be nice for a thanks, but that would be too much for a *Demolisherian*. I'll settle for not having my throat slit during the night."

Goliagoth swatted at Arash but missed. "You'll have to wait, slave. I'm too weak to do it properly. You're safe for a few days."

Arash winked at Yasamin and nodded toward the still man. "I suppose that's *Demolisherian* humor," he whispered. "We need to get back to camp and see what we can do."

Yasamin nodded and took Fleuise's hand. "Come, sweet, we'll go build a nice fire and get something to eat." She started to turn.

Arash had bent over Goliagoth to help him to his feet when he noticed a rope knotted around the man's waist. "What's this?" He looked over the edge and saw a large bundle tied to the end. It hung against the rock. "More surprises? No wonder you were so heavy." Arash reached for the rope to pull the bag up, but Goliagoth's hand snaked out and gripped him by the wrist.

"I'll take care of it. Don't touch it."

"All right. Let me help you up."

Goliagoth shrugged him away. "I can manage. You two go."

Arash looked at Yasamin. She shrugged. "We have done all we can. Oh, I found a chest with rations in it. At least we can eat. Let me show you where it is, and you can carry it back."

"Good idea."

Arash and Yasamin climbed back across the rocks and headed up the beach. After they were gone, the giant slowly sat up. For a long time, he simply stared out to sea. At last, he began pulling the bundle up to where he sat. It was neither something he wanted to do nor something he looked forward to, but he had promised. There was no other option. Untying the rope from his waist, he cradled the sack in his arms and headed for camp.

Chapter 9

There were no others. Arash searched the beach, while Yasamin tended the wounded soldiers and comforted Fleuise. She knew by the slump of his shoulders as he trudged back along the white sand that his search had been in vain.

"None?" Yasamin whispered as he approached. She hoped against hope Arash had come back to get help for more wounded.

"Not alive." He sat down on a piece of driftwood and shook his head. "There are many bodies. There'll be more after the tide's rise." Arash sighed, "I had hoped for more survivors. There's more safety in numbers."

Yasamin glanced over her shoulder at the forest edging the beach. "You think we're in danger?"

"I really don't know since I've never been here. I am sure there are wild animals in the woods, but I doubt they would venture onto the beach, especially if we have a fire. I have no idea about natives. Perhaps Goliagoth will. Where is he, anyway?"

"He was here for a few minutes to look at these men. Then he told me not to move from this spot and went into the woods. Do you think he's in danger?"

Arash shrugged. "He knows how to take care of himself. If there are any natives in there, I think they'll be the ones in trouble. I have to say, as much as I dislike Dragonval and its soldiers, I'd rather have Goliagoth on our side than the other."

"What do you mean?"

"Goliagoth is a smart man—he would have to be to make *Demolisherian*. While we're in this predicament, he knows we have to stick together for safety's sake. He'll do anything to protect you, it's his duty. Once this is over …" Arash trailed off his sentence.

"What? When this is over what?"

Arash just shook his head. "The only thing that matters is you and your safety. I don't matter, and neither do these soldiers if it comes to that. If he had to leave them to get you to King Amir, he would."

"Surely he would not leave his own men."

"We are talking about King Amir's soldiers. They are ruthless and heartless, and would slit each other's throats if it would benefit them."

"You sound as if you have first-hand knowledge."

"I have. My land's had many encounters with King Amir. He wants our wealth. We're fairly strong and have been able to turn him back, but we need to unite with more countries. If we did so, we might defeat him."

"Perhaps. Perhaps things will change. Tell me more about your land."

Arash stared at the ocean, at some distant horizon Yasamin couldn't see. "It is beautiful, green and lush. In many ways, it is like Gwendomere. In some ways it's different. I think we are more aggressive about protecting ourselves."

"We protect ourselves!"

"Highness, I mean no disrespect. I only meant we have larger cities and more of them than your country. Thus, we need larger, organized armies. Gwendomere is more rural."

"This is true. We have many small villages but no large cities. Each village does what it can to protect itself, but they usually don't unite with others to fight."

"They would for the right cause. They've proven that."

"How?"

"They would have fought for you. Isn't it obvious? There were several villages at your castle willing to protect you."

Yasamin shook her head. "That would not have been a fight. That would have been a slaughter. They're no match for an army like King Amir's."

Arash nodded in agreement. "You are probably right. Many would have died, but they would have died fighting for something they loved. You should understand, aren't you doing the same thing?"

Yasamin frowned at the young man. His dark hair was still damp and curled around his face. The soggy shirt clung to his broad shoulders, emphasizing his muscular arms. Even in tattered clothes, he was handsome. She forced her mind back to his question. "What do you mean? I'm not fighting; I'm trying to prevent the slaughter of innocent people."

"You are sacrificing yourself to save them, aren't you? That's what I'd call it. Someone like you marrying a tyrant like him. Surely there is another way.

You could marry someone from another country, and unite to stand against him instead—"

"How dare you! I will protect my people the way I see most beneficial. That is not—"

"Do you love him?"

"That is none of your business. But I am sure I will come to love him quite well. And who are you to ask such a thing? Are all of your kind so presumptive?"

Arash bowed his head. "I'm sorry, Highness. I overstepped my bounds. I am no one and certainly haven't represented my country well by my rashness. It was presumptive, and I beg your forgiveness."

Yasamin stared at the bowed head. He had been presumptive and overbearing, but he seemed to be sincere in his apology. It was too hard to stay angry with him. "Your apology is accepted, Arash. All of us have been through a great deal today and are lucky to be alive. We shall chalk this conversation up to the … uh … the unusual circumstances. But you are not to mention it again. Understand?"

"Yes, Your Highness."

"Very well." Yasamin straightened her shoulders and glanced at Fleuise who was playing with some shells she had discovered on the beach. "Do you think we'll get out of here?"

"I don't know. The land is far off the normal route, but if any of the ships survived the storm, I'm sure they will either come looking for us or go for help."

"Our ship and the one behind us was destroyed. Goliagoth said—"

"What did I say?"

Yasamin and Arash both jumped. Neither had heard the soldier, who moved silently despite his size.

"Goliagoth! Thank goodness you're all right," Yasamin exclaimed.

"Why wouldn't I be? And what is it I said?" Goliagoth carried an armload of dried wood mixed with twigs and dumped them unceremoniously beside the couple. He turned to glare at them.

"I was just asking Arash if he thought we'd get off this beach. He said if any of the ships survived, they would either come or go for help. I was telling him you had told me two ships had been lost earlier. Then our ship and the one behind us was destroyed."

"Which leaves two," Goliagoth added. "Who knows if they survived. If they had, we would have seen their sails by now. They would be searching for us; however, there's the possibility the storm drove them off course, and it was more expedient to sail for Dragonval. If so, rest assured King Amir will send a fleet to look for you."

"That's comforting," Arash murmured to himself.

Goliagoth kicked sand toward the young man. "Not for you, slave. You will be back in chains. But until then, I will not shackle you if you give me your word you won't cause any trouble."

Arash brushed the sand from his damp clothes and glanced up through his eyebrows at the man looming over him. "I doubt I could cause more trouble than we're already in, but if you mean what you say, you have my word. I will not stab you in the back while we are here."

Goliagoth threw his head back and barked a laugh. "As if you could, slave. I'd hear someone like you coming a mile off."

"I might surprise you."

Goliagoth grew serious and stared at Arash a long moment. "You just might, I give you that. You're a brazen, hard-headed fool, but I admit you have courage."

"Can the two of you quit acting like boys trying to outspit the other? It is late afternoon, and I am cold. What can we do?"

"At your service, Highness." The big soldier knelt and began arranging the logs lattice-wise in a circle. Then he placed the twigs beneath them. Finishing that, he reached into his vest and pulled out a small pouch. From the pouch, he produced two black stones.

"What are they?" Yasamin nodded to the two small rocks.

"Something a good soldier never is without." Goliagoth grabbed a handful of soft, white, dry moss, and placed it atop the twigs. He laid the longer, rectangular rock point down into the moss and began striking it with the other. Sparks flew as the two stones collided with other. A spiral of smoke puffed from the dry moss. Goliagoth leaned forward and blew gently. A small flame burst from the moss and jumped to the twigs. Within a few minutes, a fire burned brightly.

Yasamin rubbed her hands over it, grateful for the warmth. "That feels good."

"We'll keep it going day and night, so it'll be visible at sea." Goliagoth rose and walked toward the wounded soldiers. He knelt and examined each briefly. After a few minutes he returned. Grimness pulled at his features. "Doesn't look good for any of them. The one with the head wound would already be dead if you hadn't stopped the bleeding."

"I wasn't sure what to do. It seemed logical. Will he make it?"

Goliagoth glanced back at the still figure. "To be truthful, I do not know if any of them will. The one with the broken leg seems least hurt so long as he doesn't develop the fever poisoning. If he does, he'll die. Either way he is of little help to us." Goliagoth glanced at the child. "How is she?"

"She won't speak." Yasamin's face grew solemn. "I don't know what to do."

"Probably in shock. Being young, she may come out of it after warm food and a night's sleep. There is nothing you can do except wait." Goliagoth looked at the distant ocean. "Right now, that is all any of us can do."

"Goliagoth," Yasamin's voice wavered. "Thank you for saving her ... and for trying to save my dowry. That was a brave thing—"

"It was nothing," Goliagoth growled and sprang to his feet. For such a huge man, he could move quickly and as gracefully as a panther. "I told you I would." He stomped to a distant log where he had deposited the bundle he had brought with him. Sitting on the log with his back to Yasamin and Arash, he put his head in his hands.

Arash stared at the giant. "I have to admit, 'twas a good thing he did, saving the child. I would have thought he'd simply save himself. But what amazes me most is the chest. Anybody else would have drowned trying to bring something that heavy to shore. By the gods, he almost did and still wouldn't let go of it. He doesn't strike me as the greedy type. Wonder why he did it?"

Yasamin looked at Arash with unshed tears in her eyes, then turned her gaze at the lone man. "He swore to me he'd get my dowry to King Amir. I believe he would have died trying to do just that if I hadn't commanded him to let it go. He saved Fleuise and tried to save my dowry because he gave me his word."

* * * * *

It was still an hour until sundown, but the air had chilled considerably. Yasamin was thankful for the fire. It snapped and crackled cheerily, the only lively thing on the beach. She had finally gotten Fleuise to eat something, and the child had drifted off into a deep sleep with her head in Yasamin's lap. Yasamin finished the last bite of dried *yanisemire,* a meat laced with berries and honey then dried in the sun until preserved. She licked her fingers.

"Not the fanciest meal, but I swear it tastes better than anything I've ever had."

Arash nodded, his mouth full of *yanisemire* as well. He swallowed and smiled. "Limited circumstances make the most meager table into a feast. I cannot believe our luck that there was the small bottle of mead in that chest. Tomorrow I'll find a stream of fresh water. We can water the ale down to make it last longer."

Yasamin laughed. "I hope you do find water, but not only for drinking. I cannot tell you how I would love a nice, long, wonderful bath."

The image of how Yasamin might look in a pool flashed across Arash's mind and he blushed, thankful the color wouldn't be noticeable in the rosy glow of the fire. The sudden appearance of Goliagoth saved him from having to think of a reply.

"Highness?"

Yasamin looked up at the soldier. "Goliagoth, you haven't eaten. Have some food. You must be hungry."

He shook his head. "Maybe later. I have things to do. I need to speak with you." He glanced at Arash. "Alone."

Yasamin frowned, looked from Goliagoth to Arash, then back to Goliagoth. "Cannot you talk to me here?"

"I need for you to come with me. Arash can watch the child." He turned and walked back to the driftwood where he had been sitting.

"Don't go, Your Highness," Arash whispered. "Stay here."

Carefully, in order not to wake her, Yasamin eased Fleuise's head from her lap onto a small pile of clothes and struggled to her feet. "I am not in any danger from him, Arash. I think he's clearly proven that. But I can't imagine why he can't talk to me here. Watch Fleuise. I'll be back shortly."

Rubbing her arms to warm them, the slender woman followed in the soldier's footsteps. He was standing by the driftwood with his back to her. "Goliagoth?" She slowed as she came beside him. "What's so important you couldn't tell me by the fire?"

Goliagoth stared at the distant cliff and remained quiet so long Yasamin thought he had not heard her. She placed her hand on his arm. "Goliagoth, what is it?"

He would not look at her but continued to stare at the cliff's darkening silhouette. "I couldn't save her."

"Who?"

"I went to the cabin, I got the child." He hesitated, then glanced at the bundle on the ground. "She was already dead."

Yasamin looked in the direction of his gaze. The bundle was one of the ship's blankets with a rope bound around it. Yasamin's blood grew cold. She knew what was in it but hoped he would deny it.

"Nitae?"

Goliagoth nodded. "She was already dead, lying on the bunk. I think she died of fright, perhaps her heart gave out. I didn't know what ... I promised you I'd bring them both. I wrapped her in the blanket and tied—"

Yasamin's eyes grew wide. "You tied her to yourself! My god, you swam from the ship with *both* of them?"

Again he nodded. "You said both. I promised *both*. I thought you would want to see her again. I know the importance you put on proper burial." At last Goliagoth looked at Yasamin. "You want to see her?" Yasamin's breath caught in her throat and unshed tears choked her, but she managed a nod.

The soldier moved to the bundle, which at first had seemed so large but now so pathetically small. Removing a knife from his belt, he cut the rope and rose. "I will leave you now to say your goodbyes. If you need me, I'll be by the fire." He moved past her.

Yasamin was alone. For a long moment, she simply stared at the blanket, unable to move. She bit her lip to keep the sobs from bursting forth. Finally, she went to the bundle and slowly sank to her knees. She reached for the edge of the material. Her long, slender fingers shook violently, then hesitated. At last, she gently folded the blanket back and saw Nitae's pale face. "Oh, *Mamia*," she whispered and the dam broke. Tears flowed from Yasamin's eyes, down her cheeks and over her hands, which she pressed tightly to her mouth to keep from crying out loud. "Oh, *Mamia*, what have I done?" Yasamin's body shook as her silent sobs racked it.

Sniffing, she reached out a hand and gently touched the old nurse's face. Nitae's face was cold, and the cold reached out and wrapped itself around Yasamin. Loneliness and loss settled like a heavy cloak on her shoulders. She softly traced the lips of the old woman. Never again would she hear the old nurse whisper words of comfort to her. Never again would she hear her laughter ring through the room or her grumblings about being an old woman who couldn't keep up. The pain clutched hard at her heart, until Yasamin thought it would burst. "Oh, *Mamia*, I'm so sorry. I promised you I would come back for you, and I didn't. I wasn't there when you needed me. I'm so sorry. Please forgive me," she moaned. Yasamin gently smoothed the hair back from Nitae's face. "Please forgive me. I should have left you in Gwendomere where you could have been happy in your own bed, surrounded by your grandchildren. Not in some—" Yasamin's voice broke but she continued to smooth the old nurse's hair "-not in some dark hole. I'm so sorry." Grief was a rocking chair that rocked Yasamin back and forth on her knees. She wrapped her arms around herself for there was no longer anyone else to comfort her. She raised her tear-stained face to the fading sky. "Why?" she whispered. "Why her? She was a good woman, kind to everyone. Why?" Her eyes searched the faint stars. They twinkled but offered no answer.

Yasamin shivered from the cold night air, yet the chill was not as cold as the emptiness inside her. She was alone; the last tie to her old life and her country had been taken from her. The loneliness and pain stabbed through her chest. She buried her face in her hands and wept.

"*Yase*". The sound was nothing more than the murmur of wind.

Yasamin raised her head. There was no one around, yet she thought someone had spoken.

"*Yase.*" Again the whisper, and again Yasamin looked around her. Nothing. No one. *I must be insane with grief*, she thought.

There was the sound again, no louder than a leaf twirling along the ground, but it *was* there. Yasamin held her breath. It was then she noticed. For a moment, she thought a night bug had flown by, but it was too pale to be an insect. It was just a lightness, so faint that Yasamin was afraid to blink. It floated in the air a few inches above Nitae's heart. She slowly put her hand out to touch it, but her hand went right through the area. She pulled her hand back. The glow remained. Yasamin stared at it trying to make sense of what she was seeing. The glow hovered a second longer, then rose upward and directly toward her. Faster than she could gasp, the light circled her twice. It hovered for a heartbeat in front of her eyes, then touched her forehead and shot toward the heavens. Yasamin watched it until it disappeared in the night sky and became indistinguishable from the stars.

Yasamin wiped the tears from her face and again looked at Nitae. Slowly, she bent and kissed the old woman's forehead. "I'll never forget you, *Mamia*, this I swear," she whispered.

She gently covered the old nurse's face. Tomorrow she would see Nitae had a proper burial.

Yasamin rose, took a deep breath and slowly walked back to the fire and the two men who waited for her. She did not know why the gods had taken Nitae from her. She did not know why she had survived the shipwreck totally unharmed.

But of two things she was sure: she *had* seen the light that touched her and she *had* heard her old nurse's voice speak to her before the light disappeared into the heavens. Those words were engraved in her heart forever. *Remember, Yase, you are a queen. Remember, Yase, remember the road of silk.*

Chapter 10

"What do you mean we have to stay here? There must be another option." Yasamin stood facing the two men. A good night's sleep had revived her, and she was anxious to move. Having both men tell her she needed to wait did not sit well.

Goliagoth squatted on the beach and picked up a short stick. "There's one, Your Highness, but I think it best we stay here for the present."

"Why?"

"Several reasons. If one of the ships survived the storm, it would take them two or three days to search the coastline, but rescue would be at hand. If they were blown off course and headed for Dragonval, here is where King Amir will send his fleet. Then there is the injured. They are in no shape to travel. Either we stay and see if they survive, or we leave them behind." The entire time he had been talking, Goliagoth had been drawing in the sand. "Last, is this." He pointed the stick at the map he had drawn. "We are here." He made a dot in the sand. "On this finger of land jutting into the sea. It is a tangle of forests and swamps. There are few inhabitants, and those here are mostly inhospitable. For *us* to reach Dragonval, we would have to travel this direction." He began tracing a line on the map. "It is rough terrain with deep crevasses, swift-moving rivers and a high mountain called Sorania"

"*Sorania?*" Surprise infused Arash's face. "The same Sorania? It's here?"

"Yes."

"What is Sorania?" Yasamin interjected, looking from the young man to the older one.

At last Arash spoke. "Sorania is the most holy of holy mountains. It was the home of the ancient ones who followed the way of light. It was their last stronghold as they fought the dark powers. There was a tremendous battle there, and many of the light-followers lost their lives. Legend says their spirit light sanctified the ground and is so powerful that at night one may see the ground actually glowing."

"Claptrap. But it is the same mountain. There was a great battle, but legends have a way of embellishing facts. The land is inhospitable, and no one goes there, so the story grows with each telling."

"You don't believe the legend, Goliagoth?"

The soldier looked at the slender woman and worry threaded its way into his thoughts. He was afraid she would never survive the trip if they had to go inland or the beach if they had to remain too long. There'd be no help if a ship hadn't survived. They had traveled so far in such a short time that any fleet would look for them much farther west. He had sworn to deliver her safe, and he would ... or die trying. He cleared his throat. "The only thing I *believe* in is my hand and my sword."

"How can you not believe in Sorania? It is a *shrine*." Incredulity covered Arash's face. He thought everyone believed the history concerning the holy mountain.

"If you want to discuss beliefs, we can do it later, slave. We have more pressing needs."

"You are right. What about this inland route?" Arash returned his attention to the map.

"Like I said, it is rough terrain. I was through here once when I was a wet nose lad, and it was bad then. Time could only have made it worse; however, if we get through this inland route, it'll take us to the coastline of Mandemeria. It's a small country, but it has several villages on the ocean. We can get a boat in one of those villages and sail to Dragonval." He stabbed the spot indicating the fishing village and then drew a small curve indicating the direction of his homeland.

"We should proceed without delay. King Amir is waiting for me. There is the wedding and—"

"Queen Yasamin, this route is a last resort. We have a much better chance of rescue if we stay close to the beach."

"Really? Well, it is near high noon, and we have not seen any ships. They probably all sank."

"As I said, it is possible one survived but was so damaged it found it more expedient to sail directly to Dragonval. If all sank, when we don't arrive, the King will realize what happened and will send out his fleet. When they do come, it'll be easier to see us on the beach with the fire and smoke."

"But how long will that take?"

Goliagoth searched the ocean's horizon because it seemed the safest place to look. He could feel Yasamin's stare as she waited for his answer.

"How long, Goliagoth?"

"If a ship survived the storm without too much damage, it would make Dragonval in about two weeks. If heavily damaged, I'd guess three or four weeks."

"At least two weeks? And another two weeks for them to get back here. That's a month. It's too much time. I have to be there for the wedding."

"King Amir will be more relieved you are alive than having the wedding at a specific time."

"But I gave my word."

"Highness, this was beyond your control. You haven't violated your agreement. The King will understand."

"I'm afraid I agree with Goliagoth, Your Highness. We've a better chance of being rescued staying here. We must wait."

Yasamin looked from one man to the other. Neither were telling her what she wanted to hear, but both were more experienced with the world than she was and therefore knew what was best for their welfare.

She sighed. "Very well, I guess we'll wait ... for now anyway. What do we need to do?"

Goliagoth rose, confidence flowing in every movement. "First, the slave and I will clear an area in the brush there." He pointed at a small rise starting at the beach and running about ten feet into the woods. "It will put us at a higher level in case the tide rises. Being in the trees, it will give us more shade than the beach. We'll build a shelter for you and the child. That'll give you some protection from the elements. We'll keep a large bonfire for the beach ready to signal and build a smaller one in camp for cooking and protection."

"From what?" Yasamin glanced nervously around her.

"Animals, especially at night. They will not come near fire. The inhabitants should be much deeper in the forest and not bother us."

"Do you not think the inhabitants would help us?"

"I have no desire to find out. If they are unfriendly, there's only two of us who can fight. For your sake, we cannot afford the chance they might be hostile."

"I suppose you are right."

"When I was getting wood yesterday, I found a small pool and waterfall not too far from here. We can get our drinking water there."

"A pool? Do you think I could bathe?"

Goliagoth shrugged. "I see no reason why not once we have recoinnoitered

88

the area." He nodded at Arash, "He and I will take turns keeping the fire going at night in the event a ship passes. There's fish in the sea and meat in the woods, so we'll have food. If we are lucky some of the chests might float to shore, and we can confiscate anything useful."

"I can help with the wounded. We are moving them to camp as well, are we not?"

Goliagoth nodded. "Yes, but I hold little hope for any of them except Cherkis. If we can keep his leg free of infection, he'll recover." Goliagoth looked over Yasamin's head to Arash. A silent understanding passed between the two men. "Your Highness, we'll proceed to clear the area for you as soon as we finish a task which must be done immediately."

"What is that?"

"We have to gather the bodies on the beach and those near shore and burn them. There're too many to bury, so we'll have to build a large pyre and burn them all."

"Burn! Why?"

"If we don't, we will get the ghost sickness."

"Ghost sickness?"

"It comes from many bodies rotting. Something gets into the air and makes the living sick."

"Oh, but no, not Nitae! No, I forbid you to burn her with all those bodies. She must be buried in the proper manner."

Goliagoth bowed his head. "That can be done, Highness. Once we've gathered the bodies and fired them, we can dig a grave for her. Burying is an effective way for destroying the ghost sickness. There are too many soldiers. The sickness would begin before the two of us could get to them all."

"What shall I do?"

"We will take care of the bodies. You keep a lookout for ships, and notify me if you see any wreckage washing ashore. It could be something useful."

"All right. Move the injured near the trees, and I'll see to their wounds. Then I'll take Fleurise for a walk on the beach. That way I can see anything washing in, and she can be spared the sight of those corpses."

"Excellent idea." Goliagoth looked at Arash. "Move, slave. We have got a lot to do before nightfall."

The two men cleaned the area for the camp and moved the three injured soldiers. Yasamin cleaned their wounds with the limited supplies she had, while Goliagoth and Arash dug a large pit in the sand and layered it with driftwood. Then they began collecting the bodies and dragging them to the pit. It wasn't long before the hole was full, and the bodies were stacked on top of each other three deep.

Arash and Goliagoth walked toward the large cliff looking for the last of the corpses. The giant was unusually quiet as he plodded through the sand. Arash felt as though his arms would fall from his body, but he was determined to finish the gruesome task before sundown. He flexed his shoulders and arms, while Goliagoth stared at the distant horizon.

"*Demolisherian?*"

"Hmm?" The giant continued his scrutiny.

"What about that storm that sank the ship?"

"It was a rough one."

"But don't you think it was unusual? We had rain, but there was little to indicate severe weather. Then," Arash snapped his fingers, "suddenly it was as if Hades had broken loose. Then it cleared so fast, too fast."

Goliagoth glanced at Arash. "What is your point?"

Arash shrugged. "I'm not sure. I ... it ... I just don't think it seemed normal."

Goliagoth's eyes narrowed. "You think it was supernatural? Hog spittle. Don't tell me you believe in fairy tales. Granted, in all my years as a soldier, I've seen nothing like it"

"Exactly! Funnels, whirlpools, p—"

"Over there, a body." Goliagoth ignored Arash's comment and dashed into the water to grab the corpse wedged between two rocks. The tide was up, and the soldier had trouble getting it untangled. Ignoring the stench, Arash waded in to help. At last, they freed it and Goliagoth turned it over. The face was pale, swollen, contorted in a frozen scream. The creatures had already been at the eyes, but there was enough left to identify him—Nemoith. Goliagoth sighed. "Poor bastard. Looks like the old hag was right about one thing; she told him he wouldn't see home. Help me get him ashore." The two men struggled down the beach with the body toward the pyre.

"So you *do* believe Shar's prophecy came true?" Arash grunted the words out between steps.

Goliagoth came to a stop and glared at Arash. "No. I don't believe in prophecies ... or curses ... or spells. There is nothing but what we have right here, right now. What I can see and touch is what I believe in. Don't go filling the Queen's head with foolish notions. Understand? My job is to get her to King Amir safely, and you are either with me or against me—which is it? If you are against me, I will fix the problem right now."

For a long moment, Arash faced the giant soldier. Finally he spoke. "I'll do everything in my power to protect her, Goliagoth, but it is not because I am afraid of you. Her marrying the King may not be what I want, but it is her choice. She chose to marry King Amir, and I will honor her decision. The way I look at it, you and I are not enemies when it comes to protecting her. But I will tell you this: if Queen Yasamin should change her mind, I will do everything in my power to take her to safety. Take that any way you want."

Goliagoth fixed his dark stare on Arash. Silent for so long, Arash thought his end might be near. Finally the soldier grunted. "You're a feisty one, I'll give you that, slave. And more honest than most. You'd be a worthy opponent. So be it. Let's get this corpse back and finish this job." He started to move, but Arash remained still. Goliagoth's eyebrows raised in a question.

Arash spoke in a low, even voice. "One more thing, *Demolisherian*. My name is not 'slave,' it's Arash."

Goliagoth threw his head back and laughed and looked at Arash with a sliver of respect. "By the gods, you have the nerve. Too bad you aren't one of us; you've the grit for a soldier. But you'll be back in leg irons when the King's fleet arrives. Come on; let's get this carcass to the pyre."

The two arrived back at the camp to find Yasamin waiting. As they deposited Nemoith's body on the pile, she walked slowly toward them. "We lost one. I thought he was just sleeping, but when I went to change his bandage, he was dead."

"Which?"

"The head wound."

"Just as well. I'll get him."

"You seem rather callous at losing one of your men."

"We're soldiers, Highness. Death's a constant companion."

Yasamin watched the soldier stride toward camp. She sighed tiredly. "He acts like it's nothing more than an animal that died."

Arash moved closer and gently placed his hand on Yasamin's shoulder. "It's a way of life for people like him. If a soldier allows his emotions to rule him, he'll soon be dead himself. He loses his edge. You did all you could, Yasamin. The soldier wouldn't have lasted as long as he did without your care. Maybe it's just as well. If he had lived, he probably wouldn't have been right in the head. I've seen it before."

"Are you speaking from experience?"

"I've had my share of fights. All men are required to serve as soldiers for our country at least three years. They can continue if they wish, but most prefer to return home."

Yasamin continued to watch Goliagoth as he headed for the corpse. At last, she reached up and touched Arash's hand resting on her shoulder. "It must be a very lonely life, having no one. Thank you for your kind words." She wanted his hand to stay. She wanted Arash to put his arms around her and hold her to make her feel safe. She wanted—so much. But it couldn't be. She was betrothed. She gently moved so she could face him, but in the process, he had to withdraw his hand. "Arash, do you really think it best for us to stay here and wait?"

"For the time being. We can't rule out one of the ships survived. The most logical course of action would be for them to search the coast."

"I see. Well, I guess—" Yasamin was interrupted by Goliagoth's return.

He hefted the corpse atop the pile with one hand. In the other he carried a burning torch he had pulled from the fire. He stuck it into the sand.

"That's the last of them. If others wash ashore, we'll burn them later. Once we're done here, we'll dig a grave for your nurse, Highness. I'll leave it to you to pick the spot."

"I already know the place."

The soldier nodded and proceeded to add driftwood on top of the pile. He then began to stuff bundles of moss and dry weeds between and around the bodies. He picked up the torch.

"Goliagoth?" Yasamin could move no closer. The stench of the bloated bodies was already reaching out from the pile.

"Highness?" He returned to where she stood.

"Aren't you going to say a prayer for them, have some kind of ceremony?"

He shook his head. "They were soldiers. They knew the end when they began."

"But still ... some words to help them enter the hereafter?"

"I know none, Highness."

"You do not believe in the gods, a higher Power, something?"

"No." The word was harsh. Final. Realizing his rudeness, Goliagoth lowered his voice. "Highness, I believe in what I can see and touch. I believe in *this*." He nodded his head toward their surroundings. "Here. Now. It's all there is. If there is an afterlife, I've seen no hint of it."

"I see." Yasamin's voice was soft. "How sad."

"I do not want your pity."

"Nor do I give it, soldier. I meant how sad for you and your men that there is no hope of something better. Very well. If you have nothing to say to help them for the next life, perhaps you would like to acknowledge their existence in this one."

"Words are not my gift, Highness."

"*Belzabib*, you are heartless, *Demolisherian*. Fine. If you will not say anything, *I* will. They deserve something!" Yasamin bit her tongue the second she uttered the words. Her temper had gotten the best of her, and now she was cornered. She looked at Arash and saw amusement tug the corner of his mouth. He knew her predicament and thought it funny. She wanted to slap him. She glanced at Goliagoth, whose face was a study of astonishment.

92

"You want to say words for *them*?"

"I said so, did I not?"

Goliagoth got his face under control. "Very well, Highness, if you wish." He moved aside, so she could see the pile of bodies. Yasamin slowly moved forward. Her mind whirled, searched for something to say. *Mother, help me. I don't know if I can do this even though it's right.* She managed to move ten feet toward the bodies before the stench stopped her. She held her breath, trying not to gag. Abruptly, a faint breeze stirred from the ocean and blew the odor away from her. Thankful for the small reprieve, Yasamin closed her eyes to erase the horrible sight. "These soldiers," she hesitated, searching for the right words. These were the *enemy*. How could she say something good about them? The memory of an earlier conversation crystallized in her mind, and she straightened to her full height. "These *soldiers* fought for their country. They gave their life performing their duty. But these soldiers were also men, fathers, husbands or sons. Somewhere they left someone who will mourn their loss. May those people be proud these men performed their duty, that they didn't give in to fear but fought their best and, at that final moment, faced death with courage. May the gods have mercy on their souls."

The breeze faded and the stench doubled. Yasamin returned to Goliagoth. "Set the torch, *Demolisherian*. When you're finished here, you may prepare the grave for Nitae."

She turned and hurried toward the camp. It would be a long time before she forgot the sight of bloated bodies. It was then the smell overtook her. It curdled around her, fingered her hair, her clothes, her skin. It permeated everything. She grabbed Fleuise, pulled the child to her breasts and buried her face into the girl's long, dark curls. If she lived to be a thousand, she would never forget the smell of burning flesh.

* * * * *

They buried Nitae on a small rise covered with emerald green grass surrounded by tall trees covered with tiny pink blooms. Every day Yasamin carried fresh flowers to the grave and sat there talking to her old nurse. Since the night she had experienced the manifestation, Yasamin was confident Nitae heard every word she spoke. It was not as comforting as having Nitae's arms around her, but it was comforting knowing that Nitae *was* somewhere.

On the third day, when Yasamin was returning from her visit to the grave, she saw Goliagoth in the water tugging at something. Often a huge wave submerged him, but then he would burst through the surface slinging water and spewing like a whale, then return to his battle. Arash was on the beach running up and down and grabbing objects indistinguishable from her viewpoint. Yasamin hurried down the trail and ran to the beach. "What is it? What's happening?"

Arash looked up at her and grinned. "Good luck for us. The submerged ships must have finally broken up. They're spilling out their contents." He nodded at the bundles in his arms. "Usable food, some clothes that'll be fine once they're dried. We won't know everything until we've opened them all."

"Wonderful!" Yasamin hurried to grab some of the smaller bags. She nodded toward the soldier who was finally winning his battle and coming ashore. "What is Goliagoth doing?"

"Trying to get a huge chest in. Looks to be intact. Hopefully it contains lots of useful things."

Goliagoth continued to fight the swirling ocean, slowly but steadily gaining shore. Finally able to stand, he grabbed the trunk in both hands and staggered onto the beach with it. He brushed the seaweed from the top.

"Highness," he bellowed between gasps.

Yasamin looked up to see him waving for her. "Come on, Arash, let's see what he's found."

The two of them ran toward the soldier. As they neared, Goliagoth looked at her from over the top of the trunk.

"I believe this is yours, Highness."

Yasamin's eyes dropped to the lid. The House of Gwendomere's emblem covered the top. The reefs had poked holes in the chest, and Yasamin's eyes filled with unshed tears. The battered chest was a physical reminder of how she felt and of what would happen to her country if she didn't get to King Amir. "It is. Unfortunately, I don't have the key. It was lost in the shipwreck."

"I can open it." Goliagoth placed his knee on top of the chest and one huge paw on the padlock. With a mighty groan, he pulled. The metal separated from the leather, and the soldier lifted the top. "You can check it now. I'll carry it to camp when we're finished here." Without looking at her, Goliagoth walked past Yasamin and touched Arash on the shoulder. "Come on, let her have her privacy," he whispered. "We'll get the rest of what we can salvage." Goliagoth moved on without looking back. Open-mouthed Arash gaped at the retreating man's broad back. Sometimes Goliagoth infuriated him; sometimes he simply astounded him. There were times the *Demolisherian* almost seemed human. Shaking his head, Arash hurried after him.

Yasamin knelt and carefully deposited the packages she held. She slowly reached out and touched trunk's contents. The chest had taken a severe beating, and salt water had ruined much. The small trinkets placed within were all broken. There were usable clothes after they were dried. She removed them and made a pile of things to keep. Rummaging as she neared the bottom, Yasamin's hands touched soft leather. Curious, she quickly dug beneath the material. Two items were wrapped in yun's skin, a skin similar to oilskin in that it was waterproof, but yun's skin was lighter in weight and had a sweet, pungent odor much like cedar. This made it greatly prized. The moths that thrived on heavy clothes stored during summer weather never bothered items wrapped in yun's skin.

Yasamin smiled softly. This was Nitae's doing. The old nurse had taken extra care to preserve something obviously priceless to Yasamin.

Yasamin carefully unwrapped the largest package. After a few moments, the soft, blue velvet folds of her mother's dress spilled into Yasamin's lap. The young woman gasped, then pulled the garment to her. Once more the soft fragrance of *moonlitea* surrounded her. "Thank you, Nitae, thank you," she whispered. She folded the dress and placed it with the small pile.

Then she reached for the smaller package. Slowly, she unwrapped it. The box that held her mother's book emerged. She undid the top. Because of the yun's skin, box and book were in perfect condition. Yasamin reverently touched the cover, remembering the last conversation she had with Nitae. She never had a chance to talk with the old woman about it. It didn't matter as much now as the fact she had her mother's book back. The ocean had miraculously returned it to her. Perhaps some day she would find someone who could tell her more about it. She diligently rewrapped the package. Pulling everything else from the chest, she placed the usable clothes and the two wrapped packages in it. Later she would have Goliagoth carry the trunk to camp.

* * * * *

The next day, another soldier died. They buried him. The third continued to hang on. Yasamin began to think he might survive, but he would be lame. The days turned to one week, the week to two, then three. The survivors slowly settled into a routine. Every day they all searched the horizon. Every day Goliagoth climbed to the top of the cliff where he built another fire in the hope it would be seen farther at sea. Every day Yasamin made her trip to Nitae's grave and carried flowers. Every day Arash fished in the sea with a net he'd woven from vines. Twice he had captured small animals in a trap, and they had feasted on the rich meat. Fleuise gradually came out of shock; she didn't have as many nightmares and would hesitantly respond to questions. Most of the time she stayed by Yasamin's side as the young woman pondered over her mother's mysterious book.

Yasamin was intrigued. It had been important to her mother; therefore, it must have great value, if only she had the key. Sometimes when she was reading, the words would almost make sense, but for the most part, they remained a mystery.

The weeks turned to one month. The wilderness forged a bond between the three that would never have occurred under normal conditions. With each passing day, Yasamin would find herself staring at Arash almost as much as she stared at the horizon. She thought about him constantly. And she knew Arash stared at her, although he tried hard to be discreet about it.

Only Goliagoth maintained the strict formality toward her. Yasamin decided he knew no other way. His ruthless surroundings of early childhood had carved his behavior into stone. Yet, with time, even Goliagoth softened somewhat. His big barking laugh occasionally drifted through the air as he bested Arash in mock battle or when Arash spouted a retort that in previous times would have had the giant at his throat.

Another month passed, and the giant soldier went more and more to the cliff and remained for longer periods of time. Arash and Yasamin could see him, a tiny pinpoint atop the black cliff as he stared to sea. It was becoming apparent, even to Yasamin, that no ship had survived the storm to search the coast, but they continued to hope one had made it to Dragonval to report the disaster.

As the days passed, Amir became a memory, and Yasamin found herself daydreaming about Arash, partly because of her attraction to him but also because Arash took every opportunity to convince her going to Dragonval to marry a man like Amir was wrong. Daily, he talked of the advantages of her joining another country to fight Dragonval. He listened endlessly to her stories about life in her land, but when questioned about his, he usually shrugged and said there was nothing to tell. He was just a servant to Pars and led an ordinary life. Some days Yasamin thought life would be so much simpler if she had never been born a princess. She said as much one afternoon as she sat at Nitae's grave. Suddenly, a blue light glowed over the grassy knoll, and it was as if the old nurse sat beside her.

"Yase! You were born to *be* a queen. You have a gift. If you do not use it, it will be lost. Many will suffer. Remember wrong has many faces. Look into your heart. Look into the light."

As suddenly as it had appeared, the glow disappeared. Yasamin blinked. She wanted to believe she still communicated with her old nurse, but doubt fringed her certainty. She could have imagined the episode. "Maybe I'm just going crazy," Yasamin chided herself. "If only I could have a sign that was more concrete. I just don't know what's real any more."

Yasamin angrily shook her head and started to rise when a hiss froze her.

On the other side of the grave, directly in front of her, lay a small, black snake. The only thing between them was the small bouquet of flowers she had brought. So terrified she could not move, Yasamin turned into a statue but watched transfixed as the snake slowly slithered toward her. It held its pointed head aloft, its forked tongue flickered in and out, its eyes never left her face. Hypnotized, Yasamin watched it weave through the grass. Her mind screamed, but no sound emerged from her paralyzed throat. The serpent reached the flowers. Now there was less than two feet separating them. Still, Yasamin could not move. The snake slowly crawled onto the flowers. Terrified, she could no longer breathe and was certain she was going to die. As the serpent stretched across the flowers, a bolt of white light flashed upward from them. Its power thrust Yasamin backward. She sat back up and gasped. Where the snake and bouquet had been, there was nothing ... not even ashes. Shaken, Yasamin rose and headed for camp. She was not certain of the event's meaning, but one thing was crystal-clear: she had been given a sign.

*****

Yasamin hurried along the trail to tell Arash what had just happened. He had become her best friend during the past months, and she trusted his opinion. Perhaps he could shed some insight on the snake and flowers.

As she neared the camp, she heard Arash singing and the chop of blade on wood. Yasamin smiled. Now was perfect because they would have the privacy she desired. She didn't particularly want to mention the event in front of Goliagoth, he would only scoff. Turning from the trail, Yasamin hurried through the bushes into the clearing. Arash swung at small limbs with the cutlass they had salvaged. He had removed his shirt while he worked, and Yasamin drew her breathe in sharply. She had never seen him without it. Her heart quickened as she stared at his broad shoulders and muscled arms. The sun had tanned his skin bronze, and his hair lay in damp ringlets against his neck. Yasamin thought he was the most handsome man she had ever seen. She moved toward him and called his name.

Startled, Arash whirled. "Yasamin!" He half-turned from her and sat the blade down and headed for his shirt, but not before Yasamin saw the gleam of gold around his neck.

"What's that?" She moved to touch the necklace as Arash ducked beneath her arm to grab his shirt.

"Nothing. Just a trinket." He hurried to pull the shirt over his head. His frantic actions belied his words, and Yasamin becamed determined to see the necklace.

"It is no trinket. I know gold when I see it. Let me see." Quicker than Arash, she managed to grab the necklace and its golden orb before his shirt covered it. Arash stood frozen with his shirt half on. She stared at the medallion with the engraved likeness and words, and her world stood still—or spun wildly, Yasamin wasn't sure which. Nothing was the same any longer. Stunned, she looked up at Arash with wide eyes. "This is you."

Arash sighed and gently removed the medallion from Yasamin's fingers. He finished pulling his shirt on and placed the necklace inside. "Yes. I am—"

"I can read, Arash. You are not a mere citizen. You are the prince of Pars!"

He looked at the ground, the trees, anywhere but Yasamin's face and simply nodded. "I didn't expect you to come here. I didn't want you to know—"

Sudden insight flooded through Yasamin, and with it came a boiling anger. "Of course you did not want me to learn you are a prince! It all makes perfect sense. Now I know why you're always talking about how I should align myself with another country. That is why you are always telling me I should not marry Amir! You lied to me. You have lied to me all along! Our friendship is a lie."

At this, Arash's head snapped around, and he looked in her face. "No! No, Yasamin, no! I am your friend." He tried take her hand, but she pushed him away.

"Let go of me, Arash. Liar! Stop it. I have caught you in your little game. I will not listen any more!" She turned. Arash grabbed both of her shoulders and tried to get her to look at him.

"No, listen to me, Yasamin. I brought Shar to your country. She wanted to warn you, and I believed her words. I didn't know you, but when I met you, when I saw you, I knew you were the woman—I knew Shar was right. I did not tell you I was a prince because ... because I—"

Denying her accusation and twisting the truth to make him look good was the last straw for Yasamin. She struggled out of his grasp and, without thinking, slapped his face so hard her hand stung.

"Liar! Stop it. I've caught you in your little game. I won't listen to any more!" Yasamin whirled and ran toward the trail. Tears blinded her, and she tripped over vines and roots as she hurried.

"Yasamin! Highness! Wait!" Arash called after her, but she continued to dash. His cheek burned from her slap, but that pain was nothing to the one in his heart. "Yasamin, I can't lose you," he whispered to the empty air. Arash bent his head and slowly sank to his knees. He mourned for the loss of the friendship and for the loss of the woman with whom he had fallen in love.

For the next few days, Arash tried to get Yasamin alone. He had to explain, but he had no success. She was always civil, always polite but as elusive as

The Road of Silk

Arash's happiness. If Goliagoth noticed the strain between the two, he did not mention it. He continued his vigil of watching the sea.

Arash was not the only one who suffered. Although she avoided him, Yasamin was as despondent. She missed Arash, his smile, their talks. She felt betrayed and something more she couldn't quite understand. She studied her mother's book harder, but even that didn't fill the emptiness she felt. For two nights she tossed restlessly, unable to sleep. The third night she finally fell into an exhausted sleep ... and dreamed of Arash.

They stood on the cliff. Thousands of diamond stars spilled over the black velvet sky, and the moon was a huge pearl. They stood in silence, enjoying the cool evening breeze. The only noise was the crash of the waves at the cliff's base. Yasamin leaned forward to look at them, and a rock loosened beneath her foot. She started to scream. Suddenly, Arash's arms were around her, pulling her to safety.

"Yasamin, I have you. Don't be scared. You are safe," he whispered. Frightened, Yasamin turned in his arms and leaned her head against his chest. She could hear the comforting, steady thump of his heart. Sighing, she put her arms around his waist. She had never felt so safe.

"I will never let anything happen to you; you are out of harm's way with me." Arash continued to hold her and whisper in her ear. "I will take care of you, my love," he murmured against her hair. Yasamin drew back and looked into his face. The pearl moon reflected from his dark eyes, and she could see the love shining there just as brightly. Her eyes grew wide, and her heart opened to his words as a bud yearns toward the morning sun. Arash gently cradled her face in his hands and slowly leaned down to kiss her. Soft as a feather, his lips brushed hers. The bud of love in her heart burst forth into full bloom, and she kissed him back. He showered her face with kisses, and she eagerly sought his mouth with her own. Their young bodies pressed together. The couple embraced beneath the moonlight, lost in the wonder of their love. Yasamin never wanted to leave the shelter of his arms.

Suddenly, a hiss shattered the night's stillness. Yasamin turned. Below them, a large ship entered the harbor. A raging fire engulfed the boat. The burning debris falling into the water caused the hissing noise. She turned to Arash, but he was no longer there. Confused, Yasamin turned back to look at the ship and saw a skeleton run across the deck and jump in the air toward her. It flew through the sky, coming closer and closer. The skeleton's mouth opened in glee. It reached for her and Yasamin screamed.

And screamed.

And screamed.

And screamed herself awake. Tangled in the blanket, Yasamin fought the last vestige of the nightmare. Drenched in sweat, she set up. She gasped for air as she fought her way back to reality.

Sword drawn, Goliagoth ran into the makeshift tent. "What is it?"

The last tendrils of the dream dissolved, and Yasamin pushed her damp hair away from her face. "N-Nothing, Goliagoth. A horrible dream, that's all. I'm sorry for disturbing you."

The soldier second-glanced the tent, then slowly replaced his sword. "You didn't. I was awake."

Arash plunged through the doorway with a wooden club. "What's wrong? What happened?" He pushed his sleep-tousled hair back from his eyes as he glanced from Goliagoth to Yasamin. At his stare, Yasamin felt herself blush, and she pulled the blanket closer to her chin. "Nothing. I just had a nightmare and cried out in my sleep. I'm feeling silly enough without any more ado over it. Please go."

"Rest well. Good-night, Highness." Goliagoth bowed slightly and left.

Arash lingered a moment longer, concern creased his face. "Are you sure you're all right?"

"Yes, yes. I'm sure. Please go."

Arash still hesitated. "About the other day, I should have told you when I met—"

"I'm really tired, Arash. Not now. Go, please."

Arash bowed his head and reluctantly backed out of the tent.

Yasamin watched him go. Life was so complicated. She had berated Arash for lying to her, and now she was doing the same thing, lying to him. She wasn't all right. The nightmare had opened her eyes. She had fallen in love with Arash.

Chapter 11

Medusimia fidgeted as she sat on the bench waiting for her servant to fall asleep. Finally, she rose and meandered through the garden, touching the various flowers. Her irritation flared higher. She had slipped enough *dragonilla* into the drink to make a dozen servants fall asleep, but the old woman must have the constitution of a horse. She was still awake. Pretending to smell a rose, Medusimia chanced another surreptitious glance. Good, the old hag was finally nodding. If she fell asleep soon, Medusimia would have almost three hours to spend with Vulmire.

At the thought of the man-beast, her pulse quickened, and she felt the familiar moistness and heat deep within her. Being with him was a drug; she couldn't get enough. Before Vulmire, Medusimia had thought Amir an accomplished lover. Now it was all she could do to tolerate him when he shared her bed. Compared to the man-beast, Amir was an inept boy, as was every other man she had seduced. Medusimia bit her lip to keep from moaning. She physically ached to feel Vulmire thrusting himself deep inside her. It had only been two days, but it felt like two months.

Medusimia snuck another glance. The old woman's head hung to one side, and she gently snored. Her sunken mouth made little puffs with each outbreath. The Queen almost laughed out. Finally.

Checking to make sure no one else was around, she slipped through the hedge and headed for Vulmire's cave. Today was going to be absolutely wonderful. Not only would Vulmire satisfy her body, she had the most extraordinary news to share: one of Amir's ships had limped into port with news of a terrible storm. It was feared all ships had been lost. Amir was beside himself with fear and grief that his precious, little Yasamin might have been lost. At this very moment, his thoughts were on getting a fleet together to search. He would very likely not notice his own wife was gone until late tonight, if then.

Now that she was away from the palace, Medusimia laughed loudly. It looked as if the gods were smiling on her because she won either way. Yasamin was now out of the picture. There was no longer the insult of a second wife. Amir was so upset it would be easy for her to deal with him. With a little effort, some well-placed words and deals, she would have him declared incompetent, and *she* would be Queen of Dragonval. Vulmire obviously could not sit on the throne with her, but she would be free to have him service her any day or night. She would have the best of both worlds.

She reached the clearing and chanted the words for the *buzimorian* to come. She danced from one foot to the other as she waited. The longing had become a most pressing physical ache; she could hardly wait for the hardness and power of the man-beast. At last she heard the flap of heavy wings, and the *buzimorian* appeared. He knew Medusimia well. Now he never bothered to circle and exam her. He simply guided her back toward the cave.

Reaching the entrance, Medusimia hurried forward as she fumbled with the buttons of her dress. She no longer noticed the smell when she entered the lair.

Running toward the black rock in the den she shouted, "Vulmire! Where are you? Come!"

She urgently pulled the fabric over her head. Her breasts were heavy, throbbing, straining to be free of restraint. As the material cleared her face, she saw him standing in front of her.

"Oh, gods, how I've missed you! Hurry, come, take me." She pulled the string holding her skirt, and it fell around her ankles. She angrily kicked herself free, then sprawled backward onto the rock. "Hurry, I cannot stand this ache!"

"The Queen commands. I have to obey."

What passed for laughter rumbled deep in Vulmire's throat. He moved forward and grasped her breasts in his hands. As he kneaded them, his long tongue roamed her body, coiling around her curves and exploring her crevasses. Medusimia groaned and gyrated on the altar.

"Don't tease me so," she moaned.

She yanked off his loin cloth, and Vulmire slide his hands beneath her hips and pulled her onto him. Impaled on his rigid manhood, Medusimia wrapped her legs around him and thrust herself against him harder. Vulmire almost gasped. She had always enjoyed herself, but today she was *different*. It was as if she were trying to pull him inside her. The thought excited him, and he began pounding against her. She met each powerful thrust with her own, until the two were swathed in a red heat. Tiny sparks flew from Vulmire's brow as he climaxed, and his howl sent loose pebbles crashing to the floor. At last, he rocked back onto his knees, so he could look at Medusimia. Her skin glowed red, and crimson sparks danced in her eyes. Her raven hair had loosened and flew in wild curls about her head. On her brow and neck lay small wet tendrils. He had thought her beautiful before, but now, now Vulmire's mind could not even find a word to describe how beautiful she was. He felt desire stir again. Medusimia looked at him and laughed. She tantalizingly licked her full lips with the tip of her tongue.

"More," she mouthed and reached for his erection.

Vulmire's hand shot out and grasped her wrist. "What's happened to you?"

"What do you mean?"

"You are … different."

Medusimia laughed again. "Because I am ecstatic."

"Because?"

"*Because* everything is coming together. Amir got word today the ships carrying Yasamin were probably lost in a bad storm at sea. It took the boat bringing the news almost four weeks to get here . If she had somehow survived the storm, she would have to be dead by now. I no longer have to be humiliated by that little milk sop." Again she started to reach forward, and again, Vulmire stopped her.

"Then you would have King Amir to yourself again. You're first Queen. You would have what you want"

"Vulmire, not jealousy at a time like this. This is good for *us*. Amir is beside himself. With the right plan of action, I can have him declared incompetent."

Vulmire snorted. "Don't plan on it just yet. You still need me."

"What do you mean?"

"The ship sank, but Yasamin is still alive."

"What? How do you know?" Stunned, Medusimia sat upright, her urgency momentarily forgotten.

"I told you before, I have my ways. Yasamin, a young man and two of the King's soldiers are stranded about a three weeks' journey from here."

"*Belzebar*! Amir is getting a fleet together now for a search party. What if he finds them?"

"I think it would make my Queen very unhappy."

"Of course it would! It would change everything. I cannot believe it. You have powers! Do something!"

"What does it benefit me? I destroy Yasamin, and you get King Amir all to yourself. Once you're first Queen again, you won't come here."

"You do not understand. Things have *changed*. Of course I don't want to be humiliated by Amir, not in front of the people nor in private for that matter. But I do not *want* Amir anymore. Compared to you, he is nothing. He does not have your kind of power. He cannot please me like you." Medusimia leaned forward against Vulmire's chest suggestively. "Next to you, Amir is a splinter, an inept schoolboy." She began tracing circles on Vulmire's chest. "I have to tolerate him for the moment. Things can't just happen overnight. But if we get rid of Yasamin, then in a little while I can start putting rumors out about his incompetence. They will declare me Queen of Dragonval. Then you and I can be together."

"You and me?"

"Yes. But we have to destroy Yasamin first. Can you do that?"

Vulmire snorted. "That is nothing."

Medusimia kissed Vulmire's chest and circled his nipple with her tongue. "Do it," she whispered. Her hand continued its downward journey toward its mark. "Do it," she whispered between kisses. "Get rid of her. With a little time, I'll get rid of Amir. We have to do it the right way. Then I will be recognized as Queen of Dragonval." The man-beast trembled beneath Medusimia's onslaught. She licked and nibbled him, and as her mouth neared its target, she felt the heat blaze within him, and her own flared higher. "With my beauty and expertise and your intelligence and power, *we* can rule Dragonval as it should be." Her voice was hoarse with desire. Need. Craving. "We can be together like this," she murmured as her mouth closed on him. Then she had no time for words; all but her need was forgotten. And Vulmire? Savoring Medusimia's passion, Vulmire forgot to tell her there was one thing more powerful than he.

Chapter 12

Amir hurried through the dark, domed passage. The smell of old age, decay and rot permeated the air, and he held a perfumed handkerchief to his nose. Disgusted, he walked faster. His destination was a massive place, forgotten by all but a few. This dank, subterranean tunnel was the fastest way there. Despair and fear propelled him forward. The ground slowly sloped upward. Thank the gods, he was almost there.

At last the tunnel opened into an enormous chamber. Grabbing a lit candle, he picked his way through the debris scattered on the floor and walked toward the second room.

"Back so soon? What an honor." The sarcastic voice slithered and rattled like dry scales. Amir whirled and held the candle aloft.

"You said I could have her. You promised it," Amir shouted. Anger contorted his usually handsome face. "You betrayed me."

"I take it you've heard the news."

"Yes," Amir growled. He took a step forward but stopped when he heard the deadly rattles shake. "You made a deal—"

"Stop your whining, fool. She is not dead. There has been a slight delay, a little interference I didn't foresee."

"She is not dead?" Relief flooded Amir.

"Did I not just say so?"

"Then where is she?"

"Here." A bony fist appeared within the candle's light. It turned palm up, and the fingers opened. What appeared to be a small, dark, crystal ball materialized. Another hand appeared, and a long, gnarled finger tapped against the glass. Amir leaned forward and peered into the dark sphere.

"There? How did she—"

"It doesn't matter. As I said, there was some unexpected interference which I'll handle. You have only to go get her." The hands retreated from the candle's glow.

"I will." Amir turned to go, but the crackling voice halted him.

"Amir."

The king turned. "Yes?"

"Have you taken care of the other?"

Amir shook his head. "Not yet."

"I told you three days ago."

"I will get to it when I can."

The bony hand shot into the candlelight. One finger pointed at him. "*I* said take care of it immediately. The hand closed into a fist. Although Amir stood more than six feet away, he gasped and clutched at his throat. Beads of perspiration spilled down his forehead, and he rose one foot into the air in conjunction with the hand moving upward. It was as though an invisible bar connected the two. "Do it today. Understand?"

Amir's face darkened as he clawed at his throat. At last, he managed a feeble "yes" through the constriction. The hand opened, and Amir dropped to the ground. The light went out as the candle hit the floor. The king remained on his hands and knees, coughing and gasping to get his breath. Although he could no longer see the other's presence, he felt it and made no attempt to rise. At last he heard the *click click click* of movement on the rough stones, and a low hiss reached his ears.

"One more thing, Amir. Do not ever forget *who* rules Dragonval."

The king remained silent in acquiescence.

Chapter 13

Yasamin floated in the cool, crystal water. It cradled her like a cocoon. She wished she could stay there forever. It was a beautiful pool with a tiny waterfall that created thousands of diamonds as its cascade hit the surface. Small bright-colored birds sang and darted among the trees. Pale water lilies dotted the pond. Their fragrance filled the air with their sweetness. It was her favorite place, not only because of its beauty but also because of the peace and serenity infusing the area.

But there was no peace for her today. Sighing, Yasamin drifted to the waterfall, then stood beneath it, letting the cold water splash over her face and wash away any trace of the tears she had shed that morning. She fervently wished it could wash away the discovery she had made the night before.

Once acknowledged, Yasamin could not deny she had fallen in love with Arash. She dipped below the surface and swam to shore. She climbed out and wrapped herself in a fluffy blanket. Sitting on a rock, Yasamin attacked the wet tangle of her hair. It seemed her life was just like her tresses—full of snares and tangles. Everything was so complicated now. She had not planned on falling in love with Arash but she had. She had fallen for him, thinking he was a simple man, but he wasn't. She thought he had deceived her for selfish reasons, but remembering the look on his face the night before, she now believed he had spoken the truth. The long and short of it was she loved him even if he *had* deceived her for selfish reasons. She wanted to be with him; she wanted to marry him, be close to him even if it were a marriage motivated by his political reasons. Her every instinct told her if she went to him now, he would marry her. She could do it and be happy, but she had sworn to marry another.

Yasamin laid the comb in her lap and studied her hands. She remembered the smoothness of his skin when she touched him, the firmness of the muscles beneath his shirt and smiled. Yes, she could do it and be happy even if he didn't love her, even if he married her for political alliance. It might even be possible that if Gwendomere and Pars united, they could defeat Amir.

A flash of brightness caught Yasamin's eye, and she looked upward. A small bird lit on a low-lying limb and twittered about, then looked directly at her. It was miniscule and one of the most beautiful creatures she had ever seen: golden with a small, flame-red crest on its head. It turned its head back and forth, looking at her with twinkling eyes and Yasamin laughed. Suddenly, a memory flashed into her mind—the memory of golden bracelets shining in the torchlight as her people threw their valuables to her feet. Her people. Her people had given everything out of their love for her. Yasamin's blood turned cold as she remembered Amir's oath the dark messenger had brought her. If she didn't marry him, her people would suffer and, worse, be no more.

Yasamin bent her head in sorrow. She could not do that to her people. Even if she and Arash somehow defeated Amir, it would not be before he had carried out his promise. How could she ever be happy knowing her love for Arash had destroyed her people? The coldness running through her veins congealed in her chest and filled the place where her heart had been.

Her path was clear. Resigned to her duty, Yasamin rose and dressed. She must return to camp and change the bandage on the injured soldier. She had made a promise. She would keep it. She would not let her people die for her. She would never love Amir, but she could help him. She would always love Arash, but honor dictated she could not have him.

Dressed, Yasamin set out for camp with a heavy heart. No matter what happened, Arash must never suspect her true feelings; she would not endanger him as well as her people. As she walked, Yasamin prayed she'd have the strength to follow her destiny.

She never looked back. She didn't see the diminutive golden bird as it burst into tiny beads of silver that disappeared into the air.

Chapter 14

Goliagoth stepped into the ring of light cast by the fire. "We have to go." Arash and Yasamin both jumped at his sudden appearance. Yasamin stopped dishing up the stew. "Now?"

Goliagoth moved to the fire and rubbed his hands over it. The nights were becoming nippy, especially on the top of the cliff.

"In the morning. After supper, pack what you need. Keep it light; we have to carry it on our backs. We will leave at first light."

"I thought we were to stay here in case ships arrived." Arash threw a handful of kindling on the fire to revive it.

"It's been long enough for a flotilla to reach us. It concerns me the wind is shifting." He sat down on a log and took the bowl Yasamin handed him. "Thanks, Highness." For the moment, he was grateful simply to hold the warm bowl.

"What does that mean?" Yasamin asked as she ladled another bowl for Arash. Fleuise contentedly chewed her food, while she played with her makeshift doll. The adults' conversation held no meaning for her.

"Once the wind shifts to north, the *monsease* begins. The seas will become rough, almost impossible to sail in this area."

Arash frowned. "You don't think King Amir will still send his ships to find us … the Queen?"

Goliagoth studied the young man for several heartbeats. There was no sarcasm in Arash's face, only concern. The soldier sighed. "I know he will. I had hoped a ship would make it to Dragonval and return in time for us to have clear sailing. It appears that is not the case. Once the King realizes what has happened, he will send the fleet."

"If you are so positive he will, why can't we wait?"

"I believe the King will send the fleet to Gwendomere first and begin tracing the voyage. If the *monsease* has begun, they will not make it here. They'll break on the reefs. He will send more, and the same will happen."

Yasamin interrupted Goliagoth's explanation. "How long does it last?"

"Anywhere from three months to five, if it's a severe one."

Arash interjected, "So we wait it out here. When it's over, they'll find us."

Goliagoth returned his attention to Arash. "That is not my only concern." He kept his eyes on Arash but slightly nodded in Yasamin's direction. "It will be rough here as well. Once the winds and sea shift, the weather will become much colder with a good chance of snow. Animals hibernate and are harder to find. Fishing as you've been doing will become impossible. The fish will migrate to much deeper water. There'll be no fruit. Maybe some berries, but not enough to live on for several months."

Arash grasped Goliagoth's inference. Yasamin would not survive such conditions. Worry crawled in his stomach, stealing his appetite. Arash set his bowl down. He was afraid she was not capable of making the long, overland trip. "You really think our best chance is trying overland to the other coast?"

Goliagoth nodded. "If we start now, I am pretty sure we will have time to get there before the true *monsease* begins. Our biggest barrier is the mountain. We must cross it before the snows begin. Being higher, it will receive ice and snow long before the lower lands. If we do not get across it …" The soldier let the rest of his sentence trail. The meaning was clear.

Yasamin whispered, "Goliagoth, what about the soldier?" She nodded in the direction of the man sleeping by a sputter of a fire in the distance. Goliagoth had formed a splint by taking a small tree trunk and splitting it in two. He'd placed half on either side of the man's leg and wrapped the leg and splint in some heavy cloth salvaged from the ship. The fever had broken long ago. The man had been lucid for weeks; however, he had crawled about fifty feet from their camp and built a small one of his own. He accepted the food Yasamin brought him silently but, beyond that, would not associate with them.

"He is a soldier, used to rough conditions. He will either make it or he won't." At Yasamin's pained expression, Goliagoth gruffly added. "Before morning I'll make him a pair of crutches. It'll keep the bone from re-breaking."

"What about her?" Yasamin nodded toward Fleuise.

"Highness, I see you think it callous, but I am telling you a simple truth, she will either make it or she won't. The point is our only chance in the journey."

"I see." Yasamin straightened her back in that familiar gesture of stubbornness. "So be it then. We leave in the morning. I'll help Fleuise get ready."

* * * * *

Morning came much too early. It seemed Yasamin had just laid her head on her pillow when Goliagoth was calling her to rise. Yasamin sat up and rubbed her eyes. Remembering they were to leave, she jumped up and hurried to the fire. She stared in amazement. The night before, she had packed her mother's dress and book and a change of clothes into a small bag she had made by tying the four corners of canvass together. While she and Arash had slept, Goliagoth kept busy. He had added two straps to either side of her bundle, so she could carry it easily on her back instead of holding it in her arms. He had fashioned several backpacks out of leather, and they sat beside the fire. One was open, packed full of dried meat and berries, and it dawned on her why the soldier had been gone so much from camp. He had been curing food in the event they had to make the trip. She shook her head and poured herself a bowl of porridge from the pot on the fire. The simple truth was the soldier's training was probably all that had kept them alive all this time.

Sipping the hot mush, she glanced around. In the distance, she could see Goliagoth, Arash and the soldier working. She smiled. True to his word, Goliagoth had fashioned a rough pair of crutches, and the man was adapting quickly. Arash and Goliagoth were bringing large rocks to the man, and he arranged them on the ground, while the other two went back for more. She watched them a few minutes longer unable to figure out what they were doing.

She finally turned and went to wake Fleuise. She gazed at the sleeping child, wishing she could still sleep with such peace. Her heart contracted, and tears stung the back of her eyelids. She hoped Fleuise would survive the trip before them. She knelt and gently shook the girl.

"Wake up, sweetplum. Time to rise. We're going on a great discovery trip today."

Fleuise immediately opened her eyes and sat up. "Where?"

"We're going on a long trip to see a big town. There'll be all kind of exciting things to see on the way."

"Like what?"

"Oh, I don't know. Maybe deer and rabbits and pretty birds." Yasamin smiled, as she remembered the golden bird she had seen earlier. "All kinds of things. You might even get to see snow!"

By this time Fleuise was already up on her knees, all traces of sleep gone. "What's snow?"

Yasamin paused. How could she explain snow to someone who had never seen it? "Well, it's like rain except it's white and cold. And it's soft, like goose feathers."

"It comes from the sky, like rain?"

"Yes."

The little girl laughed. "That's silly. How can goose feathers fall from the sky?"

Yasamin laughed. "No, it's not feathers. It's soft like feathers, except if you hold a snowflake in your hand it melts and turns to water. If there is a lot of it, it can cover the earth and everything turns to white until it's warm enough to melt the snow."

"I want to see snow!" Fleuise danced around Yasamin, chanting the words over and over.

"You might get your wish, but we have to get ready to go now. We're going to cross a big mountain, and you might get to see snow there."

Yasamin's heart twisted again. If Fleuise did see snow, it might be the last thing she ever saw. She gently pushed the child's hair back from her face.

"Let's get you some breakfast, so you'll feel like walking. But I want you to promise me one thing first."

"What?" Fleuise stopped her dancing and came to stand in front of Yasamin.

"I want you to promise that you will stay close to me, or Arash or Goliagoth on this trip. If you get too far away, you might get lost, and we might not be able to find you. Will you promise me that?"

The little girl grew solemn, and she stared at Yasamin with huge eyes.

"Will you promise me that, Fleuise?"

"I don't like Goliagoth. He's a bad man. He killed my brother and hurt my mama."

Yasamin's eyes filled with tears, and she gently straightened the little girl's clothes. "I know, sweetheart. Sometimes people do bad things, but they're sorry later."

"I hate him! He's a bad man."

"Fleuise, he *did* do some horrible things, bad things, but I think he's truly sorry. He's done some good things, too."

"Like what?"

"Well, he saved my life, and he saved *your* life, too, did he not?"

Fleuise nodded.

"And he is very smart. He has kept all of us alive in this place. He has caught food and built fires and lots of things."

"Huh-um." The thumb went into Fleuise's mouth as she continued to stare at Yasamin.

"He knows a lot more things about being in the wild than I or even Arash do, so I want you to promise that if you cannot find me or Arash, you will stay with Goliagoth. He will protect you, no matter what. I swear. Now will you promise?"

"Will he bring me to you if I get lost? And will he find you if you get lost?"

"Yes, he will. But I am going to stay close to Goliagoth because I trust him to lead us to safety. So I want you to also. Will you do that?"

"All right."

"Good. Now let's get you a quick bite. We're leaving soon." Yasamin took the child's hand and led her to the kettle. She saw the men, turned and headed toward them.

"What were you doing there?"

Goliagoth knelt and began fastening the knapsacks, while Arash headed toward his belongings to collect them.

"Spelling the name of the town where we're headed. The rocks are heavy enough and high enough from the sea that they will last. If any ship makes it ashore, they will know where we went."

"Goliagoth, what a wonderful idea!"

The soldier grunted. "It was *his* idea." He nodded to Arash who was coming back toward them with his belongings on his back.

Arash picked up the empty kettle, rinsed it, then looped a rope through its handle and fastened it to his waist. "I'm ready."

Goliagoth nodded. "I'm through here. You're packed, Highness?"

"Yes, a small bag for Fleuise and that small bundle for me. Thank you for putting the bands on it. It'll make it easier to carry."

Goliagoth merely nodded, but Yasamin thought he blushed beneath his tan. "You need your hands free for balance." He fumbled through one of the bundles. "These are not finery for a Queen, but they are more serviceable than the ones you have." Goliagoth produced a pair of what had been men's boots. He had modified them to fit Yasamin's feet. He brusquely handed them to her. "If you wrap some cloth around your feet, they should fit."

Yasamin looked at the boots. They were probably the ugliest shoes she had ever seen. The sole was flat and the leather worn. She could see where the soldier had made the revisions to reduce their size. Goliagoth had also rubbed them with some kind of oil to repel water. They would probably come to her knees but they would fit the terrain much better than the tattered, high-heeled shoes she wore. Yasamin smiled. "Thank you, Goliagoth. This is very thoughtful of you."

"They are necessary. Your feet would be cut to ribbons within two hours in those." He nodded at her cloth shoes.

"You're right." Yasamin bent to change shoes.

Goliagoth reached back into the pack and produced another pair of boots. These were much smaller and uglier, if such were possible. He had cut part of the leather from an adult's boot and fashioned it into a size that would fit

Fleuise. As with the first, he had rubbed them with oil. He offered them to Fleuise. "Here, child, put these on."

She stared at the shoes. Both fit in the palm of Goliagoth's hand. Then she looked at Yasamin.

"Go ahead, sweet, put them on. They'll help you walk." Yasamin whispered. She nodded toward the shoes. "Go ahead."

Fleuise slowly took the shoes. "Did you make a pair for my dolly?"

Goliagoth frowned and opened his mouth for a rebuke. Instead he shook his head. "Your doll is small. You can carry her, so she doesn't need boots."

Fleuise stared at the soldier for a moment, then nodded seriously. "All right. It's best I carry her anyway, so she won't get lost." She sat down and began to lace them on.

In a few minutes, they were ready to leave. Yasamin looked around at the abandoned camp and felt a pang of sadness. As rough as it was, this had been *home*. She would miss it, as she would miss the simplicity of her life here. She turned her back on it and faced Goliagoth and the others. "I'm ready."

"Good. I'll lead the way, then you and the child. Shemar will follow you. He—" Goliagoth nodded at Arash "- will bring up the rear. Stay close together. If you need to stop for anything, let me know. Do not lag behind. We're headed into the unknown."

Yasamin nodded and took Fleuise's hand.

"We will start on the path running by the waterfall. Let's go."

Goliagoth moved toward the trail with the others following. When he reached the first line of undergrowth, he stood aside and let Yasamin and the others pass. "Keep moving, Highness. I want to make a last check."

He looked to the sea. The horizon remained vacant, and he shook his head. Just as Arash passed, Goliagoth turned.

"Slave!"

The young man turned and looked at the soldier. For a long moment Goliagoth simply stared back. Finally, he reached toward his scabbard, and Arash tensed. Goliagoth withdrew a second sword from his belt. "The way is rough and damn dangerous." The soldier moved closer and handed the second sword to the young man. "Keep a sharp lookout."

* * * * *

The way was rougher than Yasamin had ever dreamed possible—dark forests where she could see the shining eyes of beasts watching them, fast-moving streams with water so cold it took her breath, vine-strewn paths that grabbed at her feet and paths laden with razor-sharp rocks. With every step, she was thankful for the boots Goliagoth made her. Shemar had difficulty with the streams but, for the most part, managed well.

Even Arash felt the demands of the trail. His lungs told him they were slowly gaining altitude, and he prayed they would reach the mountain and cross it before the first snow.

His respect and love grew for Yasamin with each passing day. She had never experienced such a harsh environment, but she moved forward without complaint. In fact, she seemed *different* since they left camp. There was a restraint, a coldness, a steeliness, a *withdrawal* surrounding her that had not been there before. He hoped it was nothing more than the strain of the journey, which would disappear once they reached their destination.

Goliagoth was Goliagoth—the soldier. He led the way, sometimes stopping to locate a landmark he remembered. He carried the four packs of food on his back every day and, occasionally when the going was especially rough, hoisted Fleuise to his shoulders as well.

The days turned to weeks, and the terrain grew rougher— huge chasms gouged the earth's surface and tremendous boulders seemed to hang by a mere thread atop the boulder beneath. It looked as if some giant had empted a box of blocks, then left them laying.

But there was hope. What at first seemed like a low-lying cloud, grew and took shape. Soon they were able to see the form of Mount Sorania soaring against the sky. Two days later they were in the low hills surrounding its base.

And they were in luck, so far no snow blanketed its top.

* * * * *

"Tomorrow we begin our ascent." Goliagoth's voice cut through the stillness of the night as he stared at Arash and Yasamin. He knew they were exhausted, but to give them credit, they had managed to keep up the pace quite well, especially the Queen. He had admitted to himself over a week ago that he was amazed at how well she had managed. His respect for her had grown to grudging admiration and finally to well-earned adulation.

"How long will it take to cross the mountain?" Yasamin did her best to keep from yawning as she spooned out hot soup for each of them.

"Without trouble, about ten days."

Arash looked up from patching one of his boots. "Will we cross before snow?"

"Hard to say. Sometimes snow comes early, sometimes late. Was a red sunset today, means tomorrow will be clear."

"Goliagoth, what are our chances if it snows?" Yasamin's blatant question hushed both men. Both had done everything in their power to avoid mentioning this problem. In truth, they didn't want to think about the possibility. Now they had to.

Arash looked at Goliagoth because he didn't have the heart to tell her.

Goliagoth studied the fire a moment as he assimilated his thoughts. "Highness, we are going to do our best to beat the snow."

"I know, but what *if* we don't?"

"We do the best we can. If it's a light dusting, we will be uncomfortable but we will manage. If it's a heavy snowstorm, we will seek shelter and wait it out."

"But if the snow does not stop? What if it continues to snow for months?"

"We stay in the shelter. We melt the snow for water. We ration the food."

"What if we run out even if we ration, and it's still snowing?"

Goliagoth stared at Yasamin for a long time. She would accept nothing less than the truth, yet the thought of her dying in a distant place, alone, in the snow made an unprecedented lump rise in his throat. Unable to meet her stare, Goliagoth dropped his gaze to the fire before he spoke. "Then, Highness, we die."

Chapter 15

True to Goliagoth's prediction, the next morning dawned bright. The sun burned away the mist as the group began their onward journey. As the early hours progressed, Yasamin and Arash became aware of a low rumble that grew louder as they traveled. At midday, Goliagoth called a halt, so they could rest and eat. He knew this group would make better time in the long run if they rested briefly instead of marching all day.

"Shemar, we'll stop here. Post outlook on that small rise." Goliagoth pointed to a small knoll twenty paces from where they stood.

"Sir." The soldier saluted and hobbled toward the mound.

Goliagoth slowly turned and searched the perimeter of the clearing where they stood.

"Goliagoth, what's the noise?" Both Arash and Yasamin moved toward him. The sound made hearing difficult.

The giant continued his surveillance as he explained. "It is the mouth of the river Bethock. The water spouts from granite rock forming the base of Sorania and falls a thousand feet into a gorge that holds the river. From there it flows eastward into the sea."

Arash raised his eyebrows in question. "If it comes from the rock, how do we cross it?"

"A hand bridge spans the river. It was built by the inhabitants of this area." Goliagoth whirled to look at the forest behind Arash. "Did you hear that?"

Arash half-turned and looked at the area Goliagoth was scrutinizing. He saw nothing. "What? I didn't hear anything."

"Nor did I," echoed Yasamin, but she drew Fleuise closer to her. "What was it?"

"I thought I heard some—"

"*Demolisherian!*" Shemar shouted.

All three adults turned to look at him. The soldier pointed toward the trees where Goliagoth had been staring. They waited for him to speak. Instead of words, bright crimson spurted from his mouth, and he slowly tumbled headfirst down the knoll. The shaft of a black arrow protruded from his back. A blood-red feather shuddered on its end.

Yasamin screamed. Fleuise cried and buried her face in the woman's skirt. As he drew his sword, Goliagoth roughly pushed the Queen and little girl to the ground.

"Arash, my back! Keep the Queen between us."

Arash responded quickly. Pulling his sword, he moved so his back was toward Goliagoth, and the two soldiers faced the perimeter with Yasamin and Fleuise between them. Without taking his gaze from the surrounding forest, Goliagoth removed a small dagger from his belt and dropped it on the ground beside Yasamin.

"Highness, take it. If Arash and I are killed, it would be best if you do not let them take either of you captive." Then he drew another sword so both his hands were armed.

It was quiet, too quiet. Even the birds had stopped singing. If it had not been for Shemar lying on the ground less than ten paces from them and the dagger gripped in her hand, Yasamin might have thought she imagined the whole thing. The two men slowly circled round her, their backs to each other, weapons pointed at the trees.

Nothing happened. Yasamin began to think whoever it was had been scared away.

She was wrong.

The forest abruptly erupted with howling creatures, and Yasamin screamed again. They were hideous. Yasamin pulled Fleuise closer to her breast. She didn't want the child to see these things for her own heart thudded with terror.

They were short, barely three feet in height and dark like shadows. They seemed to be nothing more than bone and ligament. Their skeletal heads were too large for their bodies, the eye sockets empty, except for a red glow. When they emitted their ear-splitting screams, smoke erupted from their grinning mouths. Both soldiers swore under their breath. Neither had ever seen creatures like these. They braced for the onslaught. The things seemed to hobble and jump more than run.

When the creatures reached them, Goliagoth and Arash slashed at them.

When the soldiers' swords hit bone, the blades bounced off it as if the bone were black granite. When they thrust into the chest, the sword penetrated, the creature fell to the ground, then got up again. Arash felt a momentary panic. How could he kill these things if his sword had no effect?

He swung at one of the creatures who leapt through the air toward him. The sword's arc swept across its neck, decapitating the creature. It fell to the ground and dissipated. Momentarily stunned by the sight, Arash gaped. Another creature aimed its spear and missed Arash only by inches. Regaining his senses, Arash yelled: "Goliagoth. Their head's their weakness! Decapitate them!" He had no time to check if the giant had heard him for three of the things merged on him.

Goliagoth had heard him and began attacking with a vengeance. Using both hands, he swung at the creatures on either side of him. The tide slowly began to turn. The things began to retreat to the darkness of the forest with the soldiers following, still trying to kill the creatures. The one Arash fought emitted another ear-splitting scream cut short as Arash's blade sliced through its neck. The young man continued to watch for a second or so, then turned.

Yasamin was safe, although he could see her shaking violently. Goliagoth was just beyond her still fighting three more of the creatures. Engaged, Goliagoth failed to notice a fourth monster hop into an overhanging branch. Arash began to run. He knew that between the squeals and the roar of the river the giant would never hear his warning. By the time he reached Yasamin, he knew he could not get to Goliagoth in time.

At that moment, two things happened simultaneously. Goliagoth struck one of the creatures so hard the blade went through the first's neck, and the momentum carried it through the second's as well, and with his other hand, he decapitated the third. He turned toward Yasamin just as the fourth creature prepared to jump on him.

"Goliagoth!" Arash shouted and threw his sword toward the attacker. The blade swirled through the air and hit it. Goliagoth swiveled his head at Arash's shout and saw the sword hit the creature mid-jump. As it fell to the ground stunned, Goliagoth quickly dispatched it and ran back to Yasamin and Arash.

Both men were breathing heavily as they searched the forest.

"Are … those the … local … inhabitants?" Arash puffed.

"No. I have … no idea … what those *things* were. But we need to get out of here now. The bridge isn't far." Goliagoth looked toward Shemar and shook his head. "Dead." He hastily reached down and drew Yasamin to her feet. "Highness, quickly."

Pale and shaken, Yasamin nodded and almost trod on Goliagoth's heels as they ran down the trail. Arash brought up the rear, almost running backward, so he could keep a sharp lookout.

The roaring grew louder, and the ground beneath their feet trembled. They emerged into another clearing a mile farther. Goliagoth slowly reconnoitered the area, then cautiously approached the bridge. He warily crossed it and checked the other side. Satisfied by his findings, he returned to the group. He bellowed so they could hear him over the roar of the waterfall. Drops of water clung to his hair and beard and small bubbles flew as he shouted.

"Think we got all of them. Don't see any signs across the bridge, but we need a plan in case they've laid a trap ahead of us."

"What do you want us to do?" Arash's heart still trembled from what he had seen, although he believed they had killed them all.

Goliagoth leaned closer and continued to shout. "I will cross first and will stand guard on the forest yonder." He pointed at the trees on the other side of the chasm. "Highness, you come next. Arash keep watch over our backs. Once the Queen has crossed, you carry the child, but keep your sword arm free."

Arash nodded his understanding. Goliagoth turned to go, then stopped and glanced back at him. "You saved my life back there. I will not forget." He quickly ran toward the bridge, then across it. He waved them forward, then turned to watch the woods.

Arash took Fleuise's hand and nudged Yasamin onward. "You're next."

Yasamin edged forward. With each step more of the deep chasm came into view. Her heart hammered harder against her ribcage. She was deathly afraid of heights. Her stomach began to flutter and her head swam. She looked at the bridge. It was a flimsy thing, made of two hand-held ropes attached to boulders on either side of the abyss. The bottom of the bridge consisted of old, rough-hewn planks held together by yet two more ropes on either side then running through holes drilled in each end of the board. It shimmied and swayed from the wind created by the thundering waterfall. It glistened in the sunlight, wet from the spraying mist. Arash continued to gently nudge her forward, and Yasamin moved slower and slower until she was almost to the edge. Suddenly, she pushed back and whirled behind Arash.

"I c-can't. I can't do it."

"Can't do what?"

"I can't cross that thing, Arash. I can't do it."

"You have to. It's the only way out of here."

"Don't you understand? It is not that I won't do it. I *cannot* do it. I am too afraid of heights." She sat on a large rock behind her, her knees were too weak to hold her. Tears filled her eyes.

Arash looked toward Goliagoth, but his back was to them. Arash knelt before her. "You have to. We've got to cross the mountain before snow. We won't leave you here. Think of Fleuise."

"I know, I know!" Yasamin looked at the heavens, at Arash's face, then dropped her gaze to her lap. You go with her, but I cannot cross that thing." Tears were now streaming down her cheeks and splashing on her arms as she hugged herself.

The tears tore Arash's heart. He gently took one of her hands. "Look at me."

She wouldn't, embarrassed he had seen the tears. "I'm a coward, Arash. My fear of heights overwhelms me."

"Yasamin," Arash gently touched beneath her chin and raised her face, "Look at me." This time she did and he smiled. "You are no coward; you have proven that many times. You can cross this bridge." Yasamin shook her head. "Yes, you can. I'm going to carry Fleuise across the bridge. I'm coming back for you. We will walk across the bridge together."

"But—"

Arash overrode her protest. "I'm coming back for you. We'll walk across the bridge together. You will look into my eyes, just as you're doing now. You won't look anywhere else, just my face. You'll be safe. I won't let anything happen to you." He wiped the tears from her cheeks. "I promise I'll keep you safe. Do you believe me?"

Mute, Yasamin nodded.

"Good. I'm going to take Fleuise now. You stay here on this boulder. Don't move. I'll be right back for you, and we will cross the bridge together." Arash reluctantly removed his hand from her face. He wanted nothing more than to kiss the tears away, although to do so was impossible. He rose, picked up Fleuise and smiled at her. "All right, Fleuise. We're going to have some fun on the swinging bridge."

The little girl clung to him but looked at Yasamin. "I want her to come. I want Yasamin to come with us."

"She will. I'm going to take you, then I'm going to bring her, all right?" The child nodded. Arash gazed into Yasamin's eyes. "I will return in a few minutes. You'll be all right until then?"

"Yes, but hurry."

Arash hurried toward the bridge, and Yasamin watched as he started across. The bridge swayed beneath his movement, but he kept talking, and she could see Fleuise laughing. She watched until he was almost halfway, but the swaying made her dizzy. She *would* be able to cross if Arash were with her. The aloneness crawled over her, and she became uneasy. Yasamin looked back at the woods. They were quiet. She saw birds darting in the trees overhead, and she watched them a few moments, trying to calm herself.

At last, she looked back. Arash had just reached the other side as Goliagoth turned. She saw him run toward Arash and gesture toward her. Arash knelt, trying to get Fleuise to turn loose of his neck. From their gestures, she knew he was explaining to Goliagoth what had happened.

It was at that moment she smelt it.

Smoke.

Yasamin glanced around. What could possibly be burning? Her gaze fell upon the source, but her mind could not comprehend what she saw. Her heart felt as though it would burst. Both ropes tied to the boulders were smoking. She could see the glow of embers as the heat frayed the hemp. At that moment, Arash turned and started across the bridge. Frantic, Yasamin jumped and gestured wildly for him to go back. If he continued forward, when the ropes burned through, he would fall to his death.

Arash paused, confused by her signals. She ran forward screaming, even though she knew he couldn't hear her. "Go back, go back!"

Arash took another step.

"No! Go back. The bridge is burning." It made no sense. They would think her crazy, but she saw it and smelt it. "Go bac—"

Yasamin stopped short as a huge burst of fire erupted from the ground directly in front of her. She halted, then moved backward, confused and dazed. This couldn't be happening. She stared at the fire. It was a living thing. It writhed, coiled and inched its way toward her. Flames resembling arms reached for her. Yasamin's mind screamed silently as the fire drove her back farther from the bridge. She could no longer see the men, for a thick, black smoke rolled from the flames. The smoke twisted around her, shutting out the view, and she lost her sense of direction. It clogged her nose and lungs and stung her eyes. Frantic, Yasamin rubbed her eyes, stumbling over vines and pebbles as she moved. Now that she was disoriented, fear swelled within her that she might be headed toward the cliff. She slowed, too petrified to move. Coughing and wheezing, Yasamin stood still, certain she would be dead within minutes.

"Yasamin." The voice was calm and familiar.

Yasamin knew she must be dying. There was no one around her.

"Yasamin." The voice became more urgent and snapped her out of her daze. She glanced around wildly. To her left, superimposed over the black smoke, was her mother's face. White light suffused it.

"Mama?" Yasamin took a hesitant step forward, then stopped. It couldn't be. Her mother was dead.

"Yasamin, this way. Hurry." The light brightened, and the old Queen's face became more radiant. "Come, now. There is safety."

Suddenly, all doubt fled Yasamin. It *was* her mother. She didn't know how, but in her heart she *knew*. She hurried toward the image, and it retreated before her along a small, almost invisible trail. The black smoke coiled and thickened, trying to hold her. She heard the fire's crackle and hiss as it followed. She didn't look. Yasamin kept her eyes on her mother. The thicker the smoke became, the more radiant and solid the Queen's face became, until it filled her vision. The Queen smiled at her daughter.

"Yes, my darling, come. I will take you to safety. Do not fear."

The entrance to a cave abruptly appeared. The Queen's face disappeared through the opening. "In here, Yasamin. Come to safety."

Without hesitation, Yasamin plunged through the entrance. The air was clean and clear. She looked behind her where the smoke twisted and writhed. It grew blacker and heavier but did not enter the cave. Yasamin could hear the fire roaring outside, but she was no longer afraid. Turning, she saw her mother's face drifting down the long tunnel. It grew fainter.

"Mother? Mother, wait for me." Yasamin called as she hurried forward.

Yasamin edged her way along. It seemed like hours since she had left the cave's entrance. The tunnel twisted and wound deeper into the mountain. She had not seen her mother's face since entering. She was alone, but she felt no fear. In fact, she felt *safe*.

Yasamin stopped and glanced around. Something wasn't right and the reason suddenly registered. She was deep underground and going deeper, yet she could *see*. She gently touched the rocks. They felt normal, not warm, but they emitted a soft glow, enough for her to see how to walk. Perhaps she wasn't going deeper into the cave but toward another entrance. Even as Yasamin thought of the possibility, she dismissed it. The glow was coming from *within* the rocks, not reflecting from them, and the path was definitely sloping downward.

She continued.

The glow grew brighter.

The tunnel ended in a high, multi-vaulted chamber. Stunned, Yasamin stopped. The place was as beautiful as any room in her home. The stalactites and stalagmites were glowing crystals, illuminating the space with a beautiful soft light. The walls were lutescent, with flecks of gold twinkling like the night stars. The worn granite floor gleamed like black ice. The room smelt of herbs and flowers, and Yasamin thought she caught the faint whiff of *moonlitea*. In several places, running water trickled into round, smooth stones, creating miniature waterfalls. In awe, she moved through the hall and into the next room. It was the same, except here, flowers bloomed. Amazed, Yasamin approached them. They were alive, and the source of the scent she had noticed earlier. A twinkling light darted by. Yasamin glanced up and gasped. In the dark recesses of the chamber's heights, hundreds of tiny lights winked in every color imaginable. They reminded her of the lighting bugs of her homeland. A cluster of them hovered over her head. She darted backward, and they followed her. She stepped right, then left, and the lights trailed.

"They will not harm you."

Yasamin jumped and whirled to face the voice.

An old man stood in the doorway of the next chamber. Slightly stooped, he appeared as ancient as the rocks of the cavern. Wispy, white hair haloed his thin, angular face, and his arms were unusually long and ended in large, capable hands. He moved toward her, and she noticed he had a slight limp. As he neared, she could see the deep laugh lines around his mouth and golden eyes, which were so knowing Yasamin felt he could look into her soul.

The cluster of lights hovering above her head flew to him. They circled him, twinkling more rapidly, then returned to their former position above Yasamin.

He smiled. "They are impressed with you."

"They? What are they?"

"I'll tell you all, my child, but first let's get you some nourishment. You must be exhausted after your ordeal. I am Mosesra." He turned. "This way, Yasamin, I'll fix you some nice *berrirouge* tea, and you can relieve yourself of that backpack."

Without thought, Yasamin followed him. As he prepared the tea, Yasamin surveyed the room. It was as the others except for a few pieces of furniture. She removed the backpack and set it on the table. The lights whirled around it excitedly, then resumed their position above her.

"Is this your home?"

Mosesra smiled. "Yes. Has been for about four hundred years."

Yasamin sought control of her expression. "Four hundred years! You're four hundred years old?"

"Actually, I am four hundred and forty-six to be exact." The faint smell of sweet berries reached Yasamin, and she realized she was famished. "Honey for your tea, child?"

"Yes, thank you. How do you know my name?" Yasamin felt no fear of this stranger. In fact, she felt quite at home and safe. She even thought he must be slightly daft thinking he was so ancient.

Mosesra smiled again. "When one gets to be my age, one spends time studying small details. You have met one of my friends."

"Who?"

"Shar. She was quite impressed with you." Mosesra came to the table with a cup of ruby-red tea and set the steaming mug in front of her. He added a small saucer of cakes.

The thought then occurred to Yasamin that he might not be so daft. "You know Shar?"

"Quite well."

"How did she—"

Mosesra nodded toward her food. "First things first, child. Eat. I'll begin by explaining a little about myself. If you haven't already guessed, you are inside Sorania, the Holy Mountain. I am su—"

"You are a holy man?"

Mosesra chuckled. "I suppose some call me that, among other things. I am one of the few remaining Gwedosharians left on earth. So is Shar. We have continued to keep the old ways and knowledge alive, but it gets harder with time as our numbers dwindle."

"You *do* exist!"

"Unfortunately, too many have stumbled from the way of light and think we're just a legend. But the stories are true. The one here at Mount Sorania is perhaps the best-known."

"So I heard. Many of you were lost. Ara—I have a friend who says so many lives were lost here, the ground became so holy it glows."

Mosesra laughed. "Arash has a good heart. But *technically* he is not quite right."

"What do you mean?"

"Why, child, our lives were not lost. We simply moved to our next level of existence. That's why the non-Gwelowsharians say the ground 'glows' from holiness.'"

"I don't understand."

"You just have not grasped it yet." Mosesra glanced up at the pinpoint lights hovering above Yasamin's head. She looked up as well. The tiny lights glowed and jiggled, almost as if they were *laughing*. Yasamin watched them flit about for a moment, then her eyes grew wide with wonder. She looked back at Mosesra. "That's the glow?"

"Yes. We don't call ourselves 'holy,' although we always strive to reach for the light. When we pass from this physical world, we go to the next. We *become* light and energy. Each of those—" Mosesra glanced at the dancing orbs "- was once an individual here. You see—"

One of the smaller lights, a bright blue one, darted from the group above Yasamin's head and flew to him. It danced in front of his face for several seconds and he nodded. The light fluttered back to Yasamin, touched her hand, dipped slightly, then rejoined the group.

"I've been asked to clarify something. One does not have to be *born* Gwedosharin, or in Gwendomere for that matter, to become a follower of the light. It is above and beyond a physical place or country—it is for all. To be a follower, one simply strives toward light and shies from the dark side, not as easy as it sounds, but I'm digressing. Babes and young children are born on the right track. As they grow older, greed or jealousy or something else pulls them from the path. Innocent children who die young join us." Mosesra smiled. "That tiny blue light just now is the young boy, Mata, who was killed in your village. He wanted you to know he is happy."

Tears pricked the back of Yasamin's eyelids, and she touched her hand where the light had grazed it. Her skin tingled. "You mean …"

Mosesra nodded. "It is the same with your old nurse, Nitae."

"The lights above her corpse and the grave?"

Mosesra nodded again. "Yes. Both times Nitae was reaching out for you. The fact you were able to see her light says a lot for you. The battle between right and wrong, good and evil is still occurring today, Yasamin. Powerful forces are at work constantly. You witnessed one earlier: the fire. Did you feel it strange it started for no reason?"

Yasamin nodded. "I did."

"It was not a true fire but actually Vulmire. He is half man, half beast. He was a ruler in Dragonval long ago. He wanted to be the most powerful man on earth, so he joined the dark side. Now he has many powers. He can change into fire or call forth creatures from hell like those your friends fought earlier. They could have harmed you. Arash luckily found their weakness. As you saw, they vanished to ash."

"Vulmire sent them? What could he possibly want with me?"

"Ah, my dear, where do I begin? There is so much to tell you and so little time. We have waited for—oh dear, I'm wandering again. Let me try to straighten matters out before I turn this over to another."

He leaned forward, resting his hands on the table. He stared at Yasamin, and she could have sworn his eyes gleamed as precious gold. The tiny lights settled in a circle around Yasamin's head. They no longer startled her—she found them comforting now that she knew what they were.

"King Amir intends to marry you because his wife is barren. However, Queen Medusimia isn't at all happy about it. To her it is an insult. She has aligned herself with Vulmire in the hope he will destroy you before you reach Dragonval. Vulmire has lusted for the Queen for years. Of course he agreed, it gets him what he desires most."

"But Amir—"

"The King knows nothing of this alliance. He does not even know of Vulmire's existence. The Queen is clever in getting exactly what she wants without leaving a trail.

"But I am to marry Amir. I cannot tell him of her intentions. There is no proof. He'll think I am crazy."

"Yasamin, only you can decide if you will marry King Amir. If you choose to do so, I and the others are here for you."

"You hardly know me. Why?"

"I have known you since you were no more than a twinkle in your parents' eye. Your mother was one of us."

"What?"

Mosesra nodded. "Long ago we were given a sign a woman would be born who could become one of our greatest leaders. For a long time, we thought and hoped it was your mother. It wasn't, but that doesn't diminish the fact she was a most wonderful woman."

"Yes," Yasamin whispered. "I never remember her without a smile."

"She was kind. She healed many people, physically and in the heart."

"Except herself."

"She chose to use her strength and powers to help others. She loved this." Mosesra tapped the backpack lying on the table.

Yasamin frowned. "What?"

"The way contained in this book."

Yasamin unwrapped the bundle and withdrew the box. She carefully extracted the worn manuscript. "You're talking about the road of silk?" Her voice trembled with excitement.

"Precisely."

"Tell me everything. What is it? Why does it seem so familiar, yet I cannot read it? Why—"

Mosesra chuckled and held up a hand. "One thing at a time, child, one thing at a time. Let me start with the heart of the matter."

"Tell me everything." Yasamin leaned forward like a child waiting for her favorite bedtime story.

"First, our minds are very powerful, more powerful than most humans can imagine. With proper training, we can go beyond our physical bodies, change our form. If we are followers of the light, we do this to help others or to protect ourselves but never to hurt an innocent being. We must be selfless, not selfish. Secondly, we believe all worlds are connected, there is more than just this physical world. For example, there is the next plane of existence, which you see in the lights around you. Do you understand?"

Yasamin nodded. "Yes, so far."

"Good. Now for us, we believe it is possible to 'borrow' from another level, a place created by our actions on this earth. In this place, every blade of grass, every grain of sand, *everything* is shaped by a good deed and a good life in this world. This place is woven by our actions, just as a silkworm weaves its silk."

"It exists in our minds?"

"No. It exists between this world and the next plane—what many call heaven. To access it, yes, we need our minds, but we also need our hearts. Only those of a pure heart can travel to this place on the road of silk. All our knowledge, trials, and formulas, everything we have learned through the ages has been written in these books. When you *believe*, when your actions are pure, these words become legible to you, and you'll find what you need to help others and protect yourself."

"What do you mean?"

"Let me back up a little. In the middle of this place I've told you about is the Castle of Silk. This is the ultimate goal for anyone following The Road. Anywhere offers you some type of help, but when you reach the Castle, *this* is the ultimate center. In the Castle you are protected, not only by the bridge you've created, but everyone who has ever followed the light is there with you. Nothing, absolutely nothing, not even the evil one can touch you there. Lesser powers, for instance humans who follow the dark side, cannot follow you along the road of silk you create, for this land will not tolerate any evil-hearted souls. Do you understand?"

"I think so. But what if you're trying to help someone who is in danger but who doesn't believe?"

"If that person is not evil and you are strong enough, if *you* believe enough, you can carry people with you into the Castle of Silk. They may not *understand* where they are or what has happened, but as long as you maintain your belief and power, they'll be safe with you. After leaving, the person usually doesn't remember where they were. If they have an open heart, they might. For example, a young child may very well remember every detail."

"So you're saying it's a real place?"

"It is as real as the chair you're sitting in, if you believe as we do. The stronger your belief, the more tangible it is. If you have true faith, even if it is only the size of the seed of mustard, this world exists. It may be barely discernible but like silk, durable. A length of true translucent silk will hold a beast weighing one hundred kiltons."

Yasamin reverently touched her mother's book. "And my mother knew all this?"

Mosesra nodded. "She did. There were few like her."

"I don't remember her ever being gone. How did she visit you?"

"Remember, child, this physical world is not the only one that exists."

"Of course, she came to you on the road of silk! Is there a word for it?"

"You are partially right. Let me clarify something. The road of silk takes you to a place when you need something more, say, physical protection; it is a bridge for getting you from trouble to safety. The mind is a powerful instrument in itself. You may travel out of your physical body and communicate with another, which is what your mother did most often. We call this airtrail travel. If you concentrate hard enough, you can control the elements."

"Like the wind and water?"

"Yes. For example, let us say you were on a ship, and there was no breeze for the sails. You aren't in actual danger, yet if the ship does not move, you will stay at sea forever. You can call up a wind to fill the sails. Do you see the difference?"

"I'm beginning to understand."

"I knew you would be a fast learner, just like you dear mother." Mosesra rose from the table. "Now, child, I shall take you to another. There are things you need to know. Once you have learned all of them, *you and only you,* must make a decision. If you decide to go, I must tell you the way will be hard and very dangerous. If you decide against going, none of us will punish you. You must live with your own conscious. Being the woman I think you are, that would be the harshest punishment you could have. Come." Mosesra indicated for Yasamin to follow him. "Just leave your things there."

"Where are we going?"

Mosesra headed toward a small niche running off one side of the chamber. "Not far … or to the ends of the earth, depending on how you look at it,"

Chapter 17

The niche was narrow, only wide enough for one person at a time to pass through. It ended in a circular room, large enough for seven or eight people. One stalactite adorned the room, emitting just enough light to see how to walk. Mosesra rambled across the chamber to the opposite wall with Yasamin behind him. When he reached the wall, he stepped aside.

In front of her was a smooth, indigo rock running from floor to ceiling. At its base was a circle of small stones of the same blue.

Yasamin looked around. The room was empty. "I thought we were meeting someone."

"You are in a moment." Mosesra knelt in front of the circle. Stretching out his hands, he whispered a few words. Silkworms immediatley appeared from the crevices and began threading their way to the side opposite them. Each insect loosened a silk thread behind it. Within moments there was a woven sheet of golden, gossamer silk shimmering and swaying like a living thing.

Mosesra rose. "I'll be in the outer room when you are finished. You can come to me there." He gently rested his hand on Yasamin's shoulder, then left her alone.

She thought she was by herself.

The dark blue wall began to lighten in the center.

"I have missed you, Yasamin." The voice was just a whisper. "You've grown into a beautiful, young woman." As the light grew brighter, the voice became stronger. The face of Yasamin's mother suddenly appeared.

"Mama?"

"Yes, my dear. I'm here." The face sharpened, along with the rest of Casadra's body. She was beautiful, youthful as she had been before the disease had consumed her.

Yasamin's eyes filled with tears and her lower lip trembled. "I can see you." Yasamin gently reached for her mother. Her fingers touched rock but warmth encompassed her hand.

"Things are always clearest when in the holy mountain." Casadra reached to Yasamin's cheek. A hint of warmth caressed the girl's skin.

Yasamin put her own hand to her cheek to keep the warmth there. "I love you, Mama. I miss you so much."

"I love you, too, my Sasa." At the mention of her pet name, Yasamin burst into sobs. "Now, now, no tears, my dearest. This is not a time for sadness."

"I know. But I'm so alone. I miss you. I don't know what to do." Yasamin furtively wiped at her streaming eyes.

"You're never alone; I am always with you. Only remain still for a moment, and you will find me. "

"That isn't the same as you being here *with* me."

Casadra smiled gently. "I know, Sasa, but my time on earth is gone. My mission on Earth was accomplished. Now is your time. Try to remember the things I taught you when we were together."

"You were so smart. You knew how to do everything. I can never expect to remember half of what you knew."

"There were times I was terrified of doing the wrong thing. I guess I did a better job of hiding it than I thought."

"You were never scared. You were always so brave."

"Oh, yes I was … many times. And being brave doesn't mean not being afraid. Being brave is simply doing what you have to do despite your fear. You just need time to gain some experience. I am very proud of you, Daughter. You are willing to go into the dragon's mouth to protect our people. That is a tremendously courageous thing to do. No wonder the people of Gwendomere love you so much."

Tears threatened Yasamin again, but she controlled them. "Mosesra said there were things I needed to know. Are you the one who's going to tell me?"

"Yes. Things I should have told you long ago. I thought I had more time, but the right moment never seemed to arise, then it was too late. But now I must tell you."

"About what?"

"Your beginnings and what waits in Dragonval. Behold." Casadra pointed to the circle at her feet. The golden silk shimmered and shifted from an indiscernible breeze. As Yasamin watched, the colors altered. Pictures formed then sharpened.

She saw her mother and a man she imagined must be her father sitting in a rose garden. Casadra confirmed this as she continued speaking.

"Dragonval was not always as it is. Your father was a good man. He was ecstatic when I told him the news of you. His father—your grandfather—was very ill, and your father, Gretental, sat on the throne, acting for the old king. The people of Dragonval loved him dearly. There was dancing in the streets when he announced I was to bear a child. Everything was wonderful. In some ways, I was very naïve then. I assumed everyone was happy there would be a child born to the royal couple."

The images shifted and darkened. Yasamin saw a shadowy room, so dark she could barely discern the man's body. The rest of the images squirmed and coiled like snakes.

"I was wrong. Your grandfather was happy but not because there was a future heir. I thought him ill. No one ever saw him because he never left his room. Only your father entered, but even he didn't really see his father. The room was void of light except for one or two candles. Your grandfather said the light aggravated his condition. He would talk to Grentental, tell him matters that needed to be done. If there were papers to be signed, Serpata told his son to leave them, he would sign them when he felt able, and the papers could be picked up later."

Yasamin strained to see the images, yet they remained obscure. She could barely detect a figure deep within the curtained bed and a pair of hands within the candle's glow signing parchment.

The images shifted and grew brighter. Yasamin's eyes widened and she gasped. She looked at her mother in amazement.

"Yes, Yasamin. You are a twin. You had a brother." Casadra paused, letting the information sink in, then continued. "His name was Orando. Your father and I were beside ourselves with joy. I was so happy. But things slowly altered."

The silk shimmered and shifted to a new image.

"You knew your father died. As time passed, I grew to believe your father's death was no accident, that he was murdered. His death devastated me, but I did my best to run the country as queen and acting for your grandfather. The only consolation, the only happiness I had was you and Orando. In truth, there was a time you children were all I lived for. As I became more convinced your father was murdered, I vowed to bring his killers to justice. I began to investigate, and that is when I learned the awful truth and discovered the evil lurking in Dragonval."

"My father was murdered?" Yasamin's stomach curdled, and for a moment, she thought she would be sick.

Casadra nodded. "Yes. But the horror of it is he was killed by his own father." Casadra's voice grew hard. "Your grandfather was ill but not with a human sickness. Your grandfather, Serpata, craved power more than any thing, and he sold his soul to the devil to have it. He could rule the world if he sacrificed a child to the evil one every month in the dark of the moon. Serpata *agreed* to this monstrosity. The devil sealed the pact by kissing your grandfather on each shoulder.

Your father discovered your grandfather's secret, and Serpata couldn't let him live with the knowledge. He killed him there in the bedchamber, then arranged for it look like an accident."

"How could he do something so horrible?"

"Greed is a great motivator, Yasamin. It makes people do horrible things to obtain their goal."

"What did my father find out? What was the secret?"

"Remember I said when the evil one sealed the pact with Serpata, he kissed him on each shoulder?"

Yasamin nodded.

"From each kiss sprang a snake—the emblem of the evil one. They grew and multiplied until there were six snakes—three from each shoulder. They coiled around his arms, his neck. They could never leave him because they were a part of him. The snakes had vicious, poisonous fangs and scales they rattled to warn Serpata. This is the only reason he let your father sit on the throne: he knew no one would accept him if they saw him."

Yasamin shivered at the picture on the silk. "But if he was to become ruler of the world, what did it matter what people thought?"

Casadra smiled at her daughter. "Forgive me, darling. I get ahead of myself. I forget when one is in physical form one does not function the same as we. When you pass from earth form, things are more omnipotent and seen simultaneously. We don't have time as you know it." She nodded. "That *was* the agreement. But the evil one is jealous. Sly. He places his mark on those he owns, thus the kiss. If Serpata had kept up his end of the bargain, the snakes probably would have remained small and kept covered in public. But that is not the case.

"Serpata did sacrifice a child every new moon, but the evil one demanded even more. To prove devotion, the devil demanded your grandfather sacrifice you and your brother. Again Serpata agreed. No price was too great, and there was his fear of what might happen to him if he didn't.

"Mo—my father came and warned me of the king's plan. I spent many nights worrying about you. I tried to make arrangements to leave the city. I had a little time. The new moon had just passed. No one would help—no country offered asylum. I was frantic."

Yasamin trembled as she watched the story unfold on the silken fabric.

"One night as I was laying in bed a vision came to me: a large, black serpent crawling into the nursery, into your beds. It swallowed both of you. I had no doubt it was a sign and that I had to get out of the castle immediately. I ran to the nursery, grabbed you and returned to my bedroom. I put you on the bed and hurried back for your brother. He wasn't there. I ran down the hall toward Serpata's chambers. Before I got there I heard the voices—one, your grandfather. He had learned of my plans and decided to kidnap both of you and hold you until the dark of the moon. Serpata told the men to put Orando in his bedchamber, then search for you and

Unshed tears glistened in Casadra's eyes. Two trails of water emerged on the cobalt wall and dripped toward the floor.

"It was too late to save Orando. I rushed back to my chambers, grabbed you, some money and my book I had begun studying and a black cloak. I fled the palace."

Again the silk darkened. Queen Casadra darted from pillar to pillar in a shadowy hallway as soldiers begin searching. Shut off from the main exit, she fled to a small maid's chamber. Holding the baby tight against her, she desperately sought a hiding place. The room was too basic, no closets or chests, nothing. The sound of heavy boots grew closer as the soldiers hunted for her. She ran to the only exit from the room, the window. Opening the latch, Casadra leaned out and saw a low-lying roof was just beneath her. She scrabbled through the window and closed it behind her. Crouching, she half-walked, half-crawled across the sloping tiles. The roof led to the outer wall of the castle then ended. She heard the soldiers shouting behind her, and in the distance, she heard others slowly covering the perimeter. Only one direction remained open. The Queen clasped her baby closer, drew the black cloak tightly around her and jumped. A bed of dried flowers broke her fall. Getting to her feet, she headed toward the woods edging the road.

On the shifting silk, Yasamin watched her mother run through the dark countryside, then shadowy streets. The black cape blended with the dark alleys, and she could only see her mother's pale face as she glanced over her shoulder.

"It was only a matter of time if I didn't escape Dragonval, so I ran for the harbor. It was a long way. The castle is almost a mile from town, and I had to get through the town itself. I thought if I could get on a ship, could bribe the captain, we had a chance. At the time I didn't know enough about the road of silk to help us or to help your brother. But fate decrees some things that cannot be avoided.

"I ran and ran. You were scared and hungry, but I was afraid to stop to feed you. I continued toward the village, but I sensed someone following me. I saw no one, but I could *feel* him."

As the scene unfolded, Yasamin saw a dark form emerge from the shadows and dog her mother's trail. Her skin grew cold.

"I reached the town. I thought we were going to make it, but it was not quite so simple. I got to the harbor and saw one ship anchored. I hurried toward it, when out of the shadows a man appeared: Gargolen, the tax master. He was mostly referred to as 'The Collector' because of his perversion of 'collecting' something from a person who couldn't pay. It was rumored his rooms were full of ears, fingers, noses, and other things of the poor souls who didn't have the money due him."

Yasamin stared at the man standing at the mouth of the alley. She could not see much of him because of the long cape and hood, but she caught a glimpse of a long, hooked nose, pale skin and a blood-red mouth. The hairs on her arm rose, and she rubbed her skin to warm it.

Casadra faltered. "He was a vile man. I knew who he was, but at the time, I didn't know was he was your father's half-brother. Serpata sired him through some poor chambermaid. The Collector knew. He worshiped Serpata, would do anything for him, and Serpata was smart enough to use this to his advantage. He appointed Gargolen tax master which cemented Gargolen's idolization forever.

"I hoped he had not recognized me, and I turned to run. The cobblestones were rough, and I tripped on my cape. I fell to the ground with you. Before I could rise, he was upon us."

The silk shifted and fluttered.

Yasamin looked on as Queen Casadra fell to the hard cobblestones, throwing herself to her side at the last moment to protect her baby. Blood seeped through the Queen's gown where she gouged her knees. Yasamin curled tightly against her mother and whimpered. The Collector sauntered toward her, then stood over her as his eyes roamed her body. He suddenly bent down and roughly grabbed Casadra by the shoulder. The abrupt movement disconnected mother and child's embrace.

"Careful, my queen" he sneered, "You might bruise that lovely skin of yours."

The words were faint, like an echo, but Yasamin could hear them. His fingers remained longer than necessary on Casadra's arm. He quickly turned to the baby sitting on the stones.

Yasamin watched the silk. Even in its wavering light, she saw the desire and longing spread his thick lips wide. His tongue ran around his mouth, causing her stomach to churn once more.

"I saw his lustful smile as he grabbed you. I was so afraid for you, Yasamin, more than for myself. I knew he was capable of anything before he returned me to Serpata. And he *would* return us—both of us. It was terrible. I believe I could have handled it for myself but not *you*. If he touched you, if he had had his way with you, Serpata could not have sacrificed you. The children have to be virgins, but the price, Daughter, the price you would have paid! It would have scarred you for life.

"I was desperate. When he picked you up, I noticed a dagger in his belt. When he straightened and looked at me, I slapped him as hard as I could. 'How dare you touch *me*. You are not fit,' I screamed at him. I turned and headed toward an alley. I didn't have to look to see if he followed; I knew he would. His arrogant pride would never let such an insult go unpunished. He forgot about you. He followed me. I could feel him closing. While I was walking, I managed to loosen a few buttons of my gown. When he grabbed my shoulder, I struggled and fell in the gutter face down and pretended to be unconscious. It was almost unbearable. I heard your cries. I wanted to come to you, but I had to protect you whatever the cost. I lay still. I could hear his heavy breathing come nearer as he knelt. At last, I felt his hand on my shoulder. As he turned me over, I grabbed the dagger and stabbed him. He fell on top of me. I pushed him off and ran to you."

Yasamin's throat constricted with sobs as she watched the silken imagery. She was unconscious of the tears running down her cheeks. A waft of warmth enclosed her, and she could smell the gentle fragrance of *moonlitea*.

"Mama," she whispered.

Casadra smiled. "I ran to you and cradled you in my arms. You were crying, but I will never forget you putting your chubby, little hand to my face and rubbing my tears away. You had the gentleness in you even then.

"I thought we were safe. I gathered you, my things and started to rise. Gargolen wasn't dead, and he was furious. He drew his sword and started toward us. The way to the ship was blocked. I thought about retracing my steps, but I could already hear Serpata's hunters and their wolves searching for us ... and closing fast. I was at the water's edge. There was no escape. I reached down and found some small rocks lining the shore's perimeter. I threw one at Gargolen. It hit him in the face and broke his nose. Blood spewed. It made him even more angry. He yelled horrible things about what he was going to do to you, then me. I threw more. Each hit him. Each slowed him down. Still, he struggled toward us. He had broken teeth, a shattered cheekbone and a huge gash on his jaw, but he was like a madman. I don't think he even noticed the pain because he was so intent on destroying us. My hand closed on the last rock, larger than the rest. I threw it. It hit him in the middle of his forehead.

That rock would have killed a normal man. Not The Collector. But, it did stun him. He fell almost at my feet. He grasped for me. There was nothing left. I prayed, held you close to my heart and jumped into the sea."

Coldness surrounded Yasamin as she watched her mother jump into the black ocean. Not only could she see the water froth around them, she could feel it trying to draw them into its depths.

"Luckily, The Collector couldn't swim. He shouted obscenities at me and ran for the hunters. I swam toward the ship. The water was freezing. My arms grew heavy. My mind fogged. You were the only thing that kept me going. I had to get you to safety.

"It seemed I swam for hours, but it was only minutes. Time ceased to have any meaning as I tried to stay afloat. I grew weaker, and my clothes began to weigh me down.

"At last, I closed my eyes to sleep. In the distance, I heard a splash. Arms encircled me, lifting us back to the surface. An old fisherman, curious about a small light flitting about him had gotten into his rowboat and followed it. The light shot out and over me seconds before I went under, but he saw me. He jumped in and pulled us to safety."

"Was it one of them?" Yasamin nodded toward the other room.

Casadra nodded. "The old man was a follower of the light. He was familiar with Sorania and the Gwedosharians. He rescued us, took us to his hut. We talked long into the night. I told him everything: Serpata, how every country refused me asylum, Orando, everything. I was afraid for you, for me and for him. I knew Serpata would torture him if he found me, but the old man told me not to worry, everything would be taken care of."

Yasamin watched the white-headed man talk to her mother. In the corner, she could see herself fast asleep on a worn cot. She liked the old man; his eyes were kind and crinkled from decades of smiling. Her mother's voice interrupted Yasamin's thoughts.

"It was the fisherman who took me where I needed to go to be safe."

"Where?"

"Here, Daughter. To Sorania. He brought me here."

Chapter 17

The silken images faded. Once more the fabric was simply a piece of material.

"I spent months here learning about the way of light. You were just a baby—you don't remember. I learned so much, Yasamin. There was so much to learn. So much to do. So many to help. With Mosesra's help and the others, I learned quickly, but at last, it was time for me to leave. As long as I was here no darkness could find me because it could never have the power needed to enter this holy ground. Until I left here, I am sure Serpata thought me dead. Things had changed in Dragonval. Amir, Serpata's nephew and closest relative, had assumed the throne. I returned to Gwendomere. Two months later Mother died, and I became queen of my homeland."

"And now with this marriage," Yasamin whispered. "I repeat the pattern."

Casadra nodded. "Dear child, someday you'll realize everything is a circle, some more noticeable than others. For everything, there is a beginning and an end, and every end is a beginning. Our only choice is whether we repeat the circle or create a new one."

"I don't understand."

"You will when the time is right."

"Should I marry him, Mother?"

"I cannot tell you what to do. That decision has to come from your heart. Every circumstance has choices. Each choice results in a different outcome. It is your path, your choices that either add to the road of silk or do not."

"What happens to those who don't know about the way to light?"

"There are those who do not know about the way of light or the road of silk by *name,* yet they follow its path. Those people will never know how to borrow help from that other place as we do. Yet if they follow the light, they still help *create* it. They become a blade of grass, a leaf, a stone; therefore, they contribute after they leave their earth form."

"What about the ones who don't follow light?"

"They are lost forever. If they helped no one here or hurt people here, they are condemned to darkness, trapped in whatever their greatest fear was in this life. They will live that fear forever. But they are not our greatest worry."

"What is?"

"Those people who sell their soul to the evil one. *He* lives forever. When an individual sells his soul, he or she also receives power to live forever unless one discovers their weakness. You see, they are not quite demon, but they are more than human. If one finds their flaw, they can destroy them. It's the evil one and his followers against whom we wage the biggest battle."

"They must be very powerful if they are more than human."

"They are, but don't forget, people like Mosesra and Shar are more than human, too. They have embraced the light and receive power from it and from all those gone before. And they know the road of silk."

Yasamin sighed. "There's so much to learn. How do I know what's the right thing to do?"

"You will know. You will feel it in your heart."

"So why don't more people follow the light?"

"There are many reasons. In earth form other things take on more significance, seem more important. The way of light is not an easy way. It requires much in time and patience. Many want instant gratification. They want happiness. They think *things* or possessions will get this for them."

"Like wealth?"

"Yes. Or prestige, power, many things. Even love, Yasamin."

The young woman raised her eyes to her mother. "Love?"

"Yes. True love is selfless. It does what is best for others, but most people don't understand this. They want love for themselves. *That* is not wrong, it is human. It is when love becomes egotistical or used as manipulation to reward one's self that it becomes wrong."

Yasamin smiled. "Mama, if I ever reach the castle of silk, could I touch you? I mean, as before, when you were here alive?"

"Sasa, I am alive now, only in different form. But yes, in that place I would be as real to you as these rocks, this cave."

"Can you see the future? What it holds?"

"Not everything, Yasamin. As I have told you, humans have free choice. It is the choice they decide upon that determines which path the future takes."

"If I go to Dragonval, can I help Amir?"

Casadra hesitated, studying her daughter intently. At long last, she answered. "If you go to Dragonval, you can help."

"And if I chose not to go?"

"This much I can tell you, Amir will keep his promise, and he will hunt you to the ends of the earth."

"I see." Yasamin looked away. She didn't want her mother to see the disappointment in her eyes.

"Yasamin, humans are not perfect. If you choose to follow our road, it does not mean you will not be tempted to fulfill your own desires. In the end, it is what you *choose* to do and act upon that matters. Understand?"

Yasamin nodded her head, then raised her eyes to her mother. "Mosesra said something I don't understand. He told me they thought you might be the One they waited for. What did he mean?"

Casadra contemplated a moment. "My time is growing short, and there is still something I must tell you. Mosesra can elaborate, but I will give you the essence of it. In the beginning there were many, many followers of the light. As mankind multiplied, they grew fewer as earthly things began to distract people. There was a great book the Old Ones followed, but it was destroyed in the Great Battle. The story, however, was remembered, and the survivors told it to their children, who told it to their children through the ages. The legend is: there will be a woman born who will become a great leader. This woman is different, as she is not entirely 'human.' Our sanctified leaders seldom marry, especially with one not born a follower of the light, although it is not forbidden. This woman is descended from such a union, and she carries the seed of the dark side *and* the seed of the road to light within her. She must make a great choice that will affect the whole earth. She must choose which path she will take. If she chooses the dark side, she will become ruler of the entire world. If she chooses the road to light, she will become a great leader and lead many back to the light. She will become the greatest fear of the evil one, for she can become as strong as he is."

"But if they thought you—"

"Sasa, that is all I can tell you. My time is almost over, and there is something you must know."

Yasamin heard the urgency in her mother's voice, and it made her skin tingle. A terrible foreboding rose in her chest and heaviness settled on her like a cloak. "What is it, Mama?"

"Evil lives in Dragonval. It stretches its deadly tendrils in every direction. It is slowly poisoning the land, the people, the very air of that country. If it is not destroyed, it will devastate Dragonval. Then it will reach far beyond to other lands."

Horrified, Yasamin stared at her mother. "King Amir? The man I am supposed to marry?"

"No, child, I'm not speaking of Amir. You will be in gravest danger. You must protect yourself. This evil will reach directly for you."

"Mosesra has already told me about the queen."

"No, Yasamin! Not Medusimia. I'm talking about unadulterated evil that has to be destroyed. You are the only who can do it." Casadra's image began to fade.

"Mama, wait! If it isn't Amir or the Queen …"

The image disappeared, but Casadra's voice lingered. The words rang in the small chamber. "Amir sits on the throne, but he is not the ruler. Because you escaped sacrifice, the evil One severely punished Serpata, who is so hideous he hides in the darkness beneath the castle. Serpata *still* rules. Beware of your grandfather, Yasamin. He will kill you if possible for it is his only hope of redeeming himself. Yasamin, remember the road of silk!"

Chapter 18

Yasamin's mind spun as she returned to Mosesra. Her grandfather, alive! And he had killed her father! The thought was almost inconceivable. She moved to the chair where she'd been sitting earlier and cradled her head in her hands.

"You look tired, child. Perhaps you would like to rest a while before we talk," Mosesra started to rise from the table.

"No. I'm just overwhelmed by what my mother told me. I want to talk."

Mosesra smiled. Casadra's daughter certainly had the backbone. Now if she developed the spirit ...

"I will answer anything I can," Mosesra said.

"She told me my grandfather is still alive. "

"Yes."

"And he would kill me if he could."

Mosesra nodded. "That is true."

"How could he kill his own son? It is horrible. And he would kill me, his granddaughter, his own flesh and blood?"

"When one sells their soul to the evil One, they become less human over time and more like him. Their light departs. Darkness fills their heart. The only thing they love is themselves. Serpata has worshiped the evil One for *mileus*, his power has grown. Never underestimate his abilities, child. He is capable of great evil. He's only been unsuccessful in one thing, and until he fulfills the contract he made, Serpata cannot rule the world."

"Mother said I was the only one who could destroy him. Why me? And how?"

"I cannot say. I can only tell you that you have the ability if you chose to do so. And I cannot tell you how because I don't know. If you chose to do it, you will discover the answer in your heart."

"I don't know enough or even where to begin."

Mosesra gently touched Yasamin's hand and looked deep into her eyes. "Child, the first step to understanding is to realize you know nothing. Only then do you begin to truly learn."

"I suppose."

"You have taken the first step, Yasamin."

"When? how?"

"When you came from the alcove just now, you asked me about what you should *do*. You never questioned the fact you saw and talked with your mother who left this earth years ago. You accepted it as truth."

Yasamin smiled. "Yes. I don't exactly understand it, but I have no doubt I talked with my mother. I believe she lives someplace. Maybe there is hope for me."

"There is always hope, my child. It is part of faith."

Yasamin removed her mother's book from its box and caressed its cover. Opening it, she slowly ran her finger beneath the lines of writing. "Mosesra, I *know* the road of silk exists." She sighed and looked at him. "But although the words look familiar, I cannot read it. What am I doing wrong?"

"Child, you are doing nothing 'wrong'! But you have to realize there is a world of difference between knowing and believing. You have the seed of believing within you as evidenced by the fact the words look familiar."

"But I do believe it's true," Yasamin protested.

"I think you *believe* that you believe."

"Now I am confused. Didn't you just say I believed because I saw my mother?"

Mosesra stood and moved his chair to her side of the table. "If you are not too tired, I will try to explain."

"Please do. I want to find out everything."

The old man smiled. "You remind me so much of your mother, Yasamin, always eager learn. First of all, child, you can believe *here*," he tapped his forehead, "and you can believe *here*," he tapped his heart. "You must believe here," he tapped his chest again, "to be a true follower of light. Here, let me try to demonstrate."

Mosesra lifted his left hand, and the light dimmed. Simultaneously, the candle sitting on the table lit itself. A soft circle of light shone on the rough wood. He pointed at the circle of light. "This candlelight represents Sorania." He picked up two small grapes, lifted one to his lips and whispered something, then set both grapes on the table out of the candlelight's glow. "The table represents the world outside of Sorania." He pointed to the grapes. "This is you." He then indicated the other. "Do you see anything unusual about this grape?"

Yasamin peered at the fruit. It looked like a normal purple grape. She shook her head. "No."

Mosesra nodded, "Very well." He selected the grape representing Yasamin and set it next to the candle's base within the circle of candlelight. "Now *you* are in the center of the holiest of places for believers of the way of light. The power is extremely strong here, so strong, in fact, that if I were to bring a *good* person in here, one who was not a true follower of light, she would be able to *see* any manifestation occurring." Mosesra picked up the other grape and set it beside the grape representing her.

Yasamin gasped. Now that the second grape sat within the circle of light, she could see a miniscule star shining within it. "There is a star. I see a star in the grape."

The old man smiled and waved his hands. The lights brightened, and the candle extinguished itself. "Do you understand what I am saying?"

Yasamin nodded. "I think so. First, there must be some goodness in me, or I wouldn't be in here."

Mosesra cackled and slapped his knee. "Very good, child! Very good! That was such a simple premise I did not even think of it. What is the second thing?"

"Because I am here, I can see things I might not be able to see outside the mountain. Does that mean I am not a follower of light?"

"It simply means you have not developed your abilities in that direction. The fact you did not question seeing your mother's image shows you are capable of true belief."

"So I can learn to read this book?"

"Let us try another experiment." Mosesra pointed to the manuscript. "Pick up the book and open to any page."

Yasamin did as she was told.

"Now, to focus yourself, put your finger on a passage in it."

Again, Yasamin did as he told her.

"Good. Good. Now this is the hard part. Close your eyes. Take a moment, and think of someone you love, someone dear to you. Think hard. Imagine that person as being in the direst of danger, so much danger their very life is threatened. Go on, shut your eyes, try."

Yasamin closed her eyes and thought of Arash trying to run back across the bridge toward her. She thought of him plunging to his death when the ropes burned.

"Now keep thinking what you're thinking but listen. Keep that image sharp in your mind. Think of that person's life, how much you want *them* to be safe, even if it meant losing your life. Understand?"

Yasamin nodded.

"Good. Now I'm going to count to three. Focus. Focus hard on what I just told you to do. When I get to three, I want you to open your eyes quickly, and look at the passage where you have your finger. Understand?"

With her eyes squeezed shut, Yasamin again nodded and lowered her head toward the book.

"Very well. One ... two ... three!"

Yasamin opened her eyes and looked at the passage where her finger pointed. For a few seconds every word was comprehensible, then her perception faded. "I saw it. I could read it! How?"

Mosesra laughed. "The reason is two-fold. First, you were focused; absolutely nothing distracted you. Secondly, you were being selfless; you were thinking of someone you loved and how you could help them, even if it meant losing your own life. You lost your fear because of your love, and it opened the channel so you could read. The greatest, most selfless love anyone has would be to give his or her life to save another. That is one of the principles of the way of light."

"But I lost my ability to read."

"Only because you are not trained. When one is a true a follower, they develop the ability you experienced until it becomes a way of life."

"I understand." Yasamin closed her mother's book. "And the more I study, the better I get, the closer I come to the castle of silk, right?"

"Absolutely, child, absolutely."

"Can you go to the castle of silk, Mosesra?"

"It took me a long time, but I eventually reached that goal."

"Is it as beautiful as Mother said?"

"There are no words here on earth to describe it." Mosesra closed his eyes, remembering the last time he had been there. He was suddenly startled. "But you and I must talk. There are some things I must tell you, then you must return to the outside. Your friends are frantic about your safety."

"Friends? You mean Arash and Goliagoth?"

"Yes. They are searching for you. Out there it has been three days since they last saw you."

"Three days? But I only just came in a little while ago!"

"Remember, when on the road of silk time has no meaning; everything operates on a different premise and interconnects."

Yasamin shook her head. "I'm confused again. How does that affect me now?

"Child, you haven't figured it out yet? When you were lost in the smoke and fire, you were choking. You could not see …"

"I heard my mother's voice. Then I saw her. I ran along the trail she showed me. She led me to Yasamin's eyes grew wide. "You mean?"

Mosesra nodded his head, his eyes twinkled with joy. "Exactly! How do you think you could suddenly see and breathe, yet all that black smoke and raging fire surrounded you? Your mother pulled you from the clutches of Vulmire. She brought you to this cave on the road of silk."

Chapter 19

Mosesra and Yasamin talked for several more hours—Yasamin assumed it was hours. It was hard, trying to shift old ways of thinking. She learned much from Mosesra except for the times she asked what she should do. On each of those occasions he simply smiled and told her she had to make the choice herself.

At last, the time came to say goodbye. Yasamin felt the tears well in her eyes. In the time she had been in Sorania, she had grown to love the old man.

"Will I ever see you again, Mosesra?" Yasamin finished packing her belongings.

"Anything is possible, child. Who is to say our paths might not cross again one day?'

"I hope so."

"As do I." The old man gently patted Yasamin's shoulder and smiled. "By the way, before you leave, there is someone who would like to tell you farewell, too."

Yasamin turned in time to see the burst of silver butterflies, and Shar appeared.

"Shar!" Yasamin exclaimed. "How wonderful!"

The old woman moved forward. "You look well, Majesty, despite your ordeal."

"How do you—never mind, silly question. Of course you would know. I'm doing much better now since I've spoken with Mosesra—and my mother."

Shar glanced at Mosesra and raised her eyebrows.

"I answered what questions I could about our ways."

"I see. Yasamin, take care. There is much danger around you should you decide to go to Dragonval."

"Yes, yes, I know all about Serpata."

"He is the worst kind of evil, but there are—"

"Shar!" Mosesra moved forward and put a hand on Shar's shoulder. "The Queen needs to return to her friends. They wait for her. She must make her own decisions at every turn of the path she takes."

"Of course, Mosesra. Queen Yasamin, I shall pray for your safety."

"Thank you, Shar. I am glad the soldier didn't hurt you when he threw his spear."

"Psah!" she chortled. "It will be the day when a mere babe can hit me with his toy spear. I am much too fast for them even if I am over three hundred. Farewell, Highness."

"Goodbye, Shar." Yasamin turned to Mosesra. "Goodbye, Mosesra. I hope we meet again. Thank you for everything."

Mosesra bowed his head. "Be careful, child. Just go through the tunnel there, and you will find your friends. May the light be with you."

Yasamin nodded and began her journey toward the outside. For a long time, the two simply stared at the space where she had been.

The old woman looked at Mosesra. "Did you tell her?" He shook his head. Again Shar's eyebrows rose in surprise. "Why not? It would have helped her tremendously."

"I believe it would be too heavy a burden. She has learned so much in a short time."

"But she is strong."

"She is. But you know the story as well as I. The way is fraught with temptations of every kind, and *she* must make each decision from her heart without our help. If we are not careful, we will influence the path she chooses."

"It must have been hard, not telling her you are Casadra's father."

"It was, old friend, more than you can imagine." Mosesra looked at Shar with his tears in his eyes. "But how could I tell my own granddaughter she is the One? That she carries the seed for both good and evil within her? That if, in the end, she chooses the dark side, I will become her mortal enemy. That if she chooses the dark side, I will have to fight her to the death?"

Chapter 20

Medusimia smiled as she lounged in her bath. The water was warm and sweet with the *franpania* petals floating in it. Life could not be better. Amir, the fool, had sent a fleet to search for Yasamin, but Vulmire had promised he would take care of everything. Amir could never match wits with the man-beast. Medusimia's smile grew wider: the man-beast, she loved the sound of it. She stretched like a lazy cat and played with a bloom-laden branch hanging above her head. She had just returned from an afternoon of passion with him and was satiated.

Medusimia groaned. She *believed* she had been. Just the thought of the man-beast pounding himself into her sent the familiar warmth flooding through her. By the gods, she could not get enough of Vulmire. Medusimia swatted the water in frustration, sending bubbles in every direction. She already wanted him again—needed him.

The woman threw her sponge across the room, then the goblet of wine. The glass shattered into thousands of splinters. The red liquid ran down the wall, reminding her of the crimson fire in his eyes.

"I cannot wait," Medusimia gritted through her teeth. "I have to get Amir dethroned, so I can get Vulmire to the palace. I need him here where I can have him any time I want him." Her monologue was interrupted by the maid scurrying into the bath.

"Highness, are you all right? I heard a noise and—"

"Get out!" Medusimia screamed at the young girl. "When I need you, I'll call you, nitwit. Get out, get out!"

To emphasize her words, the Queen threw the beaker on the edge of the tub at the girl. The maid barely closed the door before the container burst into fragments.

"Fool! Brainless sop," Medusimia muttered to herself as she pulled her hair up from her neck and pinned it. The cool air felt good against her skin. Most of the time she was burning up—Vulmire kept her throbbing with desire most of the time.

Grabbing another sponge, the Queen washed herself. Amir would be with his counselors later that afternoon. If she timed it right, she could see Vulmire again for a few hours and be back before anyone noticed she was gone.

Medusimia picked up the mirror and examined her face. If anything, she was even more beautiful. It had to be because she had finally found someone who knew how to satisfy her. She smiled again. Soon she would have the best of both worlds. Medusimia continued to examine her face for any blemish but could find nothing. She scrutinized her long neck, and her smile froze. *It must be a shadow.* Medusimia sat up and leaned into the sunlight. She turned her neck to see better and sucked in her breath. It was no shadow. She would never have seen it if she had not pinned up her hair. Just behind her left ear were six perfectly-formed, glistening spots the size of a small pea. Medusimia ran her hand over them. They were not hard, but they were rough. They reminded her of Vulmire's skin below his waist where he became a beast.

Scales?

Medusimia's heart skipped a beat.

Were they scales, like Vulmire?

This must be a bad dream.

Medusimia scrambled from the soapy tub and ran beneath the skylight. She looked closer but couldn't believe her eyes. She frantically rubbed at the spots.

They remained.

Six perfectly-formed, amber scales.

She forgot Amir and her plans. She didn't care if someone told him she left the place. She had to see Vulmire immediately. She had to know what was happening. *Now.*

In one way, Medusimia was lucky. No one saw her sneak out of the palace. No one saw her running down the trail that led to Vulmire's lair. No one saw her waiting in the clearing for the giant bird to take her to the cave.

But once there, her luck ended.

Medusimia ran down the dark tunnel and into the fiery chamber.

"Vulmire! Vulmire! Where are you!" she shouted.

She heard the slither of scales and a small chuckle. "Back so soon, my Queen? You've been gone only one hand's span. You must truly love my fire."

Vulmire emerged from the darkness and headed for the black stone. He sat, his dark eyes gleamed as they roamed Medusimia's body. His tongue flickered between his lips. "I still taste you from before, but I am always ready for more."

"Never mind that," Medusimia shrieked. She moved toward him. "What is this?" She pulled up her hair and presented her neck.

Vulmire bent forward and peered to the area where she pointed. "They look like scales." He leaned back.

"I know what they look like. What are they?"

"I just told you. Scales."

"Why would I have scales? They're not contagious. I am not like you. Why would I have them? I *cannot* have them," Medusimia screamed. "I am beautiful. I cannot have these things! What would people think? What ..."

A low rumble interrupted her. It grew louder. Medusimia stopped and stared, open-mouthed, at Vulmire. He was chuckling. His entire body shook with laughter.

"What are you laughing at? This is not funny! How dare you take it so lightly!" Medusimia shouted.

"I am not the one who has been taking it lightly," he managed to speak.

"I am serious, Vulmire. This is no laughing matter. How do I get rid of these ugly things?"

Vulmire stopped laughing but smiled at Medusimia. "I never took it lightly, my Queen. You did."

"What do you mean?" A quiver of fear wound itself around her spine. "What are you talking about?"

"Tell me, Medusimia, did you think you could have everything you wanted without a price?"

"I don't know what you're talking about."

"Yes, you do. You knew about me when you came here—knew the price I paid to have what I desired most. I was the *king* of this country once, woman. You think you are an exception because you are a mere queen? You had to choose your path, as I did. You had a choice, you made it. You are receiving what you wanted. These past months you have reveled in your new power, your lust, *your* needs being met." Vulmire lost his smile. "Did you think me a fool? Did you think you could play without paying? Everything has a price."

"But this?" Medusimia pointed to her neck. "How can I replace Amir and sit on the throne with this?"

Vulmire rose and walked close to her. Medusimia could feel the heat radiating from him. His long tongue flicked out and delicately licked the scales. "Personally, I think them beautiful, but then they say beauty is in the eye of the beholder." His tongue licked one breast, then retreated. "Decide now,

Medusimia. Make no mistake, there will not be another chance. If you wish to remain one of Amir's wives and let things continue the way they are, do not come here again. I will wash my hands of you. No more scales will grow. These are small enough you may disguise them with powder."

"You will not take care of Yasamin?"

"No. You cannot have it both ways. If you do not want to be mine, you cannot have my help. And Vulmire moved until he pressed against Medusimia. She could feel his manhood rigid against her. "If you want to go back to Amir, we shall have to do something about the boy you carry."

"What?" Medusimia gasped, thinking she had misunderstood. She took a step back. "You are mistaken. I'm barren; I cannot carry a child. That is why Amir is—"

Vulmire interrupted her. "*Amir* is the one. His seed is dead. So you see, my queen, neither you nor Yasamin will bear him a son, but both of you shall share him. It is my child, and you will not take him with you. It will be very obvious he is no son of Amir."

Medusimia gaped at the man-beast. "You didn't tell me it was Amir's problem."

"That is not why you asked for my help, is it? You did not want the insult of a second wife, and Amir's being unable to have a son is no reason to dethrone a king, is it?"

"No."

"What you really want is the power of the throne, is it not? To rule Dragonval? 'Together *we* can rule Dragonval.' Isn't that what you said to me, Medusimia? Well, together we can rule the country. There will be sons, many of them. But make no mistake, you *will* pay the price that is required. The one I serve demands it. Now decide, woman, which shall it be? Amir and Yasamin or ruling with me as it use to be when the dragons ruled?"

"You can defeat Amir?" Medusimia whispered.

"His house is nothing compared to me."

"And I am carrying your child? You are sure?"

Vulmire's tongue flickered out and ran under Medusimia's gown. She could feel its wetness against her breasts, her stomach and her thighs. Then it was gone.

"Yes. I can smell him, taste him."

Medusimia stared into Vulmire's eyes for several heartbeats. A smile slowly stretched her full lips.

"So be it. I choose."

She reached for the beast man's loin cloth and ripped it from him, then dropped her dress to the ground.

"I choose this." She lowered her head. The scales gleamed in the firelight as the two merged.

Chapter 21

He'd won. They had tried every argument in the book.
It was too late in the season, too risky ...
That's why they paid their soldiers so well.
It was too costly ...
It was *his* money.
It was not known if anyone survived ...
His future wife had been on that ship. He would do what it took to find out if she survived, and he knew what they did not; she *was* alive.
In the end, they had acquiesced to his demands. There was no choice. He was king. Of course, some of them would sulk. Some of them would smile, then talk behind his back. Those would pay dearly.
Amir stood on the rampart and watched the fleet float past below him. The winds were high, and all sails were full. On the horizon, he could see the first ships already circumventing the Dragon's Mouth. There were over fifty boats leaving the harbor. They were crammed with soldiers and artillery. No one, absolutely no one, would interfere with the fleet's mission.
And if these fifty were lost, he'd send fifty more, then fifty more until there were no ships left. But he would have Yasamin.
Amir felt the familiar tightening in his groin at the mere thought of her. By the gods, he *had* to have her. His patience was wearing thin. All he could think of was possessing her, satisfying this constant burning, yearning. In his mind, he could see her lying on his bed: her pale hair spread on the golden sheets, her long limbs soft and pliable beneath him. He groaned. Yasamin was the exact opposite of Medusimia: pale, soft, almost ethereal; Medusimia was

dark, athletic and fiery. Perhaps that was part of the attraction. He wanted both, and he would have both; he didn't have to choose. And now that he knew Yasamin was alive, he'd spare no expense to get her to Dragonval.

Medusimia.

Something dark slithered through Amir's mind as he thought of her. She had been pouting ever since their argument about him marrying Yasamin. The king shrugged. She would just have to move past it if she wanted to retain her position as first Queen. If she didn't, Medusimia might find herself in a reverse role with Yasamin.

Amir hit the rock wall with his hand. It was difficult, having to wait. He'd already waited longer for Yasamin than anything he'd wanted. Hopefully, the first fleet would find her and have her at the palace soon to end the physical torture he in which he found himself. A slow grin spread across his mouth. He obviously had to wait for the ships to return; however, he didn't have to wait to relieve himself of one problem. Medusimia was already *here*.

Flinging a last look at the disappearing fleet, Amir descended the steps. The afternoon would be an endless round of useless talks, but he could have a little fun *before* they began. By now Medusimia must be regretting her rash words and yearning for his bed.

Whistling, he went looking for his wife.

It never occurred to him Medusimia might have no regrets.

It certainly never occurred to him she might make her bed with another.

Chapter 22

"Do you think she's alive?" Arash stopped to wipe sweat from his eyes. He and Goliagoth were cutting vines and weaving them into a rope. The soldier's plan was to get to the bottom of the gorge, cross the river, then scale the opposite side of the ravine. Arash didn't have much faith the plan would work, but at least it was a plan, and it beat sitting around doing nothing.

"It's possible if she found a place where animals couldn't get her and provided no more of those *things* showed up." Goliagoth didn't have much faith in his plan either, but he couldn't think of another way to reach the other side since the bridge had burned. He jerked tight knots into the vines and tested them by pulling until his muscular arms bulged with the effort. "I do know we're running out of time. She's been gone three days without food and water unless she found a spring. She'll weaken rapidly in this environment."

"Aren't you just a bundle of good news?" Arash growled.

"I assumed you'd want the facts, not pretty words."

Arash watched the soldier weave the rope. His large hands moved rapidly as they twisted the tough vine.

At last Arash sighed. "You're right, Goliagoth. My sarcasm was out of place."

The giant soldier merely nodded and continued weaving. His mind whirled from the events of the past three days. For the first time in his life, Goliagoth found he suffered indecision. He was out of his element, fighting an unseen enemy, especially an enemy like the creatures that had attacked them. They defied logic, but he had seen them. The fire defied logic as well.

Then there was Yasamin. Goliagoth felt his heart beat harder. One moment she was on the opposite end of the bridge, and the next, a raging inferno appeared from nowhere and quickly destroyed the makeshift bridge. A headache tightened its vicious grip on his skull. Any possible origin for the fire eluded him. There was no sign of her body once the flames were gone. Although they had shouted for her a hundred times, she hadn't responded.

She had vanished.

His fear for Yasamin was almost incapacitating. His stomach was in turmoil, forbidding food, even if he had time to eat. The headache's fingers stretched around and began pulling at his eyes. He hadn't slept since her disappearance, and the strain was beginning to take its toll.

"We've got to get to the other side by morning. What concerns me most is her not answering. She might be unconscious, in which case …"

The giant left the ugly thought unfinished. He stretched his shoulders and went back to weaving.

"What about that fire? What do you think started it?" Arash dreaded the silence more than the soldier's laconic answers.

The giant shrugged. "Don't know."

"You have no guess?"

Goliagoth shook his head.

"And the creatures? What about them?"

Again the soldier shook his head.

"In all my travels, I've seen nothing like them." Arash glanced around at Fleuise. She was talking with her doll and weaving tiny flowers. He didn't want to scare the child. He then resumed his thought. "I think they were supernatural."

Goliagoth stared long and hard at Arash, and for the first time, Arash saw indecision in the soldier's eyes.

Something close to fear nibbled at Goliagoth's consciousness. He tried to squash it, but it refused to disappear. It made him angry. "Instead of sitting, arguing senseless points, we need to be *doing* something about saving the Queen. Cut me some more vines, the longest ones you can find."

"Sure." Arash ignored Goliagoth's hostile tone. He understood it because he felt the same helplessness. "I'll try down the …"

"What are you two doing?" Yasamin's voice shocked the two men. Both jumped to their feet, eyes bulging and mouths open. Fleuise dropped her doll and ran for the young woman. She wrapped herself around one of Yasamin's legs.

"Yasamin." Arash forgot the plants. He ran to her and hugged her close. "Thank the gods, you're safe!"

For a moment, Yasamin hugged him back. There was no mistake; his concern and happiness were real. It felt good.

Goliagoth's happiness was just as real. He took three steps toward her but stopped. Hugging her as Arash had done seemed natural, but he couldn't. Old habits die hard.

"Highness, are you all right?"

"Yes. I'm fine."

Knowing she was safe and being the soldier he was, logic quickly returned to Goliagoth. Confusion rapidly replaced happiness. He moved to the trio. Arash stepped aside, and the soldier confronted Yasamin. His experienced eye slowly roamed over her. Except for a few minor cuts from twigs, there were no major injuries or bruises on her. In fact, she looked well-rested and well-fed. She looked *radiant*. More pieces of confusion were added to the puzzle he would think about later. Assured she was in good condition, Goliagoth asked the thought uppermost in his mind. "Highness, how did you cross the ravine?"

Yasamin's smile disappeared. "What?"

She looked at the gorge and the space where the bridge had been. In her happiness to find them, Yasamin thought she had returned to the location where she had been at the time of the fire and that it had not destroyed the bridge. She assumed the men had returned to look for her. She now realized she was on the *other* side of the ravine where they had been before the fire. Confused, she stared at Goliagoth.

"I-I don't know."

It was the truth. She believed she had exited the mountain the same way she'd entered.

Now Arash was perplexed as well. "You must have some idea. The gorge runs deep for miles. You'd have to know when you crossed it."

Yasamin suddenly knew the answer, but she couldn't tell the men. They would either think her daft from a concussion, or worse, they would believe her. The last thing Mosesra needed were people wandering into Sorania to check out her story.

The simple fact that she was disconcerted added to her credibility. "I-I'm a little confused. There was the fire, so much smoke; I couldn't see where I was going. I remember moving away from where I thought the gorge was. Then I found this little trail. I didn't think. I went down it and ended up at a tunnel. I went in. I thought it would be safe, but there was nothing to burn in it. I wandered in it for a long time, and well, I guess I came out on this side."

Arash grinned. He wanted to hug her again but didn't dare. "Thank the gods you did. We were frantic for your safety."

Goliagoth gazed at her. There was no doubt she was confused, but she wasn't telling everything. He could see it in her eyes, and there were discrepancies in her story as well. *Something* had happened, only he couldn't think of anything. He'd probe but not too much to see if he could get a clue.

"Highness …"

"Yes?"

"How did you see inside the cavern?"

"Oh. I-uh-I grabbed some branches outside the mouth of the cave, I lit one and carried the rest. When one died, I lit another."

This was a lie. Goliagoth could see it in the way she refused to look directly at him. "How did you find your way through so many tunnels?"

"There weren't too many, but I-I lit one of the torches then put it out so I had charcoal. I would make a mark at each branch as I've seen you do. That way I knew where I'd been."

Certainty grew in Goliagoth's mind—another lie. What could she possibly be hiding out here where there was nothing? By now Arash was looking unsure as well. He glanced back and forth between the two.

"You were in there three days, Highness. What did you do for food and water?"

"I had a little bit of food in my backpack that I had kept in case I needed a snack while we were walking. I-uh-I found several springs in the cavern with clear water. I drank from them."

"Why all the questions, Goliagoth? We should be thankful the Queen found her way to us."

"Yes, why so many questions? I'm lucky I found you." Yasmin hated lying, and she was quickly running out of explanations. So far she'd been lucky and able to repeat things she had seen the soldier do. Next, he might ask something she couldn't answer.

"Make no mistake, I am thankful the Queen is safe. Only it amazes me she had such presence of mind to fare so well in the wilderness. Being a Queen, she did *exceptionally* well, better than some new recruits."

"Well, I have a good example to follow. I've learned much from you, Goliagoth. But I'd say I was more blessed with finding my way."

Goliagoth bowed his head, not because of the compliment but to prevent her from seeing his face. "I'm grateful you learned so well."

Her last statement seemed to be true, but it made no sense to him, and he would get no further. Now that she was safe, they must resume their journey as soon as possible. They should have already crested the mountain. "We'll rest here today. It's too late to start out. We'll leave at first light. Highness, could you show me where you exited the mountain on this side?"

"I really do not think I can. It was very overgrown, and I made a lot of turns. I do not think I can find it again, Goliagoth. Why?"

"I thought I would check it out. If you found a tunnel leading from that side to this, maybe there would be one running through the mountain in the direction we're going."

"I am sorry. I really cannot help you. I was not paying attention when I left the tunnel. I thought I was on the other side."

"It doesn't matter. It would probably be a wild goose chase. I doubt tunnels would run that far."

"I'll get a fire going, Goliagoth. Now that the Queen has been found I, for one, am starving," Arash interrupted.

"Me, too." Fleuise wouldn't let go of Yasamin's hand. "I did just what you told me. I stayed close, so I wouldn't get lost. I'm glad you aren't lost anymore."

"Me too, sweet. Food sounds like a good idea. I'll help get it ready, Arash." Yasamin was eager to do anything that would turn the conversation. She wasn't sure what would happen to Goliagoth if he entered the cave; therefore, she wanted to get his mind on something different.

"How many days will it take us to get over the mountain from here?"

"With no trouble, four or five. Our luck has held with the snow. If we get over without a storm and enter the valley on the other side, our biggest worry is over. The town is only two days' travel." Goliagoth turned and indicated a log near the fire Arash was building. "Highness, I suggest you take advantage of the afternoon and rest while you can. We'll have food prepared shortly."

Now that they were all together again, spirits ran high as did their appetites. Goliagoth caught a *mohairna,* and they roasted it over the open flame. The meat was rich and sweet. After weeks of dried berries, the taste was decadent.

Shortly after dark, each crawled into their blankets. Morning would come soon and with it, hard travel. Quietness settled on the small group. The flame died down to a soft glow, while the stars appeared and seemed to sparkle brighter. All slept peacefully except for one.

Still as the stone against which he sat, Goliagoth studied the stars above him. Before this trip, he had never thought of them except in terms of navigation. The unusual events had raised questions for which he had no answers; however, it appeared the biggest puzzle of all would remain unanswered. The wee hours of the morning found the soldier still staring at the distant top of Mount Sorania.

* * * * *

Their luck held as they climbed the heights of the mountain. Goliagoth pushed them as hard as he could each day. Most nights, Yasamin simply wanted to fall asleep without supper, but the soldier wouldn't let her. She needed food to keep up her strength. Most of the time, Goliagoth carried Fleuise on his back along with the packs. The child would let him pick her up and place her there, but she constantly checked to make sure Yasamin followed. Arash and Yasamin felt the high altitude; they both had trouble breathing.

Goliagoth watched the sunset cast a long, red glow on them every evening, and every morning, he rose and studied the skies. Yasamin knew he was worried. Thick, black, ominous clouds covered the sky to the south and north of them. In the distance, they all could see white covering the highest peaks. The soldier was concerned the thin, snow-free corridor they traveled would soon become knee-deep in banks of snow that would hide rocks and crevasses before they crossed. His frown grew deeper in his high forehead at the impending danger.

Yasamin longed to tell him he didn't have to worry. She wanted to ease the burden she knew he bore on his shoulders, but she couldn't think of a way. He would never believe her. They would get through; the snow would not fall before they left the mountain. She had known it the moment she saw two butterflies waiting for them the day they began their ascent. The gold one flew north, the silver one south.

Chapter 23

"Goliagoth, come here! I see ships!"

Arash was perched on an outcrop of rock a few feet away from the fire where the others rested. It was the middle of their second day since leaving Mount Sorania. They had been no more than three leagues away when the two storms met over the mountain, and the trail they had descended disappeared behind them in a thick fog. Goliagoth, knowing he had pushed all of them to their limits, had slowed his pace a little in deference to the Queen and began to take noon breaks again.

The soldier scrabbled onto the rocky ledge, grappling for the spyglass he had salvaged. He peered in the direction Arash pointed.

"Part of the King's fleet." He handed the instrument to Arash who tried peering through it. Goliagoth pointed. "See the red flag with the dragon. One of the ships must have made it to Dragonval." He took the spyglass back and returned it to its container.

"Why are they here?"

"My guess: they're stopping to take on supplies before heading around the peninsula."

By this time, Yasamin had walked to the men and overheard part of the conversation. "How long will they be there?"

"It will be at least another hour before they hit port. Depending on the amount of supplies they need, I would guess a hand span. If they've a good-sported captain, he might spend the night to let the soldiers have their fling before hitting the rough ocean. For most it will probably be their last trip."

Fleuise had come and put her arms around Yasamin. The Queen drew her close but kept her eyes on Goliagoth. "Can we make it to town before they leave?"

The soldier studied her and the child, then shook his head. "If they leave tonight, none of us can make it. If they wait till morning, I can."

It was Yasamin's turn to frown. "What do you mean?"

"If I leave now and push hard, I can be there by nightfall. You and the child could not keep up with my pace. Our best chance is for you, Arash and her to camp here. Arash can protect you. If I get there in time, they will wait. I shall come back for you."

"What if they leave before you get there?"

"Worse thing I will have run my legs off for nothing. We will go back to our original plan."

"What if the Queen and I keep moving and camp tonight?"

"No. You might wander off course or run into danger and not have help. Best thing is to stay here, so I'll know exactly where you are."

"Sounds like a plan to me." Arash turned to Yasamin. "Highness?"

Yasamin bit her lower lip as she tried to find an argument; however, she could find no flaw in the soldier's reasoning. At last she nodded. "I think he is right. He will make better time without us. If they know I am here, there's no need for them to go to Gwendomere. Go. We will wait here for your return."

Goliagoth bowed his head, picked up a skin of water and trotted toward the town.

Chapter 24

There were people everywhere. After being with just a few for so long, Yasamin felt suffocated by the presence of so many. They lined the streets for a glimpse of her.

Goliagoth had reached the town in time and had notified the fleet's *Captaineer* that the Queen was camped within an half-day's march. The news spread like a fire gone mad.

The soldiers formed a barricade around her and the others as they marched through the town and aboard the lead ship.

The *Captaineer* waited on deck. As Yasamin came aboard, he removed his hat and bowed deeply.

"Your Highness, welcome to *The New Moon*. We were elated when the *Demolisherian* here notified us of your presence. I dispatched a ship yesterday to carry the good news to King Amir. He will be overjoyed you are alive and well."

Yasamin's insides rebelled at the familiar rocking motion, and the old memories flooded through her. She gritted her teeth. She would not let anyone see her fear or her loneliness. Now that she was actually aboard one of the King's ships, Amir was all too present in her mind. And any chance for being with Arash was gone forever.

Assuming her royal demeanor, Yasamin lifted her chin. "Thank you, *Captaineer*. Please, stand up. I shall have a spasm in my neck if I keep looking down at you."

The man rose and fumbled with his hat. He had never been in the presence of a queen and was unsure of himself. The fact that this Queen was stunning made it worse. He felt like a tongue-tied schoolboy. A red flush crept up his neck. "I have made my quarters available to you for our return trip. It is the largest cabin, but I'm afraid it's still much smaller than what you are use to."

"I'm sure it will be fine. After all, I have been sleeping on the ground for several months." All the talk was giving Yasamin the beginning of a headache.

"Y-yes, of course, Highness." Trying to regain his composure, the *Captaineer* turned to Goliagoth. "Who are these people?" He nodded toward Arash and Fleuise who had followed Yasamin aboard ship.

Goliagoth moved forward until he stood between the *Captaineer* and the others. "The child is the Queen's personal maid. They are not to be separated."

"She is rather young for a maid, is she not?"

Goliagoth's brows drew together in a dark line. "She was a *personal* gift to the Queen, and Her Highness has grown quite fond of her, *Captaineer*."

"I see. The cabin will accommodate both. What about him? Is he one of her servants, too?"

Goliagoth threw a hard stare at Arash who remained standing behind Yasamin. He was holding Fleuise and unable to defend himself, but it wouldn't have mattered if his hands had been free—he was surrounded by Amir's soldiers. At last the soldier looked back to the *Captaineer*.

"His name is Arash, an ambassador from Pars, I think. He sought passage with us, as he was headed for Dragonval. He paid quite handsomely for the privilege of sailing with us. Needless to say, he got more than he bargained for."

The *Captaineer* laughed. "I hope he'll pay as handsomely to me."

Goliagoth moved closer to the *Captaineer* and laid his hand loosely on the hilt of his sword. "Understand this. He has already paid for his trip. He will not pay again. He saved my life when the hostiles attacked us. I owe him. Do I make my meaning clear?"

The *Captaineer* took a step back and quit smiling. "Clearly."

"I expect him to have a room as well. Is that a problem?"

"No and the rest of your men?"

"Dead. All. The ones who survived the shipwreck died along the trail. Enough jaw-wagging. The Queen is exhausted. Show her to her room. You and I can talk later."

"Yes. I'll show her the way myself. Your Highness, this way please." The *Captaineer* turned and went below. He didn't see the look of gratitude Yasamin flashed Goliagoth as she passed nor did the *Captaineer* see the look of shock on Arash's face.

Chapter 25

Yasamin stood on the bow of the ship, staring at the approaching land. The salt air now carried the slight smell of earth in it, and she breathed deeply. This trip had gone without incident, but she could hardly wait to get back on land. She doubted she would ever sail again without the memories of the shipwreck dogging her.

"We will be there, soon." Arash moved to stand beside her. It was the first time he'd had the chance to be alone with her, and the minutes would be few before someone interrupted them.

"I know. I can smell the earth and something else. I'm not quite sure … flowers or herbs. I cannot quite put my finger on it."

"Probably *whitable*. It's the time of year for reaping. *Whitable* is one of their staples—like our wheat and barley—only it has a slightly nutty taste. You will see plenty of it at your celebration."

The reminder of what lay ahead of her caused Yasamin to involuntarily shiver, and she pulled her cloak tight. Remembering her mother's words, Yasamin knew as soon as she landed she'd constantly have to be on her guard. Danger could come from anywhere. She had no way of knowing whom he might send.

"Cold?" Arash's voice interrupted her thoughts. He moved a little closer to shield her from the wind. What he wanted was to put his arms around her.

"A little. A little nervous, too."

"Yasamin," Arash leaned a little closer and lowered his voice. "Are you really sure you want to do this? It still isn't too late."

"Arash, please, let us not start this again. I gave my word, and I will keep it.

It's for the good of my country. You, of all people, should understand duty."

"I do. But there's a difference between duty and sacrifice. You—"

"We have been over this before. I do not want to talk about it anymore. I said I would marry Amir, and I will, so just stop interfering where you don't belong."

Arash wished he could shake some sense into her, but that wasn't an option. "Will you answer one thing?"

"What?"

"Do you still think ill of me, about my not telling you I am a prince?"

Yasamin thought for a long moment, so long Arash began to fear what she had to say.

At last she whispered. "That was a long time ago and under conditions a lot different from now. We were all under a lot of pressure, Arash. But to answer your question, no, I do not think you were manipulating or using me. I believe you were concerned. But that doesn't mean you can interfere in my affairs."

"I understand. Believe me, Yasamin, I am your friend. Always. If you ever need one, remember me."

"Thank you. Arash, what is that?" Yasamin pointed toward the shoreline, which was close enough now to make out details. She was pointing at several spots in the sky. Even as she spoke, one of the specks detached itself from the others and flew swiftly toward them."

"The lookouts. Did you not know that's how Dragonval got its name?"

"What are you talking about?" Yasamin looked over her shoulder at Arash. A slight frown creased her smooth brow. "What lookouts?"

Arash merely nodded his head toward land. "Look."

Yasamin looked back toward shore and drew in her breath sharply. Startled, she took a step backward into Arash. "What—"

Arash slowly put out a hand to steady her and whispered. "Don't make any sudden movements. Try to remain calm and look it straight in the eye."

Yasamin did as he told her. Had it not been for leaning against the man behind her, she wasn't sure she could have remained standing.

Hovering directly in front of them, about three feet above the ship's rail, was a blood-red dragon. From its nose to the tip of its tail, the animal was about sixty feet long with a wing span closer to one hundred feet. Huge, shiny scales covered its body. They glinted in the sunlight. Each limb ended in a five-clawed talon, four claws in front and one opposable, like a thumb. Two rows of razor-sharp teeth lined it's alligator-like snout. Its forked tongue delicately flicked in and out of its mouth. But it was the eyes that chilled Yasamin to the bone.

She involuntarily drew her cape tighter, knowing it wouldn't help. The chill was *inside* her. It congealed around her heart and throat until she thought she would suffocate, but she could not look away from those eyes. They were mesmerizing. Amber and glowing, sparks of fire danced in their depths. In the middle of each, a small, round black pupil dilated as the beast studied them. *Human* eyes in an animal's body.

"What is it?" Yasamin whispered.

"A dragon. They guard the country. They fly over this port and the few major roads entering Dravonval."

"Dragons exist?"

"As far as I know, Dragonval is the only place they're left. I've heard that at one time the sky over the country here was black with them, but they're dying off," Arash whispered in her ear.

"What is it doing?"

"I'm not sure. From what I understand, they usually do not investigate the ships from Dragonval. They see the banner and let the ship pass. If they sense danger, they either destroy the boat or drive it toward the Dragon's Mouth where it sinks. The only thing I can think of is it's inspecting you."

As if in response to Arash's statement, the beast eased itself closer with the grace of a butterfly.

"Don't flinch and be as still as you can. I do not believe it will hurt you, but let's not take any chances." Arash could feel Yasamin trembling. Brave as he was, the creature was terrifying.

The dragon moved to within five feet of Yasamin. Its slow-moving wings stirred her hair gently. The dragon extended its long neck until it was mere inches from Yasamin. It gently sniffed, much like a dog. Small puffs of smoke came from its nostrils with each snuffle. Its eyes studied her intently. Despite her terror, Yasamin could sense the intelligence in them.

The dragon suddenly jerked backward until it was ten feet above them. Raising its huge head, the beast opened its mouth and emitted a thunderous screech. A stream of fire erupted from its mouth.

And it was gone.

Sailing through the air, toward land. In the distance, Yasamin saw the others swarm to it. Even from the ship she could hear its deafening screeches. The others danced and pivoted in the air around it—a rainbow of reds, blues, greens and gold. Then the red dragon sped toward the dark castle in the distance.

"King Amir will know of your arrival within seconds." Goliagoth's voice broke the silence. Yasamin and Arash both whirled. He stood a few feet behind them. Seeing the shock on both their faces, the soldier almost smiled. "They can be overwhelming if you've never seen one."

Yasamin regained her voice. "What was that thing doing?"

"Examining you, making sure you were the one the King is waiting for. Dragons are quite thorough in whatever they undertake."

"I thought they were just myths." Yasamin had regained her composure now that the creature was gone and curiosity had the upper hand.

Goliagoth glanced at the distant dragons. "In a few decades, they probably will be. Once they were everywhere, now they exist only in Dragonval, and then only because they are—catered to."

"How?" Arash found the creatures fearsome but majestic as well.

"Let us just say the king takes care of them. Now, Highness, if you will go below and gather your things, we'll be in port soon. Don't worry if the ride gets a little bumpy, we have still to go through the Dragon's Mouth, but our sailors are experts at it. We received word last night that the King wishes you taken to the Counsulate's Tower as soon as we arrive. There are things there waiting for you."

"I wasn't aware of any shoring last night."

Goliagoth glanced at Arash but spoke to Yasamin. "Pigeons. We use them for messages."

"What is the Counsulate's Tower?" Yasamin queried.

"It's a small castle in the port used for visiting royalty or counselors. It is more convenient since it's close to shore. The visitors travel to the castle for their meetings. King Amir knew you would want to clean up and dress appropriately before you went to the castle for dinner. When you are ready, I will have a squad take you—and you." Goliagoth nodded to Arash. "The King has extended an invitation to you as well."

Yasamin suddenly felt very alone even though Arash had an invitation to attend dinner. "Goliagoth, I wish you to take me to the castle. I want someone I know to be with me for my entrance."

Goliagoth bowed. "As you wish, Highness. Now, please go below. The waters will soon grow rough."

"Of course." Yasamin nodded good-bye to Arash. "I'll see you later at the castle." She moved past Goliagoth, and the soldier turned to follow.

"Goliagoth." Arash started to move forward, then stopped. The giant soldier turned and raised his eyebrows in question.

"I have not had the opportunity, but I would like to thank you for what you did the other day. You could've had me thrown in chains. It ..."

The soldier held up his hand, ending the conversation. "Consider the debt I owed you paid. Just remember, you are in Dragonval now. Do nothing to interfere with the King's marriage, or you will have to face my blade. Understand?"

Arash nodded.

Goliagoth turned and followed the retreating Queen.

Arash watched them for a moment, then turned and studied the sea passing below him. He truly hoped he'd never have to face Goliagoth in battle.

It was not because he feared the soldier.

Over the months, he had begun to genuinely like him.

Chapter 26

Medusimia's long, slim fingers were fisted—the tapered nails bit into her white skin. The inner courtyard had been transformed into a dazzling dreamland. The servants had erected long tables and covered them with gold cloth that twinkled in the light of hundreds of white candles adorning the tabletops. The courtyard and tables were crammed with beautiful flowers of every color imaginable. Their fragrance filled the space, along with that of baking bread, roasting meat and other delectable dishes. The aromas were stimulating to the point one could become giddy from the scents alone. Many of the villagers had scaled the walls of the enclosed patio or sat in trees waiting for the appearance of Yasamin even though she wasn't due for another two hours.

Medusimia wanted to annihilate all of it. Despite Vulmire's original prediction of Yasamin's destruction before reaching Dragonval, the woman had somehow managed to arrive. Not only had she arrived, but she was now being hailed as a superwoman as well. She had survived the wilderness unscathed. The word spread through the town like wildfire. The villagers were impatient to see her.

The Queen gritted her teeth.

They would soon be sorry—all of them, especially Amir. Once she and Vulmire gained control of the throne, the idiots would see what real power was.

Medusimia's eyes narrowed in anger. She swept down the aisle toward the main table on the dais. The working servants scurried before her fury as her rage was almost tangible. Red sparks flared from her ruby-encrusted gown as well as her dark eyes.

Arriving at the table, she stopped. The long-necked, silver wine container bearing the insignia of the King sat on the table. She had not seen it used since her marriage to Amir. She muttered an oath under her breath. Her silver glass bearing her house's crest sat on the King's left. Yasamin's new, silver glass sat on his right. *This is wrong. I'm his First Queen; I should be on his right.* Medusimia wasn't sure if she had shouted the words or just thought them, but it didn't matter. The fire within her raged out of control. She drew back her hand to swipe the offending silverware from the table.

On her forward swing, a vice-like grip grabbed her arm.

"What do you think you're doing?" Amir stood behind her. He had already changed for the ceremony. Despite her fury, Medisumia's eye still caught the broad shoulders swathed in the black velvet jacket with diamond-encrusted sleeves; the narrow hips encased in more black velvet shot with strands of silver thread. The heavy rings on his hand cut into her arm.

"I said 'what do you think you're doing'?" Amir's dark eyes flashed in rage, and his generous mouth drew tight beneath the mustache.

"You not only insult me by bringing this wench here, but you have the audacity to place her on your right where *I* should be. How dare you!" She spit out the words in a low hiss.

"For the last time, Medusimia, the law allows me a second wife, as you are barren. Yasamin has done nothing to you. As for the placement," Amir's grip tightened until Medusimia's fingers turned blue. "Yasamin is to be my new wife. This ceremony is for *her;* therefore, she will sit on my right just as you did when I married you. It is tradition."

Medusimia's hand quickly became numb, but she refused to let the pain show. "I don't care …"

"Your Highness," a red-faced officer approached the couple. Amir did not loosen his hold but lowered his hand, so the Queen's arm was between them. He glanced over his shoulder at the officer.

"What is it?"

"*Demolisherian* Goliagoth wanted me to inform you Queen Yasamin has finished her preparation and will be here within half of the hour instead of two hours. He thought you might wish to inform those who are to be present."

"Yes. That will be all." Amir dismissed the officer without another glance.

But Medusimia's glance saw the look of lust and craving that shifted across Amir's face. Her burning rage condensed into a ball of impenetrable ice. She would beat him at his own game. She would have him her servant. She would wipe her shoes on him as if he were a doormat—if she played her cards right.

The Queen purposely relaxed her arm as if the fight were gone from her.

"You know how hot-headed I am, Amir. You often told me it was my fire that attracted you. I can't help it if I'm jealous of another sharing your bed. You please me so well; I hate to think of someone else receiving that same pleasure."

His wife's sudden shift in mood surprised him. Amir studied her, trying to discover her reason but grew only more confused. She seemed genuinely contrite—something unheard of in Medusimia.

"I have to admit, husband, it pains me to say I'm not perfect. I cannot give you the one thing you most desire, an heir. But I shouldn't take my anger out on you, and we shouldn't air our dirty laundry in front of the servants. Gossip spreads so."

Amir reluctantly released his wife. He half expected her to finish her blow at him, but she simply rubbed her arm where his fingerprints marred the white flesh. He looked at the vivid red pattern on her pale skin.

"I didn't realize I held you so tightly. You'll bruise."

Medusimia glanced down at her arm. "It matters not. It doesn't hurt, really ... not nearly as much as my heart." From somewhere within, she found tears and forced them down her cheek as she looked up at Amir. "I realize you have to do this thing. I'll do my best to not fight with Yasamin, but I cannot do this tonight."

"Why not?" The King was more confused than ever. All the years they'd been married, she had *never* cried, and it caught him off guard. A mêlée of anger, satisfaction, tenderness and intolerance filled him.

Medusimia saw the confusion. She reveled in it and grew stronger. The tears flowed freely now. "I know in my *head* you must do this. But my heart cannot stand it. To know someone else will feel your touch, your kiss, it's more than I can bear. I cannot sit at this table tonight and pretend to be happy. You can say I'm ill, it's true. Say I send my regrets, but I will not be at this table tonight. I would cause you more embarrassment than I would if I were angry. I will attend the marriage ceremony in three day's time, perhaps by then I'll have better control of myself. I promise I shall be nice to Yasamin when I am around her." Medusimia tiptoed and quickly kissed Amir on the cheek. "I am sorry, husband, I cannot do this." She turned and ran from the courtyard.

Amir stood amid the candles and flowers and watched his wife run away; his confusion temporarily replaced his lust for Yasamin. He never had expected this from Medusimia. He couldn't believe he had won his battle so easily. At last a slow, satisfied grin spread across his face. It appeared he would have both after all. He rubbed his hands together as his thoughts returned to his bride-to-be.

He should have frowned instead of smiled.

He should have worried more about Medusimia's leaving than about Yasamin's arriving.

He should have worried less about Medusimia's fighting and more about her acquiescence.

He should have, but he didn't.
And by not choosing *between* them, Amir made his choice.

Chapter 27

Yasamin gazed at the profusion of beautiful dresses lying around the room and shook her head. It was decadent, this riot of color and fabrics waiting for her to wear. Knowing of the shipwreck, King Amir had brought in seamstresses to make a wardrobe fit for a new Queen— *three new Queens*, Yasamin thought. If she changed dresses twice a day for the next year, she would never wear all of them. And the style! While everything was very fashionable, it was obviously the style the King liked and not what she would have chosen for herself. But then she was to be a Queen of Dragonval, and etiquette demanded she fit the part.

She *was* grateful for the bath though. She had spent almost an hour soaking in the deep, hot tub full of fluffy bubbles. It was both heaven and a refuge. She had lingered as long as she could, dreading the upcoming dinner.

Wrapped in an oversized, white towel soft as velvet, Yasamin examined each pile of clothing. The profusion of flowers overwhelmed her, their strong fragrances each vying for her attention. Yasamin closed her eyes and rubbed her temples. Between the cornucopia of flowers and the plethora of dresses, she had the beginnings of a migraine. Although she had been Queen in Gwendomere, she was not used to such superfluity. She wondered how the common people fared when so much went toward impressing others with the wealth of Dragonval.

Yasamin went to her knapsack and removed her mother's blue dress. She buried her face in it to obliterate the riot of colors and odors around her. The worn velvet and soft scent of *moonlitea* soothed her. *I know this is the right thing to do, Mama, but I feel so weak. I need strength to follow through. Please help me.*

Warmth enveloped Yasamin almost immediately. *I am always near, daughter. Follow your heart. You will find the strength.*

Almost as quickly as it came, the warmth went, and Yasamin rose from the bed. Her country's welfare depended upon her, and she would do whatever it took to protect them even if it meant giving up the man she now knew she loved with all her heart.

Yasamin sorted through the dresses. At last, one caught her eye. It was a light rose velvet, simply cut. She drew the gown over her head and let it fall into place. The rounded neckline emphasized her long, slender neck and full bosom. Beneath her breasts, the velvet skimmed her waist then fell to the floor in a slender column, which swayed in soft folds around her long legs when she moved.

Yasamin went to the dressing table and examined the boxes of jewelry the King had sent. Again the thought flitted through her mind at the ostentatious display of wealth Amir seemed to love. She enjoyed beautiful things, but the abundance the King had lavished upon her was almost crushing. She selected a multi-stranded necklace of large and small cut garnets. She fastened the clasp and glanced at herself in the mirror. The pale, simple-cut gown showed her figure to good advantage. It was elegant but simple. The garnets sparkled in the candlelight. But against her pale skin, they almost looked like drops of blood.

Yasamin started to remove the necklace then hesitated. She studied her reflection again, and the conversation she'd had with Arash about her sacrificing herself for her country flashed in her mind. In a way, she was doing just that. She would always love Arash, but she loved her country and had a duty to them as Queen. She might never be truly happy, but she would be at peace with herself if she could save Gwendomere. She picked up the matching earrings and placed them on her ears. She would wear the garnets. They would be a reminder of her duty. She swept her long hair up in loose curls atop her head and placed the smallest crown she could find among the cascading ringlets. She didn't need the tiara to show she was a queen. It was evident in the way she held her head, the way she moved; however, for tonight's dinner, etiquette demanded it. Yasamin was ready.

Almost.

The quiver was still in her stomach, and her knees remained shaky. Yasamin went to her backpack, removed her mother's book and walked around the room taking deep breaths. With the book it felt as though Casadra was right beside her. She needed it to be with her. Yasamin glanced around the room, and her eye fell upon some silver netting. She picked it up. It was a beautiful bag, woven from silver threads and probably meant to carry a few small items a woman might want with her. Nearby lay a dress heavily encrusted in silver. Hundreds of silver cords looped around the sleeves, and a matching cord of a slightly heavier weight gathered around the waist. There was a loosely woven shawl to drape around her arms, woven in the same pattern as the bag. No doubt the purse was part of this outfit.

It didn't matter.

Yasamin quickly took the belt cord and ran it through the open weave of the bag. The cord ran across the top and exited the other side. It was a perfect match. Yasamin tied the sash around her waist. The bag hung low on her side. She placed her mother's book inside the bag, then took the shawl and loosely knotted it around her hips. She examined herself in the mirror. Unless one looked very closely, it seemed she was merely wearing a silver girdle.

She could always have her mother's book with her.

Now she was ready.

She opened the door and descended the winding staircase. Goliagoth and a squadron of men waited in the foyer. Hearing her footsteps, the men jumped to attention. Goliagoth moved forward to escort Yasamin to the waiting carriage. The setting sun blazed through the open doors and illuminated the Queen.

Goliagoth stopped, his heart in his throat as he gazed up at her. He had forgotten how beautiful she was. Now with the sun's last rays upon her, Yasamin appeared to be a pillar of crystal with fire inside. In that moment, Goliagoth's entire life passed through his mind.

Of all the women he had used and left.

Of all the lives he had destroyed.

Of the lives that could have been created but hadn't.

Of the aching, black void in his chest.

Of something forever lost for which he had no name.

As he watched the slender woman descend, Goliagoth felt a small spark grow in that black void. It grew and spread a warmth through him. He had no name for it, but he knew what it was not. It wasn't lust or desire. He had danced to that tune many times and knew it well. Two things became crystal clear in that moment: he wanted to protect her from all harm, and he would lay down his life for her.

Goliagoth realized he was staring and purposely looked back at the soldiers. "Volmanthin, form the squad on each side of the carriage. They can gawk all they want, but no villager is to get near enough to touch it."

"Aye, sir." The officer snapped a salute and called the soldiers to follow him.

Goliagoth turned back to Yasamin as she took the last step from the stairway. He bowed. "Highness. The carriage awaits." Goliagoth found he could not keep his eyes from her. He straightened.

Yasamin moved toward him and a smile lit her face. "Goliagoth, it's good to see a familiar face. I'm happy you're escorting me to the castle."

A faint flush crawled up his face but was indiscernible beneath his dark tan. Her smile reminded him of the sun's first rays after a cold, winter night. His mouth wanted to return that smile, but too many years of harsh training forbid it. He coughed, trying to rid himself of the unfamiliar lump in his throat.

"It is my honor, your Highness."

Yasamin cocked her head to one side and studied him. Something was different about him, although she couldn't quite put her finger on it.

"Is something wrong, Highness?"

"Hmm? No. I was just wondering, do you think, perhaps just this once, before we go, before I become a Queen of Dragonval, you could at least call me Queen Yasamin? It'd make me feel like I have at least one person who knows *me*. After all, we did go through a lot together."

"We did, Your Hi-, Queen Yasamin. Remember, if you ever need me, I am always at your disposal. Now if you are ready, King Amir is eagerly waiting."

"I am sure he is. Very well, let us go." Yasamin started through the door.

"Wait, please." Goliagoth moved toward a small anteroom near the front door and returned with a black velvet cape. "Something you should learn about our country this time of the year, the nights get cool quickly. You will need this." He held the cape open for her.

Yasamin backed into it and let him drape it on her shoulders. As he did, she reached up and touched one of his hands. "Thank you, *Demolisherian* ... for everything. If it were not for you, I doubt any of us would be here in Dragonval now." She smiled over her shoulder at Goliagoth.

He felt as though he were ten feet tall. His hand tingled with burning waves of fire. It was at that moment he felt that for which he had no name.

Chapter 28

Beneath the table, King Amir tapped his foot impatiently. Now the time was here, every second seemed like an hour. At last, he heard the marching steps and the creaking wheels of the carriage. He stood and nodded for his captain to line his soldiers on either side of the path from the entrance of the courtyard to the table. The men quickly did as ordered, and the soft *swwwwissssh* of drawing swords was the only sound heard. Each soldier pointed his blade just above the head of the soldier opposite him, forming a covered aisle.

The carriage stopped. Complete silence reigned for a few seconds.

Yasamin stood in the arch of the doorway with Goliagoth behind her. An audible gasp escaped from some of the older guests. For a second, they thought Casadra had returned. Almost simultaneously the populace murmured its approval. Amir could not get his breath. By the gods, she was the most stunning thing he had ever seen. She had chosen well to wear the simple gown, for she would outshine anything she wore. He waited as she slowly walked beneath the crossed swords toward him. Common man and court alike bowed as she regally strolled down the path.

Amir met her at the foot of the dais and took her hand. He carried her around the table and seated her beside him. Goliagoth took a spot behind the dais where he could see the entire courtyard.

The King was ecstatic. He had his Queen. Had it not been for the heavily populated courtyard, he wasn't sure he wouldn't have taken her right there on the table, but he could wait. It was only three days. With a benevolent smile, Amir raised his hands in the air.

"People of Dragonval, I present to you my bride-to-be, Queen Yasamin of the House of Gwendomere."

He turned and nodded for Yasamin to rise. The crowd went wild with cheers and applause. The slender woman stood silently as the ovation washed over her. People she glanced at felt as if she had truly seen them.

After some time, the noise died to a low muttering. Yasamin began in a gentle voice that rang clear throughout the courtyard.

"People of Dragonval, thank you for your most generous welcome. As you know, in three days' time I will become Second Queen to your King. It is a great honor, an honor which I will not take lightly. It'll take me a little time to grow accustomed to all of your ways, but I promise you this: I will always strive to do my very best for the good of this country and for your King. I shall always conduct myself in a manner befitting a Queen of Dragonval toward any and all with whom I come in contact so that Dragonval's honor and glory shall shine throughout the world."

And then...

Yasamin smiled that dazzling smile of hers.

And captured the hearts of young and old, commoner and royalty, men and women.

The audience leaped to their feet, applauding wildly. The villagers did the same, those on the fence and branches almost losing their balance.

King Amir applauded. He was pleased. Not only was he going to have a beautiful wife but an intelligent one.

Arash, sitting at the end of the table, rose and applauded. His heart was breaking, but he admired the slender woman and her determination.

Even Goliagoth, soldier that he was, found himself applauding.

Everyone loved the Queen-to-be.

Everyone was captivated by her.

Everyone but one. From a darkened room, a pair of eyes narrowed in anger. "You will never rule. You shall soon die as will that fool who sits beside you. You will rue the day you were born, Yasamin. And oh, how you will suffer. I shall see to it personally."

The shutter closed against the festivities below.

Chapter 29

The next three days were a flurry of activities. To Yasamin it seemed she no sooner put her head on her pillow than it was time to rise.

She smiled until her smile felt frozen in place.

She shook hands until her fingers were numb.

She tried to remember names, but there were so many advisors, counselors, dignitaries. They were all very forgiving when she forgot.

She had had her first argument with Amir, but he had capitulated in the end. She wasn't happy she'd had to argue, but she was happy he had relented and agreed Fleuise could be in her wedding.

Surprisingly, Medusimia had been very friendly the few times she had encountered her.

She had tried to see Arash, but he was always busy talking with dignitaries or out of the castle.

Even Goliagoth was hard to find.

The only true happiness she had was the child. Fleuise was ecstatic about being in the wedding and having a new dress made just for her. She was with Yasamin constantly, even sleeping in the same bed with her at night.

Something Yasamin knew would soon change.

And then, the day was there.

Too soon.

Too quickly she was being dressed for the wedding. Yasamin vowed the gown must have had hundreds of yards of material for as soon as the maid slipped it over Yasamin's head, it felt someone had placed an anchor on her shoulders.

"You're beautiful, Queen." Fleuise clapped her hands and jumped with delight. She had already donned her gown. It was hard to believe she was the same child who would barely talk only three months before.

"You're beautiful ... the most beautiful bride in the whole world." The little girl continued her song. "Everybody will love you and want to marry you."

Yasamin's heart chipped. *There is only one I want to love me but he cannot,* but she smiled at the child. "I think everyone will think you are the most beautiful girl in the world and will want to marry *you*," she countered.

"You think I'm beautiful?" The child was so amazed, she stopped her dance. "Really? You think I'm pretty?"

Yasamin shooed the maid away who was fussing with the many layers of silk and knelt beside Fleuise. "Yes, I do. You are a beautiful little girl, Fleuise. Don't you every forget it. Someday you will find a special person, and you will marry them."

"But what if you say I cannot?"

"Now why would I do such a thing?"

"Because you are the Queen. You can do anything."

Yasamin drew the little girl close and hugged her tightly. "I would not do that to you, precious. Someday you will find someone you love very much, and I would never stop you from marrying him. That is a promise."

"Cross your heart?"

"And hope to die. Love is very precious. If you find it, never let it go."

"All right." Fleuise turned and solemnly examined her reflection in the mirror. "I still think you are beautiful though."

Yasamin laughed. It was good to have someone she could laugh with. She reached for the silver cord and purse.

"Highness, you are not going to wear that, are you? It will mess your gown."

"Yes, I am." Yasamin gave the maid a look that brooked no further conversation. "Bring me the veil."

The maid scurried to get the covering. Yasamin tied the silk cord around her waist and let the purse hang behind her. She'd forego the shawl. People had already become use to seeing her wear the purse. Out of deference to the ceremony, she tugged the purse until it was in the back. The thirty-foot veil would completely hide it, but at least she would have the comfort of the book being on her.

The maid returned, and Yasamin sat down so the girls could arrange her hair. Exhaustion pounded at every muscle, and the ceremony had not yet begun. It felt good to let anyone take over who could help her.

She was finally prepared. Yasamin walked to the full-length mirror. She hardly recognized the young woman staring back at her. The wedding dress was made of hundreds of yards of silk so white that next to it even her pale skin appeared slightly tan. The dressing woman had brushed a tiny bit of rouge on her cheeks and lips and lined her eyes with a minute trace of kohl. As a result, her eyes were breathtaking, as luminous as opals and as light as the strands of pearls adorning her slender neck. Her upswept hair was a concoction of silver curls beaded with more pearls and white flowers; the veil, waves of white tulle studded with more of the white gems as well as diamonds.

She was no longer a child. It was time to put away childish dreams.

She was a naïve, young girl about to become a woman and wife.

Yasamin bid a silent farewell to the young girl in the mirror. After tonight she would never see her again.

"I am ready."

She turned and picked up her bouquet of white roses. She noticed a tiny bunch of *moonlitea* tucked among the white petals. Someone knew. Someone remembered—her mother.

Chapter 30

He wanted to take her. It might not be proper, but over the past few days, he'd found the old rules didn't hold the meaning and gratification they once did.

She had asked him once. Perhaps she would ask him again. If she didn't want him, she would say so without hesitation.

He paced back and forth.

He wondered if she found the flowers. He couldn't ask. It had taken all his skill to get them in her chambers without detection.

He would go. He had to see that smile once more. Something told him he wouldn't see it much in the future.

He headed for the door.

And stopped.

What if she didn't want him to take her? It would be awkward.

It could court danger.

It could lead to his demise if improperly handled.

Or worse.

He fingered the black leather strap. He had to be careful with his words.

He had worked long and hard to get where he was. A few seconds could unravel everything.

It didn't matter. But *she* did.

He checked his clothes. Everything was perfect.

He *would* do it.

Before he could change his mind again, he jerked the door open and slammed it behind him. He swiftly marched toward Yasamin's chambers.

* * * * *

Yasamin headed for the bedroom door and jumped when someone outside pounded on it.

"Wonder who that is?"

"I'll get it." Fleuise ran for the door and opened it a bit. "Oh, it's you. Why are you here?"

Yasamin couldn't see the stranger, so she moved a little closer. "Who is it, Fleuise? Open the door."

The child looked back at her then out the door. "Do you think I look beautiful? You have to tell me now before I open the door because after you see *her*, you won't be able to look at anything else. She is gorgeous."

Yasamin couldn't hear the reply, but she saw Fleuise giggle.

"Fleuise, open the door. Don't leave them just standing there."

Fleuise shoved the door wide open and pointed at Yasamin. "Look! Didn't I tell you she was gorgeous? Didn't I?"

Goliagoth stood in the hallway, helmet in hand. Following the little girl's finger, he stared at Yasamin.

"Goliagoth! What a surprise! What are you doing here?"

He didn't answer; he only continued to stare at her.

"Told you. Told you." Fleuise danced around the giant. "Cat's got your tongue. Isn't she the most beautiful thing you've ever seen? Isn't she gorgeous? Isn't she *beeeeautiful*?"

He glanced at the child, then back to Yasamin.

"Fleuise! Hush, now. You're embarrassing me. Goliagoth, come in, please." Yasamin smiled at the soldier. "She's so excited about the wedding. Don't be upset with her teasing you."

Goliagoth took two steps into the room, drawn toward her as a seedling toward the sunlight. He could think of no words to describe her. "I-I'm not, Your Highness. If you will forgive me for being so brazen, the child *is* right; you are beautiful. The most beautiful thing I have ever seen in my life."

It was Yasamin's turn to be speechless. She didn't think Goliagoth had a compliment in him. A soft pink flush crept up her cheek. "I think you exaggerate, but thank you. What are you doing here?"

Goliagoth might have regained his composure outwardly, but inside, everything, especially his heart, was trembling. "I came to escort you to the castle's chapel, if you desire it. I thought today being your wedding day you might … uh, not want to … uh, go there by yourself, that is, if you do not have someone to escort you, I will."

"I would appreciate that very much, *Demolisherian*." She smiled. His title rolled across her tongue like a caress, the exact opposite of the first time she had used it. "I can think of no one more suitable to get me there safely."

She could, but that person could no longer be a part of her life. That person was a precious memory tucked away in a corner of her mind to be brought out on a lonely afternoon. "Shall we?"

He bowed. The three of them headed for the chapel and their futures.

Chapter 31

"Do you understand what to do? I must have her *before* tonight."

"I know."

"If you wait until he gets her, she won't do me any good."

"I understand. I'm not an idiot. I'll get her and take her to my place. I'll hold her there until you tell me to bring her to you."

"Good. Timing is everything."

"I said I would get it done. What about *him*?" The man scratched his neck. He always felt as though things were crawling on him when he entered this place, yet his love for the other continually drew him here. "Do you think he will interfere?"

A low hiss and rattle echoed through the darkness. The man realized the other one was chuckling. "He might throw a temper fit, but it will do him naught. He knows my power, and he will not test it to the limit. He's a fool who *thinks* he knows everything."

"But if he does … ?"

"I'd kill him. What else? He's a useful tool, but I can always find another."

"Maybe I could …"

The chuckle became a belly laugh, which ended in a spasm of coughing.

"*You*? Surely you jest. Take a look in the mirror. You aren't fit for the position."

Anger flared in the man but quickly dissipated into wanting to please the other. Sometimes he wondered if it was because he feared the consequences if he didn't.

"Of course. You're right."

"I will not need anyone in my place when I have accomplished the deed. I shall assume my rightful place. Now go, watch her carefully and get her before that crazy fool has his way with her."

"Yes, Highness." The man bowed and scurried backward from the chamber. He couldn't wait to get above ground. Although only a few feet below the surface, the atmosphere of the place made it feel miles deep in the belly of the earth.

He would get her. He would get her because he didn't even want to think about what would happen to him if he didn't. Failure was never an option when it came to serving *him*.

The man pulled his hat lower over his ruined face, so no one would notice him. His was a visage no one easily forgot. There were a couple of fellows who would help him. They were scared enough of him to keep their mouths shut.

Within twenty-four hours, everything would change. His life would definitely change for the better.

Within twenty-four hours, everything *would* change but not the way he thought.

Chapter 32

Yasamin thought her head would explode. Everything had become a blur since Goliagoth delivered her and Fleuise to the castle's chapel.

She remembered the ceremony. Twice she'd thought she was about to faint from the heat, the closeness of the packed bodies, the narrow confines of the stone chapel. She had managed her vows without stumbling and remembered wondering how her hand could feel so cold as Amir held it to place his ring upon her finger when she was burning.

She was suffocating.

And the party afterward was worse. Everyone congratulated her, pressed around her and hemmed her in. Her bridal veil felt as though it had turned to granite, and her feet ached from the tight shoes. She just wanted to escape to some place quiet and rest.

She couldn't. She was Second Queen of Dragonval.

Yasamin smiled at the old man who was attempting to tell her about his hunting accident. He rambled in disjointed sentences, and Yasamin became lost in the story, but she continued to smile and nod when it seemed appropriate.

She looked for Arash. She'd seen him when she had entered, but it appeared he had left.

She couldn't find Goliagoth either and found herself wishing the soldier would just pick her up and carry her from the milling crowd.

But she couldn't. She was Second Queen of Dragonval.

Fleuise tugged at her gown. Yasamin excused herself and bent down.

Fleuise cupped her hand to Yasamin's ear and whispered, "He's smelly. Why do you talk to him?"

Yasamin glanced at the old diplomat who was already engrossed in a conversation with another man.

"Because, sugarplum, it is the polite thing to do."

"But he smells bad. And he drinks too much."

"As a Queen, I have certain obligations to fulfill. One of them is talking to diplomats, even if they are smelly. Besides, I feel sorry for him. He's old and probably lonely."

"Ugh. I'm glad I'm not a queen."

"Why, don't you go get yourself another sweet?" Yasamin whispered to the little girl. "Just be careful not to eat too many. You don't want a tummy ache."

"All right." She scampered off, and Yasamin straightened, only to find King Amir beside her. He put his arm around her waist and murmured into her other ear. "You look tired, my dear." His breath was strong with wine as he grazed a kiss on her cheek.

"I am."

"But not too tired for later?"

That was the last thing Yasamin wanted, but she had a duty to perform and she would. She forced a smile to her numb lips. "I only hope I do not disappoint you too much. I know little about these things."

He grew a little bolder and kissed her on the side of her mouth. "That's what makes it all the more delicious, my sweetness. I shall be the first, and I will teach you things that you have never dreamed of."

Yasamin was naïve but not so innocent she didn't know what the hardness was between them. He rubbed himself slightly against her.

Yasamin wasn't sure how she kept the smile on her lips. She was sure he would see through her lies. "I am sure you will, dear. I look forward to—to our time together."

King Amir threw back his head and laughed. "My little dove, so innocent. But I shall teach you. After tonight, Yasamin, you'll beg me to come to you every night."

"I probably shall." She tried to laugh, but it was more of a squeak. She moved slightly from him. "But, my dearest, since I am so innocent, could we please wait until the bedroom? Everyone here is going to know what is on your mind."

He laughed again. He was in good humor now that his desire was about to be consummated. "A prim and proper Queen. By the gods, how utterly delightful. You realize, of course, everyone here *knows* what is going to happen in a very short time. And I will wager most of them will find someone to bed tonight as well."

Yasamin blushed. "Perhaps. With your permission I'd like to leave and go to our chambers. It will take me a little time to get ready for you." She saw Amir's eyes narrow slightly. She had said it the wrong way. "I did not mean that as it sounded, husband. I meant I would like to bathe and have the maids prepare me to be beautiful for you. And I thought maybe one of them might, you know, tell me, well, I mean …"

Amir relaxed and patted Yasamin on the derriere. "Tell you how to please a man? Don't worry about it, Yasamin. I will teach you everything you need to know about pleasing me. But if you'd like to bathe and have the maids gown you, I've no objection. Perhaps it will relax you somewhat. Being a virgin, I imagine you are nervous. Go. I will be up in half of an hour."

He pulled her close and kissed her on the mouth. His sour wine breath almost choked her. She could feel his tongue searching, probing against her lips. Steeling herself, Yasamin opened her own and let him kiss her as he wanted. Closing her eyes, she pretended it was Arash kissing her—so much easier. Yasamin actually felt herself melting against Amir until she realized what she was doing.

She pulled away, her face beet red. Fortunately, Amir thought the blush was over the public display of affection and not the guilt overwhelming her.

"Go on, my dumpling. Beautify yourself if it will make you feel better. You are already beautiful." He turned to the crowd and beckoned the waiter to fill his goblet.

Yasamin took a deep breathe and headed for the exit. The dark hallway's coolness felt wonderful against her hot skin. She picked up her skirts and headed for the stairway.

"I'm coming with you." Fleuise stood two feet behind her.

"But, Fleuise, I am going to my bedchamber."

"I know."

"I mean I am going to my bedchamber to get ready for Amir."

"I know. I'm not *that* dumb."

Yasamin turned back toward the child and knelt. She pulled Fleuise close and hugged her. "I have never thought you were dumb. But there are things children …"

Fleuise pulled back, so she could look into Yasamin's face. "I'm not stupid. I come from the village, remember? Our house doesn't have a lot of rooms like your castle. I know what Mama and Papa did. I know where babies come from. And besides, there are cows, pigs and goats, they all—"

"All right, you have made your point, Fleuise." Yasamin wiped a lump of cream from the child's mouth. "I know I let you sleep in my room until now. But the king does things differently here. I do not think Amir will want you around when he … is with me," Yasamin finished lamely.

The look on Fleuise's face was enough to break the Queen's heart. "I know. He doesn't really want me around anyway."

"It has nothing to do with you, sweetheart. He just wants to be alone with me."

"I guess." Fleuise's eyes were full of tears when she looked up at Yasamin. "Please, please let me just go with you, while you get ready for bed. I promise I'll be good. I promise I'll leave when you tell me. I just don't want to be alone all night. I'm scared. Please, Queen Yasamin, please let me come. I'll leave when you say to."

Yasamin couldn't say no to those tears. "All right, you can come with me and stay while the maids prepare for tonight. I'll tell one of them to stay with you in my old bedchamber. But you do have to leave. Promise?"

"Yes."

"Come on, then." Yasamin lifted her skirts and ran up the stairs with Fleuise following. They twisted and turned through the dark hallways where only a few candles burned to show the way.

"It is dark up here."

"Yes, it is, but I am pretty sure we are going the right way. I remember these big columns here. The doors should be just a little beyond them on the left."

Yasamin turned; Fleuise was right on her heels. The twin doors lay a few feet down the hallway. "See, I told you."

"Yasamin." A figure emerged from the shadow of the first column.

The Queen jumped and grabbed for Fleuise's hand. She almost screamed but didn't when she saw who it was.

"Arash! You almost scared me to death. What are you doing here? Amir will have your head if he finds you," she whispered furiously.

"I hoped to talk some sense into you before it's too late."

"Arash! My mind is made up. There is nothing you can say that will make me change it."

"You do not love him." Arash moved closer and took Yasamin in his arms. "Tell me you do not care for me, that you do not love me. I saw it in your eyes in the wilderness. I love you, Yasamin. I can take you away from this nightmare."

He stared into her pale eyes, saw his reflection in their depths, saw the unshed tears and saw her mouth tremble. He brushed his lips across hers. "I will give my life to save you. I have enough men to take you away. I have ships that can carry you to my land, my father's home, where you'll be safe. Just come before it's too late."

"Are we going with him?" Fleuise's whisper cut through the darkness.

Yasamin leaned against Arash.
This was her dream.
This is what she'd waited for forever.
She wanted to go.
She wanted to spend her life with him.
She wanted his love and to give him love.
Then Yasamin remembered where she was.

She pushed away from him. Drawing herself up to her full height, Yasamin stared at Arash. Her eyes briefly flared blue-pink, then turned to ice. Arash could feel their coldness from where he stood. They were lifeless, cold chunks of frost. Her voice was even flatter and icier. "That was another lifetime. Different circumstances. I was a foolish girl with childish daydreams. I am married now. I am Second Queen of Dragonval, and you are out of line, Prince. I will not dishonor this house."

Arash took two steps back from her frigid anger.

He had seen her angry but never like this.

Yet his love would not let him walk away.

He tried once more. "Yasamin, listen, you are just a pawn here. Queen Medusimia will always have the upper hand, and she will make sure your life is miserable even if you produce an heir. I love you, Yasamin; tell me you don't love me. Tell me you love *him*."

Yasamin thought her heart would shatter. She had to get Arash away before someone saw him. Amir would kill him on the spot. From somewhere deep inside, she found the strength she needed. She narrowed her eyes. "I do not love you, Arash. I do not know how to make it any plainer. For the sake of our old friendship, I will say nothing of your impertinence if you will just leave. Now."

"You haven't told me you love him." Arash was desperate.

"Love is not the issue here. What is import—" Yasamin's reply was cut short by a dark-gloved hand covering her mouth. Someone jerked her arms behind her and bound them. A gag quickly replaced the hand on her mouth, and a black hood was jammed over her head as she struggled and kicked her assailant. She felt herself lifted high in the air and thrown over someone's shoulder. The bag was heavy and foul smelling. Her stomach churned at the odor.

At last she felt the cool night air against her skin. They were outside the castle. Terrified, Yasamin struggled harder against the ropes and gag. A rough blow landed against her temple. Yasamin drifted toward the waiting darkness. Her last memory was Arash lying on the rock floor and two shadowy thugs pounding his motionless body.

Chapter 33

"Wake up, please wake up," the persistent voice slowly penetrated Yasamin's consciousness as did the nudging, but it was a long way away. Her mind drifted upward.

She recognized the voice.

Fleuise.

Fleuise whimpered and shook her.

Memories pierced her awareness.

The shadows.

The hand.

The hood.

The blow.

Arash lying, bleeding on the floor.

Yasamin sat upright on the cot. Her head immediately protested by swimming crazily, and her stomach stirred. She lay back down and closed her eyes.

"What happened?"

"We've been kidnapped. Why? Do you think it's for ransom? Do you think they hurt Arash? Why do they have us in this place? It's scary." The little girl's voice trembled, but she refused to cry. She nestled closer to Yasamin. "Do you think they'll hurt us?"

"Who are 'they'?" Yasamin sat up again but much slower. Her head still throbbed but didn't spin quite so wildly.

"I don't know. There are this many." Fleuise held up five fingers. "They have hoods on. And they're dressed all in black. They don't talk. One of them just points what he wants done."

"Where are we?"

Again, the child shook her head. "I don't know. They put something over my head, but it's scary—especially in the other room. I don't like it here. I want to go home. Do you think Goliagoth will find us? You told me in the woods to stay close. He'd always find you or me."

Yasamin continued her examination of herself. Except for a slight bump on her head, a queasy stomach and a foul taste in her mouth, she was in good condition. She turned to examine Fleuise. "I hope he does. This is not the woods, and we are dealing with people, not wild animals. It is not quite the same."

The look of terror that filled Fleuise's eyes chilled Yasamin, and she hastened to add some comforting words. "But we both know he's very good at what he does. I imagine as soon as King Amir knows we are missing, he will have Goliagoth tracking us in no time. We just need to be patient."

"I hope he finds us soon. I don't like this place. It's bad. It's *wrong*. It's scarier than the woods." Fleuise drew her knees up to her chin and stuck her thumb into her mouth. She began rocking back and forth.

The simple motion worried Yasamin more than immediate danger to herself. "Fleuise, where are the men?"

It took a second for the thumb to come out, but she responded after a few moments. "They're not here right now. They left. I tried the door; it's locked."

"How long have they been gone? Did they say anything about when they would return?"

"They didn't say *anything*. They don't talk. That's why they're so scary. They're like ... like ... I don't know. They dropped you on the bed and walked out. I don't know how long. But we have to get out now. This place is *wrong*. It's bad. It's evil." The thumb went back into the mouth.

"Why do you say that?"

This time the thumb didn't come out. Fleuise glanced toward the other room. She finally spoke around the appendage. "Because bad things, there." She nodded her head toward the door.

Yasamin knew she had to investigate. Perhaps there was a way out the child had overlooked. "Fleuise, you stay here. I'm going into the other room to look around."

"No!" She shrieked the single word as she lunged and wrapped her arms around the woman.

"I have to. Maybe I can find a way out."

"No. Don't go in there." Fleuise burrowed closer to Yasamin.

"I must. You can stay here. If I find a way out, I'll come get you."

"No, don't leave me here. I'm afraid of being alone."

"Then you have to come with me, but I am going to check the other room." Yasamin disentangled herself from the child and stood. "I have to see what I can find. Are you coming?" Fleuise rose and put her hand in Yasamin's. The thumb remained in the mouth.

Fleuise's body language sent a tremor of fear down Yasamin's backbone. She could not imagine why the child was so scared of a room. She slowly walked to the door, then through it.

And stopped dead-still.

No wonder the child was terrified.

The room was enormous. In one glance, she could see its owner was wealthy. Handcrafted art filled the chamber. Candles in two candelabras cast a dim, flickering light on the vast expanse, but it was more than enough for her to see.

The walls were blood red, the floor and furniture ebony, as were the pedestals holding the statues.

The statues.

It was the statues that sent a chill into Yasamin's blood. It was the statues that drained the color from her already pale cheeks and made her knees tremble. Perfectly detailed, each portrayed a horrifying subject: a wolf holding a half-chewed, bleeding child in its mouth; a vulture ripping at the entrails of a fallen soldier, the soldier's bronze hands frozen forever in a futile attempt to push the bird away; a laughing, naked girl spread-eagle beneath two men, one fondling her breasts, the other preparing to thrust himself into her, each of the three perfect in detail, down to the girl's erect nipples.

Yasamin closed her eyes against the obscenities, but it did little good. Each statue was ingrained in her memory as surely as if it had been etched into the cells with acid. Without saying a word, she drew Fleuise close to her and shielded the child's face against her own body.

"It's all right, sweetheart. We'll find a way out of here. These statues are horrible and ugly, but they can't hurt you." Fleuise's response was to pull herself closer to Yasamin.

Moving slowly, holding the child close to her in a parody of a waltz, Yasamin moved to the door—bolted from the outside. She turned toward the high windows to her left and froze. She didn't know her exact location, but she now knew where she was.

Her mother's words drifted back to her: *He was mostly referred to as "The Collector" because of his perversion of "collecting" something from people who couldn't pay. It was rumored his rooms were full of ears, fingers, noses and worse, of the poor souls who didn't have the money due him.*

Nailed to the blood-red wall were hundreds of ears, noses, fingers and some shriveled things she didn't want to examine any closer.

The Road of Silk

Her mother had escaped The Collector, but she hadn't. She was locked in a sub-chamber of The Collector's house.

Chapter 34

"Idiots! Worthless sows! What do you mean she isn't here? How could you lose her? How in heaven's name could you lose my Queen?" King Amir paced to and fro in front of the three chambermaids. All three were on their knees, heads bowed to the floor. The veins on Amir's neck bulged as did his eyes. His face was apoplectic. His screams echoed down the corridor as Goliagoth ran for the chamber. He entered just in time to see the king kick one of the maids savagely in her side. "Answer me, Sow!" Glancing up, he saw the soldier enter. Reaching down, Amir grasped the youngest maid by the hair and pulled her head up. "Answer me!" he screamed again, "Or by the gods, I'll have the *Demolisherian* cut out your tongue!"

The hapless girl, already terrorized beyond reason, could only stare at the soldier. Foam ran from her mouth. The second maid, her older sister, managed to stutter a few words. "Your Highness, mercy, please! We d-didn't lo-lose her. She never arrived."

The king kicked, and the second maid fell backward, blood gushed from her split lip. "You lying bitch. She told me she was coming here. You're lying to cover up your own ineptness." He raised his foot to kick her again.

Goliagoth stepped between him and the maid. "Highness. Let me question them. Why don't you sit and have a glass of wine. I will get your answers."

Amir pushed his face into Goliagoth's. Spittle from his mouth sprayed the soldier, but he didn't flinch. "I don't want to sit down! I don't want a drink! I *want* my Queen! Now!"

"Highness, you're upset and rightly so. It would be almost impossible to remain clear-headed in such conditions. Perhaps there is something I can find that is useful. Let me question the maids. While I do, settle yourself, so you can best decide how to proceed once we've ascertained what happened."

For a moment, Goliagoth thought the king was going to hit him, but he didn't care. His heart was pounding with fear for Yasamin. If it meant receiving blows from Amir until the king spent his rage, he'd suffer it. Amir's actions would never get them answers.

Amir sighed. "So be it. Find out what you can. After all, questioning is your forte. I'll have a goblet. I have a horrible headache." Loosening his hold on the maid, he settled himself in a cushioned chair. Pouring a drink, Amir drained it, laid his head against the chair's back and gently massaged the bridge of his nose.

Goliagoth glanced at the second maid trying to staunch the blood's flow with her hand. He stepped to the vanity, picked up a towel and knelt beside her. "Use this." He handed her the towel. "Keep pressure on it. It will stop."

Turning slightly, he looked at the third maid still cringing on her hands and knees. "What's your name?"

"M-Madinina."

"What happened here, Madinina?"

"The Queen was to come. We were to prepare her for her marriage bed. We waited. We didn't know how long the festivities would be. We didn't know anything was amiss until the King came."

Goliagoth looked at the second maid who stared at him over the rag. "True?"

The maid nodded. "Yes, sir," she whispered around the towel.

"You never left this room? Tell me the truth right now, and I will not punish you. Lie, and I promise all of you will regret it for a very long time. Torture always loosens a tongue to wag the truth."

"No, sir, we never left." Both girls answered in unison.

Goliagoth studied them closely. He believed them. His gut instinct said they were as bewildered as he was. He glanced at the youngest maid. She lay shivering on the floor. The foam no longer drooled from her lips, but her eyes were slightly glazed. "What's wrong with her?"

"My sister has a sickness. When she's badly frightened or hurt, this happens. When she quietens, it gets better."

"Was she here the entire time?'

"Yes, sir. We have all been here since sunset. I swear none of us ever left."

"Did anyone come to the room asking for the Queen?"

"No, sir."

"Nothing unusual happened?"

The maid with the towel shook her head, "No, sir, except …" she hesitated and looked at the other girl.

"Except?"

"Yolanda," the maid nodded to the other girl, "thought she heard something once."

Goliagoth turned his attention toward Yolanda. "What did you hear?"

"I am not sure. I thought I heard a cry, maybe a shout. All of us went to the door and looked out, but we did not see anything. We didn't go into the hall, just looked. I decided it must have been a bird."

"When?"

"I think about half of an hour ago."

Goliagoth nodded. "Stay here. Do what you can for your sister to make her comfortable, but she remains in this room. I may have questions for her later."

He rose and grabbed a candle from a sconce on the wall. "Get a candle and come with me," he ordered one of the soldiers standing in the doorway.

Goliagoth slowly paced the hallway, scouring the floor and walls for anything unusual. When he neared the immense columns he stopped, then knelt.

"Bring that candle here, soldier!" he shouted to the following warrior.

The man hurried forward. "Where, sir?"

"Hold it close to the floor here." Goliagoth pointed to the faint circle of illumination on the floor caused by his own candle. The man did so. Goliagoth frowned at the few droplets on the floor. He touched one of them. Smelt it. Tasted it. He knew that coppery taste anywhere.

Blood.

Someone had been hurt at this spot not too long ago. The blood was just starting to clot. Goliagoth began to rise but hesitated. Something was still pulling him here. He moved his candle to enlarge the search area. That's when he saw it. His heart hammered against his ribs.

Grabbing it, Goliagoth jumped to his feet and ran for the bedchamber.

"Highness, I've reason to believe the Queen has been abducted, possibly injured."

Amir opened his eyes. "Preposterous. What would give you such an idea?"

Goliagoth held out his hand with his fingertips covered in blood. "I found this in the hallway outside the chamber."

Amir's eyes widened and he sat upright. "Yasamin's?"

"I've reason to believe so. One of the maids thought she heard a faint cry. They looked out the door but saw naught. They didn't venture into the hall."

"When?"

"About half of an hour ago."

Amir rubbed his face to clear the cobwebs from his dazed mind. "That's around the time Yasamin said she was coming here. But blood by itself—"

"There is more." Goliagoth opened his other hand. Within his huge palm lay a minute spray of *moonlitea*. "This was in the Queen's bouquet. I'm guessing she dropped it when attacked. The assailants grabbed the flowers but missed these few that fell out."

Amir grabbed the wilted blooms from Goliagoth's palm and studied them. His hand trembled so violently several of the tiny petals fell to the floor. "Whoever did this, I'll have their heads. They will be sorry they were born," he swore.

"Do you have any idea who might wish to harm the Queen?"

Amir thought. "Medusimia."

"If so, she was not here, herself, and she did not contact anyone this afternoon or tonight."

"How can you be so positive, *Demolisherian*."

"Highness, I've been aware of her displeasure with this second marriage. I observed her at the wedding and the party. She never disappeared. She only talked to a few visiting dignitaries who are two of your strongest allies. She left the festivities over two hours ago, went to her chambers and never left. I, and a few of my men, stood watch outside her chambers should she make any attempt to interfere tonight."

"Which is why you got here so quickly."

Goliagoth nodded.

"You should have been watching my Yasamin!" Amir screamed at Goliagoth. "Fool, she's the one missing!"

The giant soldier bowed his head. "You are right, sire, I was only aware of the First Queen's displeasure. The thought anyone else might wish the Second Queen harm, occurred not to me. If you wish to relieve me of my command ..." Goliagoth made to remove his sword.

"No! No, you're the best in Dragonval. I need you. You had the presence of mind to watch a source of trouble you knew about." Amir poured himself another goblet of wine and gulped it. He glanced at the maids on the floor. "You think they were involved?"

"No, sire, they are only guilty of being terrified. I would place my reputation on it."

Amir downed another cup of wine. By now the room was half-filled with soldiers and a few of the King's advisors who had heard the commotion. He glanced at them.

"Get out! All of you! You, too, you useless sows. Get out!"

The sudden shift in Amir paralyzed the crowd for a moment.

"I said 'GET OUT'!" He threw his goblet at them. The cavorting goblet with its spraying red wine galvanized them into action. Within seconds the room was empty.

"Shut the door, *Demolisherian*. Lock it. I have something to tell you. It may be the answer to this quandary. But if you repeat a word of it, I swear I *will* have your head and nail it to my front gate. Come here."

Little did the king know a similar conversation was occurring in the basement of the palace.

Chapter 35

She tried everything, covered every inch of the wall. There were no hidden exits. The only two windows were high up the wall—both barred. The door at the top of the stairs was bolted from the outside.

Frustrated and sickened by the statues, Yasamin returned to the windowless bedroom with Fleuise. For a while, she tried to entertain the child by letting her wear her wedding veil and telling stories. Nothing totally removed Fleuise's fear, but she finally fell into a restless sleep.

Yasamin watched the sleeping child. She realized where she was but not why The Collector had abducted them and brought them to his house. The one thing of which she was certain was it had something to do with her grandfather. Mosesra had warned her, but she had let her guard down. Now it appeared she and Fleuise might pay the penalty.

A slight sound penetrated Yasamin's contemplation. Someone had entered the outer room and was moving toward the door where they were. She glanced around the room for a weapon. There was nothing except one small statue of a naked woman near the bed. It wasn't large, but it was heavy. Yasamin grabbed it, moved closer to Fleuise and placed the statue beneath her torn wedding gown.

A heavy wheezing announced the person's approach. He soon filled the doorway.

"I see Your Highness is awake."

He entered the room and approached the bed. As he did so, the candlelight revealed him more clearly. Yasamin involuntarily drew back, not so much from the disfigurement as the sense of evil emanating from him.

He wore a black cape with a hood, which he now threw back. He laughed a hoarse cackle that sounded like a wounded crow. "Your Highness is offended by things not so beautiful, is she?"

Yasamin's stomach crawled, but she fought back the bile and forced herself to look directly at him. His left eye was missing, the lid rudely sewn shut. The right cheekbone had been shattered and caved in, so the right side of his face appeared flattened with no structure beneath. Above his broken nose, a huge knot nestled in the middle of his forehead that twisted to the left. His lips were blood-red against his fishbelly-white skin, and they drew back as he cackled. Yasamin could see the black gaps of missing teeth.

"I am not offended by things unsightly; I am offended by sick, evil people who prey on hapless victims."

His laugh ended abruptly, and his eye narrowed in fury. "Don't push your luck, bitch. You're only alive because *I* say so. You're not a ruler in this house."

"Perhaps, but neither are you. I am alive because my grandfather wishes it."

For a moment, The Collector gaped at Yasamin, his mouth slack in surprise. He moved a little closer. His foul breath almost gagged her. "*You* know about your grandfather? How?"

"Does it matter? I know he is alive, that he is your ruler and that he wants me."

Rage exploded through The Collector. "You're just a stupid woman. You think you know everything, but you know nothing. Serpata is the supreme ruler, and when he's through with you, you'll be sorry—you'll be dead."

Yasamin shrugged, exhibiting a calmness she did not feel. "If I am dead, then I am dead. There is nothing more you can do."

"Really? That just shows how little you know. Serpata's going to make you suffer, more than you'll ever guess."

"How?"

The Collector's eye shifted toward Fleuise, and he grinned. "Serpata has his ways."

Yasamin's mind flashed back to the scene on the silk screen and how The Collector had looked at her when she was a baby. "What do you mean?" Her voice trembled despite her brave front.

"You'll see, *Highness*." The man let the title drip in sarcasm. "You'll see." The man moved closer and let his one good eye roam over Yasamin. "Such soft skin." He reached out one dirt-encrusted hand and rubbed Yasamin's arm. "Just like your mother. I bet you're sweet-tasting like her, too." He moved nearer and ran his hand upon her shoulder. He leaned into her hair and breathed deeply. "Sweet, like melons. I bet these are like melons, too." He reached one hand down and grasped one of her breasts.

Yasamin almost gagged and thought she would throw up. He was so revolting. She shoved him away. "Do not touch me, Collector. How dare you put your hands on me."

"Feisty, too, just like your mother. Maybe that's why you interest me. I like a lot of fire."

"You will burn in it if my grandfather finds out your plans. I am not a fool. My grandfather wants me a virgin. That's the reason he had you abduct me on my wedding night—before my husband came to me. He will kill you if you defile me." Yasamin's heart raced. She hoped she was saying the right thing, was on the right track. If she wasn't, both she and Fleuise might die in this room within minutes.

She evidently said the right thing.

The Collector reluctantly removed his hand. "Stupid woman. Maybe he just wants you for himself. Ever think of that? And he's a lot uglier than I am. There'll come a time when you'll wish you'd been a lot nicer to me."

Yasamin could think of nothing to say.

"Not so high and mighty are we now, Highness? Like I said, Serpata has a big surprise for you, and you'll suffer plenty," he guffawed. "Oh, yes, you'll suffer plenty, and I'll enjoy every second of it."

His glance again strayed to Fleuise who stirred in her sleep, and the stare grew bolder. He spread his lips in a lewd grin.

"Don't even think about it," Yasamin's words were low but authoritative.

"You're in no place to tell me what to do."

"Touch her, and I'll tell Serpata what you tried to do with me."

"So what? I didn't do anything with you. Serpata'll know I didn't. He has ways he can tell I didn't."

The Collector started to reach across the bed toward Fleuise.

"I said leave her alone." Yasamin pulled the figurine from beneath her skirt and brought it down on the man's left arm with all her force.

"*Yeooohw*!" The Collector screamed. He jumped back from the bed and cradled his injured arm. "You broke it."

"I doubt it, but I swear I will if you touch her. The only way you'll get her is over my dead body. What will Serpata say to that?"

The man hopped from foot to foot. "You stupid, stupid, bitch. You'll be sorry, I promise you." His shouts dwindled to a whine. "You'll see. You'll be sorry. So sorry. I'm going to enjoy every minute. As for the girl, I'll have her when we're through with you and him."

"*Him*? Who?" A cold knot of fear tied itself around the base of her spine. "Who?"

The Collector realized he'd said too much. "You'll see," he repeated. "You'll see, and you'll be sorry."

He started to go. "Oh, yes, I almost forgot." He fumbled with a small bag tied to his belt. "Serpata said wear this." The Collector tossed something at her feet. "So put it on. If you don't, I'll rip that wedding dress off you and dress you myself. I'll be back later."

He hobbled out the door. Yasamin heard the distance *click* as he bolted the outer door behind him.

The young woman bent over and picked up the cloth. It was a simple, black, cotton dress much like the older peasants wore. She gripped it as she remembered her last vision: Arash on the ground with the thugs beating him. Her thoughts ran rampant.

She was deathly afraid but not just for herself.

She was afraid for Arash. She knew Serpata had him, would torture him.

He would torture Fleuise as well.

He would torture both the people she loved before he sacrificed her.

With a heavy heart, Yasamin began undressing.

* * * * *

It had been at least half of an hour since her encounter with The Collector. Thankfully, Fleuise had slept through it all and had no idea what lay before her. Yasamin sat on the bed in the black outfit. She had discarded the torn wedding gown but tied the cord and purse around her waist. She needed her mother's book as close as possible. She stared at it now as her mind sought ways to escape. She could think of nothing.

With the book lying on her knees, Yasamin looked at the sleeping child: the picture of perfect innocence. Yasamin gently smoothed Fleuise's hair away from her face. She had to protect her somehow. She must never let Fleuise fall into the hands of her grandfather or The Collector, for what they would do to her was far worse than death. She had to get the child to safety even if it meant loosing her own life. Yasamin continued to softly caress Fleuise's head. She had to get her free. If only she could find a secret passage or overlooked key.

Sighing, Yasamin looked back at the open book lying in her lap.

There was a time when people knew many things closer to the true way of life. Unfortunately, much of that knowledge fell victim to the relentless march of time. Mighty civilizations rose and crumbled. Peoples came and vanished. For many ages, this knowledge from those distant times was kept alive by the ones who remained pure in heart. Handed down from generation to generation, this knowledge was revered, respected and, most of all, believed.

Yasamin's breath caught in her throat. She had just *read* the passage. She quickly grabbed the manuscript with both hands and thumbed through the manuscript. Just so many meaningless words again. Yasamin frowned. Why had the knowledge disappeared? Time was rapidly running out.

Frustrated, Yasamin laid her head back on the pillow and closed her eyes. What could she do? Something. Something to help Fleuise.

Believe, Yasamin.

Yasamin opened her eyes. Where had that come from? Someone had spoken.

Believers become fewer and fewer, destroyed by conquerors. Another voice, a different voice from the first, whispered the words.

… By progress demanding facts and data that delegated such things to the arena of folklore or fairy tales. Yet another voice whispered.

… And, unfortunately, destroyed simply by the growth of human greed. Yet a fourth voice murmured.

Yasamin sat up in bed and grabbed the candlestick. She held it high in the air. There was no one in the room.

"Believe, Yasamin." Mosesra's voice was beside her ear.

"Yasamin, believe." Shar's voice came from above her.

The young woman looked up. Against the dark ceiling, she saw the twinkling of tiny lights. A shiver ran across her skin, leaving goosebumps in its wake—not from fear, but from sudden awareness.

The tiny, blue light detached itself from the rest and descended. It bounced in front of her, then moved to Fleuise. For a second, it gently lay on the sleeping girl's cheek, and she smiled. The blue dot slowly circled Fleuise, then flew back to the rest. As suddenly as they appeared, they were gone.

Yasamin gently smoothed Fleuise's brow once more.

Love.

Love was the answer. When she had been so worried about saving this child, the book made sense.

She *could* get Fleuise to a safe place.

With that thought in mind, Yasamin went back to the book.

* * * * *

Half of an hour later, Yasamin knew she was right. There was much to learn, and she would. The most pressing thing was to get Fleuise to safety and find Arash. She had to do it alone. No one would believe what she had learned from the book, and that disbelief would counter her work.

She started to wake Fleuise. At the same time, she heard movement at the door.

"Fleuise, sweetheart, wake up. Wake up. We must go."

The child stirred and tried to rub the sleep from her eyes. "Where?"

"We're going to get out of here. Come on."

"But ..."

"Trust me, Fleuise. Just trust me."

Yasamin heard the scraping of a key against metal. She placed her hand, palm outward, in that direction and imagined a iron padlock on the door. She heard the scraping of the key a few seconds longer, then it was replaced by a loud thumping as if someone were throwing himself against the stout door.

Fleuise stood with mouth hanging open. "Did you do that?"

"I'll explain everything later. Just trust me for now, please?"

Fleuise nodded. "I do. I'm not so scared when I'm with you."

Yasamin drew the child against her. "I love you, Fleuise. I'm going to get you out of here. Just don't be scared by anything you see. It will not hurt you. I promise."

"All right."

The thumping became louder. It sounded like more people had joined the onslaught against the door.

"Here goes."

Yasamin turned toward the bedroom door and put Fleuise in front of her. She stared at the door and believed it opened to a tunnel that ran through the outer room, through the outer wall and to another place.

She believed it so.

She willed it so.

She willed it, so Fleuise would be safe.

As Yasamin stared at the wooden doorway, a soft light began to shine around the edges of the door—a dim, twinkling, blue light.

"What's that?" Fleuise whispered in awe.

"Shsssh. Just watch."

The light grew brighter.

"Let's go." Yasamin held out her hand to Fleuise. "Don't be afraid, sugar-plum. Everything you will see is good. Believe me."

The small child unhesitatingly placed her tiny hand in Yasamin's and said, "I do."

Yasamin walked to the bedroom door and opened it.

She could still faintly see the horrendous statues. She could still faintly hear the splintering of wood as more bodies threw themselves against it.

But the tunnel ...

The tunnel was crystal clear, made of gleaming golden silk that shimmered and danced with twinkling lights. It formed a passageway through the outer room and the outer wall.

"Let's go." She walked forward.

The two of them moved through the sparkling passageway, floating three feet above the floor. They walked toward the shining gold door, terminating on the other end of the tunnel.

Yasamin knew where she was going.

She was taking Fleuise out of the castle.

To a place where there was no darkness.

To a place where the child would be safe no matter what happened.

And then,

And then she would return for Arash.

Chapter 37

"What do you mean she's gone? How can she be gone?"

"I don't know. I swear I don't. She just vanished. I bolted the door from the outside. I swear it. I left her in there, sitting on the bed with the dress you wanted her to wear. The door was still bolted when I returned. It wouldn't open. It took three of us to knock it down. I swear it. Ask them. They're just outside."

Rattles vibrated violently in the darkness. "You brought them here, fool?"

The Collector was trembling. He had never heard the snakes rattle so loudly. "Y-yes. I'll show you I'm telling you the truth. They can vouch for it. I'm not lying."

A single, gnarled hand appeared in the dim light. The sight stopped the man as surely as if it had flattened itself against his mouth.

"Quit jibbering. Bring them."

"Yes, Highness." The Collector scrabbled to the entrance of the tunnel that led directly to the outside. "Come here. He wants to talk with you."

Three men crept in the room. They were big, tough-looking thugs with faces that evidenced many battles, yet they trembled like palsied, old men as they slinked into the chamber. They peered through the gloom, trying to fathom their surroundings.

"He tells me he had trouble with his door." The voice hissed through the silence.

The bravest of three spoke up. "That be right, sire. The bar still be on the door and the key still in the lock."

"And it took all of you to knock it down?"

"Right you are. Don't know why. It were an oak door and it be tough. There weren't nothing barring it on the inside neither."

"Yeah," the second man piped up, "it was a sturdy one, all right. I bruised my shoulder on it."

"Never seen nothing like it. We ain't weaklings, but it took us a good while to bust it down."

"I see. Well, it seems you're telling the truth."

"Yes, sire. I told you I wasn't lying."

The man who had spoken first peered through the darkness but couldn't see anything. "I was wondering. It was hard work and all."

"Yes?" The word was almost a hiss, a sound that sent a chill up The Collector's spine, and he took a step back.

"Well, we worked hard to get that door down for The Collector and all. And Bothwelly, here, stove up his shoulder fairly bad. I was wondering if we might get paid a little something for our efforts?"

"You want payment?"

"That's right. Just a little something. For our effort and time, you know."

"I believe that can be arranged. The three of you come up here. I'll see that you get your reward, each of you for your effort."

The mention of reward emboldened the men. They straightened and headed toward the voice.

They moved four feet.

It was the last move each of them made.

Before they knew what was happening, huge snakes lunged into the circle of faint light and coiled around each. The huge spirals of the snakes' bodies wrapped around arms and legs, rendering the men immobile. They then continued up to the neck where the serpents tightened their hold, cutting off the men's air and their shouts for help. As the men struggled within the coils, the snakes bared their poisoned fangs and struck at the men's faces. Each strike ripped a huge gash into the skin as if it were mere paper. The men's eyes grew wider in terror, and they opened their mouths in mindless screams.

After delivering at least a dozen blows to each human, the snakes drew their heads up into the air and plunged into the mouth of each man. They went down the throats and bit their way through until they exited each man's chest with his heart in their mouth.

Even The Collector, as cruel as he was, closed his eyes at the gruesome sight.

But not Serpata. Through the entire ritual, his hissing laugh was heard, accompanied by the steady beat of the pulsating rattles.

Chapter 38

Yasamin reached for the handle of the golden door. She gently pushed the latch, and it swung open. "Come, Fleuise, you'll be safe here."

The child followed her through the door into the glowing cavern. "Where are we?"

"Somewhere you will be safe from everything. I have wonderful friends here who will protect you. This way. Come."

They went through the outer chamber and into the second where the flowers grew.

"It's beautiful. I like it here," Fleuise whispered as she looked around.

Yasamin studied the child. She never asked how she got from a prison to the cavern but accepted it as real. Mosesra had been right about children, especially this one.

"I'm glad. You are going to stay here for just a little while with my friends."

"But I want to go with you. I want to help you."

"I need you to stay here for now, Fleuise. I know you will be protected here better than I could ever do. 'Tis a good place. Come on, let's find my friend."

Holding Fleuise's hand, Yasamin entered the third room. Mosesra sat at the table. "Yasamin. It's good to see you."

"And you, Mosesra. Thank you for your help."

The old man shook his head. "I didn't do anything really, except encourage you a little. Everything else you did on your own."

"You and Shar were there for me when I thought I was defeated. You gave me hope."

Mosesra bowed his head in acknowledgment then looked at Fleuise. "And this lovely child?" He winked at Fleuise. She blushed.

"Fleuise. Mosesra, I have a great favor to ask of you."

"You have but to ask. You know I shall do it if I can."

"I would like Fleuise to stay here at Sorania with you. I must return to Dragonval to help my friend. He's a prisoner there. I know she will be safe as long as she is here."

Mosesra smiled. "Of course, my dear. We shall take good care of her." He grew solemn. "You realize what you are up against? You will be facing your grandfather, Yasamin. He is very powerful."

"I know, Mosesra, but I will not leave Arash there."

"Serpata is a most evil power, but there are others who have chosen the dark side. They will try to destroy you as well."

"I have to try and save Arash. Do you know where he is?"

The old man hesitated. "He's in Serpata's dungeon beneath the palace. The entire subfloor is a labyrinth of tunnels and cells. Your grandfather's quarters lie beneath the oldest part of the palace directly below the Counsel Chambers. There are two entrances, one lies through the numerous old burrows beneath the castle. Another is slightly shorter—an outside exit that begins near the tunnels carrying water to the kitchen."

"Thank you. I have to go. He's hurt, and Serpata will torture him. I—"

Mosesra grew solemn. "I know you care for Arash, Yasamin, but remember there are others in Dragonval who are victims too. Be careful not to narrow your vision so much you miss the truth before you."

"I will remember. Now I must go."

"May the light go with you. Come, Fleuise, I have someone I'd like you to meet."

Yasamin was afraid the little girl would hesitate, but once again, she was surprised. Fleuise went straight to Mosesra. Yasamin's last glance before she opened the door to the tunnel was that of the old man with Fleuise on his knee watching a small blue light bobbing in front of her. The sound of laughter followed her as she closed the door.

Chapter 39

Goliagoth fastened a third sword to his belt. His head was still reeling from the information King Amir had given him. The story was too incredible to believe, yet he believed every word of it. To think King Serpata still lived beneath the palace was staggering, but the rest of the story Amir told him chilled Goliagoth to the bone.

All these years he had not been serving Amir but a man who was suppose to have been dead: a man who had supposedly sold his soul to the evil one.

Goliagoth shook his head, trying to clear his thoughts. He could only handle one thing at a time. At the moment, the most pressing was to find Yasamin and get her out of Serpata's hands, if, in fact, that was where she was. The oath he'd sworn to the King compounded the situation. He had decided not to take any soldiers with him. If he did and they discovered Yasamin in Serpata's chambers, the King had ordered him to kill the soldiers once Yasamin was free, as they would have forbidden knowledge.

Goliagoth frowned. What kind of man was Amir? If everything he'd said was true, if Serpata did live underground, if he *had* sold his soul as Amir had indicated, if such a thing could be done, why had Amir forbidden him to kill such a monstrosity? Instead Amir had ordered him to kill his own men, good men, so they couldn't tell anyone of the monster.

Because he's just as bad. He'd rather serve a bad master to keep his power than be a just man. The thought blasted into Goliagoth's mind. He grunted. Thoughts like that bordered on treason and would get him killed.

Truth is truth. Acknowledging truth shouldn't be treason. Better to die for the truth than live lies. Goliagoth hit his head against the stone wall of his cell. He didn't have time for debates—with himself or anyone else. Yasamin's life was at stake, and he was the only one who had the means to free her.

Lighting a torch from the hearth in his quarters, Goliagoth grabbed his shield and headed for the oldest part of the castle. Somewhere there were stairs leading to the subchambers. He had to find them, then find his way to Serpata.

For the first time, Goliagoth prayed; he prayed he'd be in time to save Yasamin.

After a long search, he found the stairs tucked away behind a grand staircase rising to the second floor. They were old, rough and lichen-covered. Each step had a dent worn in the middle from the thousands of passing footsteps through the centuries. He quietly descended. The air was stale, full of mold and dust and the hint of decay.

Gritting his teeth, Goliagoth moved forward. He wandered for what seemed hours. He took a right turn and ran into a dead end. Backtracking, he turned left: another dead end. Swearing under his breath, Goliagoth retraced his steps. He could spend years down here and never find the way. For the thousandth time, he wished the King could have been more specific about the way. Time was not a luxury. It was running out for his Queen.

Chapter 40

Yasamin cautiously opened the tunnel door. No one was around. She was in the courtyard, not too far from the castle's kitchens. Breathing a sigh of relief, she pushed the door open a little farther and squeezed herself through. She closed it and heard a small pop. The door was gone. She stood in the middle of the courtyard.

Alone.

Staying in the shadows, Yasamin ran toward the pipes coming from the river. Mosesra said the entrance to Serpata's quarters was near them. She followed the ducts away from the castle.

At last she heard the murmuring of water and saw the river. The entrance must be near. She searched among the boulders for the entrance into the hillock beneath the pipes. She had almost given up hope when a small *delitere* ran across her path. It squeaked and scurried toward a bush where it abruptly disappeared.

Disappeared.

How could it just disappear?

Yasamin slowly approached the bush. Gently pushing it aside, she discovered a small hole in the hillside. The *delitere* had obviously gone into the opening. She would never had discovered it if it had not been for the small animal.

Warily, she entered. It was dark, dank and muddy. Yasamin wished she had thought to bring a torch. She would feel her way forward, and if it got too dark, she'd have to take the time to go back and find a light.

"*Why, Yasamin? You have the means.*"

The slender woman jumped. For a second, she thought Mosesra was in the tunnel with her. He wasn't.

But he's right. Yasamin smiled. She stopped and picked up small branch blown in from some ancient breeze. Holding it before her, Yasamin gently blew. A faint glow gleamed at the edges. She continued to blow, and the luminosity grew brighter until she saw the floor. Holding the torch above her head, she slowly moved forward.

The path sloped downward. Yasamin continued, her eyes glued to each turn in the tunnel. She didn't want to barge into Serpata's chambers. In her concentration, she didn't see the *delitere*. She stepped on its long tail, and it squealed.

Yasamin jumped backward just biting off the scream about to emerge from her own mouth. The *delitere* scurried for the cave's opening.

Breathing a sigh of relief, Yasamin rounded the bend.

Right into The Collector's arms.

"Well, well, Highness, ain't we lucky. Here you are right at our front door. You've got some explaining to do. And we've got something special for you. Come on."

The Collector roughly twisted Yasamin's arm behind her and pushed her forward.

Chapter 41

Another dead end. Goliagoth swore for what must have been the hundredth time and brushed the cobwebs from his face. If there were a hell, it must be like this place. Sunlight and fresh air were nothing but distant memories. His whole life was composed of nothing but ancient rocks, dust and darkness.

Despite his impatience, Goliagoth retraced his steps and looked for the last mark he had made. Time had no meaning down here, for there was no light or dark, only the heavy blackness, which his torch barely penetrated. The hair on the back of Goliagoth's neck rose. *If this torch goes out down here, I'll never find my way out.* Goliagoth forced the thought from his mind. The torch wouldn't go out. He'd brought another. If the second one burned low, he'd go back and get more, but he would not give up the search.

Somewhere down here in this hell, Yasamin was a prisoner.

He would find her.

He would find her ... or die trying.

Chapter 42

For him, time had ceased long ago. He faded in and out of consciousness. It was always black, even with his eyes open; therefore, he no longer opened them.

The pain was always with him.

Relentless.

Excruciating.

Death would be a relief. He wondered if he could will himself to die.

On the heels of that thought came another.

He couldn't. He had to know what had happened to her.

If it meant bearing unbearable torture, he'd bear it.

He'd hang on, somehow, someway.

Despite his pain, he managed a weak smile. He'd hang on just as he was hanging suspended in air.

His arms had long ago grown numb. He knew they still existed because of the agonizing pain in his ribs.

It was hard to breathe hanging this way.

And getting harder.

What was the point?

And where was he?

More importantly, where was Yasamin?

He would hang on. He would hang on until he learned what had happened to the woman he loved.

And with that thought, he drifted back into blessed unconsciousness.

Chapter 43

"Look what we have here. She stumbled right in our front door. Can you believe it?" The Collector laughed.

Yasamin peered into the darkness. She saw nothing but the outlines of things in the dark chamber.

"Where are we?" she whispered.

"Well, your Highness, you're so smart. You should know." The Collector cackled again. "You're right where you were supposed to be: your new home ... for a while."

"Gargolen, put her in the red chamber until it's time."

Yasamin's mouth grew dry at the sound of the voice. It slid and slithered through the darkness toward her. Despite her resolve to find Arash, she shivered.

This fact did not go unnoticed by The Collector.

"Ha-ha. Not so brave are we now, your royal bitch. Know where you are, do you?"

"Gargolen! Your mouth flaps loosely." A soft rattle underlay the hissing voice.

"But she knows who you are already. She told me. How does she know?"

"We'll find out. There are preparations waiting. We must do the ceremony properly, and we do not have a lot of time. Do as I ordered."

"Yes, Highness." Gargolen tightened his grip on Yasamin's arm and savagely twisted it higher. "Come on, Queen, your room awaits." He roughly pushed her forward. "You'll find your accommodations not quite as fancy as what you're use to, but they'll just have to do." He pushed her through an open door and slammed it behind her. She heard the bar slide into place.

Yasamin shifted to a sitting position and rubbed her aching arm. It was pitch black, and she had lost her torch in the scuffle.

Yasamin slowly felt around. She sat on a cold, stone floor. She reached outward.

Nothing.

Crawling slowly, she kept investigating. At last, her fingertips encountered a table leg. She rose, finding her way by touch. On the top, she found a candelabra. Closing her eyes, she concentrated.

She couldn't hear Mosesra's voice.

She couldn't hear anyone's voice.

Yasamin shivered. She felt alone.

Abandoned.

No, she was here for a reason.

Somewhere down here was Arash.

She was here to save him.

Concentrating on Arash's face, Yasamin tried to forget her own fear.

She touched the candle and thought of Arash.

She could find him if she could see him.

She could save him if she could find him.

The wick exploded into a weak flame, but the effort exhausted Yasamin. She slowly took the burning candle and lit the others. Glancing around the room, she saw more. She went around the chamber lighting every candle.

There wasn't much to see. The walls were hewn rock as was the floor. A bed, a bedside table, a desk and a chair comprised the only furnishings. By the one door, she noticed a mirror. There was nothing else.

Yasamin moved to the bed and lay on the crimson covers. She was terrified. Simply lighting the candled had depleted all her energy.

If she concentrated, she might be able to construct another tunnel and escape.

But if she did, she would be leaving Arash to die in this underground prison.

Of that there was no doubt.

She couldn't. Love wouldn't let her. She might not be able to marry him, but she could not leave him to die.

Never.

Her grandfather had mentioned preparations and a ceremony. What kind of ceremony could he possibly mean? It had to be important if he was willing to keep her prisoner, while he attended it.

Yasamin wearily propped herself up on the pillows and reached for her mother's book. Pulling the candles closer, she began to read. Perhaps she could learn enough in whatever time she had to save Arash.

Chapter 44

She must have slept because the rattling of the door awakened her. Yasamin slid the book beneath her.

Gargolen entered with a tray. "Here. Eat. His Majesty wants to talk to you soon. He wants you to keep up your strength," the deformed man snickered. "Not that it matters much." He dumped the tray on the bedside table and left.

Yasamin glanced at the tray. She did need her strength if she was going to fight. The food surprised her: fresh apples, apricots, grapes and peaches lay on the plate, dewdrops still on them. In a small bowl was a hunk of white goat cheese and a piece of bread. A goblet of wine finished the meal. Yasamin cautiously sniffed the fare. She could detect no unusual odor on the food or in the wine. The thought hit her that if her grandfather wanted to talk to her, he probably wouldn't drug her beforehand.

Yasamin nibbled the food as she continued to read her mother's book.

All too soon, she heard the bar being removed from the door. She hastily stuffed the manuscript into its bag.

"King Serpata wants to talk now. Come on." The Collector left the door open and disappeared. She heard his voice from the other room. "Come on, or I'll drag you out."

Yasamin rose from the bed and smoothed the cotton dress. As she passed the gilded mirror, she automatically glanced at it to arrange her hair. There wasn't much she could do without a comb, but it didn't matter. What mattered was her grandfather seeing her calmness and dignity. Out of habit, she reached for one errant curl to push it from her forehead. She froze. Casadra's reflection stared back at her.

"Come on, we don't have all day." The Collector's voice cut through the silence. "You want me to carry you out here?"

Yasamin blinked, and the image was gone. Her own reflection stared back at her. Turning, she walked into the outer chamber. One lone chair sat in the middle of the floor, flanked by two candelabras. Beyond it sat a huge, bulky desk.

The Collector appeared in the spotlight. "Sit there." He pointed to the chair.

Yasamin moved toward it. As she did, she noticed two things that struck terror in her heart. Four masked men stood in the shadows. Leather masks covered their heads; the leather formed to resemble a dog's head topped by two horns.

The second thing was far worse. What she had thought to be a desk was a huge, black stone. Two sets of chains and shackles were at each end.

It wasn't a desk; it was an altar.

Yasamin sat but not because she had been told to.

She sat because her knees wouldn't hold her up.

Chapter 45

"It's been a long time, Yasamin." The voice slithered toward her. "Your mother defied me and shamed you when she denied you your destiny.'"

Yasamin raised her chin defiantly. "My mother was a good woman. She didn't shame me. She saved me from your depravity."

"Silence, girl," the voice roared. It was accompanied by an angry rattling. "Your mother was a fool. She could have had power, wealth, anything in the world she wanted had she obeyed me. But she ran, like a rabbit, a scared little lamb. And she cost me. SHE COST ME A GREAT DEAL!" The room vibrated from the thunderous voice. It bounced off the stones and pounded against Yasamin's head.

Serpata moved into the candlelight, and Yasamin gripped the arms of the chair. If she had been capable of movement at that moment, she would have run.

Anywhere.

Any place away from the atrocity before her.

Serpata stood over six feet tall. His shoulders were almost four feet wide. Three huge snakes, their bodies the thickness of a man's thigh, grew from each shoulder. Their bodies coiled and squirmed around him. Each snake had slit, red eyes and fangs over three inches long. The heads snapped at the air, at her, at each other. They were in constant movement. She could see the tails of the snakes hanging from the back of Serpata's shoulders. The tails reached the floor. At the end of each tail was a vivid green rattle the size of her hand.

"Do you see, girl? Do you see what your fool of a mother cost me?" Serpata glared at her. His own eyes were slit like a snake. His skull was bald, his ears nothing more than slits in the bone. He was covered head to toe in scales. He pointed at her. In the feeble light, Yasamin saw each finger was gnarled like a twig and ended in a talon. "But your mother wasn't as smart as she thought. I am more powerful than she imagined. I arranged to have you brought back. I will finish what I started, and I will rule the world." He smiled, revealing pointed teeth: his incisors long and curved just like the serpents coiling around him.

"My mother was no fool. After all, she got away from you. I chose to come here. I chose to help the people of Dragonval."

Serpata's laughter roared. "You? A mere child? Help the people of Dragonval? Pathetic. You are nothimg more than a sheep walking into the wolf's mouth."

"Really? I knew you were here. I chose to come in spite of you."

"How could you possibly know?"

"She told me. Everything." Yasamin nodded toward The Collector. "Even about him and how he wanted to have her and me before he brought us to you."

Serpata frowned and looked at Gargolen.

The Collector cringed. "She's lying. She's just trying to cause trouble, your Highness. I would never cross you."

"Not if you value your life." Serpata looked back at Yasamin. "It does not matter. You are here, and you will meet your fate. Then I will become ruler of the world."

"I don't think my husband would approve of your plan. Once he finds out what you plan to do."

"Amir?" Once again Serpata laughed. "You had almost convinced me you had some sense. You are a stupid child. Amir is mine. I rule Dragonval from here. All I have to do is offer Amir a little more power, a little more land, and he'll forget all about you. He'll find another pretty face to fall in love with."

Yasamin's mouth went dry, but she kept a brave face. "Amir loves me. He went to great lengths to get me here in order to marry me. He has told me so many times."

"Amir loves himself. He loves power, money. He may lust for you, girl, but love? He doesn't know the meaning of the word. But I tire of this fruitless conversation. The dark moon will soon commence. At that time, I will offer you to my ruler and fulfill my pact. He will then grant me what I desire and return me to my glory."

"You plan to sacrifice me like you did my brother years ago."

"So your mother did tell you everything."

"As I told you."

"The sow hurt me. Unfortunately she died before I could have my vengeance on her, but I will have something almost as sweet."

"What is that?"

"I will see you suffer before I kill you. Not as good as seeing your mother suffer but almost."

"And how do you plan to do that? When you kill me, it's over."

"Oh no, girl. I'll watch you suffer terribly before you die without touching *you*."

Something dark fluttered through Yasamin's heart. "How would you do that?"

"Like this." Serpata raised one twisted finger toward the high-domed ceiling, and a light appeared.

Now that she could see better, Yasamin gasped in spite of herself.

Arash hung suspended from the ceiling. His shirt was torn away. Wires twisted around his wrists pulled his arms above his head and hung him from the distant beam over them. Blood dripped from gashes in his head. Despite the distance, Yasamin could see the terrible bruises on his body.

"A-ha. I see the fear in your eyes. That's a foolish move on your part, child. It lets me know I have the upper hand."

"What are you going to do to him?"

Serpata chuckled. "Why, have some fun." He grew serious. "And when I tire of that, I will kill him."

"You are heartless."

"Yes, gives me more power. Behold and learn a little something, girl."

Serpata pointed his hand toward Arash and balled it into a fist. He swatted the air so hard, Yasamin could hear the *swwissssh*. Twelve feet above them, Arash's head bounced backward from an unseen blow, then fell forward. Yasamin saw a new wound on his face.

"Or this." Serpata put his hands side-by-side and began to twist.

High above them, Arash's torso began to contort, and he screamed in pain.

"Or one of my favorites." Serpata made a half circle with his right hand and began closing the gap between his thumb and fingers. Arash's head raised, and the veins bulged. His mouth opened in a soundless scream as he gasped for the air that couldn't pass down his throat.

"Stop it. Stop it, now." Yasamin screamed. She could not bear to watch the torture inflicted on Arash by the monster before her. "You've proven your point. You're powerful."

"*I* know that, girl. And now so do you. I enjoy having the fun." He raised his hand to deliver another blow.

Yasamin stood. She straightened her back and lifted her chin. "Serpata, I *demand* you release him."

Stunned by her defiance, Serpata forgot about the blow. He simply stared at her. His body began to shake, and Yasamin thought he was having an attack. Then laughter erupted from his mouth as it flowed up from his belly.

"You *demand*?" He alternated between spasms of laughter and coughs. The snakes twisted wildly. "You *demand*?" As suddenly as it started, it stopped.

The silence was deafening.

Serpata glared at Yasamin. "You are more foolish than I thought. You are in no position to demand anything. I am ruler here."

"Let him down, Serpata. Let him down, and let him go."

"Or what? What do you think you have to bargain with, fool?"

"What you need most, myself."

"What jibberish is this? What are you talking about?"

"Let Arash go, and I will willingly lay myself on your altar."

Serpata started to laugh but stopped. Uncertainty flashed across his face. He leaned forward slightly, and his forked tongue flashed toward her. He leaned back and sniffed again. "You have nothing to bargain with. You are still a virgin. I smell it. I will kill him, and I will slay you on my altar."

"No, you won't."

Serpata looked at The Collector. "Did you hit the bitch on the head?"

"No, Highness. We never hurt her in any way."

"Then she's crazy."

"I am not crazy, and look at me when you speak about me, Serpata. I answer for myself. I will say it once more. Free Arash and I will stay."

"You tire me with your meaningless jabber." Serpata raised his hand toward Arash.

Yasamin's eyes followed it, then continued upward to look at the hanging man. Tears filled her eyes. His pain was her pain. Without moving her gaze, Yasamin whispered. "I mean it. If you hurt him again, I *will* walk out of here now, and you cannot stop me. You'll lose everything, again. Your power is no stronger than mine."

"You *are* crazy." Serpata's eyes narrowed with fury. "I will not tolerate such impertinence. I am sore put not to slay you now!" he screamed.

Yasamin glanced at the monster, then raised her arms outward until she formed a cross with her body. "Try it. See what happens."

"Get her!" Serpata screamed at Gorgolen.

The Collector grabbed a metal bar and ran toward her. He swung it at her head, then fell back screaming. The pole dropped at his feet and disintegrated.

Serpata roared in anger. "I'll kill you now!" He moved forward and swung one mighty arm toward her. "Die!" His hand stopped about one foot from Yasamin's head. White lightening wrapped itself around his hand. Serpata screeched and backed away. The snakes snapped at Yasamin, their rattles vibrating furiously.

"What is it?" he shouted. He rubbed his smoking hand.

"As I said, set Arash free, and I will give myself up for your sacrifice; otherwise, you have nothing."

"What trick is this, girl?"

"It is no trick. It is truth. It is light. I travel the road of silk."

If such a thing were possible, Serpata appeared to shrink in on himself. "You're too young to know such a thing," he whispered as much to himself as her.

"No one is too young to know right from wrong, *Grandfather*. You chose darkness for your own selfish end. I choose light to help those I love. Let him go if you want me."

Serpata stared at his granddaughter for a long time. At last, he nodded toward The Collector. "Release the wires."

"You're setting him free?"

"Do it."

The Collector stepped toward two wheels on the wall. Winding them counterclockwise, Arash's body began to lower to the floor. When he reached the concrete, Arash lay lifeless.

"Arash!" Yasamin cried. She rushed to him and cradled his head in her lap. "Arash, can you hear me? Open your eyes, please. Talk to me."

Arash's lids fluttered open. He gazed at Yasamin. His cracked lips tried to form her name.

"Arash, you must get up. You must leave now while there's time." Even as Yasamin spoke the words, she saw Arash's gaze drift past her.

She turned just as The Collector grabbed her and pulled her to her feet. "Got you now, bitch. Not as good as you think. You can't do two things at once."

It was at that exact moment someone else spoke. "Let her go."

The Collector swung Yasamin around and hit her on the jaw. As she went down, she saw Goliagoth, sword in hand, standing in the doorway. She thought it, but she couldn't get her mouth to form the words "look out."

* * * * *

After countless wrong turns, Goliagoth had heard a noise. He had slowly crept toward the sound and saw a feeble light. It had to be Serpata's chambers. Extinguishing his torch, he had slipped forward and hidden behind the curtains hanging in the doorway.

He had heard most of the conversation.

He had heard more than he had wanted from Serpata.

He had not heard enough from Yasamin.

His mind had worried furiously, trying to think of a way to save both her and Arash. He could think of nothing until Yasamin had demanded Serpata free Arash. Calmly. Rationally. Queenly. She had *demanded* the monster free him. Unable to believe the drastic change in the conversation, Goliagoth had peeked through the curtains.

He had seen Yasamin facing the monstrosity standing before her.

He had seen her outstretched arms and heard her quite voice.

He had seen the white fire flicker around her as The Collector had swung the metal bar at her.

He had seen the white lightening flash around her as Serpata had slashed his monstrous hand at her.

He had seen it all.

But he did not understand.

It defied all reason.

For a moment, he was hopeful they would all escape … until Arash was lowered to the ground and lay unmoving, until Yasamin hovered over his motionless body, oblivious to the communication between Serpata and Gorgolen, and The Collector had grabbed her.

He had to act fast. Sword drawn, he dashed through the curtain.

"Let her go!" he shouted.

The Collector hit her, and Yasamin went down but not before Goliagoth saw her glance to his left and her mouth move. He swung and saw the four men moving toward him with swords of their own. He charged.

The blow did not knock Yasamin unconscious. She was dimly aware of Arash's body next to her, of The Collector running and of Goliagoth fighting the four dog-headed men. She was also aware of Serpata withdrawing to the shadows. She pushed herself up and tugged at the wires wrapped around Arash's wrists. The metal had dug into his skin, and it was slippery with his blood, but she managed to get him free.

"Arash," she whispered. "Arash you must get up. We have to get out of here." She frantically rubbed his face and his arms, trying to get the sluggish blood moving. After a few moments, he opened his eyes.

"Yasamin? Am I dreaming?"

"No, darling. I'm here. Goliagoth's here. We've got to get out now. Try to get up, please. Try."

Arash tried to rise, but his extremities had minds of their own. "I can't. You go."

"I will not leave without you." Yasamin tried pulling him to a sitting position. Arash struggled with his heedless limbs.

Goliagoth saw them from the corner of his eye. The man was lucky to be alive but was in no condition to run. He was going to have to get to them and carry Arash out.

The men's masks worked to his advantage. It didn't take long to dispatch them.

He whirled and started for Yasamin.

He then heard the hiss. "Don't let her escape."

Goliagoth whirled but couldn't see Serpata. He turned back to Yasamin and saw The Collector running toward her with a dagger. Trying to help Arash, Yasamin didn't see him coming.

There wasn't time to yell a warning and her be able to respond.

Goliagoth sprinted.

Yasamin stood and turned to see Gorgolen upon her.

Goliagoth yelled "Highness!" He wrapped himself around her and was pushing her down as The Collector struck.

For a second, time stood still. Goliagoth held Yasamin in his left arm. He turned and slashed backward with his right hand.

The Collector's head fell to the floor.

"Are you all right, Highness?"

"I-I think so. We have to help Arash. He can't walk."

Goliagoth stared at her. "I know." His eyes glazed slightly and he stumbled. Yasamin put her hand out to steady him, then drew it back. Blood covered her hand.

"You're wounded! Goliagoth, here

"It is nothing. Just a flesh wound." He knelt to pick up Arash.

"You will not leave this place alive."

Yasamin whirled and saw Serpata reemerging from the shadows. Anger contorted his face, and the snakes hissed and struck the air around him. He appeared to glow red. His voice grew louder and began to change: became rougher, like hundreds of voices speaking.

The evil one was coming. He was coming through Serpata.

Neither Arash nor Goliagoth would live if she failed them now.

"Be still. Do not move—remain exactly where you are." Yasamin's voice was low but commanding. "Whatever you do, do not move from the spot you are in."

She bent her head. Her silver hair covered her face and reflected the flames now coming through vents in the ground. She whispered something and straightened. She walked around the two men—Goliagoth on his knees with Arash half on his shoulder—and touched each. She then returned to the spot where she had stood. Once more, she raised her arms so she formed a cross. A pale blue light burst from her fingertips and followed the trail she had made. The light went around the three of them, then through them—bouncing and refracting until it encased them in a dome that gleamed in the darkness.

"You are not wanted here," Yasamin intoned. "Go back to the depths from which you crawled. I will not be your sacrifice. You cannot touch me here in the Castle of Silk. You cannot touch me or my loved ones. Leave, I command you. Your servant, Serpata, has failed you once more. You shall not have your sacrifice. Return to your hole."

The earth trembled. The rock walls shivered. The flames lowered, then hissed out.

Serpata stood alone.

"It is finished, Serpata. Your ruler has left you alone. Let us go."

"Never. You haven't won. Not yet. He left me to fight the battle to prove my loyalty. I still have my powers."

To prove his point, Serpata pointed to a jagged rock hanging from the ceiling.

It fell.

It landed on top of the lighted dome and shattered.

But Yasamin could feel the weight. She could not withstand that kind of pressure long without crumbling.

If she crumbled, the two men would die.

She desperately prayed. There had to be a way to destroy Serpata. Mosesra had told her there was a way; she would find it in her heart. She had to find it fast. She was in Serpata's domain where his power was strongest. She could feel the darkness of the place squeezing at the Castle's walls.

Serpata laughed. "It's a losing battle for you, girl. You haven't the intelligence to outthink me."

He pointed at a boulder lying on the ground. He swiftly pointed from it to Yasamin. The boulder flew through the air and hit the side of the Castle. Yasamin felt a slight pain in her temple.

He could not win. She was in the Castle of Silk where the powers of all followers of the light were with her.

She shook her head. She thought her ears were ringing from the blow.

The noise grew louder.

It wasn't a ringing; it was thousands of voices whispering—*samin, Yasa —lig—Yas—li.*

The voices grew stronger. Clearer.

Yasamin, Yas—lig—Yasamin, light, light, the light.

The whispers flew around her.

Through her.

Inside her head.

Outside her head.

Yasamin saw Serpata move his hand toward another gigantic boulder. He was laughing. Evidently, he did not hear the voices. "I told you, girl, you're nothing. This is *my* domain. Down here in the darkness you're nothing. The darkness is my domain, *my* power." Relishing the moment, he paused and grinned at her. "Mine, all mine."

The meaning clicked.

She understood the voices.

The darkness was his domain.

The light was hers.

Yasamin smiled. "You're wrong, Grandfather. You're wrong about my mother, and you're wrong about me. Behold."

Yasamin pointed at the high-vaulted ceiling. There was a slight shift, a drizzle of loose dirt.

"Behold your grandaughter, Serpata."

A rock fell from the ceiling, then another. A shaft of daylight streamed through the opening and lit Yasamin.

Another rock fell and another one. The sun began to shine through.

Bright, dazzling sunlight.

"Behold your enemy, Grandfather."

A large section of the roof fell. Brilliant sunshine flooded the room. Serpata screamed and threw his hands over his eyes. Rocks continued to plunge down. None touched the Castle of Silk.

None of them hit Serpata.

It didn't matter.

The scales of his skin began to glow, then hiss. Small puffs of smoke crawled from beneath them. The hissing became louder, transforming to sizzle. Serpata screamed. The snakes squirmed wildly. They coiled and twisted around his body. In their agony, they began striking Serpata. Huge slits appeared. He futilely tried to shove the serpents away. That failing, he sought to wrap his huge hands around their necks and choke them. Again, his attempts were futile. The rattling of their scales grew more violent until the chamber vibrated from the noise.

A great ripping noise echoed over the rattling. Serpata threw back his head and howled. The snakes detached themselves from the man and squirmed toward one of the vents in the floor, leaving gaping holes in each of Serpata's shoulders. He tried to staunch the ooze flowing from the wounds. In a vain attempt to hide from the sun, Serpata turned for one of the tunnels.

His legs could no longer hold him. His toes and fingers burst into flames.

The flames grew.

Serpata's unearthly screams filled the room as he combusted into a human torch.

Yasamin turned from the sight. "Come, we need to leave now."

Goliagoth hefted Arash over his shoulder. "Lead, your Highness. I'll follow."

Yasamin quickly picked her way amid the falling rocks toward the outer tunnel. They then ran through the passageway.

Serpata's screams followed them but soon ceased.

Her grandfather was nothing more than ashes and the stench of sulphur.

Chapter 46

The battle between Yasamin and Serpata did not go unobserved. Vulmire and Medusimia watched the confrontation in the pool of lava deep in the man-beast's cave.

Seeing Serpata's destruction, Vulmire laughed. "One of our stumbling blocks crushed. The throne will soon be ours." He waved his hand over the glowing magma, and the images disappeared.

"How can you be so sure? And what is this thing the wench has, this road of silk she mentioned?"

The morning after the ceremony Medusimia had packed a few things and moved to Vulmire's cave because the scales were becoming more noticeable. She didn't want Amir to see them. She scratched at the scales behind her ear, then those on her thigh. The things were irritating as they grew.

"I've never heard of it. Is it some sort of magic?"

Vulmire murmured low in his throat as he rubbed Medusimia's belly. The child was already beginning to show. His hand went lower, and he nibbled at her ear. "Just so much smoke and mirrors, my queen."

"But she destroyed Serpata. He's ruled Dragonval for decades. It worries me." Medusimia felt her juices stir as they always did at the man-beast's touch, but at the moment, her desire for power had the upper hand—one thing at a time. She took his hand and stopped its downward trail. "If she can do that, shouldn't we worry?"

Vulmire sighed and removed his hand. "No. Come, Medusimia, I want some wine. I'll explain why."

The two of them moved to the large chamber. The beast man poured each of them of goblet of blood-red wine. "I've already explained how Serpata received his power."

She nodded. "I have to say I am amazed how he ruled for so long, and I didn't know he existed. All this time, I thought Amir was the strong one."

"His ambition combined with his ego was Serpata's downfall."

"I don't understand."

"Serpata agreed to sacrifice his two grandchildren. He thought himself so powerful he didn't take precautions to make sure that would happen, and Yasamin escaped. For that reason, Serpata was punished."

"That much I grasp."

"Serpata never thought he deserved that punishment, so he didn't actively pursue a course that would rectify it as soon as possible. He simply sat back and dreamed of the day Yasamin would fall into his hands. In his mind he would then instantaneously become ruler of the world."

"Meaning?"

"Meaning if he had sent someone to kidnap Yasamin while she was yet a babe when he learned where she was, he could very well be the supreme ruler of the world today."

"But he didn't."

"No, he did not. If he had, we would have a harder time gaining the throne. The second biggest mistake Serpata made was thinking he was the most powerful man on earth. Bezembu has many followers, and he rewards them as to their allegiance. Serpata was not his only follower. I serve him, too. You've seen my power. Whatever kind of human we were before choosing Bezembu as our lord also dictates the extent of our power. Serpata was a selfish, lazy man before he chose Bezembu; therefore, he opted to use his power for immediate gratification instead of thinking things through and choosing a wise course."

"But if he is all-powerful ..."

Vulmire sighed. Sometimes the woman had a one-track mind that could not see the whole picture. "That is precisely it, Medusimia, none of us who follow Bezembu are all-powerful. If we were, he knows we'd be tempted to try and overthrow him. Of course, we are more powerful than any human, but being all-powerful does not mean simply being the strongest. We still need to act wisely. We're capable of greater thought than mere men are, so we must think prudently. Serpata didn't want to join me. Together we might have overthrown the world, but he wanted it all to himself. I decided to use my wit. I made one mistake by acting in haste; I will not make the same mistake twice."

"What did you do?"

"I tricked Serpata. I put what he wanted most in his hands. His ego did the rest."

"Vulmire, don't be so obtuse. Explain yourself. Why don't we have to worry?"

The man-beast drained his glass and poured another. "Forgive me if I'm boring you, but I think a little boasting is in order, seeing how my plan worked perfectly."

The Queen sighed. "You're not boring me. I'm sorry. I don't know why I seem more irritable lately and snap at things I shouldn't."

Vulmire smiled and patted her stomach. "It's natural. After all, you are to be a mother; irritability is just part of the package."

"So what did you do?"

"I worked a spell on Amir. It worked very well."

"What kind of spell?"

"A love spell, my darling. Why do you think Amir is so besotted with Yasamin?"

Medusimia sat upright, anger flashing in her eyes. "You worked a love spell on my husband? You're the reason he married that milksop of a girl? How dare you?" She raised her hand. She wanted to slap the smile from his face. Vulmire grabbed her wrist.

"Not so fast, my lovely. Let me explain. I think you'll come to realize it was to your benefit as well. I would hate to ruin this celebration with a fight. But if you want to start something, I will finish it."

Medusimia lowered her hand. Fury coursed through her veins, but she was not in a position to do anything about it. "Very well. Explain."

"I knew if Amir got Yasamin to Dragonval, Serpata's ego would take over. Here's the girl who escaped now in his territory. Serpata thought he only had to destroy her, and he would be returned to his full glory. He never stopped to analyze why Amir was so in love with *her* of all people. I'd bet he thought Bezembu was giving him another chance to show his loyalty."

"So you wanted the throne for yourself. It didn't matter to you that I had to suffer the humiliation of having to share Amir?"

"Medusimia, listen carefully. You never loved Amir; you loved the *power* you thought he had. You love the power being Queen gives you. The humiliation was and is simply in your mind. As for the throne, yes, I want to rule, but unlike Amir, I want you as well. I watched you for years, biding my time until the opportunity presented itself. I knew you craved the power as I craved you."

"Vulmire?"

"Yes?"

"Did you work a spell on me as well? Is all of this because of some words you mumbled?"

"Do not belittle what I can do. But no, Medusimia, I did not. I wanted you to come to me by your own free will. I wanted you to choose me over the King because of my power, because of what I could offer you that Amir couldn't."

"But what if Serpata hadn't tried to destroy Yasamin? Why did you tell me you would destroy her before she reached Dragonval?"

"You'll have to forgive me for that little lie. Honestly, at the time, I wasn't sure where you loyalties truly were. I couldn't have you running to Amir and saying something that might ruin my plans."

"Maybe. I was furious. The only thing that got me through that time was the thought she would be dead. But what about Serpata? What if he hadn't—"

"I study my enemy. I knew Serpata would not pass up the opportunity to restore his former power. If for some reason he didn't try, I would have destroyed Yasamin at the appropriate time. I don't want her gaining too much strength."

"Which brings me to my original question? What is this power?"

"There are those of us who follow Bezembu, and we are many. On the other hand, there are those who are followers of what they call 'the Light.' Not as many as there use to be. We destroyed a great many, and far too many humans prefer an easier road. But there are a few. Yasamin's mother was one. Somehow Mosesra got hold of Yasamin and taught her some of their teachings. She knows some things, but it's obvious from what we saw she's a novice."

"Who is Mosesra?"

"He is recognized as the leader of the followers of the Light, if that word can be used. They don't like ranking titles."

"You said you thought he was the one who taught her."

"There are strengths and weaknesses on both sides, Medusimia. This is why I'm careful with my plans."

"How?"

The core, or heartland, for these people is Mount Sorania. Whenever they do something outside this mountain I can track them. But there is too much power in the mountain. I cannot see what happens inside their holy place. The same is true with me. Unlike Serpata, who enjoyed making his power known, I do my planning and most of my work here in the cave where I cannot be seen by Mosesra or anyone else. The power is too strong; however, outside they can track *me*. They know of my existence, but they have only seen what I wanted them to see. They think I am a simple man-beast who goes out at night to grab livestock or some hapless human to feed myself. They know nothing of my plans. In fact, Serpata took much of the blame for my strategy."

"Yours?"

"Yes. Until our power is stronger, I don't want them to know anything about me. Unlike Serpata, I have planned every step of this scheme."

Medusimia found her anger was subsiding as admiration grew for the plan unfolding before her. "So with Serpata dead, we can take the throne?"

"Patience. There are a few pieces of groundwork that still remain, especially since I've learned Yasamin follows the road of silk. I want to catch all the players and destroy them. Then it will be too late for Mosesra or anyone else to interfere."

"But her power?"

"I study my adversary, Medusimia. Perhaps you did not notice that there is a flaw in the belief of the followers of the Light. I plan to use it to my advantage."

"What flaw?"

"Didn't you notice Yasamin and the two men? Had she been by herself, I doubt she would have had the strength to save herself. It was her will to save those she loved that gave her the strength to escape."

"How is that a flaw?"

"The light followers believe in doing only *good*." The word dripped from Vulmire's mouth as if it were something repulsive, then he grinned. "They cannot use the power for selfish purposes. This is where Serpata made his big mistake. He tortured Arash. Everything he did to hurt Arash and the soldier only fueled Yasamin's power. As I said, she hasn't had the time to study the road of silk for long. Someone like Mosesra would be a real threat for he has been around hundreds of years and has the experience."

Medusimia frowned. "I am lost."

Again Vulmire sighed. Sometimes she was like a child, incapable of seeing things that were so obvious, but he had the patience. After all, she carried his baby.

"We do not do anything that would fuel Yasamin's power. The idea is to make her feel as if *she has* done wrong. And that, my darling queen, is where you come in."

"Really? What do you want me to do?"

Vulmire smiled and placed his goblet on the altar. "Come here, Medusimia. Pleasure me first, then I'll tell you exactly what you are to do. Once you've laid the groundwork, the throne will be ours in a short time."

Medusimia grinned and pulled the beast man's loincloth from him. She climbed into his lap. "I look forward to sitting on the throne *almost* as much as I enjoy sitting on this."

She slowly began rocking back and forth in Vulmire's lap.

Chapter 47

She has passed one hurdle.

Mosesra moved to the fire and poured water for some tea. He cradled the warm cup in his hands and savored the brew's sweet smell. He was proud of Yasamin. She had demonstrated the goodness deep in her heart, but worry still nagged him. Her powers were amazing, their depth almost overwhelming for the short time she had been studying, but she would also have to learn discipline to be able to control them and not let them control her. There was much heartache ahead, and he prayed she would have the courage to face it. The powers would not reveal her final choice, and that worried him somewhat. His biggest fear was she might turn from her path, might turn sour over some of the losses she had to face.

Mosesra closed his eyes. If he had to fight Yasamin, she would be a formidable enemy, but that wasn't what scared him. She was his own flesh and blood, the one he had placed his faith in as being The One. Everyone believed him a holy man, and although he tried his best to follow the Light, he was a man as well. The thought of having to destroy his granddaughter tasted sour in the back of his throat.

Mosesra set his tea down. He wished Shar were with him. She was the only one who would listen and not judge him any less a holy man for having these doubts. But even Shar couldn't help him with this. If Yasamin turned, he was the only one strong enough to destroy her. And he couldn't hesitate. If Yasamin turned, she would be strong enough to destroy the world as they knew it.

He bowed his head and prayed Yasamin would find the strength she needed. And that he would, too.

Chapter 48

Medusimia hurried through the courtyard and up the back stairs to Amir's chambers. With all that had happened, she was positive her husband had not noticed her absence.

Vulmire's plan was perfect.

It would rid them of Amir and Yasamin.

Composing her face to be a mask of wifely concern, Medusimia entered Amir's sitting room.

He was pacing back and forth on the balcony. He occasionally glanced toward the main avenue to the castle.

"Amir?"

He jumped and swung toward her. "Medusimia? What are you doing here?"

"I thought I'd come see how you were doing." In truth, Amir looked terrible. She wasn't sure if the strain that deepened the ridges on either side of his mouth and clouded his eyes was due to losing his benefactor or Yasamin. She could almost understand the first, but she had no pity for the second; however, that didn't matter. What mattered was to set Vulmire's plan into motion.

"Have you eaten anything?"

Amir came inside and poured another glass of wine. "No. I cannot. I'm too upset."

"Perhaps I could get the cook to prepare you something special. Is there anything—"

"I don't want any food!" Amir shouted. Realizing how foolish he must appear, he amended his tone. "Thank you for your concern, but I can't stomach anything until I have learned about Yasamin."

"Oh. Yes. I am so sorry about that, Amir, but how could you have known?"

"How could such a terrible thing happen here in my own castle under my nose?"

"You must admit that I did try to warn you. A pretty face can hide a lot of secrets."

"Secrets? What are you talking about?"

Medusimia forced a look of contriteness on her face. "I'm sorry. I spoke out of line."

Amir moved toward her. "What are you talking about?"

"Perhaps I should ask that of you. What terrible thing are you talking about?"

"Fool! The kidnapping, of course. The fact someone could steal my wife from me on my wedding night. The fact someone could kidnap her from right under my nose."

"Oh. I am sorry, Amir. I did not realize you didn't know. I spoke in haste. I should leave." Medusimia bowed her head to hide her smile, then quickly turned. She hadn't taken two steps before Amir's voice lashed out.

"Wait! Come here."

Medusimia turned. "I didn't mean to cause you more grief. I really should go. I-I thought you knew; otherwise, I would have kept my mouth shut."

Amir's face had already crimsoned. "I said 'come here.' Now, Medusimia."

She slowly turned and moved back toward him. She had chosen her wardrobe carefully to hide her filling figure and left her hair down to cover the scales. The next few minutes would be crucial. She had to get him angry but not angry enough to grab her. She stood before Amir with her head bowed. She carefully forced tears to her eyes and fidgeted with her hands, so she would appear anxious.

"Look at me."

She did as she was told.

"Now tell me what you are talking about before I beat it out of you."

"I heard part of it from one of the dignitaries, the rest …"

"I don't care about where. *What* did you hear?"

"Arash is a prince from the land of Pars. He was with Yasamin in Gwendomere. The reason she disappeared on your wedding night is … well … she didn't want you to find out she is not a virgin."

"What?"

"Yasamin and Arash are lovers, husband. She has played you for a fool. She agreed to the marriage, so you would not attack Gwendomere. They were together all the time after the shipwreck. Perhaps she lost her nerve when faced with bedding with you."

"You're lying, whore! She would not insult me so. She is innocent."

"She has a beautiful face, an innocent face, but that does not mean she cannot lie. I am sorry, Amir. I thought this was why you were so upset."

"It cannot be true. You're jealous. You're the one lying."

Medusimia lowered her eyes, then glanced back up at Amir. Tears ran down her cheek. "I understand why you would think that, Amir. I wasn't very pleasant about the situation, but I didn't trust her the moment I laid eyes on her. If you don't want to believe me, there are others who have seen her who will tell you it is true."

"The Demolisherian was there with them. He would not have let anything untoward happen."

"Perhaps she dazzled him as well. He's been seen with her quite often. Remember he is the one who brought her to the chapel for the wedding. Do you think that was just coincidence? And where was he after the wedding? Don't you think that odd?"

"He was wa—" Amir stopped. He only had Goliagoth's word where he had been. A small doubt began to worm itself through his mind.

"But she wanted to marry *me*. Why?"

Medusimia shrugged. "I don't know. As I said, perhaps it was to keep you from attacking her country. Maybe she didn't think her plan through and only realized her one flaw when she was to bed you on the wedding night. She panicked. Or perhaps Arash decided he didn't want her to be with you."

The Queen took the goblet from Amir's hand and filled it. While her back was turned to him, she dropped a white powder into the glass. It contained the antedote for the spell Vulmire had placed on Amir. "Drink this, darling. You look as though you need it."

Amir drained the cup and shook his head.

Medusimia sighed. "I did not want to believe it either, for your sake. It's horrible for her to make you suffer so much anxiety, while she's so happy. I wanted those rumors to be wrong. I thought I could prove them wrong, but ..."

"Go on."

"I went to Arash's chambers. He wasn't there. I know why now. Anyway, I looked around, and that's when I happened to see this on the table by the bed." Medusimia unwrapped the handerchief in her hand and held the contents up to Amir. "Do you recognize this?"

Amir took the jewelry and held it closer. "This is the garnet necklace I gave her. She wore it the night of our betrothal ceremony."

Medusimia nodded. "I thought it was. It was on the stand beside the bed. I don't think Arash stole it. Since he's a wealthy prince, he has no need to steal. I can think of only one explanation why it would be there."

"But it doesn't make sense. How could she explain having been with a man? I would know immediately."

"Amir! Think! She was 'kidnapped' before you bed her. All she has to do is claim one of the attackers raped her. Then she is a victim, a poor victim for you and the entire country to grieve for."

It sounded plausible. A burning rage ignited in the pit of Amir's stomach and boiled its way upward. "How do you know Arash is a prince? He has nothing and said nothing since he's been here."

"Of course not. He couldn't have you knowing he was royalty." Medusimia began to relax. All of this was this was the truth and easy enough to check if Amir chose. She was thankful Vulmire had filled her in with some vital information to make the story believable.

Amir's temples throbbed as the veins popped into bold relief beneath his flushed face. He could hear his heart pounding in his ears as the image of Yasamin writhing beneath Arash flooded his brain. He threw the necklace across the room where it shattered.

He looked at Medusimia. The pupils of his eyes shrank to pinpoints, then exploded until they filled his entire eye. Pupil and iris were one—a cold, black void, a bottomless pit of hatred and rage. Amir had given his entire heart to the dark side. Had there ever been any love within him, it was dead. He would not stop until he had his revenge.

"The lying bitch made a fool of me. I'll have her head. I'll throw her to the soldiers first and let every man in the barracks have his way with her. I'll nail her naked body on the door for all to see what happens to one who betrays me." Amir trembled so violently dregs of wine sloshed from the goblet. He threw the cup across the room where it shattered beside the necklace. "I'll drag her through the streets, so the citizens can see her for the trollop she is." Spittle flew from his mouth and sprayed Medusimia. She moved back. "Amir, calm yourself. Think, then act rationally. Make the citizens see you as the victim, not Yasamin. You have no 'attackers' to bring forth as witnesses, but you can prove your case by simply proving Arash is a prince. On that alone, everyone will believe the rest. Say nothing to anyone until you have gotten Yasamin and Arash here. Then confront her before witnesses. If you are careful, you win this situation. Do not attack Arash. Portray him a victim, the same as you. We do not need to go to war with Pars at this time. Put the blame where it belongs, directly on Yasamin's head."

"Yes, yes, you are right." Amir's hands clasped and unclasped as if he were imagining them around Yasamin's thin neck. "He will be grateful to be returned to his country with his head. He'll go along with me to save his own hide. Yes, I see it clearly now. Thank you, Medusimia. I will not forget your loyalty."

"I love you, my darling. I may not always behave as I do—I have a bad temper—but I do love you. I hate seeing you embarrassed in such a manner. What is best is always foremost in my mind."

Medusimia bowed her head and closed the door behind her. *So easy. So easy when you know the way.* She smiled in the darkness.

Amir sat in the shadows plotting his revenge. Thank the stars Medusimia put his best interests first.

Had he known whose best interests were at stake, Amir wouldn't have been calculating how to ruin Yasamin, Amir would have been calculating how to save his life.

Chapter 49

Goliagoth laid Arash on the grassy hillock outside the tunnel. The young man's color was returning, but his lips were parched, and several of his wounds still oozed.

"I'll get some water. Keep him still." The soldier rose and headed for the river.

Yasamin knelt beside Arash. "How are you feeling?"

Arash's lids fluttered, but as he focused on Yasamin, he smiled weakly. "Better than I was."

"You took a terrible beating. I am so sorry, Arash. It's all my fault."

He shook his head. "No, it wasn't. Don't blame yourself."

"I should have been more careful. I knew about Serpata. I knew he wanted to kill me. I just didn't think he'd go after anyone else."

"How could you know about him?"

"It doesn't matter, darling. I'll explain later. Right now we need to take care of you. Just lie still. Goliagoth is bringing some water."

As if on cue, the soldier appeared. He had his helmet full of the cool liquid. He knelt. "Lift his head slightly. Let's see if we can get some of this down him."

Yasamin raised Arash's head, and Goliagoth tilted his headgear to the boy's lips. Arash began to drink greedily.

"Easy, boy, not so fast, or it'll come back up. Take your time."

Arash slowed his gulps.

"Enough for now. You can have some more in a few minutes." Goliagoth set the helmet aside and, with experienced hands, began checking Arash's wounds. After a quick exam, the soldier looked at Yasamin. "Not too bad considering what he's been through. He's got some bad bruising but no broken bones. I need a rag of some kind."

Yasamin grabbed the hem of her gown and ripped part of it away. "Here, will this do?"

"Better than nothing." Goliagoth took the cloth and dipped it in the water. He blotted the bleeding wounds. "These aren't as bad as they appear, mostly superficial. Head cuts always bleed the most. Hold on." Once more, the giant moved toward the tunnel's entrance. He disappeared inside for a second, then reemerged with a handful of cobwebs. He placed them on the wounds. "These will help staunch the flow. I have some powders in my quarters that will stop it altogether. When we get back to the castle, I'll get them."

Yasamin watched the soldier administer the primitive first aid to Arash. His skill and dexterity amazed her. "Thank you, Goliagoth."

"Just trying to keep him in one piece. You feel any better, boy?"

Arash nodded. "I could use some more water."

Yasamin frowned at the soldier. "Can he?"

"As long as he takes it slow. Lift his head."

Yasamin did, and Goliagoth lifted the helmet. This time Arash drank slowly but deeply. At last he sighed. "Better." He closed his eyes, and Yasamin shifted, so he could lay his head in her lap. Arash drifted to sleep.

Yasamin watched him for a moment, then glanced at Goliagoth. "Is he all right?"

"I think so. Just exhausted. Rest is the best thing."

Yasamin continued to stare at Arash and gently smoothed his hair, oblivious to the fact Goliagoth studied her.

In time, he spoke. "Highness?"

"Yes, Goliagoth?"

"How did you end up in Serpata's chambers?"

"The Collector kidnapped me outside Amir's rooms. He was Serpata's son."

"I didn't know Serpata had one." Goliagoth hesitated, then began once more. "Arash was with you in the hallway when you were attacked."

"How did you know?"

"Blood on the floor. You have no wounds. It is the only explanation."

"Yes, he was there."

"Why? Tell me the truth, Queen Yasamin."

Yasamin stared at the soldier. If she told him the truth, Goliagoth could destroy both of them, yet she detected no animosity in him. And he had just saved both their lives. He had done so much for her he deserved no less than the truth. She sighed.

"Arash was trying to talk me out of staying in Dragonval with Amir. He thought I was in danger, and I was making a terrible mistake by becoming Second Queen." That much was the truth.

"From who?"

Yasamin shrugged. "From Queen Medusimia and I guess others who might see me as a threat. I cannot say. We were interrupted during the conversation." Half a truth but still she couldn't place Arash in danger.

"I don't understand why Serpata saw you as a threat to his position. Amir's on the throne, and as king his orders, whether from him or Serpata, couldn't be usurped by you."

"Serpata was evil and powerful, and he ruled Dragonval through Amir. He didn't see me as a threat; he saw me as sort of a salvation."

Goliagoth frowned. "I do not understand."

"There are a lot of things happening right now, Goliagoth—too many for me to try to explain everything to you at this moment, but I will. I promise. I can tell you this much: Serpata was my grandfather. He sold his soul to the evil one to have power. He killed my father, his own son, when my father found out. Serpata had also promised to sacrifice my twin brother and me to further his own power. My mother found out and escaped with me."

Goliagoth shook his head. "Your father was killed in an accident."

"No, he was not. Trust me. I am telling you the truth. I heard it from someone who knows. But that's not the point. Serpata became the monster he was because he failed to sacrifice me. That was his punishment from the evil one. He thought if he could sacrifice me, while I was still virgin, he would regain his favor and be restored to power."

Goliagoth rubbed the frown creasing his forehead. "Nothing is as it seems. Nothing's as I was told, yet your words have the ring of truth in them."

Yasamin reached over and touched the soldier's arm. "Goliagoth, I am telling you the truth. In your heart, you know it is. Now tell me how you found me."

"King Amir. He told me about Serpata, except he said Serpata saw you as a threat. He was afraid if you produced an heir, when the time came, Amir would pull away from him in favor of putting his own son on the throne. He said he'd had several arguments with his uncle over the issue."

"I do not believe that. I'm sorry, Goliagoth. I know you owe your allegiance to Amir, and I don't know why he would tell you this, but Amir *served* Serpata. He wouldn't do anything to endanger himself, even if it meant giving up his own son. At least that's what I believe."

"Whichever it might be, King Amir wanted you back bad enough to send me to get you. If what you say is true, the king would be endangering his own life."

Yasamin thought about it for a moment. "You're right. If Amir sent you to save me, he would be defying Serpata. There is some part of the puzzle missing. I need to figure it out." She gazed at Arash. "And he almost lost his life because of me. I should have sent him away when we first arrived." She gently touched Arash's face, much as a mother would a child. "I should've insisted he return home the minute we landed. I never thought about him being in danger."

The soldier watched Yasamin's delicate fingers outline Arash's eye, nose and full lips. He watched her and heard the softness of her voice.

"You love him." It wasn't a question; it was a statement.

"I accepted his proposal. I married him, Goliagoth. And I will be a good wife."

"I was not talking about King Amir."

Yasamin's hand stopped mid-movement. She glanced at Goliagoth. "What?"

"You love Arash." It was a statement that offered no egress.

"Yes. But you must believe me, Goliagoth; I have never been disloyal to Amir. Arash and I have done nothing to shame the king. Absolutely nothing. I came to Amir as I was when I left Gwendomere."

"I believe you. What I don't understand is why you followed through on King Amir's proposal. You've had several opportunities to get out of the contract."

"Because of something you should understand, Goliagoth—duty. And a love of something greater than myself."

"Duty?"

"Yes. I have a duty to Gwendomere. I love my people, Goliagoth. I love my country. I would do anything to protect it, them. Amir made it clear if I did not marry him, there would be nothing left of Gwendomere. I could not abandon them.

"I love Arash, but I would never be at peace or have any happiness if my love destroyed my country. Some day I would grow to hate him or blame him for that disaster. No, I love Arash enough to let him go, to find someone who can make him happy."

"I understand duty but not this *love* you speak of."

"Love? Surely you remember how it must feel. Can't you remember your mother, how she felt about you?"

Goliagoth laughed. He threw a fleeting look at Yasamin, then directed his stare at some distant horizon. "My mother was a whore who pleasured soldiers for money. She wasn't careful enough once. When I was born, she took me and made a deal with the *Demolisherian* of the post. If he would pay her six *shinas* a month, she would raise me until I was old enough for the barracks. I guess the man saw my potential. Maybe he was the father. Who knows. For whatever reason, he agreed. I know all about duty, your Highness. But love? 'Tis nothing I can see or touch. It has no meaning."

"I am sorry, Goliagoth. I had no idea."

"I need not your pity, Queen. I've done well for myself. Now I'm *Demolisherian* of the post. Not too bad for a bastard from the trash heap."

Yasamin reached for Goliagoth's arm, but he moved away. "Goliagoth, listen, I …"

"What we need to do is decide the best course of action and move on it."

Yasamin sighed. She had blundered. Nothing she could say now would rectify the situation; it would make it more painful. "If we can get Arash attended to, you need to take me to King Amir."

"You're going back?"

"Yes, Goliagoth. He sent you to get me, didn't he? I married him. He's my husband, for better or worse. I will honor my vows."

"Yes. But Arash …"

"What about him?"

"I don't believe King Amir knows about him nor that the boy was in Serpata's domain. He would've asked for Arash's head if he had known. We can get him to my quarters. I'll attend his wounds. When he can travel, I will get him back to his own country."

"You would do this?"

"Yes. It serves no purpose to muddy the swirling waters. The less said, the better. I will take you to the king."

"Thank you. How can I ever repay you, Goliagoth?"

"It is my duty, your Highness."

* * * * *

After several false starts, because Arash's knees were still rubber, Goliagoth once more hefted him over his shoulder. They hurried to the soldier's quarters.

"This powder will stop the bleeding." Goliagoth spoke to Yasamin as he quickly worked on Arash.

The white powder stank and slightly smoked as the soldier sprinkled it on the open wounds. Arash groaned in his stupor. The bleeding stopped immediately.

"Help me sit him up." Once Arash was in a sitting position, Goliagoth deftly wrapped a length of gauze around his ribs. "This will help support him while he heals. I don't think anything's broken, but he's bruised bad. Highness, please hand me that shirt."

Goliagoth quickly pulled the shirt over Arash's head and buttoned it into place. He gently laid the young man back and covered him with a wool blanket. "He needs to stay warm. Watch him while I prepare some medicine."

Moving to the fireplace, Goliagoth reached into an old, battered, wooden box and extracted a small bag. Sprinkling some of the yellow powder in a cup, he filled it with water and stirred. He returned to the bed and lifted Arash's head. "Here, boy, drink this. All of it." Arash tasted it, made a face but finished the bitter brew. Goliagoth laid him back on the cot.

"That's all we can do now. The powder will help him. I got it off an old, silver-haired gypsy. Don't know what it is, but it works. Within an hour or two, his strength will be back. Soon as he's able, I'll get him aboard a ship."

"Why are you doing this for him?"

"I owe him, your Highness. He saved my life. The least I can do is try to save him to even the score. If you are ready, I will take you to the king. I'm sure he's anxious as to your safety."

"Of course. Let's go."

With one last glance at Arash, Yasamin turned and proceeded out the door.

She knew it best if she didn't look back, just as she knew it best not to remind Goliagoth he had repaid his debt to Arash several times over.

Chapter 50

Maybe it was because his mind was still whirling from the things he'd seen Yasamin do in Serpata's chambers.

Maybe it was because his mind was already spinning a way to get Arash out of the country.

Maybe it was because his mind was so troubled trying to comprehend this love of which Yasamin spoke.

Maybe it was simply because he thought all danger was over with Serpata dead.

Whatever the reason, Goliagoth didn't notice the odd stares people gave them as they passed. His intent was to get Queen Yasamin to King Amir safely. He knew the King was worried about her safety and anxious for her concern.

In the outer chamber, the guards at the door snapped to attention as Goliagoth approached.

"Is the King within?"

"Yes, sir."

"Is he with audience?"

"Not that you can't interrupt, sir."

"Good. Let no one enter until I leave. This meeting is private. Understand?"

"Yes, sir!" both soldiers yelled.

Goliagoth opened the door and stood aside for Yasamin to enter. She passed through and walked toward the throne. Goliagoth closed the door and followed.

The room was darker than usual. Only a few lit candles adorned the cavernous room, and their light did little to dispel the gloom.

"I see you found her." Amir's voice reached from the shadows surrounding the dais. Yasamin and Goliagoth headed for him.

"Yes, your Highness. She was where you said."

"I understand you destroyed Serpata."

"He was destroyed, Excellency." Better not to elaborate too much on how; otherwise, the King would question the Queen about her powers.

"And the little lamb is returned to her loving husband."

"As you requested, sire."

Yasamin reached the area before the throne and stopped so suddenly Goliagoth almost ran into her. At the last moment, he stepped aside and avoided the collision. He glanced at Yasamin, saw her blanch, then looked to the king to see what had caused this reaction in her.

Amir sat on his elaborately carved throne of pure gold. His black clothes rendered him almost invisible. Medusimia sat in a smaller version of Amir's throne to his right. It was then the hairs on the back of Goliagoth's neck tingled and stood erect.

He knew why Yasamin had paled and now stood silent.

The twin chair to Medusimia's throne that had sat to the left of King Amir had been removed.

Something was very wrong.

A movement caught Goliagoth's eye. He glanced to his left and saw several of the King's advisors huddled in the shadows.

"Come, Yasamin. One would think you weren't happy to see your husband."

Yasamin hesitantly moved until she was at the foot of Amir's chair. "I'm very happy to be back, Amir. The whole thing was a nightmare."

"I'm sure. Having someone try to kill you can be quite terrifying." Amir's voice was cold—diamond hard. He stood and stepped down. He slowly circled Yasamin. "You look fine. Not a scratch on you. Except for being filthy and in rags, no one would know what an ordeal you must have suffered."

Amir stopped in front of Yasamin, put a finger beneath her chin and lifted her face, so she had to stare in his eyes.

His eyes terrified her. The black irises were so large almost no white was visible. It was like looking into an eyeless mask.

Or a soulless man.

"Did you suffer, Yasamin?" he whispered.

Her lips trembled, but she maintained her eye contact. "Yes, I was terrified."

"So was I, Yasamin. Can you imagine? Can you even *begin* to imagine how alarmed I was when you disappeared? I thought my heart would burst from its frantic beating. My Queen, my *wife*, kidnapped on our wedding night." He swept his arm toward the advisors. "Everyone here can tell you how upset I was."

"But you sent Goliagoth. You told him where to find me. You had—"

"Silence!" His scream shattered the quietness of the room. "Do not speak unless I tell you to."

"A lucky guess on my part. I saved you, Yasamin. I sent my man into danger to save you." Amir returned to his throne and sat. He looked at Yasamin.

He looked at the advisors.

He returned his glance to Yasamin. "I saved my loving wife, light of my life, saved her to bring her home to my bosom. Didn't I? Speak, Yasamin! Didn't I?"

"Yes," she whispered.

"And you're thankful to be home with your loving husband—you do love me?"

"Amir, I married you. Of course."

"Liar!" Again, his shout shattered the quiet.

Goliagoth felt unease squeeze his lungs. His hand subconsciously moved toward the hilt of his sword, then he removed it. There was no one here he could fight, at least with his sword.

King Amir leaned forward. "You married me to save your precious country."

"You knew this. It was our agreement," Yasamin barely managed the words between her dry lips.

"And in return for my protection of your country, you would marry me and honor that bond. Correct?"

"I have done so."

Amir leapt to his feet. His face crimsoned. "You lying whore! You can stand before me and lie without blinking an eye!"

Medusimia touched his arm. Amir glanced back at her, then sat. He still trembled, but he lowered his voice. "You played me for a fool."

Horrified, Yasamin could only stare. At last, she found her voice. "I have not lied to you, Amir. I surely have not played you for a fool. Never."

The King smiled sourly. "Really?"

"Yes."

"Stand there and look me in the eye and tell me you do not love Arash."

Not only did Yasamin's mouth drop open, but Goliagoth momentarily lost control of his own. He quickly closed it and again placed his hand on his sword. He could not use it, but it was the only comfort he knew.

"Silence? You don't speak, Yasamin. That is because I speak the truth. Answer me, woman. Do you love Arash?"

A lone tear wandered down Yasamin's pale cheek. She raised her head and straightened her back. Despite the filthy torn garment, she never looked more like a queen than at that moment.

"Yes, husband. It's true. I loved Arash, but …"

"You admit it. You played me for the fool, gaining protection for Gwendomere, a title for yourself and all the while rolling in bed like a common whore with a prince from Pars."

"No! That is not true. I admit I loved Arash. I am a woman and capable of love, of desire. But I am a woman of honor and decency, Amir. I have never been with Arash that way. I remain as virgin as the day I left my country."

"What you mean is you lost your virginity before you left Gwendomere. That is where you met him."

"That is a lie. I swear to you I have never been with Arash that way. He …"

"What was your plan, Yasamin? Did you think you could keep up the charade with me? No. So you batted your eyes at this prince to keep him besotted with you. Then you would have another country to help you once I found you out for the tart you are. Or perhaps you thought you could convince him that together the two of you could overcome Dragonval and reign in my place."

"That was never my plan!"

"Which? To keep the Prince on the hook or to overcome my country?"

"Neither. I never played either of you for a fool, I swear. I never had any desire to fight your country."

"Lies fall so easily from your lips. You don't know the false from the true."

"I do not lie. I admit I loved Arash. We were alone in the wilderness for a long time. I am no different from anyone else. I am a woman. I have feelings. I cannot prevent a thought from entering my head. This does not mean I act upon them. I value honor and truth too much. I have done nothing to dishonor you, husband. Never. You musn't punish Arash. He's innocent. He has done noth—"

Amir held up his hand to stop her. "You are beautiful, Yasamin, so beautiful it obscures your black heart. I am not going to punish Arash. I pity him. He fell for you as I did. He is as much a victim as I." Amir's voice was full of poison. Black and crawling with sarcasm and hate. He glanced at Goliagoth, and his eyes narrowed. "And as for you, *Demolisherian*, you had knowledge of this prince, yet you did not feel it necessary to inform me of his identity. In fact, didn't you take him prisoner for attacking one of your men?"

Goliagoth stared at the man he had served for decades. The King already knew the truth, even if he asked it in question form. It would do no good to lie. "Yes, your Highness. I did. He tried to prevent one of my soldiers from attacking—"

Once more Amir exploded. "I don't want excuses, *Demolisherian*! I asked you a question, answer yes or no! Did you take him prisoner?"

"Yes, Highness."

"Yet when you arrived here, you introduced him as a prince. You made no mention he had been taken a slave."

"No, Highness."

"You are an arrogant bastard, *Demolisherian*. Who gave you the power to free him?" Amir was losing control of his anger once more. He kicked his footstool from its position in front of the throne. His rage was almost palpable. He leaned forward. "Answer me, soldier! Did I give you the order to free him?"

"No, Highness."

"Then you—" Medusimia grasped Amir's arm. He leaned back, and she whispered into his ear. The two of them exchanged words with an occasional nod toward the soldier. At last the King nodded and returned his attention to Goliagoth again.

"*Demolisherian*, you have served me well over twenty years. Your record has been exceptional. Even though I am King, I am aware of the respect and awe most of the soldiers have for you. You have never given me reason to doubt you. For that reason, I am willing to listen to your explanation. Why did you free the man by your own volition?"

"He saved my life, Highness. I owed him. By letting him enter Dragonval without chains, I believed the debt paid."

"I see. A life for a life so to speak?"

"Something like that, sire."

"Hmm."

"Your Highness?"

"Yes, soldier?"

"I was with Arash and Queen Yasamin the entire trip. They never acted inappropriately. In fa—"

"Silence! As a soldier you are outstanding. If my wife wanted to couple with the man, she is capable of outsmarting you."

"But, your …"

Yasamin turned to Goliagoth. The tears glistening in her eyes clawed at his chest. "*Demolisherian*, don't. There is nothing you can say that will change his mind. You will only endanger your reputation and your life," she whispered.

The soldier wanted to pick her up and carry her out of the room. He wanted to put his hands around the throat of Medusimia who sat smirking beside Amir. And he wanted to choke back the ugly words spewing from the King's mouth.

He wanted—he didn't know *what* he wanted. He stood mute.

Yasamin turned back and faced Amir.

"You will believe what you want to believe, husband. But I swear to you on all that is holy, on my very life, I have never dishonored you. I gave you my word, and I have kept it even though it meant sacrificing my own personal wishes.

"If thinking something makes me guilty, then I am guilty. I cannot stop a thought any more than you can stop the sun from rising in the morning, Amir, and you are *King*. If you have never been guilty of having thoughts contrary to your duty then perhaps you have a right to point a finger at me." Yasamin looked at the other women by his side. "And the same goes for you, Queen Medusimia. You never wanted Amir to marry me. I believe you would do anything to prevent me from being Second Queen. Are you the one who has poisoned his mind against me with these ludicrous accusations?"

Unseen by the King, Medusimia merely lifted one eyebrow and smiled wider. "Don't try to shift your misdoings to me. I'm innocent."

Before anyone could blink, before Goliagoth could react, Amir lunged from his throne and slapped Yasamin. The sound was sharp in the silent room. "Keep your mouth shut. You can't squirm out of this. I'll send Arash home on the next boat. I have no quarrel with his country. You, on the other hand, you are a different story. You lied and cheated. You defiled our marriage bed, and you will pay. Oh, you'll pay, wench. I will amass my army, and I will march on Gwendomere. I will destroy every person, every building, every animal, every blade of grass until there is nothing. And I will salt it so there will never again be anything that will grow on that cursed land.

"And you'll see the fruits of my labor. I will bring the head of every man, woman and child and place it in the courtyard in front of your prison window. And after I've done that, I will march you through the streets naked for all to see your shame. And I will have your head. It shall adorn my front gate to show all what happens to those who betray me." He glanced at Goliagoth. "Take her away. Put her in the dungeon. Feed her enough to keep her alive. I want her to see the consequences of her actions."

Stunned, Goliagoth simply stared at the King. That infuriated Amir even more. "Now, Soldier! If you don't, I'll be forced to think you shared her bed as well and no longer owe allegiance to your king."

"Amir! Listen, please don't hurt my people. They've done nothing. If you believe I have betrayed you, punish me, not them."

But Amir did not listen.

"Amir! Please! I beg you!"

The King took Queen Medusimia's arm and escorted her from the room.

Neither looked back.

Neither saw the giant gently take Yasamin by the shoulder and lead her from the room.

Neither saw her tears.

Neither saw the tight jaw or the fury in Goliagoth's eyes.

If they had, they would have trembled.

And rightly so.

Goliagoth had made his choice.

Chapter 51

It had gone better than she had ever dreamed. She would soon be rid of both of them.

She had made the right choice. She would have everything she wanted or could want.

A smile widened her lips. *Everything* she wanted.

Medusimia lifted the goblet to her lips, drained it and poured herself another. The palace wine seemed so weak. Not full and heady like Vulmire's.

She had the maids draw the shades against the hot afternoon sun and dismissed them. She stretched out on the lounge chair. It was so much better dark. Lately, the sunlight hurt her eyes.

She longed for a bath. It would be nice to stretch out in the warm water and soak until time to return to the man-beast. She couldn't afford the risk of one of the maids entering and catching her undressed. The scales were beautiful and delicate, but they were definitely scales covering most of her body. She couldn't let Amir find out. It had taken all of her wiles to get him to leave her bedroom earlier. He had wanted her, wanted to make love to her. He had been so *grateful* for her help.

Medusimia laughed. Not that she wasn't in the mood but not for Amir. The thought of his pasty white hands and inept proddings was almost revolting. He was such a child compared to Vulmire.

She stretched again. She wished she were with him now, could feel his heat around her and within her. She tugged at the bodice of the gown. Gods, how she hated the confinement of these dresses. They were so binding and unyielding. She longed for the freedom of nothing against her skin. That wouldn't be long. In five or six hours, when it was dark, she'd sneak away. She had done what she had come to do.

The stage was set.

Amir would send the prince home.

He would destroy Yasamin.

Vulmire and she would destroy Amir.

The only remaining player was the soldier.

A wicked grin caused her to chuckle. If he sided with Amir, the man-beast would destroy him instantly. On the other hand, if he chose to follow her and Vulmire, he would be very handy, in more ways than one. She had noticed him today, standing behind the little milk-sop Queen. He was huge, almost as large as Vulmire. He was virile, and he was handsome. Medusimia felt the familiar juices stir. She hoped he would side with them. She'd like to sample him and see if he was as good a lover as he was a soldier.

She drained her glass. It didn't matter. If he did side with Amir, she could still toy with him, then kill him. Either way, she'd get what she wanted.

She laughed again and reached for the decanter.

It was then the pain struck.

Excruciating.

Unrelenting.

Red-hot and searing.

Medusimia bent double, biting back her scream. She tried to rise, grabbing for the table to help lift herself. Another wave of pain hit her, and she fumbled, knocking the decanter to the floor. The crimson wine ran on the tiles. The Queen fell to her knees cradling her stomach, biting her lip until blood came.

The agony was vicious. It crawled around her belly and into her lower back until it encircled her entire abdomen in the blazing fury.

It couldn't get any worse. Medusimia tried to breathe deeply. For a few moments, it seemed to help. She thought once of crying for help but didn't dare.

If she had been poisoned, they would call the physician. He would discover her secret. She couldn't let that happen. Better to die than fail when this close to reaching her goal.

The pain subsided slightly, and she started to pull herself back onto the couch.

The next wave hit, more excruciating than the previous, and she moaned. It engulfed her in blinding agony, and with it came the urge to push, to push away the clawing hell that tore at her entrails.

The urge became overwhelming.

She pushed.

And pushed.

It spewed forth on the floor among the red wine and Medusimia's blood. It wiggled, coiled and waved its arms wildly in the air. With disbelieving eyes, the Queen stared, unable to move. Too early. Surely too early. The urge to push came again, and Medusimia pushed the afterbirth from her body.

It continued to squirm, trying to move its extremities. At last, it turned its head and looked at her. Its face was perfect: a minute replica of her own.

Its movements became less agitated. It mewed, a soft *'mm-mm'* and grew still.

Something burst in Medusimia's heart. She quickly grabbed the tiny thing and wrapped it in a velvet throw. The umbilical cord dissolved to ash.

Pulling herself to her feet, Medusimia stood still for a moment to let the spinning in her head slow. She was already regaining her strength. She hastily snatched some cloths and water and cleaned the wine and blood from the floor. She put the dirty rags in a small bag, along with the afterbirth.

She could leave no trace of what had happened.

She could not wait until dark to leave the castle.

She could not let anyone see her leave, or she and the child would both be in danger.

Peeking through the door, Medusimia saw no one. It appeared the hallway was empty. She headed for a back exit.

She had to get to safety.

She had to get to Vulmire. He would protect them.

The plan set in motion would still work, more perfectly now.

She and Vulmire would rule.

She would be Queen of Dragonval without a doubt.

She carried the heir of the country in her arms.

Chapter 52

The torches barely lit the passage leading to the cells. Perhaps it was just as well. Dark splotches of blood, mold and fungi grew on the ancient stones. The floor beneath their feet crunched with grit and the debris of hundreds of years.

Goliagoth held Yasamin's arm, not because he thought she'd try to escape but to support her. He occassionally glanced at her. As strong as he was, he hated this place—these dank, murky cells buried in the bowels of the castle made his skin crawl. He had feared the Queen might swoon or hesitate once they entered the gate.

He sneaked another glance at her.

He had underestimated her. She was light as a feather, a wisp of a girl, yet her back was ramrod straight, and she moved forward without hesitation.

She never took her eyes from the path before her.

She never made a murmur of protest.

She never pleaded with him to let her go.

She walked in quiet dignity toward the dark unknown.

The further they descended, the greater the stench and the darkness, yet Yasamin gave no indication she noticed. Goliagoth stopped and removed a torch from its sconce.

"We'll need this to see how to proceed. There are some steps ahead."

Yasamin stood still, while he removed the torch. The flame did little to dispel the gloom. Again, he took her arm. She didn't move.

This was it.

She was going to turn those beautiful eyes on him and beg to let her go.

Goliagoth felt his breath catch in his throat. He knew what he should do. It wasn't the same as what he wanted to do.

"Goliagoth."

"Yes, Highness?"

She turned toward him. Her face was a wraith in the darkness. Despite the dimness of the light, he could see the pain and sorrow in her eyes. He thought his own must reflect the same.

And then …

She smiled: a soft, tender smile.

"I doubt the King would consider that a fitting title for me now, Goliagoth. Before we get to where the others are, I want to thank you for what you tried to do for me. I truly appreciate it, but promise you won't do something to jeopardize your own life. Amir's mind is made up. Nothing you can say will change it. You'll only end up sacrificing yourself and ruining your career."

Whatever he had expected, it was not this. The soldier simply stared at her. He cleared his throat. "I wanted him to know the truth. You were—are his wife. He didn't grant you a trial. The lowest criminal in Dragonval is entitled to that much. It isn't just."

"It doesn't matter. He has the right to dispense justice as he sees fit. He has decided my fate. If you still consider me a queen and to be obeyed, I ask three things from you."

"I will do them."

"You don't know what they are yet."

"I said I will do them."

"Thank you. The first is get Arash safely out of Dragonval. I know Amir said he would send him home, but I don't trust him to keep his word. It would be easy enough to kill Arash and say he left the country."

"I will personally see to it."

Again that beautiful smile. "Secondly, promise me you won't do anything else for me that will jeopardize your life or your career. I don't want to die knowing I was responsible for something happening to you."

"But, your—"

Yasamin lifted her chin in the familiar defiant gesture. "You said you still considered me Queen. I'm ordering you to obey. Understood? Not a thing."

Goliagoth nodded.

"Good. It's settled. I guess we should go on." She turned to proceed.

This time, Goliagoth remained immobile. "You said three things. What's the third?"

Yasamin turned back. "So I did. The third thing I cannot command as your Queen, but I ask it as a friend. It would mean a great deal to me."

"You have only to ask, Queen Yasamin."

"When the time comes, when Amir has destroyed my country and is ready to destroy me, I ask you be the one to behead me. I would rather spend my last second on earth with a friend. I know you will be swift and sure."

Goliagoth stood mute. He had promised to do her bidding. The vision of her head falling to the ground filled his mind. The pain that shot through Goliagoth's heart was searing, excruciating, consuming. It was a demon clawing and tearing his heart and lungs from his chest. It was more terrifying and sickening than any wound Goliagoth had ever received. The soldier trembled as though ill with a fever.

"I cannot, your Highness."

"Goliagoth, please. I'm not trying to be cruel. But I know you, of all people, would not torture me and make my pain last as long as possible to satisfy Amir or provide amusement for the crowd. If I have to die for my people, I will gladly. I only wish to be spared the humiliation of being the source of sick enjoyment for him and his cohorts."

"I'm not—"

"Goliagoth, if you are my friend, you will do this for me, and I will bless you for it. You will not hurt me. I go to a better place. You'll only open the door." Yasamin laid her hand on the soldier's arm. "Please say you will, my friend."

Friend?

Her hand opened a door in his mind.

They no longer stood in a putrid, dark passage.

A rainbow of light enveloped them. The colors were glorious, dazzling. The gentle fragrance of flowers surrounded them. A sense of contentment enclosed the soldier.

She removed her hand.

Again, they were in the dank passage.

The giant understood why she was not afraid of the death awaiting her.

He understood there was something more for her. He wouldn't be ending her life, merely opening the door to another.

He mutely nodded.

"Thank you, Goliagoth. We really should proceed. The guards will be wondering where we are." Yasamin turned to descend the stairs. The giant followed her.

He wasn't sure what had happened there in the darkness.

He didn't understand what had happened.

He wished he could, but he couldn't.

The one thing of which he was certain was the Queen didn't deserve to die, and if he could prevent it, he would.

They entered a large chamber of soldiers lounging, playing cards and drinking. As soon as the two entered, the soldiers snapped to attention.

Goliagoth moved forward. "Guards, there has been some trouble. Her Highness will be put in a cell here until it's resolved."

At the mention of her name, all the men knelt. Yasamin peeked at Goliagoth with a slight frown. He avoided her glance.

He kept his attention on the men. "Enough. Rise. Put her in the largest cell." He pointed to the nearest soldier. "You, get a broom and make sure it's clean. Put extra torches within for light." The soldier scurried away, cowed by the force in Goliagoth's voice.

He looked at the others. "None of you leave here. The Queen will have constant protection. Allow no one in but me. Do I make myself clear—no one. I will bring the food for her myself." He saw the glances the men threw among themselves. "I'll not take any chances of someone slipping her poison. There is such a threat.

"If anyone is disrespectful of our Queen, if you let anything happen to her, rest assured, I will have your head but not before you wish you were dead. I'll cut you to pieces myself, starting with fingers and toes. You'll cry to die long before you do. Am I clear?" he shouted.

"Aye, sir," they cried in unison.

"Good."

The soldier appointed to clean the cell returned. "Cell's clean, sir."

"Excellent." Goliagoth walked toward a wooden cupboard against the wall and yanked the door open. Inside were several bottles, wooden cups and plates. There were also several bundles of candles. He picked up one of the bottles and uncorked it. He sniffed. "King's wine?" He grabbed one of the wooden cups. "Soldier, put these in the cell. Light two or three of the candles and put them in there also."

The soldier hastened to do as he was ordered.

Goliagoth glanced toward a smaller room where several cots were visible. He pointed to the man nearest the door. "Two blankets. Put one on the cot. Hang the other over the bars for privacy."

The soldier stood still. "If she's been sent here—"

"Now." Goliagoth rested his hand on his sword's hilt. The man knocked over a chair in his haste to get the items.

Within seconds everything was in place. Goliagoth returned to Yasamin. He took her arm and led her to the cell. He pushed her in but not so hard she'd fall and followed her in. He removed his dagger and, using its hilt, hammered one of the nails holding the blanket into the wall more securely.

He raised his voice. "You'll remain here until the matter's resolved. You will not be harmed by anyone, on that you have my word." Goliagoth started backing out of the cell and dropped his knife. He knelt to retrieve it. "I'll be back, your Majesty," he whispered.

Standing, Goliagoth returned to the guards. "Lock the cell. Remember, she is still your Queen until this matter is cleared. Protect her with your lives or answer to me."

Without a backward glance, Goliagoth grabbed a torch and headed up the long, black passageway.

He didn't have time to look back.

He was too busy planning the future.

Chapter 53

"What do you mean she's in prison?" Arash was still weak, but the news about Yasamin's incarceration caused him to bolt upright on the cot.

"King Amir accused her of infidelity. Says it renders their contract null and void. Went so far as to hint she wasn't kidnapped but staged it, so she'd have an excuse as to why she wasn't a virgin."

"That's ludicrous. Of course she's a virgin. You and I both know she was kidnapped by Serpata."

"As does the King, but King Amir has twisted it around to make the facts fit his story. With Serpata destroyed, there's no way to disprove his claim."

"We have to. You and I were with her the whole trip. We both know she was not with any man." Arash rubbed his forehead, trying to absorb this new information.

Goliagoth stared at the young man for a few seconds, then shook his head. "You do not grasp it, do you?"

"What?" Arash looked up at the soldier.

"King Amir accuses you of being her lover."

"What?" Arash jumped from the bed, then fell back on it when his knees wouldn't hold him. He settled for sitting on the cot. "You are serious?"

"Dead serious. The king is furious and wants to hurt her any way he can. The only thing surprising me is he claims you are a victim the same as he. Says she played you the fool, too, so she'd have someone to fall back on in case their marriage fell through. Says he's going to send you back to Pars."

Arash shook his head. "This is a never-ending nightmare. The man is crazy.

You know I never touched her—not in that way." Arash glanced up at the soldier. "Don't you?"

"I do not think you slept with her."

"Do I hear a 'but' in that sentence?"

"I think you would have if you could have. That about right?"

"Well ... I ... it ... I wouldn't dishonor her."

"You'd make a good politician, boy. Seems to me if you love each other, 'tis a joint thing. Nothing dishonorable about it."

"Nobody said anything above love, Goliagoth."

"You don't have to, boy. I see it in your eyes when you look at her. I know the Queen is an honorable woman. She's in love with you, too, but she had to keep her word to the King. And furthermo—"

"Wait a minute. She's in love with me?"

"Did I slur my words? I said it clear enough."

"Did she tell you that?"

"Not in so many words."

Arash felt a stone lift from his heart. Yasamin loved him. Together they could do anything. The next moment he plunged into the deepest despair. Yasamin was imprisoned, and Amir wanted to kill her.

"I have to get her out before something happens to her. I cannot let Amir kill her. If I can free her and get to my father, maybe we can help protect Gwendomere."

Arash suddenly remembered Goliagoth was a soldier for the enemy. He looked at the man who had just saved his life. They might end up facing each other with swords. He didn't want that. He spoke slowly, picking his words with great care. "Goliagoth, you know Queen Yasamin is innocent of these charges, do you not?"

"Aye."

"She kept her pact between herself and Amir. What he's doing isn't right. It's not right to her or Gwendomere. Thousands will die for no reason."

"Aye."

"I have to stand beside Yasamin and her country. You're one of Amir's soldiers, but I hope we don't face each other on the battlefield. I have come to respect you, *Demolisherian*, in spite of whom you serve. But if there is no other choice, I will fight you to save Yasamin and her country."

"I'd expect no less of you, boy."

Arash hesitated. The next question was crucial; everything and everyone's future pivoted on it. But he had chosen his path.

"Goliagoth, I won't ask you to show me where they're holding Queen Yasamin. It'd put you in jeopardy. But for old time's sake, I will ask one last favor of you: tell me how to get there? And—will you give me enough time to get her out? I'm not asking you to keep quiet forever, just give me enough time to get her out of the castle and into the country. At least there we'd have a fighting chance. If we're going to die, let it be in the sunshine, not in some rat's hole. Will you do that?"

Goliagoth contemplated the small fire. For a few seconds, Arash thought he hadn't heard him or was debating whether to kill him on the spot. The firelight flickered over his face, casting it first into light, then into darkness as it played across his features.

After what seemed like eternity, Goliagoth looked at Arash. "No."

Arash struggled to the edge of the cot. "All right. I thought you respected the Queen, guess I misjudged you. I'll find it myself." He pulled on one boot, then the other. He glanced toward the chair beside the bed. "Where's my sword?" He started to rise.

Goliagoth pushed Arash back onto the cot. "Not so fast, boy."

Arash made to push Goliagoth's massive hand from his shoulder. "If you're not going to tell me how to find her …"

"I'm not going to *tell* you where to find her; I am going to take you."

Arash's mouth fell open. "What?"

"The blow on your head affected you more than I thought. You're going deaf. I said I'm going to *take* you. Then I'm getting the two of you out of Dragonval and back to Gwendomere. And I'll not be fightin' you face to face, boy; I'll be fightin' beside you."

Stunned by the giant's words, Arash simply stared. At last, he stammered, "If you do this, King Amir'll have your head on a pole right along with ours."

"Most likely."

"The chances of us getting out of Dragonval are pretty slim."

"Odds just got better." The giant went to a small chest and pulled out two swords. He bucked on a second one and brought the other back to Arash and handed it to him.

Arash slowly reached up to take it. "Why? You'll be losing everything you've worked for, maybe even your life."

"Could be."

"Then why?"

Goliagoth pulled his sword from its scabbard and caressed it as if it were a lover. He studied the blade as he spoke. "All my life, this is the only thing I have known. It brought me power, respect, helped me put order in my life. Only thing I have ever trusted. Aye, I owe allegiance to the King because I serve in his army. It's a way to pull myself out of the gutter.

"Lately, I've realized something's missing," Goliagoth chuckled and resheathed the sword. "Don't even know what it is, don't have a name for it, but I can feel it." Goliagoth tapped his chest. "Here. It is a black hole, like something has been ripped out." Goliagoth sighed and sat on the cot beside Arash. He stared at the fire. "Real power doesn't come from my blade, and the respect I have is not for me. People do what I ask because they are terrified of me.

"Being around Queen Yasamin, well, it's like that fire," Goliagoth nodded to the small blaze. "I see her dignity, her honor, how she lives what she believes. It put a spark in that black hole. Made me realize the sword's not the answer to everything."

Arash wanted to put his hand on the soldier's arm for comfort but didn't—afraid he would ruin the moment. He doubted the giant had ever revealed anything of himself to anyone. He sat and listened.

Goliagoth continued, "Today, watching him and her, I finally saw the difference. Amir feeds on power, deceit. He's like the Dragon's Mouth—sucks everything in to satisfy himself, even if it destroys everything. I may not know what love is, boy, but I know what it isn't. It is not the way he treated her today. Can't figure out why he wanted to marry her. Gwendomere has no resources to speak of."

Goliagoth looked at Arash. "Today, when the King accused her of infidelity, the Queen told him the truth."

"It'd be easy enough to prove."

The soldier laughed. "Don't you think I thought the same thing? It'd be easy to prove. The King does not *care*. I would bet my last deniaer Queen Medusimia's at the bottom of it. Whatever the reason, the King doesn't want Queen Yasamin around now."

"The more reason to get her out of here now."

Oblivious, the giant continued. "He called her names. He exulted in hurting her by telling her what he was going to do to her country. She never pleaded for herself just for her country."

"Why didn't you do something, Goliagoth? You could've told Amir nothing happened."

"Tried. He didn't want to hear anything from me. And Queen Yasamin," Goliagoth looked at Arash with confusion in his eyes, "she turned to me and told me not to say anything else because it would jeopardize *me*."

"It is what makes her different from anyone I have ever known."

"Aye." Goliagoth nodded. "That's why we're not letting that black-hearted bastard destroy her. Enough talk. We've work to do. You up to coming with me? If not, I'll show you where to wait for us."

"I'm coming. Let's go."

The Road of Silk

The two men went into the darkness for the same woman.
For the same reason.
Only one of them didn't know it.

Chapter 54

He was satisfied. Word had already gone through the troops they would march against Gwendomere. From his window, he could already see soldiers moving through their drills. When he was through with that pitiful country, the whole world would shake when they heard his name. Rulers would know his power and respect him. They would bow before him in terror at what he could do.

Amir toyed with a chess piece as he watched the distant fields dotted with the moving figures. Everything moved at his command.

He smiled and drained the cup of wine beside him.

The only problem he had was his own quandary.

Did he want to send the troops immediately and destroy Gwendomere within two months' time?

Or did he want to draw out the troops' maneuvers and drills for several months, then send them to destroy the country. If he did the latter, the bitch would suffer longer with the anticipation of what awaited her country.

He tossed the chess piece onto the board and laughed. He'd just thought of a better plan. He'd send the troops and annihilate the country now and have the *Demolisherian* bring back the nobles and everyone else the lying bitch knew and torture them here in Dragonval before her eyes. *Then* he would behead them as he promised he would do.

Amir poured himself another goblet of wine. Perfect. His lust for blood would be gratified immediately, and he could still prolong her suffering as long as he wanted. Yes, life was good. He would have it all, and no one could stop him.

Chapter 55

The moon was a white saucer on a black velvet tablecloth sprinkled with stars. The two men crept from shadow to shadow as they made their way to the castle's dungeon. Several times Goliagoth waited for Arash to catch his breath. The young man was still weak but determined. Each dislodged pebble sounded like a canon shot in the stillness to the men, but no one appeared. At last, the door to the dungeon became visible.

"Wait behind that bush. I'll go get her."

"I'll go with you. You'll need help if the guards attack."

Goliagoth shook his head. "If you go, they'll become suspicious. They won't think anything of me coming. I'll tell them the King wants to talk to her."

"In the middle of the night? That should raise their suspicions."

"Not where the King is concerned. He's known for doing far more bizarre things. They won't think twice about it. Wait here. If anyone approaches, don't let them come down. I don't expect anyone, but if somebody shows up, stop them."

"What do you want me to do?"

"Whatever it takes. If you have to use your sword, do it quickly before they raise an alarm. We should be back in a few minutes."

Arash put his hand on the giant's arm. "If someone comes, more than likely it'll be one of your men."

Goliagoth stared at the young man a second. "Do what you have to. We've got to keep them off our trail as long as we can and get the Queen to safety."

Arash nodded. "The sooner we're out of here, the better."

"Aye." Goliagoth disappeared into the tunnel. He walked quickly and precisely. If someone approached him, he had to act boldly in order not to arouse suspicion. No one would think twice about the *Demolisherian* on an errand for the King.

Goliagoth grimaced as he took a deep breath. The knife wound throbbed relentlessly. He had staunched the flow of blood and changed shirts, but he needed rest. The injury was taking its toll. As soon as he got the Queen past Dragonval's boundary, they'd find a place to rest for a few days. With any luck the soldiers wouldn't pick up their trail for a while, and the three of them could have a chance to regain their strength.

The sound of soldiers laughing grew louder, and Goliagoth laid his hand on the hilt of his sword. He had hoped more of them would be asleep, but it sounded as if they had a game going. He'd deal with all of them if he had to.

The door to the guard's room was partially open. He pushed it wide and stood in the entry.

"What's going on? I ordered you to keep the door locked."

Four of the guards sat around the table playing a game of *swabbern*. At his roar, the men staggered to attention, knocking over several of the chairs in their haste. Evidently, they had been drinking as well—a point in his favor if he had to fight.

"Yes, sir," the braver of the men shouted. "We had it closed, sir, but the Queen seemed faint with the smell, sir. We thought it would be best to let a little fresh air in for her, sir."

"She's ill?"

"No, sir," the soldier shouted. Goliagoth could see the quiver in his hand that remained in the salute. "Her Highness is not sick, sir. The air is foul down here. We don't notice it, but for someone with her—uh, station it's overpowering. You told us to take care of her, sir, and that's what we're doing. We opened the door a little to let air in." The soldier maintained his rigid stance, but his eyes remained glued on Goliagoth's hand that rested on his sword's hilt.

"Very well, soldier. I'll let it pass this time, as the Queen's well-being is paramount, and your standing order. However," Goliagoth let his eyes slide toward the three soldiers who had obviously been drinking, "you two are lucky I don't have your heads on a stake. With the door unlocked, you're open to a surprise attack. You're drunk. I should run you through where you stand. I would if I had enough man power down here."

His words and tone were enough to almost sober the three men. They remained at attention with their eyes pasted somewhere on the wall to Goliagoth's left shoulder. "No more drinking on duty. Be found this way again, you'll regret the day you were born. Understood?"

"Yes, sir!" the three shouted.

"Very well." Goliagoth turned to the officer in charge. "The other four guards are asleep?"

"Yes, sir."

"When I bring the Queen back, wake three of them and replace these dogs."

"Bring the Queen back, sir?"

"The King wants to see her."

"Now, sir?"

"Stupid ass." If looks could turn a man to stone, the soldier would have become granite in that instant. "The King wants her now. Bring her. I'm to escort her to his chambers."

"Yes, sir. Right away, sir." The man fumbled with the keys on his belt, literally running to the cell.

Goliagoth glareed at the other men. Hopefully, his intimidation would be enough to keep the soldiers from further questions. He pretended a nonchalance he didn't feel. His heart hammered a tune in his ears. He stepped to the table, grabbed the flask and threw it against the stones where it shattered into thousands of shards.

"From now on, only enough wine to wash down your food. That's all. You're a disgrace to the King's army. It's a good thing no one tried to harm the Queen. Once the King has discovered the trick played on him —and he will discover the plot—he will want her restored to her rightful place. I guarantee I wouldn't want to be the one to tell him she'd been harmed. You don't know what pain is until the King wants his pound of flesh. I'll take you directly to the King myself. He'd take great delight in seeing you skinned alive ... almost as much as I'd get in using the knife myself."

He continued to move around the room, grabbing a couple of dirty bowls left on the second table. He threw them at the men. "Pigs. You are soldiers. I expect you to act like it at all times." The left-over food splattered on the men. They flinched but continued to stand at attention. "The next tim—"

The soldier in charge returned with Yasamin who was rubbing her eyes and sleepily stumbling. She abruptly stopped when she saw Goliagoth. Confusion clouded her gaze.

The giant moved to her and grabbed her arm. "Come, the King wants you. Now."

Yasamin hesitated, and Goliagoth saw the anxiety in her eyes.

"Tonight? Is he preparing to move on Gwendomere already? Why—"

Goliagoth roughly pulled her to him. "I'm your guard, not your counselor. Ask him yourself when you get there," he growled. The words forced themselves through his tight lips, and his heart constricted when he saw the hurt his harshness caused. "Now. We don't have all night."

Goliagoth glanced at the soldier in charge. "Get these swine to clean up while we're gone." Goliagoth pushed Yasamin through the door. "Lock the door until I return."

"Yes, sir." The soldier saluted.

Goliagoth loosened his grasp on Yasamin but continued to pull her forward. She struggled to keep up.

"Surely Amir hasn't amassed his army this quickly. What more can he want from me? Is Arash all right?"

"Keep quiet and hurry. We don't have much time."

Goliagoth continued to glance behind them and scrutinize the two intersecting passageways. No one appeared. When they reached the last flight of stairs to exit, he stopped and released Yasamin's arm.

"Forgive me if I hurt you."

"You didn't. Just tell me Arash is better and what Amir wants with me."

"Boy's fine. The King doesn't want to see you."

"What do you mean he doesn't Yasamin stopped mid-sentence, and her eyes widened. "Goliagoth, what are you doing?"

"What needs to be," he turned to go, but Yasamin stopped him.

She put her hand on his arm. "Goliagoth, answer me."

The giant took a quick glance in both directions. "Arash is waiting outside the door above. I'm getting both of you out of Dragonval. The King has sent drill orders to the army. They'll march within two months. We need to go."

Still Yasamin didn't move. "You cannot do this. Not only will Amir have your head, he will destroy Gwendomere some way even more horrible than he already has planned when he finds me gone."

"Only if he catches me. He'll have to find another *Demolisherian* to lead his army. With Arash and his country and me, the King will find it won't be as easy to obliterate Gwendomere as he thinks."

"You?"

The soldier nodded. "I'm defending you and Gwendomere. Arash will contact his father for help as soon as we get out of the country. Amir will find he has one fine fight on his hands."

"You're staying—in Gwendomere?"

He nodded. "We need to hurry. We need to put as much distance between us and the city as possible before dawn."

"Why, Goliagoth?"

The giant looked into Yasamin's wide eyes. He saw the surprise and, more importantly, the hope growing in them.

"I've no longer the stomach for Amir's ways. I will train your men best I can and lead them against Dragonval."

"There are no words to thank you."

"Be better to spend your words on your prayers. Even with me fighting, it won't be an easy battle. The King could still win. But it won't be the slaughter he has planned, I promise you that. Let's go. Arash's probably wondering what's happened. I don't want the fool raising a disturbance."

Goliagoth took Yasamin's arm and helped her up the stairs. At the door, he restrained her as he surveyed the courtyard. No one was around. "This way," he whispered.

Shielding her between his body and the castle wall, Goliagoth headed toward the heavy bush to the left. Arash emerged.

"Arash!" Forgetting protocol, Yasamin ran to the young man and clung to him. "I was so worried about you. I was afraid your wounds were worse than I imagined." She hugged him tightly.

Arash wrapped his arms around Yasamin's slender waist and pulled her close. He buried his head in her hair. "I'm fine, my love. Whatever medicine Goliagoth gave me worked quickly. Other than a little weak, I'm good as new and thankful to see you're safe." Words failed him, and he satisfied himself with holding her close and breathing in the fragrance of her silver locks. They needed no words. Their minds had finally recognized what their hearts had discovered long ago.

They loved each other.

Even Goliagoth, who had no word for the emotion, felt the strength of what was between them. He turned away and scanned the courtyard. In truth, he didn't expect to see anyone, but the overwhelming void expanding in his chest as he watched Arash and Yasamin was more painful than anything he'd ever felt. He found himself wondering what his life might have been had he ever experienced such an emotion.

After a moment, he turned. "We have to go. We need miles between town and us before sunrise. I've already put a few things outside the north gate. It'll give them a false start. We're leaving out the south."

Arash and Yasamin were reluctant to part, but they knew the giant was right. Arash settled for holding Yasamin's hand.

Goliagoth grunted. "Boy, if you want to hold the Queen's hand, it's all right with me but use your left. You need your sword hand free in case of trouble."

Arash grinned but did as the soldier suggested.

"If we run into trouble, do like before. Put her between us, your back to mine." Goliagoth hesitated, then moved to Yasamin. He pulled a small dagger from his belt and held it toward her. "Queen Yasamin, I'll give this to you. You decide its use. If we fail, two things I can promise you. The King will destroy Gwendomere no matter what, and what he will do to you is unimaginable."

Yasamin blanched but took the small dagger and stuck it in her sash. "Thank you, Goliagoth." She straightened into the familiar defiant stance he'd come to recognize and respect. "One thing I pledge is we will all escape or none of us will. I will not leave Dragonval without you and Arash."

Goliagoth nodded, his voice lost beneath the lump in his throat. The Queen amazed him. Any other woman, whether queen or not, would have fallen to pieces at being thrown into prison. Yet Yasamin absorbed the blow and came back stronger. She was such a marvelous wonder; he knew she would never cease to astound him.

"Let's go. Keep behind me until we clear the city." The soldier crept forward, eyes constantly scanning streets and alleys. The only movement was a stray dog who crept forward to nose them as they passed. Smelling no food, he quickly lost interest and wandered down an alley in search of supper.

At last, they reached the south gate. Only one guard was visible in the tiny hut above the wooden doors. Goliagoth held up his hand, and the others stopped.

"Let's hope this works," he whispered. "There will be two guards on duty by early morn. Edge around the bushes. Wait behind the one next to the exit door. It opens outward. There's no handle on the other side so it can't be accessed from outside." Goliagoth pulled a small flask from inside his shirt. "I'm going up to the guard house and share my bottle of wine with him. It's drugged. He should be asleep within a few minutes. I'm not giving him much. Stuff wears off quickly, but it should give us just enough time to get through the door and to the first line of trees. The last thing he'll remember is me saying I'm going to check the north gate."

"What if he doesn't want a drink or the powder doesn't affect him." Arash cast a worried look at Yasamin.

"Then we go to plan B."

"What's that?"

"Have to knock him out. Then our ruse that we went north is worthless."

"Let's hope he wants a dram or two." Arash pulled Yasamin closer to him to head for the bushes . Goliagoth pulled the cork from the flask and splashed some of the liquid on his cheeks. "Need to smell like I've drank a bit." He turned.

Yasamin grabbed Goliagoth's arm. "Goliagoth, be careful."

The giant nodded his understanding. He headed for the ladder to the guard house. He purposely missed a couple of rungs climbing to make it appear he was drunk. He reached the top and lunged to the door of the hut.

"*Gemonisus*, it's been a night," he grumbled and fumbled at the flask's cork. "I've walked the entire city, but I think it a fool's errand."

The guard jumped from his stool and snapped to attention. "Sir."

"At ease, soldier. Just taking a break." He saw the soldier's eyes drop toward the flask. His nostrils dilated at the smell emanating from Goliagoth. The man relaxed but remained standing.

"Nights getting a nip to them, soldier."

"Yes, sir. Be winter soon."

"Aye. Guess most of us will spend it in Gwendomere. Be warmer there."

"Yes, sir. Hope I get to go, sir."

Goliagoth pretended to take a drink from the flask, then handed it to the soldier. He hesitated, looking from it to the *Demolisherian*. Goliagoth saw the desire in his eyes. He nodded his head and pushed the flask forward.

"Ever been in battle?"

The soldier took the flask and a deep draw. He wiped his lips and handed it back to Goliagoth. "No, sir. Not a real one anyway."

"Nothing like it, boy. Gets the blood running high." Goliagoth pretended to take another drink and belched. He handed the flask back. The soldier accepted it more readily the second time and took another draw. Goliagoth kept up his monologue. "One of the most exciting things in life, feeling that blade in your hand, the power it yields. Nothing like it … except maybe a good woman."

The soldier handed back the bottle. "Had my share of them, sir. Guess, in one way, you could say I've wielded my sword," he laughed.

Goliagoth grunted his agreement. "Aye. But I'd still take the battle. It don't argue back."

The soldier laughed again and stumbled against the stool. Goliagoth saw the glaze forming in his eyes.

"Look forward to the battle. Partly why I'm out tonight. Wanted to check the walls and gates. See if I could find any weaknesses an enemy might could use at night. Nothing so far but don't hurt to be careful. Those Gwendomere sheep might try something cowardly like slipping in here to try and assassinate the King."

The soldier grinned, and his words became slightly slurred. "They better not try it at this gate, sir. I'll have their heads 'fore they take two feet in." He tried to focus on Goliagoth's face. The drug was working quickly.

"I can see that, soldier. Keep it up. You've a promising career. Most gate guards get sloppy. Go to sleep on the job. Ought to cut their eyes out for being derelict in their duty."

"Yes, sir. Won't catch me sleeping on the job. Don't matter if it's dull, never know when somethin' might happen." Despite his words, the soldier could barely keep his own eyes open.

Goliagoth made a show of corking the flask. "Well, soldier, guess I'd better finish. Be daylight soon. Want to check the north gate; guard there is notorious for falling asleep on duty. Ought to be put out of his misery or put in a rocking chair."

"Aye, sir. No good … to do … to fall asleep." The soldier saluted and sat down on the stool hard. Goliagoth had to spring forward and catch him before he hit the floor. He propped the boy on the stool wedged in the corner to keep him from toppling sideways. He ran for the door and slid down the ladder. Yasamin and Arash were waiting for him at the door.

"It worked. He thinks I left for the north gate. Let's get out of here. He'll swear he never fell asleep."

The three of them hurried through the gate, and Goliagoth shoved it to make the latch fall into place. No one would know he and the others left through it. The three ran for the woods.

* * * * *

The rosy fingers of dawn crawled over the distant mountaintops, slowly pulling the fiery red sun behind them. The darkness lightened and birds began stirring. Soon the orb grew white and drove the chill of the night into the deep crevices.

They had escaped the city undetected by all but one.

Vulmire watched their progress in his pool of lava and frowned. Amir was a fool. The King always let his personal emotions get in the way of good judgment. He was willing to waste manpower, money and everything else simply because he wanted to hurt the woman.

The man-beast sniffed and waved his hand over the magma mirror. The images disappeared. Gwendomere was a small country without any resources to speak of and certainly not worth the time and effort the King would spend to destroy it. And now there was a new element: the *Demolisherian* was going with the Queen. He was a formidable soldier, and one Vulmire had hoped would serve him. Now it appeared that would not be the case. In addition, with Goliagoth fighting for Gwendomere, Amir would find he did, indeed, have a fight on his hands, and even more wealth and manpower would be expended. The entire situation was becoming ludicrous. Amir would drag his country into poverty and for what—to hurt Yasamin.

Vulmire rubbed his jaw. He'd have to keep a close eye on the situation. He had no intention of letting Amir ruin Dragonval out of pure stupidity and childish antics. If it came to it, he'd take care of Amir himself instead of letting his original plan open the path for him to assume the throne again.

Things were different now. He had more to think of than himself. The throne belonged to him and his. Vulmire turned and ambled toward the outer chamber. Yes, he'd definitely have to keep a close eye on the situation. But for now, Medusimia was waiting, ready for him as she always was.

And his son, the next heir of Dragonval, waited for him. Vulmire planned to have many more. Medusimia was more than willing, and she was extremely fertile. Between the two of them, they would rebuild Dragonval to the glory it once had.

Chapter 56

"Are we safe? Are we far enough from the city?" Yasamin panted as she ran behind Goliagoth.

"We've made about three dectares. If they fell for the ruse, we've a good head start. If they search north, they'll lose at least a day, maybe more." Goliagoth's experienced eye examined the countryside for a hiding place. "We'll rest a while, then continue off the main road."

"How long before we're across the boundary?" Arash was tired but more concerned for Yasamin. She was making a brave effort, but he knew she was exhausted.

"Two days, maybe three. Depends on how far we have to detour to avoid detection." Goliagoth scanned the sky. "Long as the dragons don't see us, we're in good shape. We need to stay near cover where we can hide." He pointed at a small trail leading into a nest of huge boulders. "Up there."

The three of them slipped through the narrow crevice formed by two tremendous boulders. After a few feet, they entered a diminutive grove of trees with a small spring flowing through it.

"We'll stop here." Goliagoth nodded toward the spring. "Get some water but don't drink too fast; it'll cramp your stomach. Then head for the thickest trees. We'll rest there." He turned and tugged at an eight-foot boulder. Putting his shoulder against it, he finally rolled the rock in front of the crevice they had come through. "If they come up that trail, it'll look like a dead end. They'll go back to the road. It should buy us some time."

They knelt at the spring and drank slowly.

"What about the dragons?" Arash asked between sips.

"They will recognize my uniform. Hopefully, since you are with me it will not be a problem. If they discover my desertion, they will either attack or send out an alarm. I think it best if we can avoid detection altogether. If they spot us, they can pinpoint our last location."

"Can we kill them?"

Goliagoth shook his head. "Doubt it. They'll be too high to hit, and we don't have the kind of weapon it'd take. Best defense is to avoid detection. Come on." He led the way to the thicket and knelt. Yasamin and Arash lay on the soft, green grass beside him.

"Don't get too comfortable yet." The soldier pulled the small pack from his back and withdrew some old clothing. He pitched a pair of pants and shirt to Arash. "Put these on. Your red shirt's a flag to dragon and man."

Goliagoth reached into the bag again and pulled out another set of garments. He handed these to Yasamin. "Highness, you need to wear these. Your yellow dress is almost as bad as his shirt for drawing attention. These clothes were dyed with fruits and vegetables. The colors will blend with the countryside." He held them awkwardly. "Sorry they're not of better quality, but safety is paramount."

Yasamin sat up and took the pro-offered clothes, then smiled at Goliagoth. "Don't apologize for trying to help us." The trust in her smile pierced the soldier's heart. Despite the dangerous situation they were in, Goliagoth wanted to sit in the warmth of her smile forever.

But he couldn't if he was going to save her.

"Dragons are excellent hunters when their prey's moving, cannot outrun them. Dressed in these, if you remain motionless, the dragon will bypass you.

"Countryside and trees are to our benefit. If you see a dragon and have time, get under the nearest tree. If you can't, drop to your knees and roll into a tight ball. Chances are he'll pass over."

"Then we'd better change quickly." Yasamin pulled herself up and headed for a wide tree. Arash changed where he sat. The two men waited for her return.

A few minutes later, she reappeared holding her dress. "What do I do with this?"

"Give it to me." Goliagoth looked at the shirt laying beside Arash. "You, too, boy." The soldier stuffed their clothes into the small pack. "I'll carry them. Don't want to leave any trace. Now, you two rest while I scout. We'll take some short breaks, but we need to keep moving as much as possible."

The trio moved off and on throughout the day, keeping close to rocks and trees. After what seemed an eternity, the sun began its descent toward the western horizon.

Goliagoth watched the red ball sink toward the twin peaks in the distance. "Once the sun sets, we don't have to worry about the dragons any more. They have no night vision to speak of. We'll travel a little longer, then camp. I don't know if we'll be able to have a fire; maybe we can if we find a cave. Don't want to give away our location."

"We need to. She's shivering, and it's bound to get colder." Arash wrapped his arm around Yasamin, trying to share his body warmth with her.

"It will—we're in hill country. I'm not too familiar with it. Most of my travels were west and north. We'll need to stay near a road, so we don't wander aimlessly."

"Good idea." Arash rubbed Yasamin's arms, trying to bring some warmth to them. He was thankful she had on the heavier clothes. In her original gown, she would be in much worse shape than she was.

The crimson sun had reached the peaks and nestled between them. In the distance, they could hear the twittering of the settling birds.

"You two stay. I'll scout ahead." Goliagoth pulled the pack from his back and dropped it. "Be back in a few minutes." He moved wearily forward.

"Goliagoth, wait!" Yasamin pulled from Arash's arms and ran toward the giant. She put her hand to his back then removed it. Her fingers were crimson. "You're bleeding." She glanced down at the pack he had placed on the ground. Even in the gathering darkness, she could see the dark stain spread across it. "You said it was nothing."

"It is, just a flesh wound. It still oozes. Just as well, keeps the infection down."

"This is more than oozing. Look." She held her hand out.

Arash moved forward, peering first at Yasamin's fingertips, then the soldier's shirt. "She's right, Goliagoth. That's fresh, and there's plenty of it."

"Let me change your bandage. We need to stop it."

Arash took Goliagoth's arm and made to pull him toward the boulder where he and Yasamin had been sitting. "We should take care of it. Come on. Sit down. Let's have a look."

The soldier pushed Arash's hand away. "'Tis nothing, boy. I am fine."

"Goliagoth, please, let me tend it." Yasamin's eyes were wide in her pale face. He could see the concern and the fear swirling in their depths.

Their worry for him warmed Goliagoth, but he didn't have time to bask in that affection if he was going to get them out of the country. He softened his voice. "Not now, Highness. I need to scout first. Once we've secured for the night, I'll let you attend it if it will ease your mind. Don't worry. I've had far worse and lived to tell about it."

Yasamin sighed. She knew she would not win the argument, and ordering him would not work under the circumstances. She looked deep into his eyes as tears filled hers.

"You can go only if you promise you'll let me tend it later. Promise me, Goliagoth."

"I swear. Now rest. All of us are tired, and we need to sleep—we can't be vulnerable. I'll be back as soon as I find a secure spot."

Once more, he moved forward. It was the truth. He was weary, wearier than he'd ever been in his life. He hoped he could get them out of the country soon. After that he could sleep in peace.

But until then, he had a duty to perform.

He went into the night.

Chapter 57

He rubbed his hands together in front of the small fire. The cold bothered him more than it did when he was younger, but all in all, there was little to complain about. Other than the ache in his joints, he was in excellent shape.

A cup of tea would help.

He started toward the stove, then paused to sniff the air. Danger was forming. He closed his eyes and concentrated. The menace was not coming toward the Holy Mountain; Yasamin was its target. He massaged his forehead where his inner eye was located and let his mind chase along the tendrils reaching toward him. Amir was part of it, but that part he already knew. There was more, but for some reason, he was unable to pinpoint the bigger threat. The fact it was blocked meant someone as powerful as he was instigating the trouble.

The tea forgotten, he stumbled toward the chair and pulled it near the fire. He closed his eyes and focused on the white spot of light in his third eye. He saw the trio huddled around a small flame in a cave. For the moment, they were safe but unaware Amir had discovered their escape and was whipping his soldiers into a frenzy to find them. His chest ached for his granddaughter. She had a rough trial in front of her, and he prayed she'd handle it the right way. If only she did not turn from the light in anger, she might well be on her way to becoming The One.

He shook his head. The earlier menace that had touched him was greater. It wasn't Amir, of that he was sure. It had been a long time since he felt such power, not since the ruler of darkness had punished his old enemy, Vulmire.

Mosesra sucked in his breath. Was it possible they were wrong about the former ruler of Dragonval? Since the evil one had changed him into a man-beast, Vulmire had appeared nothing more than a demented soul, living in caves and existing on animals and an occasional lost human.

The sage turned his attention to Vulmire and opened his mind, sending splinters of light traveling toward the man-beast and his lair. The light waves hit a solid black wall and refracted, knocking Mosesra backward. He leaned forward and concentrated harder, sending a continuous beam to drill through the barrier. Sweat beaded his brow, and he trembled with the effort. Gritting his teeth, he pushed harder. He was vaguely aware of his collar dampening from the sweat running down his neck. He pushed again and groaned.

"What are you doing?" Shar's voice broke the stillness. So intense in his focus, Mosesra had not been aware of her arrival. "You're pale as a ghost. What is it?"

Mosesra startled. "Shar, I did not hear you enter." He forced the thoughts from his mind. "I'll make us a cup of tea." He started to rise.

"No. Sit there. You don't look well. I'll make it. First, tell me what has happened."

Mosesra smiled and willed his mind to close. Better not to say anything for the moment. "Why? Nothing to speak of."

Shar studied him as she prepared the tea. "I have known you a long time, Mosesra. I can see when something is bothering you. Now tell me."

"I am an old man, my friend. Surely, at my age, I'm allowed a few twinges." He laughed but could see she wasn't totally convinced.

"Mosesra, what is it?"

"Just a touch of something, my dear. Just a touch, it's already gone. I'll be fine."

"I think you're growing a bit cantankerous in your old age, is what I think." Shar brought a steaming mug to Mosesra and drew up another chair in front of the fireplace. "You were bent over like a crab trying to crawl back into its shell and pale as a sheet, but if you want to pretend its nothing ..." she let the sentence drift off and sipped her tea, hoping he'd volunteer more information.

He didn't.

Mosesra knew she'd help; she had a good heart. But sometimes she tried to help too much, bless her. He smiled. She'd always been spunky, ever since she'd come to him so many years ago. He needed to keep her focused on the present instead of dredging up old, wounding memories from a long time past. He reached over and patted her hand. "You're a good woman, Shar."

She sputtered over her tea. Compliments had always embarrassed her, even when they were true and came from old friends. She sought to change the subject.

"What has happened with Yasamin?"

"She has escaped the prison and is being helped to leave the country."

"How is that possible?"

"We had help from a most unexpected ally. Seems Yasamin has touched Goliagoth. He has chosen to help her and Arash escape."

"The *Demolisherian*? What a surprise. Wonders never cease."

Mosesra nodded. "I would call it a miracle. They do still happen occasionally. This one has certainly changed the direction of things."

"Especially for him."

"Particularly for him. He made his choice by free will. He is aware of the consequences. I do not think he will shrink from his decision no matter the cost."

"Have you had another vision, Mosesra?"

"Yes. It makes me worry all the more for Yasamin."

"She seems to be making her choices toward the light."

"For the moment."

"How is her progress with her powers? I've been so busy with the situation in *Aneminorea* that I've had no chance to monitor her advancement."

"She is remarkable. I am sometimes overcome by how quickly she learns; however, it is sporadic. She has a difficult time accepting her own importance."

"In what way?"

"When someone she loves is threatened, her powers are so far advanced I truly believe she is The One. She has already built one Castle of Silk."

Shar's mouth dropped into a round 'O'. "At her age? You cannot mean it!"

"Yes. I didn't give you all the details earlier when I notified you she had defeated Serpata. She built it to protect Goliagoth, Arash and herself against him."

"Then she should have no trouble defeating her enemies. Why do you doubt?"

"She has not been able to do it for just herself. It is only under extreme duress she has demonstrated these abilities. And then there is the other."

Shar frowned. "What's that?"

"She's not suffered a true loss and had her faith challenged. When she does, it could still go either way."

"You think she could turn after all the choices she's made toward our side?"

"It is possible, my friend. Look at the *Demolisherian*. Did you think he would ever turn away from darkness?"

"In truth, no. But she is your granddaughter. Surely she would not turn."

"Anger and pain make humans unpredictable. I believe if she gets through the trial she faces tomorrow, she will be with us." Mosesra stared into the flames. The cup of tea in his hand grew tepid.

"You'd best drink your tea before it grows cold." Shar watched her friend. She was worried about him, even if he was pretending nothing was wrong. She spoke softly. "It must be hard, I would imagine, wondering what Yasamin will do."

"It is. So many think I know all the answers because I am a seer. But it is not so. Man always has a choice, and depending on what he chooses, the path is always different. I wish I could see into the future and know if my granddaughter is The One, but the gods have not allowed it."

"There must be a reason why it is not revealed to you."

"I believe it is a reminder that I do not influence Yasamin in her decision-making. So by not knowing how she will choose, I end up sitting here and doing nothing because I'm afraid I might inadvertently say or do something to push her one way or another."

"As I often seem to do?"

Mosesra smiled. "Your intentions are good, Shar. Sometimes your enthusiasm just gets a little ahead of your better judgment."

"I was always a woman of action, but I'm learning to evaluate the situation more thoroughly before I act."

"Perhaps that is why we are so good together. I have a tendency to think things to death before I act. Somewhere between us there's a good balance."

It was Shar's turn to laugh. "In all our years together, I think that's the first time you've referred to us as a team."

"Like I said, I have a tendency to over-think things before I act. You are very special to me, Shar, always have been. It's time I told you so."

Shar sobered quickly. She had loved Mosesra for as long as she could remember. She never considered he might have feelings for her other than friends. Not sure how to respond, she quickly changed the subject.

"This situation I've been observing has gotten ugly. Children are disappearing nightly. I'm afraid the dark forces are sacrificing them. What do you want me to do?"

"Monitor it for the next day or two. See if you can get any leads, but don't make any moves. Yasamin will decide her fate within twenty-four hours. If she comes to us, it will be her place to make the decisions."

"So your vision does involve Yasamin?"

He nodded sadly. "Yes. I know the terrible thing that will happen tomorrow, but I was not allowed to know her reaction. I will learn soon enough."

Shar wanted to comfort Mosesra but found she was suddenly self-conscious. She sat down her cup and patted his hand. "Everything will work out, Mosesra. She's a good girl. Don't worry so much."

The old mystic looked at Shar with pained eyes. "But I do. The dark forces are as powerful as ever, and I'm growing older. There is much to do and much teaching to pass along. I have waited a long time for The One. I hope she comes before I

"Hush, Mosesra. Don't speak such. You will outlive all of us. Why, you're as strong as these rocks." Shar couldn't imagine her world without Mosesra. He had been everything to her for as long as she could remember. She gave him a quick hug. "Now you just go take a nap. You're tired, that's all. You're worring about your granddaughter which is only natural. I'm going back now, but if you need me."

Mosesra smiled at Shar. "I know you are only a thought away. Be careful, my dear. I feel the dark forces are gathering for something. Watch out for yourself."

"And you do the same." Shar waved and burst into hundreds of crystal butterflies that fluttered in the cave a moment before they disappeared into the dark.

Mosesra stared into the depths of the flames for a long time. He hadn't realized how fond he'd grown of Shar. There had been only two women in his life—his first wife, killed in the beginning wars between Dragonval and his country, and Sena, the mother of Casadra. She had long since passed to the light.

He sighed. Maybe he should let someone into his life. Perhaps it was just loneliness making him feel so old and tired. Maybe the three of them would be able to turn the darkness back upon itself.

He prayed so. It would take every ounce of their combined strengths to fight that which he'd seen in his vision earlier. They had underestimated their enemy.

But in the meantime, there *was* one small thing he could do for Yasamin. It was all he could do for her until she made her choice.

He slowly got up from the chair.

It had to be done now.

* * * * *

She was asleep, but it was a fitful sleep. She turned on the hard ground, making small mewing sounds. He watched her for a few moments.

He moved toward Arash. The boy was pale and slept like the dead. He was close to Yasamin, within arm's reach. His sword was next to him on the other side. They both lay close to the tiny fire the soldier built inside the cave. A few bones beside the pit indicated he had caught supper.

Mosesra flew to the mouth of the cave. Goliagoth sat at the entrance, back against the rocks, tiredness etched into every line of his face. Yet his eyes were alert to every movement. He occasionally flexed his shoulders and rotated his neck, but for the most part, he was as still as the boulders.

Mosesra moved back to Yasamin. Tomorrow would be the turning point for her. That much he knew. What she would do, he did not. He hoped the price would not be so great she would lose her faith. Despite their vast knowledge, there were still limitations for those who followed the light.

Tonight, right now, he would do the only thing he could for he.

He circled her clockwise three times, then counterclockwise three times. On the last circle, he shot straight up in the air through the center of the circles he made. A fountain of stardust sprayed upward from where he hovered, then drifted downward against the perimeter of the circles he had drawn in the air. The stardust settled in a circle around her.

Yasamin sighed, turned over and sank into a peaceful sleep. A smile hovered on her lips.

The sage prepared to depart but stopped abruptly.

Thank you, Mosesra. Yasamin's voice echoed softly in his mind. From some level, the girl knew him in his guise. *Can you help Goliagoth?*

Mosesra hesitated. He could do nothing to change the future. Still, there should be something he could do that would not interfere. Then he smiled. It wasn't what Yasamin was asking for, but it *was* something Goliagoth needed. He formed the words into a light beam and sent it to her. *I'll do what I can, child.*

Yasamin settled into the soft leaves, and Mosesra flew back to the cave's entrance. Goliagoth turned to look in. Somehow he'd sensed a difference inside the cavern.

With a puzzled look, he watched Mosesra fly toward him. When he reached the soldier, Mosesra hovered for a second, then rapidly flew through the air spelling a word. At the end of the word, he flew straight at Goliagoth and tapped him on the forehead.

He then disappeared into the darkness.

* * * * *

Goliagoth settled back against the rocks and stared at the empty sky above him.

He didn't understand what had just happened.

He had been keeping watch when something transpired in the cave. He wasn't sure if it had been movement or the change in the light, but he had become aware of a flickering and turned to look, thinking perhaps the fire had rekindled or one of the logs had fallen sending a shower of sparks.

Neither had been the case.

Above Yasamin, there was a glittering of something like powder. The twinkling began about eight feet above her and flowed to the ground. The hairs on Goliagoth's neck tingled. From where he watched, it appeared to be a cascading, three-tiered water fountain, but there was no water, just the glittering powder. As he had watched, the dust fell to the ground and faded, except one small light that came straight at him.

At first he thought it a fire-fly, although it was too late in the year for insects. As he watched, the insect reached him and hovered a few feet from his face. It wasn't like anything he'd ever seen. Closer, he realized it wasn't one color but a myriad of colors twinkling within the tiny body. He'd normally have swatted an insect buzzing in his face. Not this one. He sat mesmerized by the sight.

Suddenly, the light—he really couldn't call it an insect—gyrated wildly through the air and flew directly at him again. It bumped him on the forehead before bouncing up into the air and into the darkness of the night where it disappeared.

Goliagoth rubbed his chest and took a deep breath, oblivious to the shooting pain in his back.

He didn't understand what just happened.

To him.

To the insect.

All he knew was when the light disappeared into the blackness, it had taken the darkness in his chest with it.

There was no longer a void in his chest.

And he now understood that for which he had had no name.

Chapter 58

The morning dawned bright, clear and cold. Emerging from a thicket, Goliagoth entered the cave and handed a few berries to Yasamin and Arash. "Eat these. It will help to have something in your belly when we move. We're going to have to travel hard and fast today."

Each took a few of the fruits and nibbled on them. To Yasamin they tasted better than any fare she'd had at her table. Licking her fingers, she looked at Goliagoth. "Any signs of soldiers or dragons?"

"No. Dragons don't particularly like the cold. They will wait until it warms up a bit before they fly."

Arash stood and stretched. "Think your ruse worked?"

"Have no way of knowing for sure. If Amir thought about it he might realize I'd purposely lay a false trail. We have to get out of Dragonval."

Yasamin rose and folded her discarded clothes Goliagoth had spread over her the night before. She handed them to him. "I guess you'll want to put these back in the bag."

He nodded. "Will come in handy again if tonight's as cold." He stuffed them into the pack. "I've already scouted ahead. The main road forks about a mile from here—one north, the other south. We'll opt for the southern one. It should get us out of the country sooner. Since I don't know the country, I figure we'll stay near it, so we don't get lost."

The two nodded their understanding. Arash knelt and extinguished the fire. When the flame died, he scattered the debris and covered it with dirt. He then took a branch and smoothed the surface. The cave floor appeared undisturbed. Goliagoth watched with appreciation. The boy knew a lot more than he credited him.

"If you're ready, Highness, we'll head out."

"Yes. We need to get home and get ready for Amir's assault."

"As soon as we get to a town outside of Dragonval, I'll get word to my father, so he can send men and ships." Arash was also eager to get defenses set up for Gwendomere. He already felt much better about the whole situation knowing Goliagoth was on their side.

The trio headed south.

The sun grew higher and drove away the coldness. The terrain grew rougher. Huge boulders dotted the landscape, left there by a long-forgotten glacier. They edged nearer the road, as it was the only smooth passage through the maze of rocks.

At noon they stopped for a rest. Goliagoth again found them a few berries. A small spring trickled down a rough boulder nearby. He patiently gathered the drops into his bottle and brought it to the others.

He scanned the surroundings, while Yasamin and Arash ate. The boy watched the soldier. "You look troubled, Goliagoth. What is it?"

"I don't like this terrain. It is forcing us onto the road and hemming us in. We can only go forward or backward."

"How about trying to find a way through the rocks?"

"Too time-consuming. What worries me is we're headed south, which should be toward Chimethra. The land ought to be leveling out as it's dropping toward the ocean."

Yasamin looked up from her food. "Are we going in the wrong direction?"

Goliagoth eyed the sun's position. "No. We are headed south. Hopefully this is just an anomaly, and the land'll smooth out in a couple of miles."

"I hope so; I don't like being exposed on the road." Arash's hand drifted toward his sword for comfort.

"My sentiments, too, but we've not much choice. I don't think the Queen could climb some of these hills. I'd be hard put on some of them myself."

Yasamin felt a cold wind from nowhere swirl around her. She shivered. With the wind came an sense of danger, disaster. She lost her appetite. "Let's go. I don't like it here. It doesn't feel right."

Goliagoth nodded. He had the same feeling.

The three of them crept along the narrow strip of grass beside the road. The earth grew more narrow, the rocks taller. At last the boulders forced them onto the lane itself.

Goliagoth paused. The road lay straight before them bound on either side by the rocky walls. Ahead it curved out of sight. He rested his hand on his sword. "It's forward or backward. Maybe the rocks recede beyond the bend. This is not a place to be caught."

As if in response to his words, the ground quivered beneath their feet. Yasamin's eyes widened as she glanced first to Arash, then to Goliagoth. "What's that?"

The soldier stood still for a second. Panic filled his blood, not for himself but for the two with him. He and Arash exchanged quick glances, sharing the message: "Horses. Riding hard. Has to be soldiers. Run!"

The trio dashed toward the curve. They couldn't outrun the horses, but perhaps they could find a better place to take a stand. There was no doubt in their minds who the riders were.

They reached the curve, and Yasamin's mind reeled. She almost stopped, but Arash grabbed her hand and pulled her forward.

The land didn't level out. The road ahead narrowed even more and lead to a dilapidated hanging bridge connecting the two bluffs. A chasm over one hundred feet deep separated the two cliffs.

"Come on, hurry." Goliagoth ran for the bridge. His experienced eye quickly took in its sorry condition. One of the hand ropes had rotted away, leaving only the right one to hold onto. Both bottom ropes were there, but many of the planks were missing or looked rotten. It was a sorry sight, but the only hope they had.

He returned to Arash and Yasamin. He saw the terror in her eyes and mistook it for fear of the oncoming soldiers. "The bridge is dangerous, but it's our only hope. You two get across it and wait for me there."

The earlier chill Yasamin felt tightened itself around her spine. "Goliagoth, what are you thinking? You're coming."

The soldier held her eyes with his own. "We've no time for discussion. You two get across. I'm staying here and holding off the soldiers until you reach the other side."

"We're not leaving you behind!" Yasamin cried.

"Soon as you're over, I'll come. When I've reached you, we'll cut the ropes. That'll stop them."

"Goliagoth—" Yasamin grabbed his arm.

"I'll come if I can. The important thing is your safety." He looked at Arash. "Go. Take her. They're almost upon us."

Arash pulled Yasamin toward the bridge. "Come, love. We've no choice." They turned.

"Arash." The boy turned back to the giant. Goliagoth had drawn his sword. "Take care of her. If I go down, cut the ropes. Don't let them get her."

Arash's mouth tightened, but he understood the order, both spoken and unspoken. "They won't get her."

Goliagoth ran back toward the curve and took his stance just as a handful of soldiers rounded the bend. The huge horses' nostrils flared wide, and sweat glistened on their black skin. They had been ridden hard and were jumpy.

The men pulled up sharp when they saw the *Demolisherian* blocking the road. Behind him they could see Arash and Yasamin hurrying for the bridge.

"So you have turned traitor, have you," the leader of the soldiers snarled. He dismounted and stood hands on hips as he stared at Goliagoth.

"I stand for the truth. If that's treason, I'm guilty."

The other soldiers dismounted and stood behind Anraxe. They were more familiar with Goliagoth's reputation than the new man was. They were in no hurry to meet the giant's blade.

"The king has ordered we bring the bitch and you back."

"Watch your tongue. She's still the Queen."

"I'm using the King's own words."

"It doesn't change the fact."

"What he called her is better than the words he has for you. To say the King's furious with you is putting it mildly."

Goliagoth's smile would have turned a reasonable man's blood to ice. He had to buy time for the others to reach the bridge and cross it. He dearly wanted to turn and see if they were all right but dared not take his eyes from the leader. Anraxe swaggered another step toward Goliagoth.

"What happened to you? Was she so good in bed you lost your mind?"

"Silence!" Goliagoth roared. The insult to Yasamin set his blood on fire. "You're not fit to speak her name, let alone issue insults. I'll slice out your tongue."

All but Anraxe took a step back. The fury in the giant was overwhelming. The leader unsheathed his sword, then met Goliagoth's blow with one of his own. The *swish* of the slicing of air, the clang of metal against metal and the men's grunts were the only sound in the silence. Blow met blow, advance met retreat, only to be repeated in reverse in a parody of a dance.

In the meantime, Yasamin and Arash had reached the bridge. Yasamin gasped as she saw the deep chasm and eyed the decaying wood and ropes. "It'll never hold us; it's too fragile." With worried eyes, she glanced at Arash. "What are we going to do?"

"What Goliagoth said to do. It's the only chance we have." He glanced over his shoulder as he heard the clash of swords. Goliagoth was battling the leader of the soldiers. "We don't have much time. I'll go first. Let me get about five or six feet out, then start, so all the weight won't be in one place."

Before Yasamin could speak, Arash grabbed the right hand rope and ran about two feet onto the bridge.

The two bottom ropes snapped, and the bridge collapsed into the chasm.

If Arash had not been holding onto the rope, he would have fallen with the rotten wood. He dangled a few feet below the cliff.

"Arash!" Yasamin dropped to her knees and reached for him. He swung on the short rope, trying to find purchase for his feet. "Grab my hand. Here!" She tried to get hold of his arm but couldn't reach him. "Arash, don't fall. I can't lose you."

The boy scrabbled against the rocky ledge and found a small niche for his toes. He dug in and started pulling himself up, hand-over-hand, on the rope. At last he reached the top. Yasamin grabbed his sleeve and helped him over the top. Both were gasping from the effort.

"Gods, what are we going to do?" Yasamin cast worried looks from Arash to Goliagoth who battled with the leader.

"I don't know. That was the only way. We're trapped. Better to die fighting." Arash rose and drew his sword.

Yasamin closed her eyes and took a deep breath. "Wait!" She stood. "There is a way."

"There isn't. The bridge is gone."

"We will build another one."

Arash looked at Yasamin as if she had lost her mind. "Impossible."

Yasamin moved to him and took both his arms. "Remember the last bridge, when you told me to look in your eyes and trust you?"

Arash nodded.

"I'm asking that of you now. You won't understand, but trust me. Just trust me. Look into my eyes and believe what is going to happen is real. You don't have to understand, just believe."

"I trust you."

Yasamin nodded and turned to the posts of the ruined bridge. She bowed her head. Arash cast a worried look over his shoulder. Goliagoth was holding the leader in check. The rest of the soldiers stood spellbound, watching the two warriors. He looked back to Yasamin. She hadn't moved.

They hadn't moved, but the sounds seemed farther away.

Arash frowned. There was a difference in the air. Movement at Yasamin's feet caught his eye. He looked down.

The ground between the two posts glistened with moving bodies. He peered closer. Silkworms were gathering, thousands swarmed in front of Yasamin. Goosebumps raced across Arash's skin.

She held out her hand to him. He clasped it. "Come."

She took a step forward with the silkworms swarming in front of her, leaving their silken trail.

Yasamin took another step over the edge of the cliff.

She didn't fall.

She stood on a silken footbridge.

Arash stopped at the cliff's edge. This could not happen.

"Come on, Arash." He remained rooted. He couldn't walk into air.

Yasamin let go of his hand. "You said you trusted me." She ran three feet farther into the air, while the silkworms churned a beautiful, silken bridge before her. It glistened like silver in the sunlight. She turned toward him and held out her arms. "I love you, Arash. If you love me, come."

He did.

Love her.

Went to her.

He never took his eyes from her as they ran. The silk worms sped before them, weaving the silvery, silk bridge.

They crossed the chasm.

They looked back. The bridge was beautiful, a shimmering replica of the bridge that had been there once upon a time. Beyond it they saw the soldiers fighting, blades ringing in the silence.

Goliagoth was gaining on the leader, who had fallen back toward his men. Engaged, Goliagoth had not seen the episode with the bridge but thought they had had enough time to cross. He began working his way backward.

Anraxe, furious at being bested in the swordfight, realized Goliagoth's plan. He screamed at the soldiers. "Spineless jackasses don't stand there. Gutless babies, afraid of one man. Get him. Get him, or the King will have your heads."

Goaded by Anraxe's words, the soldiers drew their swords and charged.

Yasamin grabbed Arash's arm. "Oh, my god, Arash, they'll kill him." She moved forward, but Arash grabbed her. "No. Stay here."

Yasamin tugged against him. "I have to go. We can't—"

Arash pulled her to him. "Goliagoth said stay. Don't make his efforts for naught. He's doing this for you, Yasamin."

The Queen looked back at the fight, her eyes full of unshed tears. Goliagoth was edging toward the bridge. He had already killed three of the slower soldiers and slashed at the others.

Anraxe stepped back to catch his breath and let the other soldiers move in on the giant to wear him out. The *Demolisherian* was an experienced fighter—the best he'd ever seen—but he was determined to have his reward promised by the King. Running to his stallion, he mounted and spurred the horse toward the knot of soldiers.

Two of them had circumvented Goliagoth with the purpose of attacking him from the rear. His sixth sense told the giant they were coming. He twisted and swung his sword in an arc behind him. He hit both men, and they went down, but the pain from the old wound flared, taking his breath and he hesitated.

A second.

An eternity.

When he swung back to the soldiers in front of him, it was just in time to see them part and the lance headed at him.

It didn't hurt.

He thought Anraxe had missed him.

He couldn't understand why his knees wouldn't hold him.

From a great distance, he heard Yasamin's scream.

Heard her scream his name.

Then there was darkness.

Chapter 59

Yasamin saw the rider on the black horse. She saw him thrust his lance at Goliagoth. For a moment, she thought that by some miracle he had missed the giant.

And then she saw him fall.

"*No-oooooo*, Goliagoth!" she screamed. Her grief gave her extra strength, and she pulled away from Arash. She took two steps before her knees collapsed, and she fell. The soldiers had moved away from Goliagoth, who lay on the ground motionless.

Arash stood behind her. He was unable to believe what his eyes saw. He had come to believe Goliagoth invincible.

Yasamin's hands were over her mouth, and she rocked back and forth. Silent sobs shook her. Tears poured from her eyes. It was impossible. He was the pillar of strength she had relied upon for so long— it seemed he had been in her life forever. Goliagoth couldn't be dead. Not when he had turned from the darkness. Surely the gods would not take him at the time she needed him most.

The sobs went deeper, deep into her chest. They choked her, filled her throat. She could not breathe. The sobs suffocated her. They filled her heart so that it was drowning. It tried to stop beating, wanted to stop. Daylight withdrew as darkness closed its tight fist around her. Coldness settled inside her chest. A coldness so frigid it burned.

With unseeing eyes, she saw the leader on the horse gather his men and point to her. They were coming for her.

She didn't care. She no longer cared about anything.

She had failed Goliagoth.

Just as the powers had failed her.

She had been a fool for thinking she could make a difference.

She had been a fool to put her faith in something she couldn't see.

A fool to believe in a faith that would take away someone so precious, someone who had turned and given his heart to the light.

"Come, Yasamin, we must run. They'll be upon us soon." Arash tried to pull her to her feet, but she remained limp. She continued to rock back and forth on her knees, hugging herself tightly, eyes focused on another world. She made no effort to rise.

"Yasamin, run. They're coming." Again he tried pulling her to her feet.

"Go, Arash. Go. Save yourself. I don't care if they get me."

Her lifeless voice pierced his heart. Her grief had temporarily deranged her. Across the chasm, Arash saw the horseman whipping up his soldiers' courage to cross the bridge.

He had to get through to her.

He roughly dragged her to her feet and swung her around. "You're a Queen, Yasamin, for the gods sakes act like one. And you're more—I've just seen that."

"I'm nothing. I couldn't save Goliagoth. I couldn't save him even though he turned to the light."

Arash cast a worried eye toward the soldiers edging closer to the bridge. He shook Yasamin, trying to reach her. "How can you say that? Think of the thousands you've helped already. The others you will."

"No."

No? The one word wrapped cold coils around Arash's heart. What had happened to the woman he loved. What thing had stolen her and left this empy shell before him?

Arash took her chin and forced her to look into his eyes. He didn't like what he saw in hers. Aside from the sorrow, he saw a hardness that frightened him. There were sparks of rage in her gaze so unlike her; his blood ran cold. He didn't want to lose her.

To the soldiers.

To the madness lurking near.

Or the dark side.

Fear added an urgency to his actions. He shook her and forced her to look at him.

"So you pity yourself? You're saying Goliagoth was wrong to believe in you?"

Something stirred in her eyes. Arash pressed his point.

"In his own way, Goliagoth loved you. You gave him something he'd never had; you gave his life meaning. He chose to die for you and your way rather than remain in the darkness. Would you mock him now, belittle his sacrifice? Would you?" He shook her again, more gently this time.

She shook her head, but uncertainty replaced the rage. "He shouldn't have died. I should have been able to save him."

"You cannot save everyone, Yasamin, even though you want to. Each has his allotted time. Goliagoth saw something in you that cleared his mind and his heart."

Yasamin finally focused on Arash. Tears formed in her eyes.

"Yasamin, in the most important way, you *did* save him. He chose life in light rather than death in darkness."

The tears spilled down her cheeks.

Arash wiped them away. "Let's go before they cross that bridge."

"Hey, *Queenie*. You're ours now. You're big protector isn't so big any more." Anraxe sat on his black stallion, a leer on his face. "Tell your little friend if he runs, we won't chase him. King only wants you and him." The soldier indicated Goliagoth's body with a nod of his head.

"Come, on." Arash began to pull Yasamin, but again, she refused to move.

Surprisingly, she turned to face the soldier. "We don't have to leave. We are safe."

"They're going to come across the bridge you constructed."

"No they are not. Watch." Her voice was calm, quiet. She was in control once more. "They belong to the dark side. They cannot follow."

Anraxe goaded his stallion forward. The other soldiers followed behind. The horse's hooves touched the bridge. Screaming, the black stallion reared up, pawing the air. It bucked and kicked, then moved backward despite Anraxe's best efforts to control it. He whipped the horse viciously.

"Come on, you worthless mount. Move."

The horse fought the bit, cavorting and rearing, mindless of the whip. The other horses joined in. Nostrils flaring, saliva foaming, they all kicked wildly at the air.

"I'll cut ya into pig bait when we get home, you worthless piece of shit." Anraxe got off, giving one last vicious slash with his whip. "Dismount. We'll get her on foot. Hurry before the bitch runs. Forward!" Anraxe screamed, pointing his sword toward the bridge.

The soldiers hesitated. They were not sure what this thing was they saw.

"Forward. NOW! Or I'll nail your hides to the front gate myself!"

The men shouted their battle cry and began running across the bridge with Anraxe bringing up the rear.

"Get her, men! Get the bitch now!"

A quarter of the way across the bridge, the men's battle cries turned to shrieks of horror as the silk turned to dust beneath their feet. Clawing and screaming, the men grasped the air as they fell. Anraxe was closest to the cliff. Seeing the puffs of smoke as the silk dissolved, he turned and ran for safety.

But in the end, good reigned.

Inches from the edge, Anraxe's luck vanished along with the bridge. He clutched at roots, rocks and, finally, emptiness. Like the rest, he fell into the chasm's depths.

Arash let out his breath. He didn't realize he'd been holding it until the last soldier fell. He was shaking from head to foot. He slowly re-sheathed his sword. "How did you know?"

Yasamin sighed. "The road of silk will not tolerate evil. The animals sensed it; they would not cross. They aren't evil, only their riders. Greed and hate blinded the soldiers to the possibility they couldn't use it."

"The road of silk?"

Yasamin touched his cheek. "My way of life. I almost lost sight of that, but your words made me realize I was turning from it. I'll tell you about it later. Right now, there is something I must do."

Yasamin slowly walked back across the bridge. This time Arash did not hesitate to follow, although he kept his eyes glued to her slender form. He believed *her*, but he wasn't sure he believed he could walk on translucent silk with the bottom hundreds of feet below. When they reached the hole in the bridge, Yasamin held forth her hands. The edges glistened, then stretched until they met and mended the tear.

As Arash quickly checked the other soldiers to make sure they were dead and no threat, Yasamin moved toward Goliagoth. He laid face-down in the dirt. She knelt beside him. Yasamin hesitated, then rolled him over.

He groaned and his eyelids fluttered.

"Gods, he's alive. Arash!" The boy ran to her and knelt on the other side of the soldier. "He's alive, Arash. We've got to do something." She frantically started to tear his bloodied shirt away. Goliagoth reached up and covered her hands with one of his.

"Highness, no use." His words were slurred. "I can feel my life force drifting. You and Arash must go."

Yasamin put her other hand on top of Goliagoth's and leaned forward. "I am not leaving you, Goliagoth. Not now, not ever. We'll take you with us. We'll get you help."

Goliagoth tried to laugh, but it got lost in a gurgle. He caught his breath. "I can see the two of you tryin' to carry the likes of me." He grew sober. "You need to go; get out of the country." He turned his glance to Arash. "Tell her, boy. Get her home."

Arash put his hand on Goliagoth's shoulder. He could feel the coldness deep beneath the skin. He tried to smile. "I've tried, but you know how headstrong she can be. She's determined to come back for you. And for once, I agree with her, my friend."

"Friend?" The giant grunted slightly.

"Well, you are, like it or not. You're stuck with me, soldier. Forever." Arash spoke gruffly, trying to hide the tears in his voice.

Goliagoth stared deeply into Arash's eyes. "I believe you, boy. Thank you."

Arash squeezed the soldier's shoulder, unable to say more.

Goliagoth turned his gaze to Yasamin. "Highness, take care of yourself. Get home to Gwendomere. Fight for what's right." He coughed and closed his eyes. "Sorry I failed you," he whispered.

The words were her undoing. Yasamin leaned closer to him to hear his faint words. The tears dripped from her cheeks onto his face.

He opened his eyes. "Tears? Not for someone like me."

"For you. Goliagoth, what would I ever have done without you? You have saved my life more than once. You have guided me, been my strength. I would not be alive today if not for you," she whispered.

He shook his head slightly. "Wish I had known ... you earlier ... fore I drifted ... dark side. Things ... been different. Maybe I'd made ... difference."

"Oh, Goliagoth, what was before does not matter. It is what you have become that matters."

Again he shook his head. "If I could believe ... that. Done too ... bad in my life. Things I'd change but ... can't."

"That was the past. You were forgiven all when you turned to the light."

He lay still a moment, too weak to shake his head. Yasamin could feel the coldness creeping into his limbs. She wanted to hold him, to warm him, to give him life. It wasn't hers to give. She held his hands tighter, wanting him to feel her nearness for as long as possible.

"Goliagoth, believe me. You're forgiven for all that was before. You've made it up many times over."

The soldier opened his eyes. "... ish I could believe ... something afterwards, like you. Felt it once ... the prison, when you touched me. It was ... beautiful ... not for me ... done ... much harm especially ..." He closed his eyes again and coughed. A small trickle of blood oozed from his mouth.

"Especially what, Goliagoth, what?" Yasamin was anxious to comfort him. She already knew in her heart he was forgiven.

"I can't forget ... child I killed, Highness ... your village. A baby ... killed him in cold blood. I was heartless bastard ... see ... now." He closed his eyes again. Yasamin heard the rattling in his throat as death crawled closer for its victim. The soldier struggled for air.

"He's in a better place, Goliagoth. He's happy. He forgives you."

He lay unmoving, his breathing shallow.

"Goliagoth, do you hear me?"

From somewhere deep within, the soldier rallied to the voice of the woman he loved. He opened his eyes. "Heard you … too much … to be … lieve he'd forgive …"

"He does. He'll tell you so." Yasamin raised her hand that covered Goliagoth's, cupped it and turned her palm toward his face. "Look at my hand."

The giant lowered his gaze to her palm. A first he saw nothing, then her skin began to glow. A tiny, blue light burst forth. He continued to stare. The dot expanded until there was a halo around it.

He suddenly saw through the light.

Yasamin watched him stare at the radiance. His face illuminated from the glow emanating from her palm. A myriad of expressions crossed his features—disbelief, confusion, wonder and, finally, acceptance. The glow faded, and Goliagoth returned his gaze to Yasamin's face.

"I believed you a wondrous woman, Highness. You are and more … so much more," he whispered. His eyes drank in her face.

And for the first time in his life, Goliagoth smiled.

"So much more," he whispered.

He closed his eyes.

And ascended into the light.

Yasamin leaned over and kissed him on the forehead. "Go in peace and light, my friend. We'll meet again."

Arash watched Yasamin in silence. There was so much about her he had yet to learn. His soul already knew she was more than just a queen, but he yearned to know more about her and what she believed. He waited quietly for her next move.

She remained still for so long he started to speak but refrained. Something was happening. He stared at Goliagoth's body. A glow was shining through the blood covering his chest. As Arash watched, the glow condensed into a small, red light that rose and hovered above the soldier's chest. After a second it moved toward Yasamin and bobbed in front of her face.

Arash was speechless, but Yasamin showed no surprise. In fact, it seemed she had waited for this very thing. She smiled, raised her left hand and opened it again. A tiny, blue light ascended from it and drifted to the red one. It flew around the crimson dot several times.

Arash peered closer at the red light. It began quivering. A spark flared in Arash's brain, and against all reason, he *knew* somehow the red light was *laughing*.

The two lights twirled around each other, then settled side-by-side in front of Yasamin's face.
She nodded.
The two lights shot into the sky.
Into the light.

Chapter 60

"We've nothing to dig with. I'll get some rocks, and we'll cover him, so the animals can't touch him." Arash ached with the loss of Goliagoth. He couldn't begin to imagine what Yasamin must have be feeling.

She still stared into the sky where the two lights disappeared. He wanted to ask her about that, but now was not the time.

"Yasamin? Do you want me to get rocks?" He had to do something. Even he, with his military experience, couldn't leave Goliagoth's body in the open, unburied, exposed to the animals.

"What?" She looked at him, her eyes focusing.

"We've no digging tools. Do you want me to find rocks? We can build a rough cairn. It'll keep the animals away ... from ... him."

"It isn't necessary." She smoothed Goliagoth's hair back from his face and touched his cheek. She gently extracted her right hand from beneath the giant's and crossed his hands on top of his chest.

Arash was surprised. He knew how much she loved the soldier. "We can't leave him here, like this, out in the open for, you know."

"We're not." She looked across Goliagoth's body and smiled at Arash. "We're not going to leave him here."

"We can't take him. We have no way, and we're not strong enough."

"We're not carrying him with us." She gazed at Goliagoth's face. His smile still remained, and she smiled in return. She softly touched his cold cheek, then returned her gaze to Arash. "We're not leaving him here. He deserves better for all he has done, something fitting." She saw Arash's worried glance and gave a small laugh. "Don't worry, I haven't gone crazy on you, at least not yet. I will need your help though."

"Any way I can."

"Help me get him onto the bridge."

"The bridge?"

She nodded. "I cannot get him there by myself."

"Of course."

Arash took Goliagoth's arms and tried to pull him, while Yasamin joined in. After an intense five minutes, they moved the giant only two inches. Crouched over the soldier, Arash mopped the sweat from his red face and looked up at Yasamin who was breathing just as hard.

"Didn't realize he weighed so much—at least sixty stones. We need to get some of his weight off the ground." He glanced around. "I've an idea."

He quickly hacked down two small trees, then attacked the growth of vines nearby. "Won't win any prize for beauty, but I've used this before to transport wounded." Yasamin watched him as he nimbly wove the long vines between the two trees, forming a rough litter. He tied the last vine, picked it up and laid it parallel to Goliagoth.

"This should work since we don't have far to go. I'm going to roll him to his side. When I do, slide this beneath him."

Yasamin ran to Arash. "Brilliant."

Arash rolled the soldier over, and she slid the makeshift litter beneath him. Each then grabbed the end of one of the trees and began pulling. The burden was still substantial, and both still strained with the effort.

"We've distributed the weight more evenly with the litter, but he's still heavy."

Yasamin nodded, too breathless to answer.

Although the way was slow, the idea worked. At last they reached the bridge.

"We only need to go onto the bridge far enough to clear land."

They pulled Goliagoth about ten feet from the cliff.

Unsure of Yasamin's intentions, Arash looked at her. "You want to remove the litter?" This was her territory, so he'd follow her instruction.

"No, it isn't necessary." Knowing Arash was uneasy on the silk bridge, Yasamin nudged him. "Wait for me on land. I won't be long."

"You sure?"

"Yes."

"I'll be at the post." Arash turned to go, then swirled to face her. "Don't do anything. We've forgotten something." Arash dashed to the spot where the soldier had fallen and returned carrying Goliagoth's sword in his hand. He started to lay it on the giant's chest but stopped and again looked up at Yasamin. "Is it all right? I mean, with whatever you're planning? It won't be inappropriate?"

Yasamin smiled. "It is most appropriate. I'm glad you thought of it. Thank you." Arash nodded and laid the sword in place. He looked at Goliagoth a long moment, then straightened. Standing at attention, he slowly brought up his hand in a military salute. "Good-bye, Goliagoth. Gods-speed," he whispered, and he hurried to the cliff.

Yasamin knelt by the soldier. She gently straightened his clothes and repositioned his hands over the sword. She caressed the giant's face, memorizing it by touch, then kissed him one last time on the cheek.

She bowed her head.

Arash watched. He believed she was praying, as her lips were moving. So much had happened in the past hour. He didn't know what to think any more.

She finally returned to Arash. A brilliant smile illuminated her face. "I received permission." At Arash's blank stare, she laughed. "I'll explain everything later, love. Patience."

"I guess I have to. I don't understand anything I've seen."

"Soon you'll understand everything."

Yasamin faced the bridge and spread her arms, so she formed a human cross. Speaking in a language Arash didn't understand, Yasamin began chanting.

The edges of the bridge loosened from both cliffs and shrank toward each other. Soon the bridge only remained beneath Goliagoth. The silk wove and looped over itself until it formed a translucent, shimmering box encasing Goliagoth's corpse. It floated in the air between the two cliffs.

Arash couldn't have asked Yasamin what was happening if he had wanted to. He stood with his mouth hanging open. From nowhere, a huge, black eagle appeared and landed on the casket. It raised its head and emitted a loud cry, which echoed down the canyon. Shivers surfed Arash's skin. He had never seen a coal black eagle; even as he watched, the black lightened to brown, bronze, then gold. The bird fluttered its feathers, and they shimmered in the sunlight. Arash slowly sank to his knees, as he realized a power far greater than he'd ever imagined was at work before him.

Two butterflies appeared—one silver, one gold. They hovered on either side of Goliagoth's casket.

Yasamin lowered her arms as she whispered, "Thank you."

The butterflies began moving southward, and the silk-encased box floated between them. The golden eagle left the box and flew toward the two on the cliff. As it neared, Arash realized its immensity. Its wing spread was at least six feet.

It flew closer until it hovered mere inches from Yasamin. Arash could feel the wind created by the powerful thrust of its wings even though he stood five feet away. Yasamin gently raised her hand and touched the eagle's breast.

"Be happy," she whispered. "Peace."

The eagle stretched its neck and screeched its deep-throated call. It slowly circled Yasamin and Arash, surveying them with golden eyes. As the boy stared at the bird, he felt his sense of loss lessen. It was almost as if—Arash shook his head. *That could not be.*

The eagle flew back and perched on the moving casket, settling at the back of the silk casket. It faced south and folded its wings.

Yasamin lifted her hand in farewell. She and Arash watched the strange procession until it became a distant spot on the horizon and disappeared.

Arash's knees were numb, and he struggled to stand. His heart believed something his mind believed impossible. He had thousands of questions needing answers but, at the moment, only one needed an answer.

"Where are they going with him?"

Yasamin lowered her arm and walked to him. She put her arms around Arash and leaned against him. "Where he belongs—the holy mountain."

Chapter 61

"Now that you've finished your work with Goliagoth, we need to decide the best way to get to Gwendomere." Arash panted as he pushed the last of Amir's dead soldiers over the cliff's edge. He wanted to destroy any evidence of the battle, as it might buy them a little more time.

He walked back to the boulder where Yasamin rested and sat at her feet. She looked exhausted. The shadows under her eyes looked like bruises. "Are you all right, Yasamin?"

"Just tired."

He reached up and touched her cheek with his fingertips. "It's been a rough day." She looked so childlike, so vulnerable. He rose and sat beside her. He gently pulled her against his shoulder. "Rest a few minutes. I doubt any more soldiers will come today. These men won't be missed before tonight at the earliest."

Yasamin sighed and nestled against him, her head beneath his chin. They sat in companionable silence.

Arash's heart wished they could sit that way forever, but his mind knew the price was too high. After a few minutes, he spoke softly.

"I don't understand anything I saw today, Yasamin, yet I believe it. Guess that doesn't make much sense."

"It's not unusual. I've felt that way many times."

"After seeing that bridge and what you did with Goliagoth, why don't you just put yourself home? You could be safe in Gwendomere in minutes."

"It's not so simple, Arash. I'm just learning. Sometimes it works; sometimes it doesn't. There's so much I don't know."

"Then we need to determine the best way for us to get there. It won't take the King long to figure out what's happened. He'll send more men after you."

Yasamin pulled away and straightened. "I know." She rose and looked back down the road they had traveled. "I'm not going back to Gwendomere."

Arash stood. "Don't be foolish. You've got to, for your own good."

"There are things more important than my personal safety."

"Like what?"

"My people. All the lands Amir will destroy if he's free to attack them."

"This is crazy." Arash moved to Yasamin and turned her toward him. "You can't do this by yourself, Yasamin. We'll get you to Gwendomere, and I'll get my father to send warriors to help protect you."

She shook her head. "Thank you for the offer, but I'm going back to the city. I'm going to face Amir."

Panic surged through Arash. "You cannot. He will have you in irons the moment you enter the gates, if not before."

"That is a chance I have to take. I hope to reason with him. He has to understand he cannot live this way. He cannot destroy people on a whim. It is evil. He's turning to the dark side more and more."

"He already belongs to the dark side. Can't you see that?"

"I *see* a boy in a grown man's body, unable to control his emotions, his tantrums. Maybe I can reach him, turn him around before it's too late. The one thing clear to me is I have to stop him *here*. He cannot be allowed to march against Gwendomere."

She turned away.

Arash grabbed her arm. "I can't let you do this. It's crazy. He'll kill you or worse."

Yasamin hugged Arash tightly. "I will always love you, Arash, but I have a path I must follow." She pulled back. "I want you safe. Get out of Dragonval. They won't stop you. You're free." She stared at him, memorizing his face. "I must go."

Arash held onto her arm. "I won't let you destroy yourself. Don't you understand? I love you. I can't lose you, especially on a fool's mission. He's not going to listen to a word you have to say."

Before his eyes, Yasamin became the Queen. She looked at Arash, then at her arm, and with that look, she didn't need words. He let go. "Understand something, Arash, as much as I love you I cannot let it turn me from my destiny. If you think this a fool's mission, so be it. But I will do whatever is necessary to protect innocent people. I'm not afraid of dying."

"Neither am I. The only thing that scares me is losing you."

She smiled softly. "You could never lose me. Haven't you seen that today?"

Arash made his choice. "I'm not sure what I saw. I'm only sure of one thing; I'm going with you."

"You don't have to. As you said, it'll be dangerous. I don't want anything to happen to you."

This time he smiled and put his hand to her face. "You could never lose me. Haven't *you* seen that today? Besides, you said you can't always use your powers. I have a sword that works any time. I'll get you to Amir."

Yasamin smiled, and with this look, again no words were needed. The two melted together with a long kiss. He covered her face with kisses and buried his face in her long hair, breathing in its fragrance. She wrapped her arms around his neck and held him tightly. His warmth enveloped her. Happiness lifted her heart.

An instant later it crashed.

Without warning, the thought wormed its way into her consciousness. Technically, she was still married to Amir, was still the Second Queen. If she was successful in getting the King to amend his ways, she was still bound by her word to honor their marriage. Coldness settled around her heart. She'd have to be very careful in her dealings with her husband. She wanted to be with Arash; she admitted the truth to herself unashamedly. But she could not do anything in her dealings with Amir to hurt him just so she could have what she desired in her heart. She had to give her husband every chance possible to turn away from the dark side, even if it meant giving up Arash.

Another choice to make.

Yasamin prayed she'd have the strength to do what had to be done.

To Amir.

To Arash

To herself.

She allowed herself one last kiss, then pulled away. "If you chose to go with me, you must let me deal with Amir. I have to do everything I can to get him to change his mind. You mustn't interfere."

"I understand."

"Let's go, then."

"Yasamin, wait. I trust you and your belief, but you need to do the same for me."

"How?"

"You say you can't always use your power, so I assume that's why we're having to physically return."

"Yes."

"Then I'll get you to Amir, but you have to trust me, and follow my instructions for getting us there."

She thought about it for a moment. "Agreed."

"Good. Here's what I suggest: Let's go back to the cave where we spent the night. There's a good six hours of daylight left, and we'll be targets for soldiers, not to mention dragons. As soon as it's dark, we'll head out. The dragons will nest, and any soldiers searching will bed down for the night. They can't track what they can't see. We should get back to the city a couple hours before sunrise. The palace will be quiet. That's our best time to catch him. He'll be alone. Besides, we could both use the rest."

Yasamin sighed. "You're right. I just want to reach him before he sends the army."

Arash smoothed her hair back from her forehead and kissed it. "I'd wager my last penny Amir's thoughts at the moment are more on catching you than sending the army. He wants you suffering in prison, knowing you can't do anything. If you escape, it ruins his plan."

"Probably." She smiled, but the worry remained in her eyes.

"If the soldiers capture you, I can promise you there won't be a chance to reason with him. You're best chance to talk is to catch him unaware. Let's go to the cave. You can rest, and I'll keep watch." He took her hand.

They went to the cave and stayed until darkness fell.

But Yasamin didn't sleep. She told Arash about her mother.

About Serpata.

About Mosesra and Shar.

And most importantly, about the road of silk.

Chapter 62

They saw the silhouette of the castle against the white moon. They traveled hard throughout the night and had almost three hours until dawn. All that remained was getting into the city and to Amir's chambers.

Keeping to the trees and low brush, they crawled toward the rock wall.

Arash whispered into Yasamin's ear. "Let's go to the west a hundred yards. See the grapevines? We'll use them for cover, and it's out of view of the guardhouse. It'll put us almost to the wall."

She nodded her understanding, and they scrabbled through the dying vines. Within minutes, they were standing against the rock barrier. Arash moved along, searching its rough surface for anything useable as hand and foot holds.

After moving fifty yards in one direction, he retraced his steps and tried the other without luck. He returned to Yasamin. "The walls are too smooth. I can't find any purchase we can use to climb over. They've cut all the close trees. They're useless."

"So what do we do?"

"I'm at a loss. We already know the gates can't be opened from the outside. Plus there'll be guards."

Arash crouched, so he'd make a smaller target. Yasamin followed suit. "I've got to get inside." She closed her eyes and rubbed her temples. Arash watched hopefully. After a minute or two, Yasamin opened her eyes. "No good. I can't make anything happen. I don't understand why."

"I can try checking the entire perimeter, but I'd guess it'll be like this. They probably check the walls constantly for this very reason. It would foil any surprise attack."

"I imagine you're right. We're back at the beginning."

Arash frowned. "I can knock on the gate and tell the guard I've got information for the king. If there's only one, maybe I can knock him out, then let you in."

"No! That's too dangerous. What if there are two guards?"

"I don't see any other choice. I'll just have to—" Arash stopped mid-sentence and nudged Yasamin's arm. "Look."

Yasamin glanced over her shoulder. A gold butterfly hovered in the bright moonlight. She turned toward it. "Mosesra?"

The butterfly flew closer, elongated, then solidified. Mosesra suddenly stood before them.

"I'm so glad to see you. Can you help us?"

Mosesra wanted to hug his granddaughter but refrained. Timing was critical. He had to be careful with everything he did and said. She still had choices to make. "That depends, child. Exactly what do you want me to do?"

"We have to get into the city. I have to get to Amir."

"Why?"

"I have to reason with him, get him to change his mind about attacking Gwendomere."

"I see." Mosesra glanced at Arash. His instinct told him the boy's heart was in the right place even though his mind had yet to comprehend. "You are going with her?" He already knew the answer, but he needed more.

"Yes, I am, your holiness."

Mosesra smiled. "No need for such a title, son." He sobered. "You realize what you're planning is extremely dangerous, even deadly. If you choose to enter the city with her, Amir will consider you an enemy and kill you if he can."

"I understand. I won't let her go alone. I'll die if it means she'll succeed."

"Strong words."

"I mean them."

"I can see you do." Mosesra turned his eyes to Yasamin. "What if the king will not call down his troops?"

"I'm hoping he'll listen to reason, that I can get him to turn from the destructive path he's following. There's been enough bloodshed."

"Yasamin, that isn't what I asked you."

She bowed her head. When she looked up, Mosesra saw the determination in her eyes. "I will do everything I can to persuade him to change. If that fails, then I will have to stop him. I cannot allow him to destroy Gwendomere nor any other country for that matter."

"I told you once I would help you any way I could. I cannot interfere with your decisions. Precisely what is it you want me to do?"

"All I ask is you help us get into the city. That's all. For some reason, I can't make my power work. Whatever happens after we're inside is through my choice. I ... we just need a chance to reach Amir."

Mosesra nodded. "Very well." He turned and bent near the wall. He stuck the index finger of his right and left hand into the ground about a foot apart. Two shafts of golden light instantly shot up the city wall. As it traveled upward, it congealed into a wooden ladder. It disappeared over the top of the wall.

"You have your entry. The rest is up to you."

"Thank you, Mosesra, for everything." Yasamin turned to climb the ladder.

Love for his granddaughter surged through Mosesra. He couldn't resist letting some of it show. He put his hand on her shoulder.

"Be careful. A dangerous path lies before you, dangers you don't even imagine. If you survive this, we will talk. I have much to tell you."

Yasamin smiled. "I will see you, Mosera, one way or the other." She began her ascent, and Arash moved to stand next to the old man.

"Can you see if she will make it?" he whispered.

Mosesra laid his hand on the boy's shoulder and glanced at his granddaughter high above them. He shook his head. "For reasons I can't tell you, the powers have kept the outcome from me," he whispered. "Contrary to legends, followers of the light are not all-knowing. Sometimes we have visions; sometimes we do not."

Arash put his hands on the ladder to follow Yasamin. "I'll do everything I can to get her out safe."

"I know you will. Peace and light go with you, son."

"And with you, Mosesra." Arash hurried up the ladder after Yasamin.

Mosesra waited until he knew the two had reached the ground on the inside, then waved his hands. The ladder disappeared. One thing he knew for certain: when it was over, they would either walk out through the gates, or they wouldn't walk out at all.

He sighed as he gathered his energy to return to the holy mountain. It had taken him almost two hundred years to learn patience was a virtue. And now, after almost another two hundred, he still had times when impatience won the battle.

Chapter 63

Arash put his finger to his lips. "Wait here," he whispered.
They kept to the outermost streets added since Casadra's time. The town now encompassed the castle and continued to grow, wedging houses and alleys into an already crowded area. The hodgepodge made it easier to hide. It took a few minutes longer to go this route, but as Arash had hoped, they saw no one, not even a stray dog.

A lone soldier guarded the entrance to the castle. Whether exhausted from maneuvers all day or simply bored, thinking there was no point to guard at this time of night, the man half-heartedly made his rounds. He glanced neither left nor right as he marched east to west and west to east.

Yasamin crouched behind the bush. Arash kissed her lightly on the lips. "I'll signal when it's safe for you to come."

He circled the open court until he was even with the guard's outermost point of guard. He wedged himself behind the tree and waited. As the soldier passed, Arash sprang forward and grabbed the man from behind. Hand over his mouth, he pulled the guard to the bushes. A quick twist of the neck and the man was no longer a threat.

Arash peeked through the leaves. No one was in sight. He quickly climbed the steps to the huge, bronze doors and carefully opened one. He took a quick glance inside. Again, no one was in sight. One more fast scan of the courtyard, and he motioned for Yasamin to come.

Crouching, she ran across the pavement and up the steps to Arash. He closed the door behind them, and they moved behind one of the massive pillars supporting the main hallway.

"Which way?"

Yasamin nodded toward the curving stairway. "Up there, to the left," she whispered.

Arash looked back. Her eyes were huge in the dimness, and his heart fluttered with fear for her. "It may not be safe to talk after this. There might be more guards upstairs. If I stop, stop. If I point and hold up fingers, it means I see that many people. If I point to you and the ground, it means you stay in that spot like you did outside until I indicate it's safe to come. Try to stay directly behind me at all times. Understand?"

"Yes."

Arash took her hand and held his knife with the other. It would be handier in closer range. If they ran into a crowd, he'd give Yasamin the knife and grab his sword. He prayed that wouldn't happen. "Let's go."

They slowly moved forward, dodging pillar to pillar in the dark hall. As they neared the stairs, sounds of approaching men reached them. Arash dove to the shadow of the pillar and pushed Yasamin behind him.

Three guards appeared, two of them half-carrying a man between them. They descended, dragging the prisoner down the steps. The third guard pushed the semi-conscious man from behind. "Go on, worthless pig. Your head will adorn the wall tomorrow. Move."

They reached the bottom step and started across the floor. Yasamin clamped her hand across her mouth to keep from crying out.

"Yeah," one of the guards carrying the man growled, "tomorrow you'll be dancing a jig before they cut off your head." He laughed at his own joke, and the other two joined in.

"Learn a lesson, you will. Too bad you won't have a chance to mend your ways," the other guard jeered. "Shouldn't have betrayed the King. Should've talked. He might've killed ya on the spot. Been more merciful."

The semi-conscious man attempted to keep up but was too weak. Hundreds of whip marks covered his body. Two fingers had been cut off, and blood dripped from the wounds. He feebly struggled. Tears ran down his face, and his lips were bruised and swollen. "Didn't know. Thought I was doing duty …" he managed to gasp through the narrow slit of his mouth.

The third soldier cuffed him on the head. "Shut up, pig. I ought to cut out your tongue, so I don't have to listen to your whining."

They dragged the man to the narrow door leading toward the dungeon. Their jeers and taunts faded as they descended. At last, silence reigned once more.

"Arash, that man, I know him," she whispered. "He was the leader of the guards in the prison when I was there. He followed Goliagoth's orders to the letter. He's innocent in my escape."

"He'll still pay. Amir considers Goliagoth a traitor; therefore, anyone who followed his orders is a traitor by association. Come on."

They darted up the grand staircase and took shelter behind the first pillar. The upper hallway was darker than the one below—a point in their favor. Peeking around the pillar, Arash hurried to the next one, pulling Yasamin behind him. They continued this method until they reached an intersecting passage.

Arash looked back at Yasamin and raised his eyebrows. The one time he came upstairs it had been from a different direction. The palace was such a maze; he had no idea of their location. She pointed to the left. They ran for the next column and continued down this hallway in the same manner.

And on they went for two more passages. They finally reached the hall he recognized. This was where they'd been attacked. Amir's quarters lay just around the corner. Gripping Yasamin's hand tighter, he eased around the corner and started toward the door.

A violent clatter stopped them in their tracks. Arash jumped for cover and pushed Yasamin behind him. The door to Amir's chambers half-opened, then stopped. Beyond, they heard him screaming.

"I don't care how many men it takes! You have to find her! Immediately! And then find the other one! Do not come back here without both of them! Do you understand me?"

There was a murmur of voices too low for Arash and Yasamin to understand. They obviously belonged to the soldier or soldiers responding to the King's command.

"Don't give me any excuses!" Amir's voice was hoarse from screaming. "If you think what you saw earlier was bad, I'll find something worse to reward you with if you come back empty-handed. I have to tell the people something today. If I had told them anything about this earlier, it would have been embarrassing. How in Hades do you think *this* will make me look? A fool at the very least! I will not have it. Find her now!" There was the sound of something breaking against the inside of the door. Arash and Yasamin involuntarily ducked at the crash.

The door jerked open, and four commanders exited. The last one carefully closed the door and hurried to catch up with his comrades.

"He's gone insane, absolutely mad," the oldest of the four whispered to his companion.

"Aye, but what can we do? Nothing," the other whispered.

"Shhh, not so loud," said the soldier who had closed the door, "he might hear you. I, for one, don't want my head departing my body."

"We've got to do something."

"We have to find her. What do you think happened?"

"Haven't a clue," murmured the oldest as the four marched down the hall. Absorbed in their conversation, they glanced only at each other.

"Where do we start?"

"Your guess is as good as mine. All I know is I'm not coming back here without her or the other one."

"Nor me. I'd slit my own throat before I'd return. Anything'd be better than what he could conjure up." The four continued their comments as they headed for the stairs until their voices and clatter of metal faded.

Arash looked at Yasamin and raised one eyebrow. "Still think you want to talk to him?"

Yasamin's face had paled to the color of cow's milk. With her fair hair, she appeared a wraith hovering in the darkness. Her eyes were stretched wide, her pupils so large he could barely see the irises. "I have to," she whispered.

"Come on, then. I think we'll be safe from interruption from what we just heard."

The two of them headed down the hallway and opened the massive door.

Chapter 64

The chamber was dim and full of the scent of smoke from candles the King had extinguished. Even in the faint light, the blood spots on the floor were visible—evidence of the earlier torture. Shards of glass and metal twinkled near the door. This was what they heard earlier.

Amir sat at his desk, his head in his hands. A decanter sat near him with an empty goblet beside it. He sighed, picked up the goblet and reached for the decanter. The odor of wine was strong.

Arash carefully shut the door behind them, but as they moved forward, the glass crunched beneath their feet.

"I said not to come back until you—" Amir shouted and turned to throw his goblet at the intruder. He stopped mid-action when he saw Yasamin and Arash.

For a moment, he sat in stunned silence, then he stood. His eyes narrowed. "What have you done with her?"

It was Arash and Yasamin's turn to stare. They thought he had been talking about finding them.

Yasamin found her voice. "Who?"

"Who?" Amir mimicked her. "Who else, the Queen. What have you done with her?"

"Nothing. What are you talking about?"

"You know what I'm talking about. You and your lover and that traitor took her. I want her back now!" His voice rose as his anger returned.

"Amir, we've done nothing with Medusimia. I haven't seen her since you put me in prison." Yasamin looked at Arash. "Have you?"

"No."

"Where's that pig traitor? He'll tell me when I get through with him."

"Goliagoth's dead, Amir. Killed by your soldiers."

The king fell into his chair and reached for the flask. "Then I'll never find her. Did he murder her?"

"No. He had no reason to."

Amir drained the contents of the decanter into the goblet. "Spite. The heartless bastard didn't need a reason."

Yasamin took a step forward. "Amir, I swear to you, Goliagoth did not do anything to Medusimia."

"And how would you know?"

"Because it would have thwarted his own plans. He and Arash have been with me. Goliagoth helped me escape. He fooled the guards, told them you wanted to see me. They knew nothing of his plans. We left the city. He was trying to get us out of Dragonval. The last thing he'd do is harm her. If Medusimia was missing, he knew he'd be the first person you'd call."

Amir stared at Yasamin. From where she stood, she could see his alcohol-glazed eyes, yet he was sober enough to realize she was right.

He hung his head on his chest. "Then where is she? I can't find her. I can't find my Queen."

Pity stirred in Yasamin's heart. He looked like a child who'd lost his favorite toy. "When did you discover she was missing?"

"Earlier, before daylight. I was lonely. She wasn't there. Her bed was undisturbed."

"What happened then?"

"I sent for the *Demolisherian*. Couldn't find him, so I sent for you. I was sure you put him up to it. That's when I found you'd escaped the fool guards." Amir suddenly lunged from the chair. He slightly wobbled on his feet.

Arash's hand went to his sword, but Yasamin didn't move.

"Damn you. It's your fault. All of it," the King snarled.

"Me?"

"Yes. She warned me about you and your conniving ways. She was unhappy with your coming here. What did you do? Be nice to me, then taunt her behind my back because she couldn't have a child?"

"I never said anything unkind to her."

"You did. She'd never leave me. *She* loved me."

"Amir, *you* wanted to marry me. You promised to destroy my country if I did not. It was no secret I did not want to marry you. You understood I did it to protect my people. Your promise not to hurt Gwendomere was my wedding present. Why would I make trouble with your first wife? It would only backfire on me."

For once, the king didn't have an answer. He staggered toward an oak cabinet and ransacked the shelves looking for another bottle. Not finding one, he turned his attention back to Yasamin.

"Yes, it would. But my mistake was trusting you in the first place. You lied to me. Played me for a fool." He moved back toward Yasamin but stopped when he saw Arash move up behind her. "You played me for a fool with *him*." He nodded at Arash. "Was he worth it, Yasamin? Was he good enough to cost you your throne to Dragonval?"

"Amir, I swear Arash and I have never been lovers."

The king's eyes darted from Yasamin to Arash. "You still think me a fool? All that time on the deserted island? No! I think you play with semantics. Maybe you two haven't been *lovers*. Perhaps you call it pleasure, whore, or just lust. Did you service the traitor, too?"

Yasamin sucked in her breath. The soldiers were right—he seemed to have lost his mind in his grief. She pushed down the rage boiling inside and tried to reason with him. "Amir, it could have been so easy to prove if you hadn't been so angry. You had only to call in the court physician. He could have told you I was—"

"Shut up!" Amir shouted. He shook his head like a dog with a rat. His thoughts were as mired in his drugged brain as his boots when they sank into the mud outside the stables. He struggled to straighten them. "You're trying to trick me. It's why you staged that kidnapping ..."

"You knew Serpata kidnapped me. You knew I was his granddaughter. You served him, Amir. You knew his plans for me."

"Lies! He promised me I'd have you. He was strong, and the throne was his. Whatever he said would happen, happened. He promised me his power and throne were mine when he was gone."

Yasamin stopped talking. Amir was not listening to her. She considered her next move.

Amir made the choice for her. He lunged to the desk and grabbed his sword. "*You* killed my uncle. I saw it. I'll avenge his death. And I will keep my promise to you, bitch. I'll destroy Gwendomere. Nothing will ever grow there again."

"No, Amir. You won't do that. It's wrong."

"You talk about wrong? I'm the one whose been wronged. First I'm going to hurt you like you hurt me—I'm going to kill your lover while you watch. Then I'll throw you back in prison where you can rot until I bring the heads of your people to you."

"No!" Yasamin barely uttered the word before Arash pushed her out of the way.

Amir lunged for him, and Arash parried the blade's thrust with one of his own. The two men fought, the clash of steel ringing in the chambers. Yasamin backed against the wall and watched in horror as each sliced toward the other.

Again and again, Amir thrust his blade toward Arash. The boy was good, but he had not had as many years as the King to perfect his swordsmanship. He barely managed to catch Amir's blade with his own and push it aside. He had no time to thrust past Amir's defense. And the King was not above using any tactic to gain advantage.

Amir shot a quick glance at Yasamin, smiled and shifted his direction. Worried for her safety, Arash tried to move in between them. Amir's deception worked. It gave him a second's advantage, and he slashed viciously. The tip of the blade caught Arash on his shoulder, and his shirt was quickly covered in blood.

It couldn't have been more than five minutes, but to Arash, it felt as if they had been fighting for hours. His arm grew heavy under the weight of the sword. The combination of his old injuries, hard travel and the new wound sapped his energy quickly.

He met a particularly hard drive from Amir and stumbled backward. He tripped over a footstool, and he unsuccessfully fought to keep his balance. His momentum carried him to the floor, and his weapon fell from his grasp. Before he could retrieve it, Amir's sword was at his throat. He looked up into the eyes of the man before him, saw the blackness, saw the hate and the insanity.

Amir laughed. "Good-bye, fool." He drew back to puncture Arash's throat.

"No!"

Amir glanced at Yasamin. She stood less than three feet away from him. "'No', you say? What would you do? Throw yourself upon your lover and take the blade? I don't think so. Watch him die."

"You will not kill him. There has been enough blood shed today." Amir looked back at Yasamin just as her right hand rose and pointed at his sword. A bolt of white lightening shot from her fingers, and the sword flew from his hand. Amir grabbed his stinging hand and stood gaping at Yasamin.

"Sit down. You *will* listen to me."

The King numbly sank into the chair beside the desk, his mind trying to absorb what he'd just seen.

"Now it's my turn. Pay attention, husband. Serpata was evil. Everything he did was evil. He has slowly poisoned your mind, so you have drifted toward the dark side. What you have planned is not only wrong, it's evil."

"What did you do to me?" Amir wasn't looking at her; he was looking at his hand.

Yasamin sighed. "I follow the light. I have powers as strong as Serpata. But mine are for good—to help, not hurt. Your hand will be fine. It only hurts so much because you were holding metal."

At the mention of the word "power," Amir looked up. "You have powers like my uncle?"

"Listen, Amir. I have no desire to hurt you. I want to help you before it's too late. Forget your plan to destroy my country. It's an evil plan spawned of Serpata's influence. I will help you. I'll stay and honor my vows to you. All you have to do is turn from your destructive path.

"Turn from the dark, and come back to the light, husband. I will help you raise Dragonval to glory, a country of good. Dragonval will reign as a country to be admired, not feared."

"You would do that?"

"Yes. I'll even help you look for Medusimia. I wish her no harm. All of us together can make this a mighty country. I swear this to you."

"What about him?" Amir nodded toward Arash.

"He will return to Pars." A lump rose in Yasamin's throat, but she didn't glance at Arash on the floor.

Amir stood. "You would forgive all the things I've said?"

"Yes."

"You would just forget them?"

"I cannot promise I will forget them, not right now. But I can forgive you. Come back to the light, Amir. Save yourself before it's too late."

The king frowned. "Save myself? Tell me, wife, what would you do if I did march against Gwendomere?"

"I will stop you. You will not be allowed to commit such an atrocity against innocent people who have done nothing to you."

"I see."

"You have to chose, Amir. Follow the dark side, and it will destroy you. Come back to the light, and I will help you in any way I can. We can make this country great."

"Yes." The king bowed his head. "I have been a fool. I see it now. How could I have been so blind?"

Yasamin was both happy and desolate—happy she could save Amir, desolate she'd lose Arash. But she had promised; she had sworn it. She moved forward to put her arm around her husband.

At the same time, Amir swung toward her. He held a knife that had been lying on the table. With one swift move, he held it aloft. "I see it clearly, bitch. It's my throne you want. Well, you can't have it."

In that instant, Yasamin saw the insanity, the blackness filling his eyes. Amir belonged to the dark side. He had no soul.

She gasped as he brought the blade down to strike.

It never reached her.

Arash had never trusted Amir. An instant before the King grabbed the knife, Arash seized his sword. He thrust upward. The blade entered Amir's chest and exited his back, its point glistening red in the candlelight.

Amir froze, disbelief crossing his features. The knife dropped from his fingers, and he clutched the sword with both hands. Arash scrambled to his feet and pulled Yasamin away from the dying man.

He fell against the desk, still trying to pull the sword from his chest, then staggered backward until he met the wall. He fell against it so hard, it pushed the blade back through his chest. With a mighty groan, Amir pulled the sword from his body. He waved it in the air above his head. Crimson droplets splattered the floor and the couple. With hate-filled eyes, he took a step toward her. "You will—" Blood spewed through his lips and dribbled down his chin. "You b—" Amir fell to the floor.

The King was dead.

Chapter 65

"I couldn't let him kill you." Arash struggled to his feet and stood uncertainly before Yasamin. He swore to let her handle matters with Amir, but that had not happened. He wasn't sure what her reaction toward him would be. "I'm sorry. I know I promised." His knees buckled, and he abruptly sat in the chair the King sat in only minutes before.

"Here, let me see." Tearing her eyes from the dead body before her, Yasamin quickly tore Arash's shirt to examine his wound. "It doesn't look too deep, but it's bleeding freely." She cast a quick glance around the room.

A white shirt lay on Amir's bed. Yasamin grabbed it and ran back to Arash. "Hold this against the wound tightly. I'll get some water."

"Yasamin, I'm sor—"

"We'll talk later. I want to get the bleeding stopped." She hurried around the room, gathering items she thought might be useful. Kneeling before him, she poured water into a basin. "Here, let me have the towel. I want to get the blood cleaned, so I can see more about the wound." She gently dabbed the wet cloth against the slice. "Do you have any of Goliagoth's powder left?"

Arash shook his head. "No." His head felt as if it were floating above him. He closed his eyes to keep the room from spinning.

Yasamin pressed a fresh cloth against his shoulder. "Hold this tightly. I'll be right back."

Arash did as told. The screeching of furniture caused him to crack one eyelid. Yasamin tugged a heavy table to the corner of the room, then pulled a chair to it.

"What are you doing?"

Yasamin hurried back to him and picked up his sword. "Helping you." Climbing on the chair, she crawled onto the table and stood. Stretching the sword into the dark corners, she swiped the walls.

She returned to Arash. "This will help." She pulled a handful of cobwebs from the sword. "Move the towel." She gently packed the cut with the gossamer threads. The flow slowed. She picked up another cloth and pressed it against the wound.

Arash rested his head against the chair. "Amazing. Where did you learn that?"

"I had a good teacher—Goliagoth did this before. You probably don't remember."

"I don't, but I will from now on." He closed his eyes again. The room slowly stopped spinning. He was afraid to break the silence, but things needed to be said.

"Yasamin, I know I agreed to let you handle ..."

"You did what you had to do. I saw it at the last. He already belonged to the darkness."

"So, what do we do now?"

"I am not sure. We have to think." Yasamin glanced down at her blood-splattered outfit, the blood on the floor and finally to Amir lying face down in the crimson pool. He still gripped the sword.

"I guess we—"

A loud knock interrupted her. She barely had time to exchange looks with Arash as the door crashed open. Beyond, they could hear the murmur of voices and the ringing of metal as they neared.

"I guess it no longer matters," she whispered as she laid her hand on Arash's shoulder, for he was too weak to rise.

But he was not too weak for a smile. "Whatever happens, Yasamin, I will love you forever. Hand me my sword."

Side by side, they awaited their fate.